ABSINTHE
WITHOUT LEAVE

Carole Nelson Douglas
and the Midnight Louie feline PI series

"Midnight Louie's contributions are insightful, humorous, and imaginative... Along with all these wonderful offbeat characters, Douglas has an interesting plot, good story, and an intriguing mystery."
—*Affaire de Coeur* on *Cat in an Alphabet Soup*

"...just about everything you might want in a mystery: glitzy Las Vegas, real characters, suspense, a tough puzzle. Plus, a fine sense of humor and some illuminating social commentary."
—*The Prime Suspect* on *Cat in an Aqua Storm*

"Midnight Louie sniffs through plenty of plausible red herrings...in this brisk tail that even mystery readers who don't love cats will relish."
—*Publishers Weekly* on *Cat on a Blue Monday*

"It's time for that old black magic, Midnight Louie by name, to dazzle his loyal fans once more, this time with a nifty foray into the occult... Ms. Douglas comes up trumps with another splendid mystery, an outstanding puzzler chock full of scintillating wit and clever sleuthing. Another bravura performance!"
—*Romantic Times* on *Cat with an Emerald Eye*

"a dazzling blend of witty prose, clever plotting. No wonder Midnight Louie is everyone's cat's meow"
—*RT Book Reviews* on *Cat in a Flamingo Fedora*

"Fun, frothy, and charming."
—*Publishers Weekly* on *Cat in a Yellow Spotlight*

ALSO BY CAROLE NELSON DOUGLAS
IRENE ADLER SHERLOCKIAN SUSPENSE

Good Night, Mr. Holmes
The Adventuress (formerly *Good Morning, Irene*)
A Soul of Steel (formerly *Irene at Large*)
Another Scandal in Bohemia (formerly *Irene's Last Waltz*)
Chapel Noir and *Castle Rouge* (Jack the Ripper duology)
Femme Fatale
Spider Dance

The Midnight Louie Mysteries
"...full of intricate plotting and sharp characterization. And Louie?
Nine lives wouldn't be nearly enough for this dude."
—*Publishers Weekly* on *Cat in a Crimson Haze*

CAT IN AN ALPHABET SOUP

AQUA STORM
BLUE MONDAY
CRIMSON HAZE
DIAMOND DAZZLE
EMERALD EYE
FLAMINGO FEDORA
GOLDEN GARLAND
HYACINTH HUNT
INDIGO MOOD
JEWELED JUMPSUIT
KIWI CON
LEOPARD SPOT
MIDNIGHT CHOIR
NEON NIGHTMARE
ORANGE TWIST
HOT PINK PURSUIT
QUICKSILVER CAPER
RED HOT RAGE
SAPPHIRE SLIPPER
TOPAZ TANGO
ULTRAMARINE SCHEME
VEGAS GOLD VENDETTA
WHITE TIE AND TAILS
ALIEN X-RAY
YELLOW SPOTLIGHT
ZEBRA ZOOT SUIT

CAT IN AN ALPHABET ENDGAME

A Café Noir Mystery

Introducing Midnight Louie's new gal pal Delilah Street and Quicksilver

Dancing with Werewolves • *Brimstone Kiss* • *Vampire Sunrise*
Silver Zombie • *Virtual Virgin*

"Exhilarating urban fantasy that puts the sin in Sin City." —*Alternate Worlds*

"Strong, smart Delilah Street keeps you engaged and entertained. The paranormal element keeps it new and fresh, yet Delilah is still solving a good, old-fashioned mystery." —*Best Fantasy Stories*

"Douglas brings a fresh and sassy voice to Delilah Street…a blend of urban fantasy and film noir brought to life." —*ParaNormalRomance.org*

"Smartly written, plot-driven, original…deftly combines elements of fantasy, mystery, and romance to the well-sated delight of the reader. Enthusiastically recommended." —*Midwest Review of Books*

"Douglas handles the premise with spectacular style and spices the action with fabulous characters. Filled with kick-ass action, Douglas's dishy style compliments the twisty plot." —Two starred *Publishers Weekly* reviews

"A brilliant eye for detail, a captivating storyline and some of the most unique supporting characters around." —*Darque Reviews*

"Smartly written, plot-driven, original…deftly combines the elements of fantasy, mystery, and romance to the well sated delight of the reader. Enthusiastically recommended —*Midwest Review of Books*

NY Times Best-selling authors say: "A wonderfully written series with a unique take on the paranormal." —KELLEY ARMSTRONG…"Charming, witty, and utterly imaginative. Carole Nelson Douglas is always ahead of the pack." —HEATHER GRAHAM …"Authors I recommend: David Drake, Carole Nelson Douglas, Jim Butcher, Isaac Asimov, and Neil Gaiman." —SHERRILYN KENYON … "An amazingly rich world of shadows come to life from one of the most fertile imaginations in fiction." —NANCY PICKARD

ABSINTHE
WITHOUT LEAVE

The First Midnight Louie Cafe Noir Mystery

by Carole Nelson Douglas

"Snaps and glitters like the town that inspired it."
—NORA ROBERTS

WISH
LIST

WISHLIST BOOKS

ABSINTHE WITHOUT LEAVE:
A MIDNIGHT LOUIE CAFÉ NOIR MYSTERY
Copyright 2018 © Carole Nelson Douglas.

Published in the United States by Wishlist Publishing

Editor: Mary Moran

Images Copyright © iStock.com

Woman and Cat image Copyright © Cindy Grundsten

Author photo Copyright © Sam Douglas

Cover and book interior design Copyright © Carole Nelson Douglas

Printed in the United States of America

Library/retail hardcover edition ISBN 978-1-1943175-17-8

Trade paperback softcover edition ISBN 978-1-1943175-18-5

Digital edition ISBN 978-1-943175-19-2

www.wishlistpublishing.com

FIRST EDITION

*For Judy McAllister, who does so much for so many, including me.
and for Topaz, small but mighty Shaded Golden Persian,
adopted at five, left us too soon at almost fifteen.*

*This book and series is also dedicated to all our wonderful
and loyal readers and their feline friends who've joined
the original inspiring Midnight Louie and me on this
incredible journey toward a thirty-third Midnight Louie
novel and the start of a new mystery series.*

*Also dedicated with gratitude to Denise Thompson
for her volunteer proof-reading work.*

Acknowledgments

We've loved and kept your cards and letters and now emails, and appreciate the thousands of stamps you've sent to help snail-mail the annual newsletter since 1995, and those of you who've bought the books and T-shirts. We're amazed you always say you know how busy we are. How do you know? We try not to whine, because we are so privileged to be doing what we're doing. Yes, a writing career is 12/7. I'm often surprised to find I'm working on an unnoticed national holiday. I'm always wishing I could answer you more and more of you, but deadlines never die! Those of you I've interacted with have been delightful and so inspiring and understanding.

Carole Nelson Douglas & Midnight Louie, Esq.

TABLE OF CONTENTS

Currently in Midnight Louie's Lives and Times...

What *is* a humble hotshot P.I. to do?

Here I sit in Las Vegas, a city that has been a Capital of Crime for eighty-five years. I find that my nearest and dearest clients I have aided and abetted through thick and thin seem to have settled into boring domestic bliss.

Anyway, how am I supposed to keep an eye on those who need it if they are planning on leaving me at home alone?

Although we just have successfully concluded the latest case of murder on our dance cards and resolved my human associates personal issues, I have not forgotten that not long ago, my posse— both human and feline members—had their lives on the line. But I rallied the Las Vegas Cat Pack and we all came through the confrontation with snaggletooth and ragged nail mostly intact.

I was not the only one among the wounded—if you count broken nails as a wound. Mr. Max Kinsella received another blow to his already banged-up head. Who knows what setbacks his recovering AWOL memory may encounter?

The Cat Pack acted as intimidating muscle, under my direction. However, their usual leader and my esteemed streetwise mother, Ma Barker, is now again firmly in control of her feral cat clowder. ("Clowder" is the correct name for a community of feral cats, but I prefer Cat Pack.) This is a group that can produce banshee howls and administer four-shiv slashes to any assailant's face as a *coup de claw*.

I should formally introduce myself as founder and CEO of Midnight Investigations, Inc. I plied the mean streets of Las Vegas for many years as a bachelor about town, and then moved into P.I. work. I had my own condo with my Titian-haired, live-in PR woman and amateur detective (thanks to me), Miss Temple Barr.

She has now wed Mr. Matt Devine as planned, alas. Our cozy condo does not need interlopers, especially on the California king-size bed, which was perfect for the two of us, with my curl-upable twenty or so pounds and her one hundred.

Yes, she is a tiny thing as humans go, but she has the heart of a mountain lion and the relentless investigative instincts of a bloodhound. Actually, she is much more attractive in human terms than this characterization sounds.

So back to me again. Yes, the Vegas Strip is my beat.

For a Las Vegas institution, I have always kept a low profile. I like my nightlife shaken, not stirred. Being short, dark, and handsome…really short…gets me overlooked and underestimated, which is what the savvy operative wants anyway. I am your perfect undercover guy.

Call me Muscle in Midnight Black. Miss Temple and I share a well-honed sense of justice and long, sharp fingernails and have cracked some cases too tough for the local fuzz. She was, after all, a freelance public relations specialist, and Las Vegas is full of public and private relations of all stripes and legalities.

So, there is much private investigative work left for me to do, as usual.

Since Las Vegas is littered with guidebooks as well as bodies, I here provide a rundown of the local landmarks on my particular map of the world. A cast of characters, so to speak:

To wit, the current status of who we are and where we are all at:

MIDNIGHT LOUIE, P.I.

None can deny that the Las Vegas crime scene is big time, and I have been treading these mean neon streets for thirty-two books now. I began with a romantic mystery Quartet in the Eighties and became an "alpha cat" with my next mystery series. Since my foundation volume, *Cat in an Alphabet Soup* (formerly *Catnap*) debuted, the title sequence features an alphabetical "color" word from A to Z. So *Cat in an Aqua Storm* (formerly *Pussyfoot*) comes next, followed by *Cat on a Blue Monday* and *Cat in a Crimson Haze*, etc. until we reached the last volumes, *Cat in a Zebra Zoot Suit* and *Cat in an Alphabet Endgame* in 2017.

There is no rest for the wicked, they say, nor for those who pursue them and justice, I have discovered. Thus I move on to new cases after the triumphant ending of the alphabet sequence. The reason for alphabetic titles was to enable readers to quickly realize the order of the series. My always alert readers will notice a new alphabet has started with this book. Though I am on Life 33, I am not able to assure you that any or all of us can keep carrying on like this to another book Z. So how long a run we get adds another element of suspense. I may do as Miss Agatha Christie did and prepare a final revelatory book ahead of time. But that is the future and we are Crime Time now.

MISS MIDNIGHT LOUISE

This streetwise black-furred minx insinuated herself into my cases, claiming to be my unacknowledged daughter, until I was forced to set up shop with her as Midnight Investigations, Inc.

MISS LILAH LANE

This new Dark Horse on the Vegas scene arrived with a bang and a biker gang on her tail, in a Fifties-vintage car with canines in tow. I am more than somewhat skeptical of the canine kind in areas of stealth, focus, and brain power, although I must bow to their superior sense of smell. Miss Lilah's identity seems sketchy, even to herself at times. She suffered a head blow while eluding the bikers, so how much she really knows is compromised. I found her dazed but game, and led her into the nearby Hellfire Hotel. My mystical cat sense digs her grit, hiss and spit, and wit. Can there be a secret Dark Side to Sin City even I have not found?

MISS TEMPLE BARR

A freelance public relations ace, my lovely roommate is Miss Nancy Drew all grown up and in killer spikes. She is now married and a daytime TV host, but she had first come to Las Vegas with her soon-to-be elusive ex-significant other...

MR. MAX KINSELLA, aka The Mystifying Max

They were a marriage-minded couple until he disappeared without a word to Miss Temple shortly after their Vegas move. All to protect her from pursuers from his past. This sometimes missing-in-action magician has finally resolved the death of his cousin Sean, killed in an Irish Republican Army bomb attack on a pub to Ireland. His mentor in magic and in undercover counterterrorism work all over Europe, Garry Randolph, aka magician Gandolph the Great, was killed by bullets meant for Max. No wonder he found his memory going a little AWOL after an attempt on his life sent him crashing into the wall of his Neon Nightmare club with lethal impact while performing. His traumatic memory loss means he knows he and my Miss Temple were once a committed couple, but recalls none of the, ahem, spicy details. The upshot of his absence from Las Vegas on secret agent activities was that Miss Temple was left alone to meet…

MR. MATT DEVINE

Mr. Matt, aka Mr. Midnight, became a radio talk show shrink on *The Midnight Hour*. The former Roman Catholic priest came to Vegas to track down his abusive stepfather and ended up making Miss Temple his Mrs. and partnering with her for a local Las Vegas morning TV show, *Las Vegas Last Night*.

I sometimes volunteer myself to aid a hard-nosed dame who previously sought Miss Temple's elusive ex-significant other Max— on suspicion of murder, no less…

LIEUTENANT C. R. MOLINA

This Las Vegas homicide detective and single mother of teenage Mariah is also highly skeptical of me and all my works, even though I have secretly assisted her on many cases. A domestic misunderstanding many years ago resulted in her raising Mariah on her own, until who should happen to come to Vegas but the girl's father…

MR. RAFI NADIR

After blowing his career at the LAPD when Miss Lt. C. R. Molina mysteriously left him, and for years the unsuspecting father of Mariah, he works Vegas hotel security jobs and is establishing a good relationship with his teen daughter. Will Mom thaw too?

MISS KATHLEEN O'CONNOR
Deservedly nicknamed "Kitty the Cutter" by my Miss Temple, she is the local lass that Max and his cousin Sean boyishly competed for in that long-ago Northern Ireland, not knowing she was born in a brutal Irish forced-work "asylum" for unwed mothers. When Max left, she turned embittered stalker. Finding Mr. Max as impossible to trace as Lieutenant Molina has, Kitty the C had settled for harassing with tooth and claw the nearest innocent bystander, primarily Mr. Matt Devine. Even with his memory sometimes AWOL, Mr. Max still managed to declaw Miss Kitty and send her far, far away out of everyone's lives. Will she stay there?

Many of us reside at a Fifties-vintage round apartment building called the Circle Ritz, owned by seventy-something free spirit, Miss Electra Lark.

All this human sex and violence makes me glad that I have a simpler social life, such as just trying to get along with my ungrateful daughter and pursuing beautiful dames of the feline sort.

So here things stand today, full of danger, angst, and confusion. However, things are seldom what they seem, and almost never that way in Las Vegas. So any surprising developments will not surprise me. Everything in Las Vegas is always up for grabs 24/7 — guilt, innocence, money, power, love, loss, death, and significant others.

Like Las Vegas, the City That Never Sleeps, Midnight Louie, private eye, also has a sobriquet: the Kitty That Never Sleeps.

With this crew, who could?

1
Midnight Musings

I have always considered myself a solo act when it comes to my profession: Midnight Louie, P.I.

Fact: "Midnight Louie" is the moniker the inhabitants gave me when I showed up at an upscale Palo Alto motel, on the road and fancy free, shadowing some fishy prey, namely the large and succulent costly koi—liquid gold—in the motel pond.

Naturally, management wanted to trap and send me to a nearby death camp called a "shelter". What a corrupt administration!

Then a classy dame I cozied up to at the outdoor snack machine area invited me in from the chilly northern California nights. My homeless condition inspired her to fly me across state lines for pet purposes. I confess I had no intentions of being a pet, but I began to see possibilities for a new career. Then news of my "rescue" hit the newspapers. Overnight my name and game were everywhere in hard print. Midnight Louie, Private Eye. I was offered my freedom if I would relocate to Las Vegas and record my various adventures for print media, and even audiobooks.

So if you are one of forty million people who visit Vegas annually…and you spy a lone figure silhouetted on a dark, neon-lit, reflective street, a mean street where nothing nice dares show its face, you can bet it will be me on patrol.

It is not hard to become an institution in Las Vegas, but I am coming to see that my cozy little arrangement for life in Sin City has changed. Now I look out at the Las Vegas Strip lights from the third-floor balcony of the Circle Ritz apartments and condominiums.

Yeah. The third floor. My friends and fans know I used to occupy the second floor unit and balcony of this round Fifties building. An only cat. With my roommate, Miss Temple Barr. Mr. Matt Devine rented the unit above.

But, as we know from romance novels, love conquers all, including Midnight Louie's housing arrangements.

A little human matrimony ceremony and remodeling has blended their Circle Ritz condo units into a two-story affair with a spiral staircase, on which I can perform gymnastics to keep in shape for my private investigator career.

But I am not used to being a third wheel, no matter how welcome, nor do I wish to share a king-size bed with other than my petite Miss Temple. Married life is not the life for me.

With my roommates out for the evening at a new Strip hotel show, I have availed myself of the only perk in this new domestic arrangement, viewing all I can survey from the third floor balcony.

The night is bright because the moon is yellow (and often a coward hiding behind any convenient cloud), and I am a trifle glum. If I had any fondness for bodies of water, I would dive down into the Circle Ritz underwater-lit pool, sparkling like an aquamarine solitaire on the patio three stories below, just to break the boredom of staying home alone.

You do not want to sit alone in your room when life is a cabaret, my friend, says a voice in my head.

The only individual I know capable of "head-hopping" is that tiresomely New Age Birman cat who lives with our esteemed landlady, Miss Electra Lark, in the Penthouse on floor five. Karma is one of the breed known as "the Sacred Cat of Burma" for protecting Tibetan monks back in ancient days, and does Miss Karma sling around that so-called distinction.

"It is *my* pity party and I will pout if I want to," I yowl back in plain cat.

A sudden shaking of palm fronds high above drives me back from the railing. I hear agitated rustling and the *screee* of claws skidding down rough bark. Has her Heavenly Highness lost her elevated mind and attempted to climb down to my level? That way lies disaster. *Hers!*

I jump atop the railing, balancing as I watch her pale furred form swinging perilously from palm-tree trunk claw-hold to claw-hold. Descending a tree takes forelimb strength. Sleeping on a faux fur pillow does not build strength for that. The Sacred One is about to lose her grip and go splat as she scrabbles past. So I jump up, curl my rear toes around the railing, and do a forward scruff retrieval and simultaneous swing-down to a four-point landing on the balcony's faux grass surface. Faux grass. *Hmm*, sounds a bit like *foie gras*, French for goose liver paté. Which Karma would be had I not interrupted her imminent fall. She is hardly grateful. She now sits there safe, squalling like a three-month-old kitten.

"Get off of me, Louie! You weigh a ton."

This is the thanks I get. I shake out my all-purpose black suit-coat while she arranges her long, silky, vanilla-colored furs. Her heavenly blue eyes grow wide and alarmed. "I am here to give you a most dire warning, Louie. You may have noticed the round full moon last night."

I nod.

"Have you heard of a bad moon rising? This is not an ordinary moon, Louie, it is a werewolf moon."

"So? I am not afraid of anything canine. My muscular twenty-something pounds makes me the Mohammed Ali of catdom."

"No butterfly or bee braggadocio will help you against the paranormal influences massing over Las Vegas right now."

"I am not bragging. You have seen me float like a butterfly down that old palm tree and I am ever ready to sting like a bee." I snick out my four right shivs. "My right hook is legendary."

Karma rolls her big blue marble (like the Earth seen from space) eyes. "You must beware of anything even slightly weird that you encounter in coming days. Your kind's long history with black magic makes you a magnet for paranormal trouble."

I decide not to tell Karma *she* is on my weird list. Just because I am a black cat does not mean I swallow all those old wives' tales about my kind or anything else. In fact, I was born on October 31, a dangerous day when mischief is abroad for one of my color, but that turned out to be a lucky day for me and my world. I tell her so.

Karma is unconvinced. She smooths her spotless white gloves and silken ruff. Her blue eyes burn as bright as Las Vegas neon in their dark brown facial mask.

Her rear white socks lift off the plastic grass one by one as she shudders. "I have done my duty. I have warned you, Louie, small good it will do you. But, oh!" She looks up the long crude sloping palm trunk above. "However shall I get up home again?"

"Not to worry." I hustle her through the open French door into the bedroom. "We will just spring down this spiral staircase, into the hall, and take the elevator up."

"Elevator?" By now she is lofting gingerly down the dizzying stairs. I take a short cut and leap down three steps at a time.

I employ the correct bounding moves to spring the lock on the hall doors and repeat my muscular leaps to hail the elevator and take it three floors up to the penthouse.

Miss Karma is thankfully silent throughout this journey. I escort her to the door of Miss Electra Lark's abode.

"Louie, I have never left Miss Electra Lark's apartment in any of my many lives, or her paltry one life. How do I explain myself being in the hallway?"

"Never explain. When she opens the door to find you outside, simply walk in, tail high. Turn around once you are in and give her your most accusing stare. You know, like if she would try to offer you Free-to-Be-Feline or other so-called 'health' muck in your dish. Since you are so psychic, she will just think you teleported out of the rooms to the hall outside and be hysterically worried that you could have wandered off."

Karma nods sagely. "Yes, I should up my 'mysterious' quotient in my mistress's eyes. I have been a bit lax in that exercise lately. This out-of-apartment appearance of mine should unnerve her just the right amount. Good luck, Louie. I hope you avoid all the disasters in store for you."

I retrace my path to what is now the "master suite" and guest bedroom second level of Mr. and Mrs. Matt Devine's condominium.

This is a Circle Ritz renovation and territory new to me. Although I have never been shy about sharing my faithful roomie's bed, this new "marriage" arrangement is not my favorite human condition.

It could lead to unforeseen consequences for me, like the one a couple years back that drove me from my post as house detective at the Crystal Phoenix hotel-casino. That unfortunate event is now a walking, talking miniature human who answers to the name of Cinna, is instructed to call me "Uncle Louie" on the rare occasions when I cannot escape her neighborhood, and who attempts to put curlers in my ears and even my second-most valuable member. Her noisy, messy (not even litter-box trained, mind you!) advent on the scene was why I was forced to decamp and relocate to room at the Circle Ritz with my Miss Temple Barr, who not only needed on-site protection but was mostly living alone then.

I fully realize that the current situation might encourage a replay of the previous situation, which is why I sit soberly on the balcony and contemplate my uncontrollable human acquaintances.

When I and Mr. Max came and went it seemed we had equal Temple Time, equal rights, you could say and forged an uneasy truce. Now, with Miss Temple and Mr. Matt working together on a live TV show, *and* living together at the CR, I feel crowded out.

I imagine Mr. Max Kinsella, magician and sometime secret agent, and Miss Temple's long-time ex, would share my feelings as a fellow bachelor who has lost out to Mr. Matt Devine, sadly too fine a fellow to hate properly.

I picture a moon-gazing Mr. Max sitting on the high roof of the Neon Nightmare building off the Strip. He owns it, but the building is shuttered and empty, and his life is set on "pause" for the moment. Will he retake the stage? Continue as a reluctant confidential investigator for Miss C. R. Molina, homicide lieutenant? Will the mysterious European agent, Revienne, capture his romantic interest now that My Miss Temple is what they call "an old, married lady"? Could he use an enterprising new partner and master of undercover disguise?

He was to meet my Too Married Twosome to critique the hot new magician's act they are viewing, "Spellbinder" at the Hellfire hotel-casino tonight. Given Karma's unusual prophetic croakings, perhaps I should examine the scene for untoward doings.

And so I shall.

2
Black Magic Ride

Well, well, well. Here I am doing a security check on the rear of the Hellfire Hotel. I provide this service to the hotel free of charge, out of the goodness of my heart.

It is also an opportunity for me to take my fee out in trade. So I am doing a discreet Dumpster Dive for escapees from the Claw 'n' Clam Seafood Spectacular buffet, when all hell breaks loose.

I mean that literally. A glass-smashing soprano's aria with high notes that could curl my ear hairs alerts me to turn. Just in time to see a vision of a silver liquid mercury wave with the black-and-chrome grille of a motor vehicle plunging through that porous wall like a circus tiger through a blazing paper ring of flames.

Instinct has me charging out of its path on all four wheels—I mean limbs—over trash and garbage piles to surmount the Dumpster. The car, and it is a big 'un—topless, like a lot of attractions in Las Vegas—lands on all four whitewalls at once, with a shudder and quiver that seems mild for its sudden appearance. The car rolls forward before stopping, even as a dark figure rolls out over the driver-side door.

And then a dog leaps from the convertible's backseat, shaking a shower of silver from its gray fur coat. Growling, snarling and barking, it whirls to face the silver wave and the thundering unseen motorcycle convention heading this way.

This is one big mutt, with paws the size of litter-box scoops, clawing sparks off the broken concrete and asphalt alley floor.

Before I can break out the Croquet Hoop defensive martial arts position and start a battle howl, the noise shatters the silver wall, with three huge Harleys coming through, the helmetless riders' long, greasy hair waving flag-like in the wind.

Harleys I can handle. Just get out of the way, or, in an emergency, leap up on the leather saddlebags and become one mean stuck-on with sixteen shivs desert burr behind the rider's tender parts. Biker two-piece leather gear leads to crack in the rear syndrome, which makes them nicely shiv-ready.

What I cannot believe is what I see next: the snarling faces hurtling toward me, fangs bared in a monstrous grimace. These are not just mean macho men. They are wolves in biker leathers!

I look up and scan the blackness above, remembering Karma's warning.

A werewolf moon, Louie.

It is there, round and full, illuminated enough to sport rough surface shadows. I back into a building and flatten to make myself one with the night and darkness. I was born wearing camouflage.

As the wolfish bikers' tires finally hit ground, a blend of greased concrete and cracked asphalt, they circle the challenging dog. I see it is guarding something. No some*one.* A still body clad in black.

The buzzing and whining motorcycles circle, growling. The dog knocks one rider and bike sideways with a single artful lunge. The solitary dog then becomes an entire pack, constantly moving, lunging and biting, grabbing and twisting legs and arms until the bikes reel, sliding drunkenly away from their riders.

And the riders…the faces that scrape concrete are not wolfish now, but human. Well, sub-human.

"Let's roll," a rough voice bellows. "She's probably dead anyway. Fresher game on the Strip."

The gang wastes no time rolling away into a distant roar—the dog remains a small weaving figure, harrying them left and right. They leave behind silence and the reek of fuel, motor oil, and mass quantities of scrumptious seafood.

Sadly, I have lost my appetite. For the moment. Maybe the few shrimp I snagged and downed were tainted, and I am in the midst of a waking nightmare. I look up.

The man in the moon tonight almost looks like a wolf at that.

The figure on the ground looks like a goner. Also like a girl. I do not go soft on those who attack the female of the species, any species. Midnight Investigations, Inc. is dedicated to being one-hundred percent diverting. Or do I mean diverse? Anyway, I pad over to sniff the kisser of the fallen person for the breath of life. Not that I am trained for CPR.

One sniff and my head jerks away. I inhale not death and alley debris, but a blast of pure dry desert air. I feel like a movie camera that has suddenly zoomed in on a scene miles away. I am on a balcony with Karma staring at the moon. She is swaying as she sits there and hums a Purr of Power. She reminds me of a statue of Bast, the Egyptian cat goddess, who was one big stone monolith monster mama in their temples.

You can move into the human mind more than you know, Louie, especially under a Werewolf Moon.

Would Karma cut out the wolf stuff? I am happily feline and fully superior to any canine on the Las Vegas Strip. Why is it not a Leopard Moon? Seems to me the wolves have been hogging the current entertainment world enough already.

But the camera of my mind has zoomed even farther into looming night. I am on a mountain ridge staring at the moon, amid medicinal scents like sage and the Peyote cactus that produces the hallucinogen mescaline, which figured in an early case of mine, and my mind is unreeling a feature film of scenes and sounds.

I rear back from the fallen female's face to no avail. I cannot keep these jumbled alien vignettes and visions of her unconscious mind from trespassing on my own mental clarity.

"Quicksilver," she is muttering. Her limbs stir, as mine do when making running motions during a nightmare.

It seems I am locked into a first-run screening of the scenario in the poor girl's brain. I try to emulate Karma, as icky and weird as that is, and purr up a soothing storm of some stupid meditative syllable, like the fabled *Om. Ommm. Ohmm.* Does not feel like my kind of mantra.

I have got it! *Iams. I am Iammmms.* I am what I am, like Popeye. Or even better. *Koi, Kwoiiiii.* My Karma-despised mystical side is cooking with gas.

Or invoking the names of pricey pet food and decorative fish is *giving* me gas.

3
Quicksilver Moon

So what's a girl lying on her back staring up at a midnight sky and full moon to think?

This is more than a daydream, it's a nightmare.

Something wispy tickles my nose. I know I've been in an accident. My body knows I've been in an accident. My reflexes want me to sneeze or twitch, but I'm held captive, immobile, by shock and the raging need to remember what happened and how and where it happened.

I page back to darkness and speed and fear, and then before that to an empty, dark plain I can see as I stand on a ridge, looking at a lightning gash far below.

Alone? Not alone. I have companions. We are about to part ways, with lurking danger for each path we take. Yet the landscape is beautiful, peaceful, full-moon lit.

In the desert dusk, I watch the last rays of the sun slash over the western mountains and disappear while the mottled full moon hangs like an etched alabaster dinner plate over the darkening valley below.

A dog, my dog, nudges his big, furry head against my hip and sniffs the arid air with a muffled whine of excitement.

"Hush, Quicksilver," I murmur.

My guy, Ric, guards my other side and puts his arm around me.

This scene might seem romantic, something Bogart and Bergman and *Casablanca* maybe, with a bit of Disney's *Lady and the Tramp*, but only if you consider danger an aphrodisiac. And I confess I sometimes do.

"The local Paiute Indians," Ric says, "called a full moon this big and clear a 'Wolf Moon.'"

Ric goes on waxing pedantic instead of passionate, trying to make me feel better about our imminent parting. "Now, thanks to the Millennium Revelation, it's called a 'Werewolf Moon.'"

I shiver, mostly from the evening coolness draping the darkening landscape, but also from the werewolf part, which still freaks out a mid-continent-born, Kansas-sensible girl like me.

At the Millennium and in the years afterward, a wave of paranormal phenomena hit the country and the world, exposing the hidden existence of pockets of such once-mythical evils as demons, vampires and werewolves. But only Las Vegas had jumped on the apparent new Darkside to exploit as the marketing opportunity of the 21st century.

So here Ric and I stand, high above Sin City, fighting the old-new evils each in our own way.

"I gotta get going," Ric says. "It's a two-mile hike to link up with the U.S.-Mexico operation, *chica*. Thanks for the ride in style to the mountains." He nods to my big black Cadillac convertible becoming more invisible in the dark by the second. Dolly is a heavy metal gas and road-eater with 325 horses under her hood. People name pets, but I name my car too.

I manage a smile that probably doesn't show in the dark. "I wouldn't have missed Camo Gear You for the moon. Head bandana, black face paint. Really, Montoya?" I tease. "*Muy macho*, but I bet you can't even French kiss me goodbye with that greasy face gook on."

"It comes in a stick just like your drugstore CoverGirl."

"Like *your* UndercoversGirl," I answer.

He hooks an arm around my neck and proceeds to French, Spanish, and Italian kiss me to the Werewolf Moon and back.

"Don't linger," he warns. He's one to talk.

"Caesar Cicero's hunting lodge is only three miles away." Ric nods to a boxy silhouette of buildings that could have been a small city on the dimming horizon. "Their monthly Change is coming.

Our joint operation will capture his killer mob when they turn werewolf to hunt down and tear apart the poor fools who've crossed their boss."

"I was once one of Cicero's 'poor fools'. Until you rescued me." Ric lightly slaps me on the butt. Good thing I'd worn my sturdy motorcycle leather leggings and jacket. "No more mooning about. *You* get going. Real wolves hunt these mountains too."

As if answering him, High-C yips echo around us.

"Coyotes, too." I study the dark valley and the lightning bolt slash of dazzling Klieg lights and neon ripping the night apart. The Las Vegas Strip. When I look back, Ric has vanished.

I smile. Ex-FBI guy, undercover, working the border to make things better on both sides.

I have to grab Quicksilver by the black leather collar to keep him from joining Ric on the forthcoming paranormal critter hunt.

What a world! Irma, my inner voice since childhood, *tsks*. Orphaned kids often create invisible friends, I'd read, and Irma and I go way back.

"Down, boy," I caution.

Quicksilver growls his discontent, but obeys. With Quicksilver beside me, I'm not worried to be alone in the desert at twilight.

We'd been "orphans of the storm", Quick and I, and beat the odds when we came together. We three had met the same lucky day in the same place, Quicksilver, Ricardo Montoya and me. Sunset Park. (Don't worry, Vegas has a Sun*rise* Park too. All comers catered to here.)

I was a former TV reporter of rural Millennium Revelation quirky paranormal events like herds of cattle transported from one field to another.

"Delilah Street of WTCH-TV in Wichita, Kansas, reporting…"

Turned out the Mexican cartel demon drug lord, El Demonio, used cows and their four stomachs as "mules" to transfer drugs across the border.

I loved my weird beat and did a good job. My name was memorable, even though I had no history but foster homes. I'd been found abandoned as an infant, supposedly on "Delilah Street". Yet no such Avenue, Place, Lane, Drive or Street was found in Wichita.

Then I saw it on TV. Not Delilah Street, the location. *Delilah Street **me**.* My exact double, as big as life, the corpse *du jour* on one of the endless *CSI* forensic TV show spin-offs. You Remember the Bismarck? Not the battleship from the WWII slogan, but *CSI – Bismarck,* North Dakota, etc.

Las Vegas had the most successful spin-off, natch. My spitting image—and likely an unpaid extra because she didn't utter a word—half nude on national TV. She became the most popular *CSI* corpse ever. Maybe it was the Snow White in the crystal coffin look. I'm black Irish and have Snow White coloring—pale skin, blue eyes and cherry-red lips (if I wear some Revlon lipstick I normally don't bother with). The Disney image is baked into the culture.

Seeing a double shook me. I had to find out if I had a family. I quit the TV station, tossed my clothes and a few precious things, including my valiant, long white-haired dog, Achilles', ashes in a vase, into Dolly's giant-size Fifties trunk and drove to Vegas, where I haunted Sunset Park, staking out *CSI-V* producer Hector Nightwine's Sunset Road estate opposite. How to get to him? Maybe approach his limo when he came or went. He'd never responded to my phone calls, email, letters begging for an interview.

Sunset Park featured shade trees and a meandering path around a small lake, an oasis of greenery for desert-embedded Las Vegas.

There were distractions. One was canine and male. And one was human and male, and how. This guy was dressed to kill, yet playing pied piper with a bunch of kids he was teaching to "dowse" for water in the park. He wore a cream-colored lightweight wool-silk suit, the pants knife-edged pressed, the jacket draping a picnic table. Gold glinted from the cufflinks on his French-cuffed custom white silk shirt, everything a frame for his dark olive complexion and black hair. A slim gold herringbone-pattern belt curled around his slim hips like a luxurious serpent.

Think the tropical white suits Ricardo Montalbán wore on the Seventies-Eighties *Fantasy Island* TV series. I always did go for vintage. Having no personal history, I bought it at estate sales—unwanted clothes, wedding photographs. I even found Dolly under hay bales at a Kansas barn auction.

The man caught me watching and asked if I'd like to dowse. That involved him standing close behind me and guiding my hands and arms on a forked twig. He was another Ricardo. Ricardo Montoya, A former FBI agent who consulted nowadays, killing time before a client meet. I consulted Irma and we agreed this was the start of a beautiful friendship. He asked for my phone number, gave me his business card, and then left.

Delinquent from duty, I rapidly checked the walled Nightwine compound. Still no action. I hadn't missed anything.

An animal shelter was holding an adoption event in the park, so I wandered among the cages as a cover while eyeing my gated objective. Amused, I watched a stray black cat "box" with the caged cats so they displayed cute batting behavior. He acted like a self-appointed feline shill, attracting kids to the cats up for adoption.

And then there was the sad spectacle of a dog so big he hunched in his crate, a silver-gray Husky type. I tapped the wire cage and bent over to see the most soulful blue eyes ever turn to me from a silver-and-cream furred face. A widow's peak of darker fur over those amazing eyes made them seem almost human.

"Too big," I heard a woman whisper behind me. "What a shame."

Am I easy? Maybe. Or maybe I'm just ambitious.

"How big?" I asked, turning to her.

"A hundred-and-fifty pounds."

Not an Achilles, that was for sure. My beloved late Lhasa Apso dog, vampire-bitten, had topped out at twenty-two pounds.

"What's a 'shame'?" I asked further.

"I'm sorry. We're closing down soon," the harried woman said. "These unadopted animals are going back to the shelter."

"What'll happen to them?"

"We'll try again another day." But she didn't look me in the eye. In the truth-demanding, bright blue, inquiring reporter eye.

The black cat was rubbing in and out around my ankles. I nodded at it. "What about this guy?"

"Not one of ours. A stray. Besides, he's too old to be an easy adoption. And some strays can be difficult to domesticate."

The cat arched his back and hissed as if understanding and insulted.

"About the dog…" I said.

"He's a beauty, but a monster dog. You'd need to exercise him daily."

"I need to exercise *myself* daily."

"And…" She eyed my casual jeggings, jean jacket and boots. "Apartments won't take dogs this size, not even with a sizable deposit and monthly fee."

I bent over the cage again. "He's a Husky?"

"Definitely of the wolf-spitz family, but really big for the breed. Siberian huskies can have blue eyes. Maybe a touch of Irish wolfhound or even wolf. You can do dog DNA nowadays. But you have to fill out a form, be approved, and pay, and we're closing down."

"If I don't take him, he dies, right?"

"He will be euthanized."

The black cat stretched its length up the cage side. The dog sniffed its nose.

"He acts like a perfect gentleman," I told her.

Then I got an idea.

"I'm surprised you don't recognize me," I added. "Actually refreshing, after all the wild publicity."

She'd been avoiding looking me in the eye and face, but now she did.

"Oh. Wait. It's *you*! The famous *CSI* dead girl."

"Yes, that's me. My income is escalating now and I do need protection, as you can imagine with everyone trying to find me. I can afford to give this big guy a huge fenced-in run, gourmet doggie treats, and a great, free, secure life. Eighty dollars, the sign says?"

"And you must promise to get him fixed."

I heard a low growl from the cage behind me.

"Of course. He will have the best of care." I leaned confidentially close. "I know you're breaking the rules, but I have an appointment with the *CSI* producer just across Sunset Road." I waved at the mansion. "Hector Nightwine, I mustn't be late. Big things brewing."

"Oh, my goodness! Congratulations."

So I gave her a hundred dollars. *Ouch, Delilah,* Irma said, *you need every penny for that apartment and oversize pet fee. Famous Dead Girls should be less lavish with fans they're trying to coerce.*

Phooey on Irma.

I left the park with a white plastic baggie of doggie items and the dog on a ridiculously thin nylon tape leash. He had greeted me with a fervent basso *arf* when I put it on and led him out of the crate.

I left the pet shelter lady scrupulously filling out a phony sheet for me, using Hector Nightwine's address and phone number, the only ones I knew in Las Vegas. I had thought of using the info on Mr. Smooth and Creamy ex-FBI guy's card, but didn't want to burn my bridges there in case a future of pheromone fireworks was possible.

I looked both ways before crossing Sunset road. No vehicles were coming, but the black cat darted across in front of me.

Bad luck, Irma opined. Irma was not welcome to share superstitions.

I found the stone Nightwine gate sported a video and voice box I could activate.

"Delilah Street to see Mr. Nightwine," I said. "And with, uh, associate."

Silence. The dog stretched up to nose the voice box and present a stunning close-up. He growled softly, ending with an interrogatory whine.

"Miss Delilah Street," came a deep, dark-chocolate baritone voice, but no image. "If only you'd presented your visage in your earlier requests to interview me. I see now I do indeed wish to encounter you. As for your associate, what big teeth he has. Most photogenic. And persuasive. My man will be down to escort you both to my office."

So not only was a black cat crossing my path lucky, but then and there my "rescued" canine "associate" rescued me and became a full partner.

Hector Nightwine not only cooperated with me, but rented me his movie-set "Enchanted Cottage" behind his estate. Cheap. And I had every expectation that Mr. Ricardo Montoya would become a very familiar visitor there.

"We need a name for you," I told the dog whose upturned face reached my hipbone.

His eyes were not just blue, like mine, but pale and luminous like a blue moon. Like moonshine.

"Quicksilver," I said.

He sat down, boxed his nose with his paws and grinned up at me, tongue lolling amiably through his dental-office-white fangs.

Quicksilver it was.

"Quicksilver," I hear myself murmuring. My head was throbbing, my mind spinning on a Tilt-a-Whirl carnival ride of words, faces and places. Past and present nightmares for sure. My body wasn't in a bed, but on a hard, bumpy surface reeking of garbage and gasoline fumes.

Spidery whiskers and a cold sniffing nose tickle my cheek.

"Quicksilver."

No, the nose was too small and the whiskers were longer. More tickling. Had my luck turned? Or had I simply fallen crossing Sunset Road and that damn lucky black cat was back, making Ric and Quicksilver and Hector Nightwine and his Enchanted Cottage just fading figments of my fever dream?

How had I gotten from Ric and me in the desert to laid-flat in a dark Vegas alley?

Could I pick up the pieces now and tease memory into reality?

4
Hell on Wheels

Girl interrupted again. My banged-up brain was in no shape to wrestle with an existential question like, "Why am I here?"

Last clear thought. Holy Hell and High Horsepower! I need to beat some bad guys back to Vegas. That was it.

Why were bad guys after me? Because I'm a reporter with the dope on them.

A new whisker tickle prods my missing-in-action memory.

No, nowadays I'm an informal private investigator, getting up to speed on a new career. I'd been snooping around Gehenna Hotel mogul Caesar Cicero's mountain lodge and he could sic his minions on me. I could hear distant motorcycles packing into a united roar.

The coyotes were still yipping and now boldly circling Dolly, with Quicksilver darting to drive them back.

Wind-stirred, dried-out sagebrush scratched the sand all around me. *Hmm.*

I fetch a roll of twine from Dolly's trunk, link several bushes like cans, then attach them on a long lead to Dolly's back bumper with a slip-knot. Post-wedding car, ready to roll.

"Quicksilver, shotgun!" I shout.

I use a lighter to set fire to the nearest bush, then hop into my big old black convertible, keys dangling from the steering column.

Someone jumps over the door into the passenger seat. Big. Gray-haired. Quite a mustache.

Quicksilver loves to ride shotgun. I glance to the moon above. Maybe not a wolf moon, maybe a Quicksilver moon.

I gun Dolly along the smoother ridge-top road, and we leave in a flash of fire as the brush burns into a long, flaming tail behind us.

Yips turn into frustrated whines and no pursuit, and the burned twine drops away.

I baby Dolly down a last rough patch of desert road onto a paved section to the main highway.

Highway I-15 cuts through desert that looks like "litter-box cake"…lots of dingy greige sand with clumps of olive-brown brush in the daylight and Dolly's headlights. We glide into traffic and I welcome overhead lights that outshine the full moon.

We make the bottom of the Las Vegas Strip in less than half an hour, but not before the darkening horizon brings out the bright lights and neon.

Some "old classic" Strip venues remain. The MGM-Grand, Caesars Palace. Since the Millennium, though, "old classic" movie monsters like Dracula and Frankenstein had inspired venues like rock star Christophe's Inferno Hotel and Cicero's Gehenna, carrying another name for Hell and most appropriate. The taste for darker, sinister hotel-casinos and attractions that made the gaudy, lusty old Strip look tame.

Vegas had gone beyond the usual moving alabaster statues at The Venetian or holographic images of Hollywood's dead film icons who appeared to "interact" with patrons. Now the attractions featured the shadowy Immortality Mob's secret recreations of 20th-century black-and-white film stars. Call the Immortality Mob Twentieth Century Foxy. With *mucho* more of the silver mojo I have a modicum of, the Immortality Mob revived the images of the actors and their characters from black-and-white movies filmed on silver nitrate on zombie "canvases" smuggled from Mexico as "living" 3-D, black and white and gray all over Cinema Simulacrums, CinSims for short.

Nobody knew if the process was magic or science. Were CinSims animatronics, androids or, icky rumor, workable Frankensteins? Bring out the Febreze!

Since the early post-millennium days these CinSims had been chipped to stay in place and leased to Vegas venues. Some thought they were enslaved workers who needed a liberation movement, including me. I treat them as real people, and they make great confidential informants for a P.I. Just think, Sam Spade ready to chat about how to avoid a tail over an Inferno Bar cocktail. Priceless.

As Dolly glides past the Mirage's long-time volcano it spits out fire and brimstone and more subterranean snorts and screeches and growls than usual.

Then I realize Quicksilver is now in the back seat, looking behind us and growling.

I check the rearview mirror. *Uh-oh.* A triangular formation of headlights that might be IDed as UFOs in the night sky was ground-bound and heading to overtake us. One-eyed monsters clustering into tight mini-formations. Members of mobster Cicero's werewolf motorcycle gang, freshly "turned" from human form.

"'Lunatics' pack on our tails, Quicksilver," I warn.

He revs a growl of his own into a snarl and jumps out onto the Strip running, then leaping to knock the leader of the Lunatics onto the street, his bike careening riderless away. The following bikes break rank to speed past Quick while he charges to take the last one out as easily as the first.

SUVs and cabs and limos are fleeing our lane all around us, so Dolly has a concrete carpet of room to race down. I floor her gas pedal, planning to peel off into the Inferno's long driveway that circles into the back parking lot where I could run big rings around the motorcycle pack.

A *thump* on my right is Quicksilver leaping into Dolly's passenger seat from the bed of a stretch Tundra racing me on my right.

Stretched pickup? This is Vegas, baby. Anything goes. And Dolly's engine is the MGM-lion roaring up the Inferno hotel entrance, pointing straight toward its mirror-walled parking facility.

As fast as Quicksilver took them out, more motorcycles took the lead in our pursuit. And they are gaining on us.

I can mirror-walk, but can I mirror-*drive*, right through the Inferno Hotel's reflective golden side? My pal Manny, the hotel parking demon and a car buff, is falling backwards out of our way, wailing in fear for Dolly's 1957-vintage glory, if not *my* survival.

I glimpse Quicksilver leaping over Dolly's trunk to knock the new lead Lunatic off his Harley, scattering the reassembled oncoming pack like they are a fresh set of bowling pins and he's a bowling ball born.

Quicksilver, no! They'll tear you apart.

Dolly's three hundred and twenty-five horses raced up the gentle incline of the entry road. The hotel's façade of looming flames reflecting against the crimson glass wall.

I frantically eye the chiming silver charm bracelet on my right wrist I could never remove.

This "Silver Familiar", an unwanted permanent "gift" of a lock of snow-white hair from Christophe that I touched because it had reminded me of my lost Achilles, could morph into anything silver or silver metal, mostly weapons—a dagger in my palm, a necklace of martial arts throwing stars, or a pair of handcuffs to confine a captured foe. Here and now it seemed to be only a silly, useless charm bracelet in my way.

In a post-Millennium Las Vegas full of supernatural twists, silver had proved to be my magical medium. I could walk through mirrors like walking through an invisible waterfall and be somewhere else (handy escape clause) because most of them had a silver backing, but were the Inferno window-wall mirrors backed with silver? Could I *drive* Dolly through them and take Toto too? Quicksilver *arf*s with excitement.

Dolly's twin chrome fender ornaments vanish into reflected flames as I wince, push the pedal to the floor, 100 mph and leave smoking asphalt in my wake.

The sound of a thousand wind chimes and walls of shattering black and red glass feel icy-hot as it caves before two-and-a-half tons of airborne Detroit metal.

Everything suspends. Sight. Sound. Time. Motion. Heartbeat. Along with my breath. We hovered in a well of silence at the shattering tornado's still center for a long, pulse-taking moment. A pause before the action and chaos begins anew. A second reel of the film unwinding.

The resulting downward arc shows Dolly's front fender vanishing slowly into thick oily silver quicksand.

Quicksilver! my mind howls as I turn to look behind. Nothing but gooey silver enveloping Dolly's sinking black trunk and now my face, cool and gelatinous, so I have to close my eyes…on a view of Quicksilver charging into a closing maw of liquid mercury. *Quick! No.*

The cool tide of swallowing silver washes over me and dissipates as it passes. Dolly's huge steel frame jolts down onto an asphalt surface, her suspension writhing with an aging stripper's desperate moves as the pool of living silver cushioning her tires shrinks away.

I feel the large pizza-size leather-covered steering wheel jerk through my leather workout-gloved palms, burning—*ouch*. Still looking backward for Quicksilver, I flip out of the roomy driver's seat—no seat belts and air bags in a vintage vehicle—curling into a ball as I kiss pavement.

Rock and roll. Good thing I'd worn biker leather for the trip to keep creeps away. I lay there in the dark, trying to judge what the impact has done to my breath and bones and body—and Dolly's frame—staring up at the faint stars of a Las Vegas night sky through a tunnel of Fourth of July fireworks and spotlights and neon soaring sixty stories high.

Huh. I read the screaming neon words swirling like visible imaginary constellations above me. The Mirage. The Bellagio. Planet Hollywood. The Magic Lantern. The Optical Illusion. Phantasmagoria. The Trumpet…no, just Trump. The impact must have knocked me silly, or some mogul just magically increased his hotel-casino portfolio. At least I hadn't landed on the Inferno hotel grounds. And I heard no pursuing growls, from motorcycle engines or walking wounded gang riders.

Or from a defending Quicksilver.

5
Alley Cat Rescue

Girl, get a grip. Once again, a brush of whiskers kisses my raw, scraped cheek and forehead, a delicate warm sniff at my nostrils searches to detect life in me.

That spurred me up into a squat, and then to my feet in one urgent move. In the dim work lights, I see my scratched and scarred leather jacket arms and jeggings are done for, showing gashes in the tough hide.

Me? I'm unscraped except for a few knuckles and that stinging temple and cheekbone. A new silver Halloween cat charm bumped my right wrist bone. The wrist-length work-out gloves had saved my palms from harm. My fingers flex, ready to make defensive fists and trouble if necessary.

Strong whiffs of grease and gas…and shrimp?

Still no sign of Quicksilver. My sensations of being inspected by his muzzle while coming fully conscious must have been an illusion my tingling skin and nerves produced.

Time for a condition check. What and where.

Dolly and I had stopped hard in a deserted dead end of Dumpsters and mechanical installations behind a major hotel-casino. What had the impact done to Dolly? I limp over to wrench—bad sign— the driver's door open and tried Dolly's keys in the ignition. *What a girl!* She coughed twice, and then turned her engine over like a pro.

I'd kept her wheels straight, so I edge her forward and park her alongside some hulking 350 trucks and vans. Putting up her black

convertible top, I wince to see gashes in the backseat's red leather...
Quicksilver's rapid-exit claw marks as he dashed over the trunk to
charge the Lunatics.

Too bad the Lunatics can't be sued for that expensive repair job,
kvetched Irma.

Strip traffic shook, rattled and rolled in the distance. I could
hear the roar of a lone motorcycle, diminishing. Surely Quicksilver
had made it, and was in hot pursuit of any stragglers. I need to get
undercover before someone came to investigate the noise. Back
alleys are no place to be penned in. Quick could find me almost
anywhere.

I'd mastered the what, now to figure out the *where*. A ten-foot
wall of mocha-colored stucco formed the bland backside of some
gaudy hotel attraction.

I pocket Dolly's keys, counting on her black body paint and
canvas top to camouflage her in the dark, and barge into the bushes
along the wall, seeking entry.

Ouch. Yeah, I hurt all over, but Vegas has a desert climate. Its
native plants pack the kick of thorns and cactus spikes. Somehow,
somewhere I had to get through the classic fairytale thorn patch like
a princeling born, then break into the main building and discreetly
merge with the crowds until I could find out which hotel I had
crashed-landed near, then return to retrieve Dolly and Quicksilver.

Quick was probably even now taking down the last rolling
Lunatic member somewhere near the Strip. Once unleashed, he's
thorough.

Much as I chaffed at my landlord, Hector Nightwine, the
rented Enchanted Cottage reconstruction in his backyard with its
Wardrobe Witch and the talking mirror from Disney's *Snow White*
had never seemed so normal and downright homey.

I survey my scuffed boots with the thick two-inch heels. These
zombie-kickers were never going to get me three heel-clicks home
anywhere, certainly not to Kansas.

We're not in Kansas anymore, Delilah, maybe not even Vegas,
Irma whispers to me and the night.

I had looked up her funky first name. One was the deliberately
ditsy blonde star, Marie Wilson, of a Fifties radio and TV sitcom

series called *My Friend Irma*. Another was Irma la Douce, a French hooker played by Las Vegas Rat Pack gal pal and New Age actress Shirley MacLaine. A wild card candidate was Erma Bombeck, 20th-century housewife turned bestselling humor book writer. Wouldn't you know I'd end up, not with funny or sexy, but ditsy.

Finally finding a lower delivery bay in the wall, I hop over. Good thing I know the underbelly inside Vegas hotels like a rat knows a maze. If I can't make it on the run here, I don't deserve to make it anywhere.

You do not want to linger in this dead-end alleyway, Miss. What a dump.

I stop. That voice didn't sound like Irma, despite, or maybe because of the polite—or condescending?—"Miss".

Do not just stand there, exposed. Slither past the Dumpster and hang a quick left. Follow the handsome black cat cleaning his spanking-white whiskers.

What? Just white *whiskers*? No white rabbit? Was I being had by my own inner self? My head was throbbing, my nerves were shot, and I didn't need Lewis Carroll animal spirit guides. Maybe Irma is hallucinating.

Yet I spot the black cat, sitting where advertised. Oh, holy claustrophobia! An air-conditioning vent opening. I'd done my fill of crawling around overhead Eye-in-the-Sky passages for casino table surveillance.

I turn, pleased to see, or not see, that Dolly is as invisible as I'd hoped she'd be.

"I don't want to leave without looking for Quicksilver," I mutter to myself.

Worry not. He out-noses you and me by the thousands of cells, my new ride-along mind-reader says. *He will find you.*

"You?" I stare at the black cat. In the low light he looks almost as big as a raccoon and he sported no Cheshire cat grin, just those white whiskers he's so proud of, glinting along with his teeth now and then.

Last one in gets to inhale the linen closet dust, he says, lips not moving. *Whoops*. He's in my mind with Irma?

You wore her out with this whirlwind chase, he says. *If she's smart, she's taking a vacation at Temple Bar Lodge on what's left of Lake Mead in this drought. Move. Dirt and dark deeds are going down in The Looking Glass Theater inside. I need an impromptu partner who looks like she can handle herself in a tight spot.*

Well, if rock star-hotel entrepreneur Cocaine/Snow could have a black woman/white tiger shapechanger heading his security team, I guess I can back up a mind-speaking lucky black cat out of Lewis Carroll.

The name is pronounced Louie. *Not* Lewis.

"So you're on nickname terms with the pseudonymous long-gone author?"

I may be or I may not be, and I may sue or may not sue, but the name that is just plain Louie is *mine. Midnight Louie, to be precise.*

"I'm not sure I can follow where you go inside. Besides, I've got a car and dog outside to reclaim. Remember, I can't get through anything smaller than the width of my shoulders."

The cat startles me by jumping atop the Dumpster, then up onto my shoulders, his claws biting into my jacket shoulder pads.

I am breaking my rule about not speaking to humans on this emergency occasion. Do not get used to it.

"Fine with me. I only talk to magic mirrors. Even that is more psychic than I want to be."

Your shoulders are as wide as I am long. I will stand sideways in the tunnels every once in a while so you don't age-scuff that leather jacket more than it already looks. It is such primo claw-caressing material. He purrs right into my left ear.

"I'm a dog person, myself, but I won't get my canine partner back until I figure out where we are and what's going on here besides a ventriloquist act."

No ventriloquist. Sorry. But maybe a tiger. Las Vegas is the home of animal acts in every variation of the phrase.

I sigh, shrug, and bend down to let the enterprising cat precede me into a hands-and-knees slog into absolute darkness and toward what might be a literal dead end.

6
Big Game Girl

This super-size Little Doll may be a bit shaken up, but so am I. (Though I never deign to show it.) I have been shocked to my socks, if I had had them, but I am a classic kind of guy, jet-black except for my distinguished white whiskers and golf-course-green eyes. Golf courses are very popular in the Age of Trump.

I am used to keeping my mind to myself, if not my opinions. Vegas hosts a triple deck of mind readers and Tarot card shufflers and the like. And my kind, besides being hunted and burned with so-called witches in the Mid-Evil Ages, are still objects of fear, superstition and even mayhem in these supposedly enlightened times, which the word "enlightened" is a bit of an iffy supposition given the current time of day and mood.

No way would I reveal myself to a human, or actually "talk" to one of such an inferior breed, but it seems I cannot stop my thoughts from linking with Miss Dead-end Driver. This dame seems to be as exceptional in her human species as I am in catkind. Not even my adored Miss Temple Barr—though sadly married now, she has kept her "maiden" name for a professional identity, perhaps as I have retained the name the staff and visitors gave me at the upscale Palo Alto motel where I was "discovered" as ripe for fame and fortune—has what one might call "extra-sensual" hearing.

All I know now is my whole human gang has been lured to the new magic show at the Hellfire Hotel, possibly and probably to no good end. There they all are this evening, in a tidy little vulnerable clump, and even staying after the last show to hobnob with this Siegfried-and-Roy-huge new Strip magician who calls himself "Spellbinder". And since my circle of protectees have all been involved in taking down some genuine bad actors in the crime sense, I must ensure they come to no harm.

I hope to soon be introducing my car-and-canine-loving new acquaintance on the run to Miss Temple Barr, Mr. Matt Devine and Mr. Max Kinsella. Etcetera.

Before they came here I did a security check of the theater stage and belowground operations such as the operational and magic act tunnels, and do not like the smell of the setup. I noticed too many different human traces in the metal maze. Now I am introducing yet another human to an already volatile mix, but she looks like an action-ready femme fatale I can make use of in a pinch.

Especially since she is even now gamely elbowing and worming her way deep into the Hellfire's labyrinthine bowels right on my tail.

7
Cat Trick

Call me trapped.

Girl on the run has become girl gone underground.

My feline guide has disappeared into the dark like a Cheshire Cat or a phantasm. I've found no exit from these understage tunnels and steep, short stairways going ever up and down. I hear faint voices in the thrumming sounds of a possible concussion in my head and am feeling like a fresh candidate for psychiatric diagnosis. I can also hear the grind of the stage machinery above. I feel the vibrations of mad applause, and hear the cacophony of a pit orchestra. And I miss my doggone dog!

Dragging myself up another claustrophobic foreshortened staircase, I can now understand the main onstage performer. His commanding baritone is announcing something. Apparently a magical appearance from the trapdoor...*whoops*, I've arrived. Light leaking through a trapdoor right above my head.

Well, I'll give him one heck of a surprise. I crouch under the door in the stage floor.

When I hear "Now, ladies and gentlemen..."

(So trite an opening, don't you think?)

Pow! One two-handed impact and I push up like a daisy in a cemetery. Well, a black leather daisy. The barrier flips up and away, and I climb into a black space I can just stand up in...a vertical coffin painted black, barely wide enough to turn around in. A line of light on one side snaps back like a door, blinding me with spotlights.

I am also deafened by the basso mic-enhanced voice of my new dancing partner holding a white-leather gauntleted hand to aid me in stepping from the darkness onto a footlight-glaring stage.

For the moment, I am standing on a box and a few inches taller than my five-foot-eight plus two inches of bootheels, face-to-face with the man onstage.

I am staring into my own tiny disheveled image reflected in the lavish rhinestone surround of black sunglasses on a face as pale as a white leather rocker-Elvis angel with long, platinum, Johnny Winter locks. I know this dude and I am positive we've had some *not* positive encounters.

Snow and I bask in the hot lights in a stunning moment of frozen mutual shock, disbelief and instant icy antagonism.

I can't be at the Inferno Hotel. It was two miles up the Strip when I began my crawl into this neon-lit Wonderland.

But the show, any show, must go on. Snow tightens his hand on mine as he swoops me off the short pedestal to the stage floor, flourishing the black velvet lining of his white cape.

"Ladies and gentlemen, look," he announces, lofting my left arm and marching me to the glaring footlights. I stand there silent (he wears a mic), stunned in the spotlights like a ripped-leather, rags-and-bone Cinderella.

"Look," his deep, magnified voice repeats, "at what the cat dragged in."

The audience, a sea of eyeglass glints and indistinguishable features, begins a sprinkle of nervous clapping.

Feeling like a fool, I manage a stage curtsey in my clumsy boots.

The sprinkle has turned into a mild drizzle.

The master of ceremonies whirls toward a matching black box onstage twenty feet from my recent dwelling.

His sweeping cloak gestures to the box door, opening now a bit to reveal the bath-mat-sized right paw of an enormous white tiger moving slowly out like a stripper's ultra-high heel. Instant deja vu.

My mind flashes to another stage. I know the white tiger and her name, *Grizelle*. And I know that gorgeous, eight-hundred-pound feline form stalking toward us, her furred shoulder blades sharp as shark fins, has never been a friend of mine.

She stops at the magician's side, heeling like a dog. Snow is wearing his usual black-leather-and-pink-diamond collar, and Grizelle sports a huge version of her own.

"I believe," Snow announces, "our shabby Cinderella deserves a magnificent carriage for an exit."

With a pull of that indomitable white-gloved hand, he guides me around the tiger in a semi-circle and assists me in mounting the tiger's back, riding "sidesaddle".

The puzzled drizzle of applause becomes a roaring waterfall as I curl my gloved hands into the tiger's neck scruff. A shudder of dislike shakes her entire frame. She stalks offstage on silent paws, uttering a long, low, unhappy growl, which I would join if I could.

Black-clad assistants swiftly lift me off the tiger's back and down with a thump of my boots onto the wooden floor, swarming the tiger to usher the Big Cat into a large, richly decorated cage backstage.

And so ends my unwelcome freaky Las Vegas stage debut.

8
Six Deadly Sins

The stage section under the boxes rotates into the set's dark rear, hidden from the audience as a dazzling "Spellbinder" curtain covers the scene change. Apparently "The Lady or the Tiger" scenario was the closing illusion, with the cat and woman exchanging boxes in a few seconds, but I am the wrong woman. I am not a "Lady" in anyone's book. My traveling outfit was chosen to warn off bad guys.

Snow struts and bows onstage, his revealed dark cloak wings swooping and swirling offstage behind him.

I am kept there between two of the crew, who are totally hooded and clothed in black body stockings so their features are as vague as the so-called "face on Mars". Mondo creepy.

"Such a fraud you are!" I tell Snow.

"Who are you?" he demands. Assistants rush to unfasten the heavy cloak. "You crashed my show. What happened to Gwen?"

"Gwen? I don't even know what happened to *me*! I was eluding the Lunatics motorcycle gang on the Strip, and then was trapped behind this hotel with no way out but following some crazy black cat crawling into the air-conditioning vents.

"And why call me a fraud? Magicians admit it's all smoke and mirrors.

"Using a shape-shifter for the girl-into-cat trick? Doesn't that qualify for fraud?"

"Shape-shifter?" He sounds uncertain for the first time, but glances stageward and realizes he has to take another bow. "I'll deal with you afterward."

I'm forced to watch him smile and stride and bow to raging applause and finally head, grim-faced, back into the wings.

"Important media people were attending this show. Your crazy, needy, attention-getting jaunt onstage ruined my finale."

"Needy, attention-getting must be *your* middle name. Get another punching bag." I turn to go. The mute faceless men in black block my exit, and he grabs my wrist from behind.

I turned and twisted my wrist from his grip. "That's assault, buddy. I got on your stage by accident, and respected your need to make my appearance look like part of the show, but you are not manhandling my wrist a moment more."

He looks at where my short, black leather glove meets the red marks from the silver charm bracelet being pressed into my skin by his steely grip.

We both stare at the bracelet. Last I'd seen it, it was a skinny "Nevertheless she persisted" pewter bar and leather cord bangle so light I forgot I was wearing it. I'm still foggy from my wild drive, but I'd never seen this charm bracelet before, until aware of it in my rush to escape the Lunatics.

"Goth Girl, are you?" he asks, still frowning.

Those expression-hiding black sunglasses are annoying me.

"I think," I say slowly, "I actually think you gave it to me."

He drops my wrist like a hot curling iron. "You 'think'. Fans give items to *me*, not the other way around."

"I am not a fan. Can't you tell?"

He glances intensely at the stage again.

"Put her in the green room and keep her there," he orders the stagehands. To me, he says, "If asked, you make your act-crashing story something, ah, amusing or harmless. Anything that doesn't put shade on me or the show. That's the least you can do."

The assistants, steps silent as a Big Cat's, shepherd me farther into this huge hotel. Keeping me in loose custody while I obsess about getting back to Dolly as soon as possible and looking for Quicksilver.

I pass the tiger cage. Grizelle stretches one rake-size clawed paw to the bars as I walk by and the black irises of her huge green eyes shrink into slits.

"See you later, Grizelle," I mutter.

"We don't bother the Big Cat with chit chat," one guy says, no longer mute.

"I wasn't talking to the *tiger*," I say with hauteur totally wasted on him.

Grizelle's low growl follows us (just like old times) through an offstage door into a room crowded with sofas and chairs with a bar on one wall. A central table holds tubs of crushed ice, high-end bottled waters, and energy drinks for the cast and crew. Green rooms aren't green, but they do provide necessities to offstage performers and sometimes guests.

I grab a water and sink into the cushy corner of an overstuffed suede couch.

Under the bright track lighting, I realize the stagehands' costumes aren't one overall outfit, like skin, but they all wear tight spandex black turtleneck hoods, Tees, tights and soft-soled black ballet slippers. And some are women.

A woman in black below the neck shakes out a strawberry-blonde Dutch cut and comes to sit by me. "Say, you really *are* mangled. The rips and dried-blood seams aren't just for style or show."

Style or show? Hellfire, no. Hellfire is what the Scuffs on my Buff burned like even now.

"Um, yeah," I said. "This big, bad wolf pack motorcycle gang chased my convertible. I had to hide her behind the hotel delivery and trash pick-up area. But not before I took a nasty spill."

"*Her?*"

"My cars are like ships, they have a gender."

A couple more crew in black came around. "That forehead wound looks nasty." With his hood off, the slim, Scandinavian-blond young guy definitely belied the sin embossed in large, glossy black letters on his back, Lust.

The hand I touched to the fire-ant migraine ache at my left temple I'd been ignoring returned with sticky, bloody fingers. "Gee, didn't see me in a mirror. You'd think wandering into a magic act I would have passed a few mirrors to look into."

Another guy came around, still hooded, with a back-advertising Gluttony, but his words were designed to relieve my worry. "Mirrors, plain and simple, are old-fashioned magic tricks. It's all holograms and light shows and technology now."

"And what hotel and what act did I crash into, crash literally?"

"Poor girl," says Strawberry Blonde. "You don't even know where you are."

"All I remember, I was fleeing a pack of werewo...*uh-oh*...of weird but mondo mean-looking bikers. Their jackets read 'Lunatics.'"

The group drew in audible breaths at the name. Great audience. I was on a roll.

"I didn't know where I was on the Strip or what hotel I had wheeled Dolly into. I did get tossed out onto the pavement, but most of my fall was rolling rather than a shake and rattle."

"You were a prime target in an open car." A red-headed guy had joined the cluster. "No wonder you're shaky. Here. Some protein bars."

I realized I was ravenous. "Thanks." Two quick bites convinced me eating was not a good thing, and I stopped chewing.

"Hey," a black woman said. "She might have a concussion."

"I don't think so, guys," I said. "I just need to get my bearings. I'm worried that my dog jumped out of my car to confront those bad-boy bikers. I did lose them, but Quicksilver is missing now. I need to get back to Dolly and find him."

"You had a friend with you?" the male redhead asked as he reclaimed the protein bars that repelled me.

"No. Like I said. That's the name of the car."

"Listen," Strawberry Blonde urged. "We can't leave until the Boss comes in for post-show critique notes, but there's a hotel doctor. Maybe she can take a look at you."

I panicked. The less information I gave the sooner I'd orient myself. "Thanks, but no. I'm feeling way better than you look in your funereal black. You've all been so nice. What do you do in the show?"

"Well..." A gorgeous Latina girl removed her hood to reveal a pixie cut. "That's classified. We are literal stage hands, sometimes that's all you can see of us. We call ourselves the Six Deadly Sins."

"The *Six* Deadly Sins. Aren't there seven? Oh, are you a rock group?"

Given "Inferno Snow" was lead singer for the Seven Deadly Sins, this was really confusing me.

"Not us. We 'invisible' cast members number six, so we each took a Deadly Sin nickname for fun." They lined up and turned around. I read the shiny black words on their shirt backs: "Sloth, Wrath, Greed, Gluttony, Lust, Envy."

"SWGGLE," I summed up as a memory device.

It took them a minute to decode that.

"SWGGLE, right." They grinned and fist bumped. "Your brain isn't scrambled in the least, girl."

"Isn't there a seventh deadly sin?"

"We leave that one unsaid, for the Boss."

I repeated the six words. Which sin was missing? An iconic sequence might be famous, but who remembers even the Seven Dwarves' names?

Sloth, Wrath, Greed, Gluttony, Lust, Envy... Irma recounted.

"Of course," I said. "The Boss. That's...Pride. Like head of the Big Cat pride. What name does he perform under, though?"

"It's out in lights and billboards on the Strip. If you hadn't come in the back way, you'd have seen it," said the red-headed guy, appropriately labeled Wrath. "Christophe is his name, but he performs as 'Spellbinder, the Strip magician who will hold you Spellbound.'"

"Magician?"

"Most successful Vegas Strip act since the magnificently tragic Siegfried and Roy."

That reference made a white tiger shapeshifter fit right in. Had *everything* done just that? *Shifted*, not just the usual Grizelle? Had the Las Vegas I knew jumped sideways on some time bend or twist? Or had my concussed brain done the job?

Whatever, I had to avoid explaining myself until I knew what was what. And following a black cat down a hole into a hotel's underground mechanical maze would not make me look sane, or believable. How was I going to get around that?

"What's your name?" the black guy named Envy asked.

I hesitated. Didn't want to be too easily traceable. Delilah Street could have some kind of record in this loony Las Vegas.

"Take your time, honey," Greed crooned, "a head injury can knock the instant recall out of you. We get plenty in this business."

"It's….it's uh, Lilah. Lilah…" Different name for "Street" needed…LaRue! *Ooh.* Sounded like a stripper name. *Lilah Lane.*

Desperate, I echoed Irma.

So I sounded like a Superman girlfriend. Way better. And if I "recovered" my memory later, I'd given a logically garbled version of my real name. Delilah Street. Not easy to redefine your name and your world on the fly.

One thing I would not ever redefine. "Spellbinder" *was* Snow, the reputed albino vampire and rock-star owner of the Inferno Hotel. Why had he opened a new venue posing as a magician?

Or had I been knocked out longer than I thought? Like a year or two.

Snow had stretched up his arms after losing the cloak. I'd noticed the black velvet interior was embroidered with jeweled versions of the zodiac symbols. *Yum.* I'd love to wear that cloak inside out.

Before I could process that silly idea, something blew the door open and sucked the air out of the room like a whirlwind.

Enter the star of the show. The black interior of the cloak swirled around Spellbinder's white-moving figure as he twirled it off onto a couch arm. One of the Six—I was unable to see the Sin name on its back—quickly gathered the garment into its ambiguous arms and vanished behind another set of double doors to the star's dressing room, from what I'd glimpsed.

Snow took a quick turn around the room without the heavy cape.

"Good show, group," he said, "considering our tiger Lady vanished and now Grizelle tells me the Green Fairy isn't in her dressing room and has gone AWOL without a word." Snow added, "Awkward. I'm expecting the producer-hosts from *Las Vegas Last Night* here in the green room shortly. Party of three, I'm told. We comped the show for them and are doing a pre-interview discussion for my TV appearance next week. I should be back in civvies by the time they're escorted here."

He turned to leave, then paused. "Hope the guests bought that crazed, ragged interloper as a part of the act. Tell Grizelle to alert hotel security and get that anomaly out of here."

He swept inside his dressing room and the double doors slammed shut behind him.

I quailed a bit in my corner, realizing the gathered Six Deadly Sins standing around me had provided camouflage. Albinism caused weak vision. While some ordinary rockers wore tinted glasses against the stage-light glare, the problem would be even worse for an albino like Snow. I'd always wondered whether he had pink eyes, like a white rabbit, behind those sunglasses. He certainly favored pink gemstones. Flaunting his difference?

The thought of his pink rabbit eyes always made me want to giggle. It was like telling shy public speakers to imagine their audience naked, but then I'd never wanted to imagine Snow naked and ardently hoped the wish was mutual.

The Six Deadly Sins bustled around as ordered. Gluttony slipped behind the bar. Envy plumped the pillows on the intimate setting of two chairs circling a stunning triangular glass cocktail table in the middle of the long, long couch I sat on.

Greed eyed me. "Glad we were able to conceal her from the Boss," he told the others. "He is not happy about her impromptu cameo role. She'll have to leave."

"Too late," said Sloth, concealing a small cell phone in its distressingly elastic garb.

My mind boggled at where the super-sleek Sins would stow anything but hairpins.

Sloth moved fast for the name. "Grizelle's en route, escorting the TV team here. No time to risk being caught smuggling out the show crasher."

9
Deadly Delusion

"We're nearly there," said the exotic Hellfire public relations woman who stood six-feet-something in spike heels.

Temple, being five-foot-zero, was always well-high-heeled for business meetings, but she was beginning to heave a pant or two after a trek from the main doors through the massive casino to the theater area. She felt like a Yorkie dog being walked by a cheetah in full flight.

"Look. That's interesting." Matt sent Temple a sympathetic glance as he stopped dead. "I've never seen a slot machine that featured the hotel's major act as a background."

Recognizing her opening, Temple also stopped and agreed. "Yes, so clever. Video of Christophe and the gorgeous performing white tiger in a slot machine game. Smart marketing using every medium in the casino for promotion."

"Thank you," Grizelle said with a regal head bow.

Matt kept the conversation, and rest period, going. "Obviously your idea, Miss, uh…"

"Grizelle," she said. Okay *purred*, Temple amended. Her husband was too darned good looking sometimes. "Just Grizelle."

"I read on a program that was the tiger's name," Temple said. One predator named after another, she guessed.

"We are *very* close." The woman smiled with, uh, pride.

Well, close in spirit perhaps, but not really similar. Grizelle, the human, was an enviably towering black woman with an Indy 500 racetrack figure, a mane of regal dreadlocks and emerald-green tigerish eyes. Temple had noticed a black person with green eyes now and then, but Grizelle's were Max Kinsella phony-contact-lenses vivid green. Temple had to wonder if anything about this woman was natural…other than her long, sharp, kindred claws with the tiger.

Temple was finally catching her breath, so she added, truthfully, "I'm so pleased you've pointed out the special attractions along the way. We'll have to explore the fabulous outdoor tiger 'playpen' later." *From outside the glass observation area*, she promised herself.

"It's also clever that Mr. Christophe's magic act pays tribute to Vegas's most iconic attractions. Siegfried and Roy's classic animal act and breeding program for white Big Cats, with, ah, your namesake white tiger, and also the newer Absinthe circus-tent cabaret venue outside Caesars."

"The name is Christophe, just Christophe, only Christophe, no titles, honorific or not, just as I and the tiger are only 'Grizelle,'" their exotic guide explained.

Temple still found a person and an animal sharing the same name a little creepy.

"As you say," Grizelle added, smiling at Matt, "it's important Las Vegas is self-referential where we can be in these days of rivaling electronic media distractions."

"Slot machine apps on your cell phone," he answered, nodding.

"Exactly." Grizelle looked again at Temple. "I understand public relations used to be your game. Yes, we pay tribute to Absinthe with the popular woman transforming into the Green Fairy magical illusion, which has become our signature act. You'll appreciate we were perplexed how to offer our guests more of that without treading on Absinthe's brand."

"I bet," Temple said fervently. The Las Vegas Strip was mined with legal turf wars.

Grizelle turned around and swept a dramatic arm at a nearby area. "Witness the Hellfire's solution."

Temple had seen the dazzling mirrored and lit entrance to the Looking Glass theater dead ahead, but now she noticed a sizable area to the left: an oasis of neon green and gold and orange, with a vintage wooden floor, small round wrought-iron and wood café tables, and matching chairs scattered here and there, some occupied by foot-weary tourists.

The cafe area extended into a bar area with a large leaf-and-vine-twined sign decorated with the small twinkling bulbs called fairy lights.

Above it all a large sinuous neon sign in script announced, *L'heure verte.*

She turned to Matt. "This bar evokes when the universal 'cocktail hour' of five o'clock was invented. Paris in the late nineteenth century converted all France, and then the world, to 'the Green Hour', and then absinthe became the Drink of the Day.

"Oh, how charming," Temple continued as she took in the area. "All those twining images evoke the Art Nouveau period, completely unexpected in a hotel with a theme of 'hellish' fun."

If a tiger-woman could be said to "beam", Grizelle was doing it.

"Wicked Wormwood Bar." Matt read aloud the sign over the long bar. "Sounds a bit dark for 'charming', Temple."

She was not to be denied. "You must have heard Alan Jackson and Jimmy Buffett singing 'It's Five O'Clock Somewhere.'"

"No. We didn't have drinking songs at St. Agatha, Virgin and Martyr, Catholic parish." Matt liked to cite his previous chaste and, to her, unhip life as a parish priest whenever Temple became too enraptured by pop culture.

"I think Jimmy Buffett was an altar boy before his misspent youth," she pointed out.

Grizelle watched their byplay with alert puzzlement, stretching her long red fingernails in and out like a flamenco dancer missing her castanets.

Temple felt bound to give Wicked Wormwood its due.

"It all started in France when there was a terrible wine shortage due to the Great Wine Blight."

"Hard to imagine that being tragic," Matt said.

"Well, no Sacramental wine for mass in a Catholic country?"

"Or for Father when he put his feet up after six masses a day."

"Can you show him a glass of absinthe?" Temple asked Grizelle, mainly to stop the woman's annoying fingernail action. It reminded her of Midnight Louie's feline "pummeling" to show contentedness. This road show cat-woman made Temple nervous.

"As you know," Grizelle said with her first small smile, "that's not so simple. Absinthe has as many whys and wherefores and methods and myths as the stars in the sky. Although its vivid green color is famous and even notorious, it also comes in orange and gold." Grizelle led them to the long bar backed by a gold-leafed framed mirror. "Gaston will enlighten you."

"Gaston? Really?" Temple asked. She informed Matt in a soft aside, "That's the iconic name for a French waiter. I think it was because Ugly Americans abroad decades ago mistook 'Garçon'— which means 'boy'—for the French name Gaston."

"No kidding. I did watch TV."

"Anyway," Temple jumped up on the vintage barstool, having conquered that feat for one of her scant size by age twenty, now a decade behind her. She really couldn't hear much in a standing group unless she had a high perch.

Matt knew better than to try to be gallant and assist her up, while Grizelle, ever the sinewy Big Cat, leaned one lean hip on a red leather stool seat and crossed her long languid paws and claws. Uh, legs and spike heels.

A PR woman like Temple lived off a love of odd historical facts. "No wine. So, in late nineteenth-century French cafés, it was the dawning of the Age of Absinthe, not Aquarius. The 'cocktail hour' and absinthe became the rage in wine-bereft Paris. The day's artists painted scenes of intellectuals lingering over their poisonously colored potions—Absinthe drinkers included Edgar Degas, Edgar Allan Poe, Oscar Wilde, and even Mark Twain and Vincent Van Gogh."

"Van Gogh before the ear-surgery incident, I suppose," Matt said, hoisting up on his own stool for storytelling time.

"Before and probably after. Absinthe became the Western world's first fashionable cocktail. It got a reputation for stimulating artistic creation, and then for sucking the soul out of artists and writers when they became addicted. That's why the Green Fairy has been portrayed as both a muse and a seductress. I think, with all these now-famous but flawed imbibers, the real obsession was the ritual."

"Ritual?" With his priestly past, Matt was ever alert to rituals.

Grizelle beckoned. "Gaston," a thirtyish blond guy with a slightly villainous curled mustache, wearing a striped jersey and beret, placed three empty crystal glasses on the mirror-polished black granite bar, which reflected a dark, barely glimpsed shadow version of the objects and motions.

He addressed Temple while also preparing the other two glasses.

"This is a *Pontarlier* glass, Madame."

The short-stemmed glass's bottom had a bubble reservoir that opened into a flaring shape.

He took a dark green glass bottle in the shape of a skull from the tiers of liquor shelves nestled against the bar mirror.

"*Oooh*," Temple said in a spooky voice. "Doubling-down on the debauched reputation of Absinthe, I see."

Gaston filled each glass to the top of the bottom "bubble" with emerald green liquor. "This holds one ounce of Absinthe," he said, then picked up a silver serving piece.

"Your spoon, Madame."

With its fancy silver trowel-like shape, an Absinthe spoon resembled a small, decoratively slotted triangular pie server.

Gaston set it atop Temple's wider glass rim in perfect balance.

"And the organic sugar plum at the top." He placed a lump of sugar on the spoon.

"Now," Gaston announced. "For *my* magic show, my illusion and your delusion. We can go with either a fire or ice effect, but each will produce the famous 'louch' effect as the absinthe green turns opalescent white and milky.

"Next, the wonder of glacier-icy water for Madame." He poured from a petite glass pitcher retrieved from a cooler under the bar top. As the cold, clear water saturated the sugar lump and spread into the emerald bowl, the absinthe turned moonstone white. Gaston topped the glass off with a few more drops of the green liquor.

For Matt's glass, he poured a few drops of absinthe atop the sugar cube, then struck an old-fashioned wooden match and touched its tip to the sugar. A lurid blue flame shot up a couple of inches. Again he poured ice water and the vivid green absinthe below metamorphosized into a ghost of itself.

Gaston repeated the flame trick with Grizelle's glass.

By now tourists had gathered around. Matt and Temple lifted their glasses and sipped carefully. Grizelle threw hers back in one swallow, shot glass style, inspiring a small round of applause.

"It tastes like licorice," Temple said after sipping her glass, sans spoon. "How unexpected."

"Yeah," Matt said. "Do you like it?"

"I don't know yet." She sipped again.

A deep voice from behind them boomed out, "Miss Temple Barr confessing to momentary indecision. Impossible!"

She blinked as she and her stool spun around for a half turn and found herself looking into the twinkling blue eyes of Danny Dove, star Vegas choreographer and good friend.

Matt had turned to shake Danny's hand. "What's brought you here? And when can we get you on our TV show?"

"My question's the same," Temple said. "We're doing a segment on Christophe and his magic acts. This is pre-appearance research. And you?"

Danny turned to the empty area between the bar and the café tables. "The management is thinking of adding Apache dances to this new Wicked Wormwood bar attraction. I actually designed the set. I'm branching out. These vagabond knees aren't going to tap 'New York, New York' forever."

"But *you'll* be forever young," Temple assured him.

Danny's curly blond hair and compact but seemingly always "on springs" frame made him seem a font of eternal energy, as professional dancers did.

Danny proved it by grabbing Temple authoritatively by the waist, lifting her up and turning to set her down, then spinning her under one arm in perfect position to make a low curtsey.

"*Whew*, Danny. I don't know if you or the absinthe is doing a tilt-a-whirl ride in my brain."

Onlookers clapped and moved forward to order at the bar.

Danny French-pecked each of Temple's cheeks, bowed to Grizelle and waved goodbye to Matt.

Again a group of three, they moved away.

Temple had seen Grizelle slap a comp card on the bar to pay for the drinks, so she pushed a twenty-dollar tip into the bar's empty brandy snifter as they left. Gaston winked at her. Folks worked hard to please guests in Las Vegas.

10
Malice in Wonderland

The green room bustle was a welcome diversion to me. This chick was tired of being the only act in the freak show, and turned with the others when the outer doors opened. A dreadlock-crowned, supermodel-tall black woman on four-inch red heels dwarfed the telegenic couple she escorted. I was too involved blinking at the woman known as Grizelle, Snow's security head at the Inferno and no friend of mine, or Quicksilver's. And a shape-shifter into a white tiger. I needed to check where the backstage tiger was ASAP. Snow could be mixing the two into the act.

The talk show hosts were the anticipated telegenic. A handsome blond man and a petite red-haired woman wearing heels almost as high as Grizelle's.

The cat-woman herself was all business.

"Ms. Barr, Mr. Devine, please be seated, Christophe will be out as soon as he's changed."

"It's Temple and Matt," the redhead said. "And it's most gracious of Christophe to let us meet with him after the rigors of the second show."

Grizelle seated them on the chairs and offered drinks. Sparkling water was their choice. Grizelle nodded at the Six Deadly Sins to fetch the drinks and offer appetizers from the table. As the Sins split to do their tasks, I was exposed, sitting quietly on the sofa.

"You," Grizelle said in a soft hiss, stalking over the plush carpeting and leaving heel stab marks in her wake. "Again. Get out. The door behind you leads to an exit from the theater area. I'll be ordering the hotel security guards to escort you to the Strip on sight."

She wafted a tiny phone from the glittering black-and-pink rhinestone belt and small purse hung around her slim hips.

Plainly, I was toast, whether it was French or cinnamon.

Then, in the silence following Grizelle's terms of banishment, came an excited lighter, kindlier voice.

"Oh, Matt, look," the intervening angel said. "This young woman is the Brothers Grimm 'Robber Girl' from the fairy tale in the flesh, who rode the back of the tiger. She'd be a fabulous interview for show background. Don't you think, Ms. Grizelle?"

Like everyone else, I turned to view the speaker.

Temple Barr was smiling with delight at the irritated giantess.

Grizelle smothered an under-breath growl and stared daggers at the "Boss's" closed doors as she stalked toward the inner sanctum.

Meanwhile, the tiny woman got up to perch by me on the long conversation pit sofa while the blond man, Matt Devine, remained in his chair. Obviously, she was in charge of "Girl Talk". They seemed perfectly nice and professional, but Chuck and Cindy had been the star Vegas talk show hosts for years. How and when had I missed hearing about these folks or their local TV interview show before? Probably at the same time I missed the ballyhoo about Snow's show changing from a rock concert with him as lead singer backed up by the Seven Deadly Sins band to a magician working with the Six Deadly Sins assistants! Things were all a bit "off". Or *I* was since hitting my head and following Alice's cat down into a rabbit hole Wonderland version of Vegas?

Also, between Temple Barr and the Clustering Six (sounded like a band) my cozy corner was getting crowded. My anxiety peaked at being trapped. I was definitely here without leave and getting ever more entangled in a backstage meeting I should never have attended.

To make the moment even more surreal, a black cat—*the* black cat—appeared out of nowhere (probably from under a sofa) and jumped up on the high couch arm next to me, swishing its radiator brush of a tail across my shoulder and into my face while I sputtered out fur.

The TV show couple laughed at his acrobatics. "You know I'm Temple, and this is Matt," the woman told me. "That fellow is Louie just living up to a cat's reputation for curiosity."

"Louie?"

"Midnight Louie. That's what Strip people have always called him. And you are—?"

The woman's warm, charming way disarmed me. I already felt guilty about having to lie. But I did it again. Fast. "Lilah. Lilah Lane."

"Is that a stage name? How clever. It sounds like it's a street name somewhere." Temple Barr leaned closer, looking concerned. "Say, your scratches aren't just stage makeup, they're real. Did the Big Cat—?"

Grizelle stepped near in one giant stride. "The tiger is highly intelligent and trained. It's perfectly safe with authorized handlers and performers. Miss Lane came to us as damaged goods."

"'Damaged goods,'" Matt repeated. "That's…kind of harsh."

"Actually," I said to encourage peace, "this Little Cat here saved me from more scrapes. I was dodging a motorcycle gang and was chased into a bad situation, a dead end behind the hotel. I stopped my convertible too fast. The sudden braking tossed me to the concrete."

"Omigosh. Did the bikers get to you once you were down?" Temple Barr was appalled.

"My dog chased them away."

Temple had leaned forward to inspect my face. "That gash on your forehead is developing a lump. You need treatment and to make a police report."

"No! No police. The gang's long gone and I don't need a hassle. I saw this cat…" I nodded to Louie, now rubbing against my leg and scratching his nose on my boot zipper tab. "He vanished into what looked like a door to an old-fashioned coal shoot, but it was an air-conditioning tunnel. The tight escape route banged me up more, but any port in a storm."

A voice boomed out right behind me, making us all jump.

"And *my* onstage act was her perfect place to emerge and go public in front of four thousand puzzled audience members."

Apparently Snow walked softly like a Big Cat, but his seasoned stage-star voice carried like vocal thunder. I twisted to see him standing right behind me, wearing white denim jeans and Filipino shirt, holding a soft drink can. That look went a lot better with the constant sunglasses than stage finery. He seemed actually relaxed.

My defender, Temple, had retreated to the chairs assigned to her and her husband, and by now had sat and produced a narrow-lined notepad and pen, and set her smart phone on audio recording. She lifted her weapons into Snow's field of vision.

"Mind if I take notes? I'm an ex TV-reporter and a confirmed combo of analog and digital. I won't use anything you want off-record, but Miss Lane's misadventure is fascinating. So are you. You covered her sudden appearance onstage with awesome cool. I totally took it for part of the act."

Beside her, Matt Devine was frowning. "The hotel mechanical tunnels must be monitored for intrusion."

Snow folded his arms and looked down on me. Nothing new. And I didn't even show any décolletage in this jacket. Snow left his disconcerting post behind me and moved around front to sprawl on the long couch opposite the chairs of his interviewers. I remained the "bad kid" under discussion in my solo sofa corner.

He turned his intimidating black sunglasses on me. "She *is* pretty banged up. It fits her story. When she showed up instead of Gwen, I just wanted to get her offstage ASAP, Miss Barr. Glad it seemed a show bit to you."

He nodded at Matt. "Her getting in without tripping any security devices bothered me also, but I have a theory. If she *followed* the black cat into the bowels of the building, as she claims, the animal would have appeared first on camera. Our human hotel monitors would likely dismiss the intrusion alerts as—"—he eyed me "—wandering vermin."

His head turned to regard the cat. "So the security team moved on to watching other monitors, not knowing this, ah, 'Midnight Louie' had an extra-long tail."

Now I'd been relegated, along with the cat, to being a "tail"? Not that I hadn't done tailing jobs for famous defense attorney Perry Mason and other clients now and again.

"The digital records will tell the truth of the 'tale'," Grizelle, Queen of Snark, said. "I'm on it, Boss." With this terse interjection, I realized that Grizelle was still looming behind me. Not a pleasant feeling, but just what she intended to instill.

Matt Devine spoke again, to me. "I'm not surprised Louie showed up to help a lady in distress. Midnight Louie is the mobile mascot of all the Strip hotels and venues. He came for the food first, of course. Once my wife had rescued him when she was a publicity rep for a big publishing convention, he became a tourist favorite. Some tourists make spotting him a contest, like being on a scavenger hunt."

"How charming for visiting Stripsters," Snow said, stretching his long arms along the couch top. His pale left hand, wearing a pink diamond in a heavy white gold setting, put me almost within his reach. I noticed a new ring charm on my bracelet.

Snow smiled. "But I don't need guest pests in my act."

Guest pests! I stiffened my sore spine and put my right arm up along the couch top too, my charm bracelet chiming softly. Midnight Louie leaped up, sat beside me to bat a charm or two, and then pointed his rear Snow-ward. He began cleaning beneath his much-discussed tail, one back leg hitched up behind his shoulder. *Hmm.* A cat's way of flashing the finger?

Snow's dark glasses reflected a light to flash me, my bracelet and the cat an invisible dirty look, no doubt. He lowered his arms as he leaned forward to deal with his invited visitors.

"As you saw, my show pays magical tribute to some of the Strip's most storied attractions."

Temple nodded ruefully. "So many of the crowd-pleasing, free Strip-side attractions from the eighties are gone, or only flash their lights on a limited schedule. The Mirage Volcano, the Treasure Island sinking ship outdoor drama, the Bellagio fountains. Nowadays the star D.J.s lead music raves to attract masses of younger visitors. And many have gone indoors after the brutal shooting tragedy."

"Exactly," Snow said. "That atrocity shattered everybody's confidence in Las Vegas's most signature feature, a walk-along Strip and Downtown panorama of exciting lights, action, music, casinos and slot machines."

Matt Devine nodded. "And now shattered public trust. We'll cover that during our live interview and intercut shots from your show with the original attractions they honor."

Temple glanced to me. "You know, that's the reason I accepted Lilah's onstage appearance so readily. Her black leather clothes reminded me of the racy 'pirate girls' show that succeeded the Treasure Island's longtime sinking-ship spectacular. That was a happy coincidence. Of course, the pirate girls wore Victoria's Secret lingerie and little of it, not modest jackets."

I patted a ripped sleeve. "This jacket saved *mucho* epidermis when I hit concrete and rolled."

"This poor woman needs medical help. Where are you staying?" Matt asked me. "We'll see you to a 24-hour clinic and home."

I stood. I'd played along long enough. "I'm staying nowhere yet and I'm not going anywhere until I'm sure my car is locked up safe and my dog is found. It's been a bumpy night and I gotta be leaving the normal way."

"Could you find her a room here?" Temple asked.

Grizelle bristled along with me.

"No," I said. "No way I sleep when Dolly and Quicksilver are out on their own. Now that you know my being here was an emergency, I apologize for disrupting your show and—" I nodded at the nice couple, "and your interview."

I moved past them, or tried. Temple Barr...well, barred the way, planting size-five high heels and five-foot height and steely gray-blue eyes right in front of me.

"No way are we abandoning you to a strange city, hurt and under stressful circumstances."

I was stunned. I had eight inches on her and a street-ruffian look, and I do believe she expected me to do exactly as she said.

Her gaze stayed on mine. "Christophe, if you don't mind, we'll stay a few minutes more until we make arrangements for Miss Lane and her car and dog."

"And the cat?" he asked in an amused voice.

"I'm sure he still wants to accompany Miss Lane too."

"'The cat walks alone', Kipling said," Snow quoted.

"Not this one."

"You know," Matt said, "Lilah needs to have someone looking at her abandoned car and for the dog pronto. I'm calling Gangsters' stretch limo ride service. The Fontana brothers know cars like cats know kibble. If you don't mind them working at the back of your hotel…"

Snow shook his sunglasses. "Tell them to ask for Manny if security bothers them."

"Manny!" Manny was my pal, the demon Manniphilpestiles. Parking valet at the Inferno Hotel. Liked me. Loved Dolly.

"You know Manny?" Snow asked suspiciously.

"I've heard he's good with cars."

"Well then, Grizelle. Text Manny to meet the Fontana boys out back. Near…what kind is your car?"

I said it proudly. My biggest estate sale find ever. "'Fifty-seven black Cadillac Eldorado Biarritz convertible, black cloth top, red leather seats."

"Awfully big car," Snow commented, leaving off "for a little girl".

"Sounds classic," Matt said. "Glad it's getting into good hands."

Temple took over. "Matt, get Gangsters on the phone. Aldo should be there, but it doesn't matter which brother's in charge. They need to secure Lilah's car and dog. They should enter the hotel grounds at—?" She looked inquiringly at Grizelle, who snapped to attention to answer.

"Service entrance behind the Hellfire Nine Circles attraction."

Big Car, Big Dog. I can handle them both. Even a Big Cat occasionally. I looked over my shoulder at Grizelle. She remained impassive, but Snow put his hand to his sunglasses bow, as if he would lower them to get a better look at me. *Oooh.* Case of Pink Eye coming.

Instead he turned to Matt. "You have the brothers on the phone?"

Matt, cell phone to ear, nodded. "Matt Devine here. Who's tending the store? *Uh-huh.* We have a young woman in distress.

Can you spare a pair or so of brothers to secure an abandoned car—" He glanced at me and held the phone out.

"Fifty-seven black Caddy Eldorado convertible, top up. And there should be a loose dog in the area. He's kinda awesome. Leave him for me to handle."

Matt took the phone back with an encouraging smile. "Call us back when you're on scene."

Temple had stowed her notebook and cell phone and approached Snow, looking like a Pomeranian facing up to a white wolf.

"I'm so sorry, Christophe, but we need to wait to make sure everything is all right out there at the car crash scene. We can take ourselves to a restaurant in the hotel to leave you in peace after an unexpectedly stressful show."

"Not happening, my dear Miss Barr. I need to wind down anyway. We have food and drink here, as well as my sincere but fervent curiosity to know how Miss Lane's predicament resolves. Better than binge-watch TV."

The mockery was classic Snow. He was tickled rabbit-eye pink to have me depending on his hospitality in a really embarrassing and, frankly, panicked moment of my life.

Snow went on, "We all need a glass of Champagne to celebrate doing a good deed in a naughty world and a successful *Las Vegas Last Night* interview coming up. It'll take the edge off our worries yet allow us all to *keep* our senses and behave sensibly."

The sunglasses were aimed at me on the last three words. If I weren't so confused about this utterly new hotel and act Snow was fronting, I'd think I really was in Wonderland.

Envy had already emerged from behind the bar with a silver tray. He passed a crystal forest of tall, thin Champagne flutes first to Snow, then to Temple and Matt, then me.

I glimpsed my reflection in the tray bottom, my face not bruised and cut, but wearing party makeup with crimson lips and shimmering navy eyeliner around my blue eyes and my black hair elaborately piled up. Didn't remember this look. Was it some unremembered Then? I refocused and saw reality in a blink. Black and blue with raw nick of dramatic red, and not in a good way.

I looked away quickly as Envy then served Grizelle and five of the Six Deadly Sins. He tilted the empty tray slightly to produce the Party Girl Me reflection and winked at me. He put down the tray and took his own glass as we all faced our host, everyone oblivious to our byplay. But my right hand was now ice-cold.

Meanwhile, Temple had sipped from her glass and left it on the table behind the long sofa, pulling out and working with her cell phone. She looked up. "They're there."

I came over to her, though I had no idea who "they" were. *Well,* said Irma, *we know they're male and brothers.* Was "Gangsters" a cutesy Vegas name for a car repair garage?

Temple lowered the phone. "They've found your car. They're not sure it can be driven yet."

"Oh, no."

"Do you have any preference for a hotel? Temple asked. "It's late, but Vegas is always open."

"Ah…"

I'd never slept in a Vegas hotel. Shortly after hitting town, I'd found the man I'd been hunting and I'd hoped to complete my quest without having to spend a night in Sin City. Instead, the creep became my landlord. I use the word "creep" loosely. He was more just plain "creepy".

"There's always a room for Miss Lane here at the Hellfire."

Horrified, I stared at Snow, looking as urbane as an Englishman with his Champagne flute gleaming like a column of yellow absinthe at his chest. At least I now had evidence that he drank more than the reputed blood. Accepting that rock star Christophe at the Inferno was now master magician Christophe at the Hellfire somehow horrified me. Was he a semi-shapeshifter? A time traveler? Was I? In the past, when I was pursuing a case that might involve his Inferno Hotel, he'd never been this benign, cooperative mega-power guy.

Temple Barr, sensing my instinctive recoil, was at my side in a flash, my social shield. She gave me a quick, conspiratorial smile. "So very generous of you, Christophe. But Miss Lane's vehicle will be in Fontana custody for repair, so she needs to be close at hand at the Crystal Phoenix."

"Will they give her the 'Ghost Suite'?" he asked.

Is that what I was, a ghost of my former self trying to get along in some cock-eyed Afterworld?

I felt Temple's hand tighten on my arm. "Not likely. I'd better check with the boys." She guided me to her sofa end to put her cell phone on Face Time. I leaned close to hear and see.

"What's happening there?" she asked when a man's visage and voice answered.

"She's a beauty," he said.

Temple flicked me an amused glance. "I'm asking about Miss Lane's *car*, Armando." She put the phone on speaker and held it between us.

"I'm *talking* about her car. For starters, a nineteen-fifty-seven Caddy Eldorado Biarritz is a classic that car collectors dream about. For a sixty-something, her mileage and suspension are superb. Paint's easily retouchable. We'll tweak and tighten anything damaged during a rough run and stop, but it was nothing like a demolition derby. We can tow her into the shop and get her in the best shape of her life. It'd be an honor. I'd like to see the babe who drove this. What a stretch limo she would make."

"*Eeek,*" I said.

"Neither Miss Lane nor her car are considering stretching, Armando."

"I meant the car, of course. Julio wants to say something. Oh, yeah, right."

Another male voice came in. "Tell her we've found a dog hanging around here. It's pretty skittish when we get near."

"A dog. Yes, Quicksilver would be wary. Leave him to me. Stay right there. I'm coming!" I looked at Temple. "Aren't I?"

"You bet your best can of Alpo."

"So you won't need a room here?" Snow actually sounded regretful.

Temple shook her head for me. "You and I can finish discussions, Christophe. Miss Lane can ride with Matt—?" she raised her eyebrows to elicit a nod from her husband, "to see her car and get her dog. They'll pick me up here, and we'll get her and her dog to the Crystal Phoenix for a room. I'm sure Aldo has contacted Van and Nicky. Pets are accommodated there."

Maybe not, I thought. Quicksilver was a hundred-fifty pounds of awesome wolf/wolfhound.

Still the indomitable organization woman, the petite Temple finished her "must" roster.

"Thanks for your generosity, Christophe. We look forward to going 'live' with you on camera."

Irma tittered in my mind. "Live!" *If only Ms. Barr knew Christophe is rumored to be a vampire and therefore undead.*

I wasn't sure I'd believed that rumor before, and I considered it even less likely here and now in Aliceworld.

Snow even saw Matt and me to the door. "Matt's car will brought around by the time you get to the entrance."

"Thanks so much." Matt shook hands and dropped back to escort me out first. I felt like a diplomat leaving a summit.

Moving from the deserted theater house into the casino and the clash, clatter and chime of coins and slots forced us to concentrate on finding the exit. All casinos are designed to waylay you into circling back to the gaming tables and machines. I knew that, but I didn't know the layout of this foreign-to-me hotel.

Matt Devine did, weaving this way and that until we finally faced, blinking, the mega-glitz of a major portal to the Strip.

He laughed at my expression as we stood under the bright lights and mirrors, waiting for the car, I dancing from foot to foot like a kid, anticipating my reunion with Quicksilver.

11
Off to see the Wizards

A silver Jaguar did a liquid mercury ooze down the exit ramp and stopped ever so smoothly.

A wiry little guy in a scaly burnt-orange demon uniform hopped out of the driver's seat to palm a high-dollar tip and see Matt inside. He dashed around to open the back passenger door for me.

"I've seen your viral hip-hop duet with KISS, Miss DeRoque." Apparently he'd taken my beat-up appearance for some rock star celebrity and Matt for my chauffeur/bodyguard.

Matt and I exchanged eye rolls over his head. I was too impatient to explain myself. However, this parking valet looked familiar.

I leaned out the open back window. The guy's facial skin was leathery and orange from a bad self-tanning lotion.

Don't tell me that's becoming a fad, Irma moaned. I ignored her, because I realized…

"Manny, it's you!" I cried. I had recognized him from the same job at the Inferno Hotel. "Mine and Dolly's favorite parking demon. What are you doing at this new hotel?"

He posture stiffened and he got all formal. "I don't know this person named Dolly, and…parking *demon*? Pardon me. That's the suit I'm required to wear. I'm a professional parking *valet*."

"I, ah, meant *speed* demon. Sorry."

"I certainly didn't 'speed' this fine ride down the ramp. There, there, I'm sure it was an innocent mistake, Miss DeRoque." He bowed me into the back seat and shut the door.

I would have fretted over Manny not recognizing me, except I'd seen the big black cat ooze past Manny's knobby green tights and into the back seat with me, belly down on the dark carpeting. Midnight Louie was hitching a ride to see my car again and meet my dog. Interesting. He certainly acted like he owned the town. But then, cats…they always had their own mysterious agendas.

Matt looked back at me to chuckle. "Okay, Miss Rock Star. It'll take longer than you'd think to access the rear of this behemoth hotel."

Midnight Louie rolled over as the Jag glided along the long circling exit road, encouraging me to bend down and pat his rather rotund tummy.

"What have you led me into, you nervy cat?" I whispered. His ears maneuvered to capture my every word. "I'd think your hijinks were deliberate if I didn't know better."

I sighed and leaned back in the cushy leather seat, my nervous fingers wearing the light workout gloves again. Somehow my hip belt and attached flat folding wallet had been scraped off during my tunneling experience. I was one shabby Cinderella fresh from the soot and the ashes riding in a fancy automotive carriage with a cat for a fairy godmother…

Not so fast, sister, in assigning gender willy-nilly. I am all boy.

"Sorry," I said.

The proper word would be 'Godfather', as in the film of that name.

"That would imply you had lower-level crooks at your command."

All my commandos are higher-level crooks.

"Are you supposed to be supplanting Irma in my mind?"

Doing what I am supposed to be doing is Rule One for all of catkind to disobey, Miss Lilah Lane. I do not know this person named Irma.

I wasn't prepared to make introductions between two figments of my mind. Irma dated from when I was an unadoptable orphan in Wichita group homes and a target for bullies. We barricaded ourselves in the TV room at night and watched old black-and-white movies.

This Louie-come-lately chatty cat could be a product of my banged-up head.

I didn't wait for someone to spring me when the Jag rolled up to a grimy Dumpster area I recognized. I pushed the car door ajar to spring the black cat and any other unintroduced figments that had hitched a ride.

First thing I saw was the back of a guy six feet tall in a subtly cut lightweight wool suit the pale, creamy color of the Albino Vampire cocktail I invented at the Inferno bar to irk Snow. So suitable for the warm Vegas climate and the signature suit for my one and only significant other, ex-FBI agent and consultant Ricardo Montoya.

Ric must have heard about this incident on the local police channels and recognized us, Dolly and Quicksilver and me.

"Ric, I'm so glad to see you here!" I put a hand on his arm and ignored the cat frantically rubbing back and forth on my ankles.

He turned. "I'm not Rick." He looked me over. "But I wish I was."

I stepped back, shocked, grazing something soft and earning a loud meow at my feet.

"Ah, Louie." The man smiled down at him. "Always an eye for the ladies." He looked at me again. "Armando Fontana, and I can see you've had a time of it."

"The dog. My dog. Where is he?"

"Milling around here somewhere. Seems to think he's guarding the car, but my bros and I are just fixing it up enough to drive it to the shop. I wish you'd tell him that. Say, Louie, better beware of the dog here." And then he chuckled.

I looked around. Quicksilver resembled a wolf or Siberian Husky. I should be seeing his curled up back-kissing tail, sharp ears and flashing teeth, or hearing his claw clicks doing a drumbeat on the concrete.

I saw a lot of backs in Ric-like ice cream-color suits. I saw a tight pack of black…yes, Tesla sedans. But no dog. *Where was my dog?*

Chill, girl, Irma advised.

If you crave canine, try the back seat of the car. Louie looked up from polishing Armando's pale trousers with a patina of black hairs.

I lurched toward Dolly's back seat, exhausted and now really worried. Quick would have been on me by now, bumping my hip and giving these stranger guys his best ice-blue major-damage-in-mind look.

"This yours, Miss Lilah?" asked another tall, dark, and handsome Fontana brother in an every-way cool Ric-like suit.

Lilah. *Uh-oh.* I'd forgotten my own alias. I peered into Dolly's backseat, the red leather now bearing Quick's claw gouges from jumping out over the back.

Okay, as long as I had Quick back.

Then I saw what else was on the floor.

The current Fontana grinned. "Your dog, Madame." For the first time in this lousy night pilgrimage of confusion and pain, my knees gave. Just folded as my leaping heartbeat seemed to suck all the blood from my body.

"Hey, hey." The guy grabbed my elbow and braced my sagging frame against Dolly's front door.

"Thank you…"

"Julio, Miss. This *isn't* your dog?"

I looked down into the bright, almost black eyes and black button nose in a dandelion fluff of floppy ears and white hair, the fall of floor-length, Veronica Lake-long, platinum-blonde body hair shimmying with recognition and greeting on the back seat carpet, and then onto the leather seat as he jumped up to swipe my face with a wet pink tongue.

"Yes but… It's my dog. But it's the wrong dog."

Julio nodded. "We were given a way different description. Hair gray, eyes blue, weight one-fifty or sixty." This cold, cop-like rundown of Quicksilver's statistics unnerved me even more.

Julio went on, oblivious. "This overgrown Maltese dog is hair white, eyes brown, weight, maybe twenty-five pounds."

"Twenty-two," I corrected like an automaton.

"That's good! You won't have problems finding lodging with this one. He's just a 'big-boned' purse pooch. Vegas is the capital city of purse pooches. A seven-pound cousin of his is a primo drug- and bomb-sniffing dog. I've held that little tattletale myself at major events where Gangsters was hired to provide discreet security."

How a pack of Fontana brothers could ever pass as "discreet", I didn't know. But his consoling words couldn't ease my shock and awe.

"I don't know why you were so worried about us handling him. We are all big boys."

Because the only dog she had left was a big one, Irma lectured the man, even though only I could hear her.

Her Quick defense was one I couldn't say now. I was about to blow my street cred and burst into tears when a low but really committed growl announced the current back-seat dog was about to lunch on Julio's arm resting on the open rear window slot.

"Achilles, no!"

"Don't worry." Julio surveyed my tear-blurred eyes and bitten-down-hard-on lower lip. Big girls don't melt down.

"Sorry for invading your space, Tiger." Julio backed off from us both, so I wasn't sure which of us scared him more. "If he's not an overgrown Maltese, what breed is your dog, a piranha?"

"Not a bad comparison," I said. Then I had to rear back as Achilles had leaped to brace his stubby forelegs on my chest and unleashed his tongue and all his recognition and affection on my face abrasions. I had to laugh with the joy and wonder of reunion until my finally falling tears stung like acid rain.

"He's a Lhasa Apso." My voice was thick and almost breaking. Seeking control, I went academic. "Lhasa is the major city of Tibet. These dogs were bred hundreds of years ago to protect the Dalai Lamas. I call him a Tibetan staple gun. If an attacker falls down in five of them, he's dog meat."

Matt had come over and raised respectful eyebrows at my white "dust mop" dog turning happy circles on the red leather. He was all wriggling doggie love ready for his close-up.

He was also dead.

12
Enchanted Journey

It's funny. No matter how coming apart you are, you can sense people looking at each other over your head and wondering what to do with you.

How could I tell Matt and Julio—or anyone—that the last time I'd seen Achilles alive, and just barely, he'd been lying on the vet's steel exam table, hair haloed out in a glorious wavy corona of white. And then I saw the one dark eye visible was dead, shiny in the overhead lights, but motionless, sightless. Dead, dead, dead.

Dead and then cremated to powder and last seen by me in a black porcelain vase with a royal five-toed dragon design.

That vase and its ashes had last been sitting on my mantle at the residence I was thinking might not even be there now. Enchanted Cottages aren't a dime a dozen. Even in Las Vegas. Maybe especially in Las Vegas.

When I'd left Wichita to drive to Las Vegas a couple years ago, I'd wrapped the urn in a soft T-shirt and put it in Dolly's glove compartment so it wouldn't rattle around and break in the car trunk with my clothes and a few other precious things, mostly silverware and jewelry from my estate sale days. If you're an orphan without a past, buy someone else's unwanted family treasures that have come to the end of the line.

All that stuff should be safe inside the Enchanted Cottage on Hector Nightwine's Sunset Road estate, but I had no leads on either location and no time now to search for it.

Sometimes I took Achilles' ashes along with me in the glove compartment, riding shotgun, as must have happened here.

Armando cleared his throat and patted my shoulder, the one farthest from Achilles. Julio and Aldo and the other unintroduced brothers had surrounded us like a protective fence of *Esquire* models. They all so freakily reminded me of Ric that I almost crumbled into the nearest Fontana brother's arms, except I didn't want to get saltwater on those luscious, almost angelic suits.

Oh, Ric, where are you? Are you *even here anymore?*

Don't complain, Irma murmured. *There are enough Fontana brothers for a harem for us both.*

She could be so cynical. Brought me back to earth, which wasn't Kansas anymore or even my old new city.

Meanwhile the brothers Fontana were easing Achilles and me away from the scene of the breakdown, Dolly's and mine.

"There, there. Your little dog's all right now…" (Which almost sent me over the edge again.) If they called me Dorothy, I'd lose it.

"Achilles," I said.

"…and the car."

"Dolly," I said.

"You named it?" Armando looked sideways at the car profile, flicked his dark eyes back and front across the huge pointy chrome "bumper bullets", and grinned.

"Dolly, huh? Miss Dolly Parton is going straight to the best car spa and make-over garage in Vegas…"

"Gangsters, check," I said, trying a smile.

"And *you're* all right. We'll get you all tucked away for a nice spa and a beauty rest at the Crystal Phoenix."

Phoenix! The phoenix was a mythical bird, symbolic of life because it rose from the ashes.

Achilles, we're not in Kansas anymore and this is decidedly not the Las Vegas I knew.

"Armando…" He leaned close and put a steadying arm around my shoulders, his Achilles-dark eyes brimming with sympathy. "When you went through the glove compartment was there a black Asian dragon vase in it? Or an old T-shirt?"

"It's a super-sized compartment and I only glanced in. Something you lost?"

"No. Something I found," I said with a big smile. "Thank you guys so much!"

Matt came over, smiling too. "I think you and the pooch have alternative transportation now. I'll drive my car back solo, so you and the dog can have room to reunite."

One brother lifted a strangely cooperative Achilles from the car into his arms (what a great Instagram image!) and another two escorted me past the parked black Teslas I'd noticed to a purring stretch limo just driving onto the scene.

"A green car?"

"Not a mere *car*. A nineteen-seventy-one stretch Porsche in racer's green."

Another dapper Fontana brother jumped out of the low driver's seat and opened one of four side doors.

"I have orders to take you back to the Looking Glass green room, now that the scene of the accident is in hand. Miss Temple Barr and our boss, Miss Van Von Rhine, have cooked up a stay for you and your mutt, ah, I mean 'Muffy' here, until you recover from your ordeal. When Miss Temple is done interviewing the magician, we'll take you to the Phoenix with us."

"Toto too?" Fontana brows furrowed en masse at my quote from a favorite film, *The Wizard of Oz*. "I mean, Achilles, as well?"

I was definitely feeling like Dorothy Gale, Toto in escort arms, being shanghaied to a movie make-over in the Merrie Old Land of Oz.

I gave a glance to the grimy, gasoline-reeking surroundings and the now four grinning fashion-plate guys surrounding me.

"How many Fontana brothers are there?"

"Ten, including Nicky, our baby brother who owns the Crystal Phoenix."

"Ten! Any twins among you?"

"No. Now you know why we are sometimes referred to as Fontana, Inc."

"The Phoenix must be a rival to Snow's place, the Hellfire," I suggested with a head-jerk backward.

"Nah, no contest, Miss Lilah," said Julio. "Not a rival, a superior. The Phoenix is the classiest boutique hotel in Vegas. You'll see."

I wasn't entirely happy about that.

I wasn't going to hole up at some hotel. Once I'd found Quicksilver and had wheels I had to find out if a certain estate on Sunset Road with a detached Enchanted Cottage was still in the hands of its owner, my landlord. And if a dragon vase still sat on the cottage mantel.

But first I was going hunting for Quicksilver. I wasn't worried about him getting hurt. Quite the contrary if he found a lone Lunatic. Or the whole pack.

I had rescued a dog so big he was unadoptable at a Humane Society event. I didn't want him to end up in the hands of Animal Control again, this time as a dangerous dog, which bless his stalwart wolf-mix heart, he surely was with anyone threatening me.

For now, I was safe here and Quicksilver was absent without leash. Not that he'd accept one.

I reclaimed Achilles into my arms and buried my repeat tears in his long-haired, furry white glory as he growled affectionately. Fontana Inc. escorted us into the jazzy green stretch limo.

I felt better about one thing. Getting Achilles back from the dead convinced me I had mirror-walked me and mirror-crashed Dolly into just the place I needed to be.

Amen, sister, Irma said. *We are gonna rock and roll this town. Again.*

If it didn't rock and sock us first.

13
Black Magic Man

Coming in the front doors of the Hellfire with everyone staring and giving way to my awesome posse of Fontana brothers… those Ermenegildo Zegna Italian designer suits were like walking spotlights, not to mention the crazy fun label name—

I'd asked Aldo about that, in case Ric needed new suits when I found him. If I found Achilles, I could even find Ric if he was at the gates of Hell. Or only Sin City.

With Achilles borne along as an over-sized purse pooch, I felt like a slightly bunged-up celebrity. Or a Mob Mama.

A hotel flunky joined the party and cleared our way to the Looking Glass Theater and the green room doors.

I felt way more in command of myself, as Julio made sure Achilles hit the floor trotting. He ran right over to Snow, growling and gnawing on his bell-bottom white leather pant leg—leather and ankles, two things Achilles had loved in life and one he was named for. He could never resist going for the ankles, or heels, of anyone who threatened me.

He had died, in fact, from blood poisoning after having bitten and chased a Wichita TV vampire anchorman out of my apartment. The vamp's idea of a dinner date was to give me flowers with X-acto knife blades hidden among the rose stems. The old Sleeping Beauty pricked -finger trick, but this chick was wide awake. I had been cast as the appetizer before we even hit a restaurant.

Now, I watched with pride as Achilles had Snow stepping back. What didn't step back was the black cat who'd played the White Rabbit role with me.

He dashed in front of Achilles and they had a short dog-cat spat, with me calling my dog off and Temple Barr ordering Louie to "back off".

"Achilles is ultra-protective of me." I said it as a fact, not an apology.

"Somebody should be protective *against* you," Snow answered.

He'd donned his gorgeous cloak again to show Temple, who had just photographed it.

Before I could retort that I took the slam as a compliment, the double doors opened to frame a super-tall dark-haired man all in black. I was beginning to find Snow and his flowing white Santa locks a huge relief from all this brunette male beauty.

"Max," Temple said.

"Max?" Snow asked. "Not a wayfaring stranger like Miss Lane, but a team member?"

"An associate," Matt said, going over to shake hands with the Very Tall Man, drawing him into the room and the green room group. "We'd planned a late supper after the show and the meeting."

"I'm a sometime magician," said the man called Max, looking directly into Snow's sunglasses as if he saw through them. "Formerly the Mystifying Max. Not a competitor. Semi-retired."

"I could take it as a competitor spying on my secrets," Snow said.

"You could, but I'm between engagements now. Not even sure I'll perform again. Temple is an old friend. I'm happy to help her out."

"Not very old," Temple said.

"That was tactless of me. Better than 'old girlfriend', though." He turned to Snow again. "Your Lady into Tiger illusion was astonishing. Unbelievable!" He gave the last word a challenging edge, and looked over his shoulder to nod at me.

Irma was not impressed, as ever. *Oh, baby, Mr. New Magic Man has noticed Little Us. Does he not believe you also?*

Max spread some cheer our way. "Your surprise onstage guest wasn't as smooth, but at least she tried to justify her presence."

Snow rose from the sofa, snapping the rippling folds of his encompassing cloak like a whip.

We all stiffened to attention, but he confronted only Max, who had not. "The more I hear the more I think the TV interviewers put a spy in the house."

"No, no." Max's fluid hand gesture made you think he'd palm a dove any moment. "They'd asked for my expert eye to identify the most spectacular illusions, that's all. Relax. Your bag of tricks were superbly executed. I admit I assigned myself a perch in the flies to better observe and report."

Max turned to regard Achilles and Louie at my feet, each one claiming a boot heel...and probably hoping to chew on them in perfect peace together at wherever I lay down my bleary eyes and weary head tonight.

"So I saw the Cat and the Lady who *weren't* part of the show work their way out of the tunnel into the empty box. It's a good thing I was up there. I also saw something much less amusing. You're missing the assistant who was supposed to appear in the box, I conclude? What was her role to be?"

"The Lady in the Lady or the Tiger illusion. I can't believe she's 'missing', as you say. Gwen is a pro."

"I'm sure there will be some explanation from her," Max said, "but not about the *other* missing-in-action lady performer."

"Oh, you can't mean Celeste Novak." Snow turned to Temple and Matt to explain. "She's the Green Fairy and penultimate act. She left the stage before the 'Lady' illusion started. I know you wanted her to appear with me on your TV program, but she wears elaborate makeup and costume and it takes quite awhile for her to change into street clothing."

"Are you sure she's coming here?" Max asked.

"Of course she is. She'll be wonderful on your interview show," Snow told Matt and Temple. "She played Peter Pan as a child. No way she'd miss a chance to promote our show. Not as the star of my tribute to Absinthe, the cabaret tent show, outside Caesars Palace. She's a former aerialist with *Cirque du Soleil*. For me, she embodies to perfection the symbol of the notorious Art Nouveau liqueur blamed as a hallucinogen destroying addicted nineteenth-century Parisian artists, the muse who hypnotized them all."

"*Le Fae Verte*," Max savored the French phrase. Most of us blinked in ignorance. "The Green Fairy," Max said to the room. "A floating and soaring woman in gossamer green trailing scarves like a sexy Tinkerbell will disappear high above the audience on her green velvet rope, and, instants later, resolve again as the Green Fairy on a giant Absinthe bottle and disappear from the glassy cage that holds her. I'm afraid *she's* missing in action."

"Of course," Snow said, "if she is, she'll be missing a paycheck from now on out. Failing to finish out a magic illusion is a cardinal sin in the magic game, as you should know."

Max nodded soberly. "You could say it's a 'deadly' sin."

Max eyed the Six Deadly Sins scattered throughout the green room.

"Anyway," he said, "she's not so far from her role as Peter Pan. She's in Neverland now, I'm afraid."

That made no sense. It suddenly did to someone.

"No! Not Celeste!" Envy broke from the Sins' usual pack to stand quivering before the two magicians, one a white and glittering presence, and a showman; one black and muted, all containment and self-effacement. Together, they comprised the Yin and Yang sides of the trickster-god magician's purpose and personality. The light and the dark.

I knew there was a lot of dark in Snow. How much was there in this Max? I wondered.

Max eyed the six deadly sins scattered throughout the green room. "I'm afraid your missing woman has appeared in someplace more unlikely. She is lying dead below stage."

"She's not dead!" Envy shouted. "Celeste wouldn't fall. She flew like a bird of paradise. The equipment was checked nightly. I did it myself."

"I'm afraid your elegant fairy is lying dead in the stage tunnel, near the tiger cage."

"Grizelle would never harm a human." Snow walked a tight, constrained circle while he absorbed and rejected the idea.

I did not reject that belief. I was living proof that Grizelle would threaten a human for Snow's sake, from previous encounters, but I couldn't refer to a past I shared with Snow that he was refusing to disclose now. Nor could I see his fierce shape-changing bodyguard messing up the boss's top act.

"I didn't see the blood at first," Max said. "She lay in the pose of a Swan Lake ballerina, the green costume scarves tendrils all around her. At first I thought she was in position to elevate up on the moveable pedestal. Then I thought she might have fallen. I didn't get close enough to mess up the scene, but this death *will* mess up all of your current TV plans. How she died is for the police to figure out."

Temple started forward. "She could have been murdered? A police investigation on any level would be a deal-breaker, unless it's resolved quickly."

"Sorry about your show schedule," Max told her, sincerely. He looked at Snow. "And yours too." Not sincerely.

Rival magicians. That was not a happy coincidence. Mr. Mystifying Max could have been sabotaging his competition's show, and accidentally have caused the aerialist's death. Or not accidentally.

I sensed he had friends here, but he was a prime candidate for the suspect pool. I bit back a smile. A local performer with a motive edged me out of the limelight.

Matt Devine had been watching the discussion and now raised his cell phone to his ear. "I'm calling Molina. She at least has some notion of what a show schedule is," he said. "The sooner a forensics team examines the site and confirms the death and its cause, the sooner all our shows can go on."

"Forensics…" Snow murmured.

"Yes." Max shrugged and looked sympathetic. "Devine's right. A homicide lieutenant is not usually present at crime scenes, but this one knows Vegas and show biz. She'll keep the local paparazzi off."

"This is disastrous," Snow said, pacing. "A police examination will tear my illusions apart. My trade secrets are bound to get out." He stopped to let the deeply dark sunglasses scowl for him at Max.

"If you're a magician of any repute, you know how destructive this is."

"I hear you, bro," Max said with another sigh.

"What's all this talk of shows and secrets?" Temple asked. "Some poor woman died in the maze of magic mechanisms below the stage while we were sitting rapt with the rest of the audience watching the show."

She stopped speaking, biting her lip.

"You said it, Temple," Max said. "We're all suspects, including the tiger, and, I guess, Midnight Louie, if you want to be all-inclusive."

I sighed. Loudly. Everyone who had forgotten me now looked my way.

I simply said, "I was the closest one to the scene of the crime."

And you're the likeliest suspect, alone, on your own, with no direction home, like a rolling stone, Irma chimed in.

She was right. Even Mr. Mystifying Max Kinsella playing secret Spy in the Sky was somewhat removed, while I was a next-door neighbor. Was that why Gwen had bowed out? Had she feared being found on the same level as the dead woman? Where I had so mysteriously come from?

I sighed and said, "So, 'Welcome to Las Vegas' to me."

No one either welcomed or contradicted me or my conclusion.

14
Ride and Seek

Achilles whimpered and laid his chin on my boot-toe. He had always heard the stress in my voice. For now he was a flattened, downcast dust-mop of a dog, with a black button nose and glimpses of worried eyes between his thick doggie bangs.

Then I felt bracing hands clasp my upper arms. "You're *not* alone, Lilah," Temple said. "We know the crazy circumstances that got you to here and now, and can testify to it. The Fontanas saw your skid marks from the motorcycle gang's pursuit near the mechanical ducts entrance. Besides, being new in town gives you no motive."

No obvious motive, Irma noted. *For now.* She was becoming quite the ride-along pessimist.

Temple Barr's eyes were the steely gray-blue of conviction as I glanced down at her, but when I looked up again I saw an expression of reluctant reservation in Matt Devine's face.

No one could really speak for me, or who I was, or where I'd come from or had been, except for the past couple of hours before I'd crawled and clawed myself onstage, leaving a DNA trail, during which time the aerialist had died or been murdered.

I consulted Snow's sunglasses after catching a tiny flash of movement in the black lenses. He'd minutely shaken his head. At me? Was he warning me to keep silent? Or was he signaling that my situation was hopeless?

A comforting pressure massaged my leg. My tunneling partner was trying to comfort me, but Midnight Louie had been off the hook from the git-go. If animals could talk I had at least two four-foots on my side. Not the white tiger's. Why could only I see, sense, that Grizelle and the tiger were two sides of the same coin in some weird way? That chilly supermodel-security staffer wore mandarin false nails two inches long painted in 'Better Red Than Dead' scarlet. If she wasn't a soul sister to a lethal Big Cat, I'd eat a case of Fancy Feast.

And now a woman lay dead below us, and not that far from the tiger's cage, either.

Matt Devine, still looking troubled, asked the question no one had thought to ask.

"Miss Lane, are your ID and driver's license in the car? A glove compartment?"

"No, I carry them on me." I slapped a hand to my right hip faster than an Old West gunslinger hoping to get lucky.

Everybody jumped a bit.

I blinked. Slapped left hand to left hip.

"Either I've lost weight," I told my mesmerized audience, "or my ID case slipped out of my jacket pocket when I was snaking through that long, low underworld of mechanical and magical tunnels."

Temple drew back to survey my jacket with an expert's eye.

"Standard issue, good quality, but not designer, women's black leather jacket," she announced to our captive audience. "Suitable for outrunning motorcycle gangs. Front zipper. Snap-up cuffs for that rakish. pushed-up-sleeve look.

"Diagonal side pockets, often called *slash* pockets, with *no* snap-shut option. Fashion no-no for The Girl on the Run. Could make it hot in a warm climate. Could make it very hot with ID tucked into those pickpocket-inviting Mama Kangaroo pockets."

Everyone laughed at her mock diagnosis of what could have happened.

I washed my face with my hands. No laughing matter. I wasn't sure what ID I actually did carry. Did I still have my genuine real Delilah Street identity in this warped Wonderland? Had I been really on the run from anything other than, well, Lunatics? Maybe the law. This Lieutenant Molina they referred to so solemnly sounded like a pretty hard-boiled representative of the long arm of said law.

I drove, therefore I must have ID. Somewhere.

"What about in Dolly's glove compartment?" Matt Devine asked, persistent. I looked around.

"Ask the Fontanas still on the scene!" Temple said in chorus with Irma in my head.

The magic of cell phones soon had another affable baritone voice on the line as she put the phone on speaker setting. "Armando here. Anything for you, Miss Temple. I love having permission to snoop further in a classic vintage glove compartment."

The purr in this unseen Fontana's voice almost had me blushing. Except all the blood had deserted my face and classically cold extremities, also known as feet.

"Now *this* is a glove compartment!" he crowed. "Roomy enough to stash plenty of skip-town cash in this baby. *Hmm.* Original owner's guide. Sweet. Ups the value. Uh, *uh-oh.* Really big, bad dog collar, black leather two inches wide with lotsa studs and spikes and dangling chains. *Uh*, might this be your personal jewelry, Miss Lane?" He is sounding even more interested.

"It's my dog's," I gritted between my teeth.

My mind flashed a cue card of memory: me equipping Quicksilver with a black leather harness against werewolf bites and a hidden pocket for a tiny .22 pistol for me in a pinch. The dog collar was for dress-up, when Quick was out on his own, with rabies tag and vet contact info.

Everybody in the green room, including the usually unobtrusive Six Sins, was staring at "my dog", Achilles, who'd plopped over on his side like a really small, miniature shaggy Shetland pony. With all that hair, nobody would see a collar no matter how butch it was. In fact, he usually sported a cute kiddie bow on his top-knot to keep all that hair out of his eyes.

"Say," Snow said, "that fluff puppet of yours could probably follow the scent of the alley cat and you through the tunnels and find where your driver's license, credit cards and cash fell out along the way. *If* that's where they went missing."

"We'd have to equip the dog with a tiny high-intensity light and camera," Max Kinsella said. "Any one of your Six Deadly Sins is limber and lean enough to slither with him through the trail from the alley to onstage boxes. They do enough of that sort of thing in your act, don't they?"

"What my assistants may do or can do is not a rival's business to learn."

Again the absent Fontana brother reported by cell phone. "Hey, another glove-box find. A matchbook reading *Set the Night on Fire* from a place called The Inferno Hotel-Casino. Never heard of that. Must be one of those pop-up joints that come-and-go overnight."

Kinda like us, Irma commented.

Now that I'd been led here, I would like a little more "going" about my business, but I was stuck on site for an interrogation when I couldn't even answer a straight question about my date of birth.

Surely Snow knew who I was, and enjoyed having me temporarily off-balance, off-kilter and off-base. He always had. Sad that a frenemy like him was my only fixed point in this weird altered Vegas. Had I driven Quicksilver and me into more danger than we were eluding? Or could handle?

15
BatCat

Dog, schmog. So they think only a canine can deal with a Lost and Found assignment in a small dark tunnel.

My tracks are already laid down in Miss Lilah's entrance tunnel. A few more wouldn't look suspicious. Also, I can carry prey like a lost driver's license in my mouth as well as any canine, although doggie canine teeth tend to be larger. Plus, I can see better any day or night than a mop-headed dog desperately needing a bangs trim.

While everyone is politely and silently mulling Miss Lilah Lane's likelihood of being an escaping murderer rather than a poor lost chick who fell on her head, I eel under various pieces of furniture. Then I drift as silently as a breath past Gluttony, who is guarding the crack in the green room's two almost-shut double doors not very well. At least the skinny Spandex legs of his, ahem, catsuit, are attired to match my more authentic leisure wear, and he is so rapt at the current scene I slip out right between their bowed opening.

Once liberated, I am in what they call the "wings" (although they cannot fly) that bracket the stage proper. Or improper, depending on the show.

No one in the green room has mentioned aloud that Mr. Max and his batlike habit of climbing into the dark immensity above the stage, makes him as likely a suspect as our supposedly confused accident victim.

He also favors black garb. Let us face it, black blends well with half of every twenty-four hours, is equally chic on man, woman, and beast. It is always a reliable abettor at the scene of every crime.

The theater seats will not be tidied up until the morrow, so able investigators like Miss Lieutenant C. as in Carmen and R. as in Regina—no wonder she goes by her initials, although some might surmise it is an attempt to be gender-neutral—and myself will have limited time before the forensic team arrives to determine the lay of the land and the deceased.

For now, I trot unseen and unheard across the great expanse of stage, over the many thin, silver metal circles marking stage areas that can raise or lower to facilitate a full deck of illusions.

I attain what a Thespian would call "stage right", which to the audience is left. Just another charming human inconsistency they so excel at creating. I imagine it refers to some olden day custom. People are seriously sentimental about retaining the oddest little things. Like purse pooches.

Luckily, my breed are some of the little things they regard with fondness.

I may not have been born in a trunk like some famous actors claim, but my mama was not one to let anything keep her from going where she preferred. She is still that way.

So I leap upon a large cabinet called a "light board" and contemplate my next landing zone. I am headed for what they call "the flies", where stage machinery is hefted and hung to produce the effects below. Since flies are a great nuisance to my kind when we are catching a quick bite to eat on the street, I am not sure how they got to name a location in our nation's theaters.

My climb was a trifle harrowing, because I am twenty-some pounds soaking wet of counterweight. I could come crashing down onstage with one wrong move. So I must leap like I am over six feet tall. Soon I have the upper ropes and high wires and such jangling lightly together at my passage. You would think I was playing "Melancholy Baby" on a chef's kitchen rack. Or Quasimodo performing on a xylophone. Bells are ringing.

Aha. I perch on an elevated narrow scaffold to sniff a hint of Mr. Max's cologne. Handy of him to cultivate a signature scent.

Then I look down, straight down, dead down. I feel like one of those ancient hermits who lived atop a pillar.

The box Miss Lilah emerged from has *no top*. Perhaps it was spun around to show another side of itself to the audience when she emerged from the black hole of its bottom, where a small pedestal below swung into place so the audience could see her step out of apparent air onto the stage floor.

And opposite that box stood another about ten feet away, only the staging area was not painted black, as all surfaces back here, but green, a swirl of green, curled like a newborn kitten into its mother. As Mr. Max did, I have a bird's-eye view into a nest of death.

I cannot claim I have abstained from eating the feline equivalent of chicken, but at least my avian prey were all free-ranging and had a chance to escape. Now that I can eat curried salmon in oyster bisque from a can I am much more politically correct, as scales do not attract the human protective instincts as much as fur and feathers. Listen, everybody has to eat something, but we can all do it with nicety.

From my lifelong experience of climbing, be it mountain or molehill—although I will leave mountains to my cousins, the Big Cats, and moles do not appeal to me, whether in ground or on face. I survey the black iron ladders at each side of the backstage side walls. Vertical ladders are difficult for most people to climb.

I spot more rolled-up scrims and scenic paintings than you would find in a wallpaper store. I am not even mentioning the swags of various electrical cables, thick ropes and elastic rigging for scene changes and acts of an aerial sort.

Here is where I confirm that any reasonably athletic human who is not acrophobic could make his or her way up and down and around here with not much trouble.

To test my theory, I leap to a vertical rod, twist around it to snag a thick cable in my mitt shivs and swing left and then right like a clock pendulum. At the end of a swing, I release my toe-curling grip on the rope and jump to a tied-back red velvet curtain, using its heavy folds to accept my weight and break my controlled fall.

Since red velvet is particularly becoming to one of my color, I slip and slide like a skier down, down, down, as the fabric moans and rips.

Voila!

The stage floor awaits my graceful four-point landing and I walk back into the wings, knowing two things.

Any human in the show or green room could have probably interfered with Miss Celeste's act and her life, and no dog could do it. Nor an overweight white tiger.

But it would be a snap for Miss Grizelle or Mr. Max Kinsella. Or Miss Lilah Lane, although I can alibi her, should anyone care to ask me.

They will not, and I took responsibility for her when I led her away from the dead-end alley into this mess of sudden death, so it is my duty to find the killer.

16
Legal Overreach

The homicide lieutenant arrived, very tall and wearing a very short businesslike, blunt-cut brunette bob and khaki jacket. She was flanked, or rather followed, by a shorter man with a graying mustache and a wrinkled gray suit coat and a black woman who was medium everything—age, height, weight and color.

The trio's tan, gray, or navy blue suits and pale shirts were equally bland and practical, showcasing belts holding concealed badges to one side. And a firearm at the back, no doubt.

I was starting to recall talking with the local fuzz in my discombobulated past. But I hadn't been a suspect then. More likely a television reporter. Had I ever been a witness via my job? The stress must be making my temporary memory issues snap, pop, and sizzle.

Greeting them was Little Miss High Heels, swift and brisk as a Yorkshire terrier declaring territory to a mastiff.

"We knew you'd want to be on scene for a major hotel fatality, Lieutenant," Temple said.

The lieutenant nodded to the "we" as Matt Devine moved beside his wife.

"Fatality?" the lieutenant questioned.

"No one's gone near the site," Temple said. "It could be a fall. The stage is riddled with rising and descending and turning levels. It's a magic show."

The tall lieutenant had squad-car headache-rack blue eyes. Bright and focused on the Liberace-level costumed Christophe. "I've seen your Strip billboards," she told him. "Son of Siegfried and Roy, with Elvis jumpsuits and the white tiger, the whole bit. Your stagehands couldn't have guided rescuers to the site?"

She flicked the Six Deadly Sins a suspicious glance. The guy detective who looked like your genial Uncle Bob, whipped a cell phone from his side suit pocket and approached them.

Lieutenant Molina surveyed me. "Detective Bellamy. Get her story. I'm sure she has a dilly."

The other magician had found a wall to lean on for support, almost fading out of view and consciousness, despite his black garb.

Not to the woman in charge.

"Mr. Kinsella." She sounded like she was announcing the third act of a drama. "Since I'm told by Mr. Devine that you had an aerial view of the suspected death, lead on."

Surprised, he straightened to attention. "It would involve climbing, Lieutenant."

"'Anything you can do…'"

"Lead on, MacDuff," he said, gesturing toward the stage.

"I doubt this is a production of *Macbeth*." She turned to the woman detective putting her cell phone on the record setting for my interview, and extracted a large sleek semiautomatic gun from behind her back. "Hold the firepower while I'm scaling Mount Magic, Bellamy. My ankle holster should be secure."

"Ankles, Lieutenant," Max mocked. "I didn't know you had any."

Good point. Between trouser legs and the black loafers Molina wore, only a small strip of gray sock showed.

I checked Achilles at my feet. He was sleeping, worn out from the excitement, and apparently found Lt. Molina's ankles too mundane to bother with.

I watched while she followed Max onto the stage to climb into the maze of ladders and light bars and rolls of hanging rolled up scrims where a killer still might lurk, or evidence of one.

17
Warning Bell

Detective Bellamy gestured me to the sofa seat. With the hand holding the gun. Gulp.

A foot-level *Grrr* attracted the detective's attention. "Cute dog. Yours?"

Detective Bellamy didn't know it, but her cordial compliment just put Achilles off of ankle-biting mode. Guess it was a big night for ankles.

Meanwhile, Detective Uncle Bob had asked Temple to introduce him to the Sins and they all retreated to the green room kitchen area behind the bar.

What a bizarre scene! I could hardly take it seriously. Except for the lieutenant's Glock or whatever sitting big and black and mechanical on the glass coffee table opposite Detective Bellamy and me.

"Name," she demanded.

Already I had an identity crisis. Might as well continue my masquerade. If someone found out that a Delilah Street was alive and well in this town, I would only seem the muddled misfit I was taken for.

Good choice. The voice was in my head, but it wasn't Irma's acerbic soprano. It was male and rough-edged. I looked down at my scuffed boots. My partner in tunneling was leaning against my leg like I was a wall and he was Max Kinsella.

Your name?" Detective Bellamy repeated.

"Lilah Lane."

"You look roughed up, Miss Lane."

"My car was pursued by a motorcycle gang as I got into town."

That perked her up. "You spot any gang insignia? The name Lobos?"

Must be the local bad boy bikers. "L-something T-shirts, that's all. It was too fast."

And the werewolf Lunatics apparently couldn't exist here. Lucky me.

"I headed into the hotel parking lot road to ditch them," I explained, "and they herded me ahead of them until I hit a bump and came down hard in the hotel's service area out back. Then I made my way in here."

"How'd you end up in the theater green room?"

"You'd be surprised how many mechanical and storage areas are strung out behind these huge hotels. Maybe not you, but I was. I just got into the back service areas and kept going forward. I was woozy from being thrown out of my car—"

"Wait. That's what banged you up? Not the gang?"

"They took off on their motorcycles once I was on foot and my dog was chasing them, barking and nipping at their wheels."

"This dog?"

"Yeah." I lied to keep my story simple. "He's been rescued since I happened on Miss Barr and Mr. Devine, and they took me under their wings. Sent some guys called 'the Fontanas' to check out my stranded car and…" My voice almost broke. As thrilled and stunned as I was to have Achilles back from the dead, it killed me that Quicksilver was still missing, still AWOL. *No time for sniveling*, Irma urged. *Distract her.*

Yes, I needed to get the detective on a different track. "Oh! That's right. They, Temple and Matt, said the guys who would work on my car were from 'Gangsters'. Is that a criminal enterprise?"

"Not so you could prosecute them." Bellamy stifled a…was it a smirk?

"What's your business in Vegas?" she asked.

"I can't just be a tourist?"

"What's your residence? Which hotel?"

I was stumped. From what I'd seen, Vegas had grown a whole new slew of hostelries I'd never heard of.

A new voice tuned in. Temple Barr's. "She's a guest at the Crystal Phoenix, Detective…Pellham?"

Temple wasn't a slouch at derailing interrogations either.

"Bellamy." She frowned the distraction. "Can anybody else in Vegas vouch for you, Miss Lane, besides the Barr-Fontana consortium?"

"Um," I repeated her last syllable to gain time. "Um, I'm hoping Hector Nightwine is still maintaining a Las Vegas enterprise."

A sinister silence from all parties ensued.

"Where did you say you were from?" Detective Bellamy asked.

"You didn't ask. Wichita."

No reaction. Had my home town just blown away or was it only fly-over country coastal dwellers knew nothing about?

"Kansas," I added.

No reaction.

"It's Dorothy Gale country. You know… *The Wizard of Oz.*"

"Oh, right." Bellamy produced her first smile, a dazzling white grin. "The MGM-Grand used to have a recreation from the movie right in the lobby. Loved that when I was a kid. Farm girl in her pinafore and her little black scruffy dog. And, girl, those ruby-red glitter shoes were the summit!"

"Weren't they, though?" Temple said, kicking up an illustrating high heel.

"Yeah, and the characters would move, like the old cackling mean-green witch. And Dorothy's dog with the funny name…"

"Toto," I cued her.

"Yeah, Toto…was just like yours." She sent Achilles at my feet a fonder glance than before. "Only smaller and black instead of white."

"Yup," I said, "Achilles is like Toto too."

And I'm feeling very like Dorothy in Oz Las Vegas.

"About this Hector Nightwine," Bellamy said. "What do you know about him?"

Huh? Irma said. '*Warning, Will Robinson*'. *Hector might be bad to know here.*

When Irma quotes lines from *Lost in Space,* I listen.

"He was once my landlord back in Wichita, Kansas."

"What did you do in Wichita, Lilah?" Temple asked me, interviewing me before the detective could come up with more awkward questions.

"I was a TV reporter, a paranorm—and a para*legal* assistant before my TV career."

"TV reporting!" Temple grinned. "Hello, sister! My first career. Then I went into public relations when I came here. Now my husband and I—he had a syndicated radio advice show, *The Midnight Hour*— host a daytime TV show together. *Las Vegas Last Night.* You can do anything, go anywhere with a TV reporting background, Lilah."

"I was planning on a career change here, actually." But not as a suspect.

"I can help with that too," Temple promised. "No worries."

Bellamy enunciated a note into her phone. "Subject is seeking gainful employment in town."

I nodded happily, sensing an end of delving into my vague presence here.

Then my relief hit a wall. One thing was not working out. I was still desperately seeking one lost dog. And I could hardly tell my new friends it was quite a different dog from Achilles.

Quicksilver, where are you?

What? I am not enough? the new inner voice demanded.

Midnight Louie deserted my leg to rub luxuriously on Detective Bellamy's er, ankles.

"Oh, what a sweet kitty." She closed her phone file and bent to scratch him between the ears.

Thank God Detective Bellamy was an animal lover.

Mission accomplished, and I will find your big dog, too.

Reassuring if you believed interior voices. The only one of my party he had "found" was me, and look at the mess he'd led me into. Black cats are unlucky and he was living up to the stereotype. In spades.

18
Sky-high View

"Show-off," Lieutenant Molina said.

Max dangled from the top of an anchored curtain pulley.

Carmen Molina stood twenty feet below him on the metal bridge between the backstage wings of the theater.

They'd both climbed the vertical ladders attached to the house walls to get to the bridge. He leaped up to snare a cable used for swinging out over the stage.

"This is the bungee cord the Green Fairy used to have fallen where you now see her. You could get a better view from up here. There's another free cable." He thrust it out at her.

"I'll make do with the forensic team's film and photos, thank you."

"I just sent a photo to your cell."

"What? How do you know my cell number?"

"Telepathic magic."

"Computer hacking, more likely."

She pulled the phone from her side jacket pocket and opened the image. The vivid emerald of the fallen woman's costume cast a sickly green hue on Molina's features, showing the sympathetic twist to her lips.

"No coming back from a fall like this," she said. "If it was just the fall."

"And there's blood."

"And there's blood." She stowed the phone in her pocket. "Now that you've got me up here, in private, you can answer a few questions."

He stayed swaying gently on his cable. Max loved heights, even after an act of sabotage had cut his cable and he'd smashed almost fatally into a wall. Fear them, and you were done. "Your questions, Lieutenant?"

"Our new star, Mr. Spellbinder. Is he really good?"

"Excellent, almost supernaturally so. I've never seen that 'The Tiger or the Woman' shtick performed so seamlessly. And the Green Fairy metamorphosis illusion is a showstopper."

"Far too literally this time." Molina gazed down on the still pool of askew limbs and shimmering green costume bits that resembled an abandoned puppet with its strings cut.

"You never worked with onstage female assistants," she mused.

"No. The Green Fairy wasn't just a leggy showgirl serving as a magician's onstage distraction. She was an enchanting ethereal and aerial presence…until she fell and landed where we see her lying now."

"What should have happened when her act ended?"

"A stage assistant or she herself would have unfastened this almost invisible harness dangling here. Then she would have used a horizontal cable to swing down to the backstage floor fifteen feet below. She was supposed to slip down a tunnel to her dressing room. The tiger would then have been positioned to emerge from the box at the other end of the stage while the Lady was stationed even farther Stage Left. Instead, Gwen went missing and Lilah Lane ended up in her spot first."

"What about this Lane woman?"

"What about her?"

"Do you believe any part of her story?"

"I believe she could be fuzzy-brained from her recent head impact in the alley. It happened to me. And the Fontanas found her car in need of a garage inspection, with burned rubber and axle grease all over the area, so the car did a controlled crash and she's lucky not to have whiplash. The motorcycle gang seems probable."

"The Fontanas hark back to the mob days of this town. Not the most Simon-pure of witnesses. My accident analyst officer is checking out the scene. I'll get an official report from her tomorrow."

"Fontanas are smoother and faster. I believe you should know that already from dating Julio Fontana."

Molina drew herself up to her full five-feet-ten. "What you believe you know is always debatable. Anyone could lurk in this area, especially the black-clad stagehands. The lighting is murky and everything is painted matte black."

Max shrugged. "Death of the Green Fairy. It's all a fairy tale until some nasty troll or wicked witch enters stage right."

Molina glanced at the ladder leading down to the stage floor. Her sensible loafers should still manage it, he thought, although backing down a straight ladder was harder than going up.

"Right now I could use a friendly dragon making a short hop."

Max swung out and down on the bungee cord, extending his left arm to encompass her. "Need a lift down?"

"Don't you dare."

She started down, step by step, and met him at the bottom.

First thing she did on returning to the green room?

Collecting her firearm from the glass table.

Not a tower of trust, Lt. C. R. Molina.

19
Home, Sweet Homeless

At last Detective Bellamy departed to assist her partner with his mass interviews in the kitchen.

Meanwhile, Temple Barr bent to pet both cat and dog. "What a cute couple!"

She straightened and smiled at me. "I get really tired about hearing that said about Matt and me."

I too had to smile down on the domestic pet relief at our feet. At least *they* weren't suspects. "Strange they're about the same size. That cat is huge."

Temple nodded. "They remind me when we had a set of black Scottie and white Westie terriers in our last case. They actually helped Louie sniff out some perps."

"Did you just say 'last case'? Is everybody here a detective?"

Temple shook her head. "We are just 'bloody amateurs', not appreciated by law types. As a public relations person, I cannot have events I coordinate disrupted by anything, especially 'bad news' like violent death."

"Are you also the hostess with the mostess? How awfully nice to provide a hotel I'm supposedly staying at. Vegas is still a mystery to me."

"And you are a mystery to Vegas, I'm afraid."

"I see the hotshot top cop has moved on," I mentioned.

"Not permanently, unfortunately. She'd taken Max to show her how he spotted the, um, fatality, came back for her firearm, and left with a frown on her face. As you now know, the unseen underground engines for these super-acts are extensive and have many secret and mysterious ways."

I flexed an arm and massaged my sore elbow. "I've probably rubbed my leather jacket elbows bare crawling through those metal conduits."

"Once Molina dismisses us, Matt and I will get you and Achilles to the Crystal Phoenix."

What a symbolic coincidence! It still unnerved me that Achilles had risen from his own ashes like the fabled Phoenix bird. Were his ashes still encased on a mantel somewhere in this town, or elsewhere on the planet? I had no idea and no known home to go to where I could install a funeral urn if I had one.

Meanwhile… "I'm afraid we both need a bath," I told Temple. "Achilles' paws are black from the Dumpster area. And mine are bloody too." I held up scraped forearms.

"*Ouch.* Not to worry about a thing. You'll get a spa pass, and Van Von Rhine and Nicky Fontana at the Phoenix have a dog groomer on call for guests. There's a special set up in the beauty parlor."

"Why are you doing all this for me?"

"My ten uncles-in-law are crazy about your car. It's as good as a reason as any. And you got a bumpy introduction to my town. The PR person in me is obsessive about putting Las Vegas in a better light for you."

"How are these mythically numerous Fontana brothers connected to you besides their very own Crystal Phoenix hotelier?"

"My aunt married the eldest, Aldo. I have *lots* of pull. And Nicky is the youngest, by the way. It's an old Las Vegas 'family', maybe a bit too much so. Their Uncle "Macho" Mario Fontana, is a legendary, permanent, floating person of interest to law enforcement."

Like the crap game. My headache was not improving.

Lots of guys, Irma crowed. *More than one for you and one for me.*

I was feeling a bit bipolar. And starting to realize what my wolf-wolfhound mix dog must be going through. If he was still out there, he'd be looking for me. I hated to change locations, but I couldn't linger in the waste management area behind the hotel just to ensure

Quicksilver found my scent. He was an expert! So why had he disappeared?

If I was going to find Quick, I eventually had to try to get "home" to the Enchanted Cottage behind Nightwine's Sunset Road estate. And like Quicksilver, Hector might suddenly not be here too.

I never thought I'd miss that sly old manipulating *CSI: Las Vegas Everlasting* producer.

20
If I Were King...

Once the police had done their preliminary inquiries and the assembled witnesses etc. were free to go, and the forensics team had arrived to begin their procedures, I slipped back down into the scene of the crime.

I had concealed my "stash" near the tiger cage. Quite clever, if I say so myself. It was still occupied, as it had been since its tenant had been hustled off stage after Miss Lilah's brief ride on its back into the stage wings.

I may not be a Big Cat in the physical sense, but in the pursuit of my Vegas Strip criminal cases, I have both aided and been aided by my massively larger cousins.

I lose patience with this convocation of individuals known to me and some not and many distinctly suspicious, and slip away from the maddening crowd. "Madding crowd" is the literary cliché, but when it comes to humans, it is always "maddening crowd" to me.

Sadly, even my brilliant Miss Temple Barr has missed an important clue for follow-up. Where was the poor deceased Green Fairy portrayer *before* she appeared on stage to perform her last illusion?

Luckily, although I am not a bloodhound, I do have better-than-human olfactory equipment. And an aversion to dogs, who have often bullied my kind. That makes me supersensitive to what the commercials call "doggy odor". You will notice felines are not accused of having any personal B.O., or body odor. That is because we are fanatic bathers. We are not responsible if our human help fails to clean our indoor outhouses as frequently as needed, however.

Given all this history, I cannot help noticing that the fallen Green Fairy not only already bears a trace of the musk of mortality, but it is overpowered by the slight whiff of Dog.

So it happens I am not noticed when I silently pad through the ajar green room double doors into the dark and silent theater of empty seats and abandoned stage.

I dart around the orchestra pit littered with the used ticket stubs and smuggled-in candy wrappers of Mr. Snow Christophe's female fans. All his music is recorded and piped-in.

There should be a set of stairs Stage Right leading down to the performers' dressing rooms. Nothing fancy. Poured concrete and a stingy set of step risers, quite the hazard for chorus girls, but this show requires another steeper and darker stair set down into the magic-trick underworld. If I were to enter that area from this side, I would soon link to the pitifully small staging area where Miss Celeste Novak met her death.

But I am not hunting death on this mission. I am hunting overlooked life.

My whiskers sweep the concrete floor leading to the dressing rooms. Hopefully, Miss Novak merited a personal room since becoming the Green Fairy required much delicate costume and body paint work. In my younger years, before I hooked up with Miss Temple Barr as my roommate and crime-solving assistant, I had my personal pillow installed on chorus girls' makeup tables all over this town. They spoiled me outrageously, considering me a lucky charm instead of the falsehoods spread for centuries about my kind being "unlucky".

Only to evildoers and crooks, my friends.

Anyway, my scent-following spirits are lifting. Since Mr. Matt Devine stole my Miss Temple right from under my king-size zebra-stripe bedspread at the Circle Ritz, I feared my life as a private eye was knocked out cold.

Now I see that my favorite humans, perhaps even more so in the dreamy state of recent wedlock, are as helpless as ever they were before I found them. I have work to do!

A deep, loud snarl interrupts my epiphany about my future lives and times. I must do the pussycat soft shoe and tread carefully. Grizelle, the eight-hundred-and-fifty pound white tiger in Mr. Snow

Christophe's act, has extensive holding cages around here that connect with a palatial outside faux-tropical garden of pools, waterfalls, and toys.

I do not wish to encounter Grizelle unplugged and become a toy.

Unfortunately Big Cat smell overpowers the odor of anything domesticated, but I persist and am soon trotting unseen beneath racks of hanging hems of silk, brocade, and ostrich-feathered costumes. I must harden my fierce jungle heart against the succulent, teasing, shivering ostrich feathers, block out all the makeup and perfume scents, and finally pluck one unmistakable scent I am searching for. Wet dog.

Oh, it is stomach-churning, the worst of two worlds, dog and mildew, but I now resume following the scent I detected on the poor, dead Miss Celeste.

Above me, the late, late bar shows around us are vibrating the area with music and merriment thumping. I whisk into an empty dressing room that smells promising and spot a rack of leotards and capes and trailing scarves, all glittery and the color of green in its most poisonous shades.

The air conditioning system sends invisible hands paging through the sheer fabrics, so they writhe as they did in the stage act, as around some faintly detectible ghost.

I am not superstitious, but shudder at the loss of a young, vibrant human life.

The sound like a saw whining back and forth, back and forth, makes my back lift into a croquet hoop of distaste. I hiss to beat the band while retreating on my highest shivs.

"Who goes there?" a raspy, raw voice from above asks.

Even spookier. There is nothing human left in this dressing room but a faint scent of perspiration and perfume.

I jump onto a light wooden ice cream chair, commonly used as dressing table seats. Then up to the cluttered tabletop surface, where I sniff open grease-paint tins of clown white and murderous red and…I pounce on a brace of centipedes lurking at the corner of my eyes. Only a pair of false eyelashes lying abandoned.

Saw-saw-saw on dry wood. I spot a large canvas tote bag with a mesh side under the table. A wide green floppy ribbon tied into a bow decorates its drooping shoulder straps.

I jump down to approach the object on a belly-crawl, then leap straight up and wrestle it onto its side. Pinned!

Unfortunately not gagged.

Arowler-ferolwer-growler!

With this snarling warning, a creature with a short, disgustingly wet black nose on a white snoot and big pointed black ears you might spot on Anubis, the Egyptian God of the Dead with the head of a jackal, pokes its tiny face out of a canvas cave. The eyes are big and brown.

I leap back. Horrified.

If there is one thing your average, or above-average in my case, feline abhors it is the creepy human brown-color eyes so often found on dogs. Be frank. Have you ever mused deeply about this? I thought not. Besides the great apes and associated monkeys, the eye color brown is never found on cats and not much to be found in animal eyes, other than on dogs. Yes, some cats sport weak-tea yellow eyes, but not brown.

This is creepy. If I am to be appealed to, I prefer it be by human brown eyes, like Mr. Matt's. Unfortunately, he is unlikely to appeal to me. My Miss Temple might and she has proper cool blue-gray eyes.

But this little critter is decidedly brown-eyed and a canine.

"You are a purse pooch," I growl. "Talk, or I will shake you by the back of your scrawny neck like a baby powder bottle."

That only encourages the little nipper to bark and lunge at me. I begin to translate its high-pitched whining sounds. And attempt to calm it.

"I do not know where your mama is." I examine the thing. Half my substantial twenty-pound weight. It may be small, but it is still a pawful and an earful. *Ouch.* My neat, more petite ears are as fine-tuned as a Bose speaker system. You could sell them in luxury cars.

"I have nothing to do with your not 'going walkies' all this evening and night."

Arowler-ferolwer-arowler!

"I see that could be stressful. I am stressed already."

Arowler-ferolwer-arowler wee-wee!

"Are you saying, 'going *wee, wee, wee* all the way home'? I believe that line is copyrighted by three petite porcines.

"Oh! *Wee, wee there.* In the corner. I see now."

It lunges with sharp foxy fangs ajar. It wears a small collar—pink, for Bast's sake—fastened to a short lead attached to the bag. I manage to get my teeth gnawing off the short leash, which is much easier to do than a collar, especially if it is not on oneself. "What is your name?" I ask, to keep it busy while I attack pink patent leather. I see his little feet are wearing knitted slippers! There ought to be law against doing that to a dude.

"Where is my Mamatina," he whines. "Where is my Mamatina?"

"I never had a 'Mamatina'. Do you mean *Mamacita?* That would figure. You've got a lot of Mexican Chihuahua in you. Or do you mean MamaMia? I do have a Mama*Meana,* such a big bad clowder queen she was named after a dog. Ma Barker. That is the kind of mama you want. One who can knock any stranger into next week and feed you its ears."

"Ooooh. Oooow." That shuts the little wimp up for about ten seconds while he decides to communicate more plainly, and then he comes out with a doozy. "I am Arthur, King of the Britons, and I order you to release me instantly!"

With three serious chomps I break the leash in two. As I work on spitting the foul taste of faux leather from my mouth, my canine ward leaps past me. He—I am not so sure about this; I think his cotton balls got harvested, but am certainly not going to examine his rear—high-tails and high-nails it to the fluffy white "bed" in the corner, which he honors with a lifted rear leg and a stream of lemonade-color water.

I have never seen a supposedly trained Dee-Oh-Gee go amok like that.

At least Arthur, King of the Britons, does not squat like a girl.

"So you wet your bed like a newborn?"

"That is not my bed," he sniffs. "It is my personal, private portable wee-wee pad, so I can be left alone and have a comfort station nearby."

I am taken aback to observe that when he is not into high-pitched ear-splitting mode he can actually be understood.

First, he finishes the doggish ritual of sniffing where he has *not* gone, which makes no sense to me. My kind do that in reverse to make sure no betraying odors remain. Then he trots to the middle of the dressing room floor and demands to know who *I* am.

"Hooo-Arrrrrre-Uuuuu," he croons like lovesick calf.

"I am King Louie the Seventeenth. You may have heard of my royal line and predecessors, Louis the fifteenth and sixteenth."

"I have heard of the esteemed French poodle," he says graciously.

I esteem neither the French nor their poodles, but educating this fellow is not worth my time.

From now on I am not going to translate from the original dog or Briton lingo, but put it into plain people English, which I excel at. That is where the dog breed has gone wrong. They try to *talk* to the Two-legs. We felines confine ourselves to short one- or two-syllable instructions these creatures can comprehend, *me-ow* or *mer-ow*, and simple forepaw gestures, or to murmuring quietly to hypnotize them into showering us with massages and trivial conversation, and also copious high-end canned seafood and the like. Pity can openers do not have a convenient foot-pedal on the floor one could jump on.

By now, putting together the portable wee-wee pad (such a shameful description—what is dirt for, for Bast's sake?), and the green tinge to the cosmetic items on the makeup table, I understand one more thing. Arthur may be King of the Britons, but his "Mamatina" is suddenly AWOL—Absent Without Leave, a major military no-no that has become a civilian expression for other unauthorized absences, like death.

I doubt she was ever in the military—but I know she will never come back here again. In fact, who may come back here in not too long would be a police forensics team.

My usually sharp associates upstairs are still shell-shocked by their close encounter with a stranger's death and are thinking more slowly than normal, which is not uncommon in times of stress. I realized at the start that a performer might have scads of clues about her life, if not her death, in her dressing room, so have hastened ahead of them to safeguard the scene.

Now I realize I must safeguard the scene from *them!*

Once the dead woman's dog is discovered, it will be carted away to the shelter. Or, if I know my Miss Temple, to her Circle Ritz rooms to be nauseatingly fussed over and, worse, when I visit, allowed to run yapping at me, as if *I* were an intruder.

Here he stands now, nine solid pounds of almost all black fur except for a white muzzle, with a tiny brain to match, full of insightful undivulged information about Miss Novak's habits, mood, friends, and enemies. Only *I* can interrogate him and solve whether her death was accidental or dastardly.

I have a no win/no win choice to make.

I can return to the not-green green room and put myself through paroxysms of miming to lure friends and strangers to this dressing room. Then I must cogitate and caper again to keep them from treating Arthur, King of the Britons, like a dog, and not a valuable, if incoherent, witness.

Not a positive scenario.

I must save this self-called aristocrat from incarceration and whisk him away. *Fast!*

So I swallow my pride and wrap a shiv-retracted paw around his shoulder, patting delicately, as if he were a spider on the floor I have refrained from exterminating.

"Your Majesty, your Mamatina has sent me here to save you from dog-nappers who would imprison you for ransom. We must escape through the Caverns of Darkness and flee to the Outside World to elude them and preserve your reign."

How lucky that the TCM classic movie channel recently reran *The Prisoner of Zenda*, so I can speak the classy dialogue and make the proper bows.

Arthur's furry forehead is an anthill of worry furrows. "My Mamatina is not coming with us?"

"No. She will hold them off here with all of her might. We must get out, *now*. We must *get outside*."

"I must see Mamatina—"

"Not now. We must get *outside*."

"Outside?" The word begins to work on His Highness's deepest desires. Dogs always want to go outside.

"Outside!" He is standing and alert. Outsize ears pricked.

"We will have a big adventure, like soldiers of fortune. We are being hunted by very bad people, Your Majesty, and what you know is most important. We must escape."

"Escape? To where?"

He has me there. Goal one. Make sure a possible witness is not shuffled off like a dumb (mute) animal to the Big House, aka an animal shelter. Done. Goal two. Get him out before he knows his mistress is dead. Almost done. Goal three. Lie and cheat like a human for the common good.

I go into my declaration mode. "Fear not, Arthur, King of the Britons. You will soon be entirely safe because you are entering a custom-tailored Midnight Louie witness protection program. I will be your knight-errant, at your service. You may call me Sir Midnight."

His little head lifts high and he takes one last sweeping look around, inhaling deeply the scents so strongly present of his absent mistress and so shallow to my less specialized nose.

"Will I ever see this place again?"

"I fear not, but you will ultimately meet your Mamatina later in a far better place." I put in this plug for the Rainbow Bridge theory. Who knows? It could be true.

"Now—" I am at a loss for words after committing that whopper.

I jump up onto the makeup table to distract him as a second thought knocks hard on my brain.

I do what my kind does when we are sitting on a table or counter thinking hard. I push something down to the floor. Something green and fluffy.

"Oh," Arthur cries as he runs over to—what else?—sniff it. "What have you done, you clumsy oaf!" He snuffles and noses at a small green velvet pillow with a white fluffy border to inhale glitter powder and strong perfume and Green Fairy dust. He sneezes, of course, and backs off. "That is my Mamatina's favorite powder puff. It is a *Big Bad Mussentouch*. It has marabou feathers."

"My apologies to your mistress and to the marabou." I leap down, well satisfied, though I regret giving up the airy soft rim of feathers so in need of a thorough teething.

Now, with Arthur's overrated snout freshly full of such heavy scents, I can shepherd the poor little fellow past the place where his mistress lies dead without him sensing the reek of mortality that comes so swiftly to one dead, and to those of his sensitive-nosed breed.

It is a far, far better thing I do to remove and distract King Arthur than let him confront the awful truth so directly.

I push the ajar dressing room door open a trifle farther. *Hmm...* how to get him moving? He looks a bit like a miniature Husky, so...

"Mush!"

He trots right out as I sigh my relief and retake the lead. We must enter the under-stage tunnels and retrace my path to the back alley. His nose has already found my scent and is vacuuming the floor as his short little legs flash like miniature black windmill vanes.

We soon reach the underground tunnel system and I take the lead, my panther-like strides forcing Arthur to trot so fast we pass the fork in the path that leads to Miss Celeste Novak's resting place without a pause as he pants on past. Faint scuffles and voices in the theater and green room above sound like a TV with the sound nearly on mute.

Whew. We circle around the white tiger's under-above ground quarters, where I have no trouble with Arthur lingering around the smell of raw meat and Big Cat.

"Where is Outside?" he asks between pants. "You promised Outside."

We are almost there, but I am not sure our combined thirty pounds can push the H-vac door open.

It is highly heavy metal and that is not referring to a rock band. It swings outward, like the steel door on a furnace. As with all forbidden entries, it is easier to tease open from without, where handles and hinges are accessible. So I am crossing my shivs that we will not have to retreat and wait many hours for the police to come and go before we can sneak out. Since I am already hungering for a wandering tidbit, this would be a problem.

"Forsooth, Your Majesty, we are at the door to outside and all we can do is lower our heads like goats and butt."

My shoulders are massive compared to the Boy King's. So... "On your third pant, we push."

Sadly, he is now edging into hyperventilating. His domestic slave collar tags yodel like a cuckoo clock, as I lower my noble brow and push. There is the slightest squeal of hinges. I hear a loud snuffle on the other side.

"Hey," a big, deep, angry voice challenges. "You dogs! Get away from there."

There is much scuffling and I hear boot steps as big and angry as the voice. Then the hatch swings open.

"Run for it!" I yowl at Arthur, and do so.

I spot the Dumpster that had attracted my attention back here in the first place and rush to belly crawl under it. Arthur, King of the Britons, shimmies under easily alongside me.

The boots follow us, kicking at the Dumpster side. We cover our ears with our forelimbs because an emptied, beaten Dumpster makes a very big drum set.

"You damn dogs," the man yells, trying to push a wooden rod underneath the Dumpster to jab us.

I resent being called canine, but am not leaving my secure Dumpster dwelling to make that point, which I would do, with my full-frontal eight shivs, had I not a...darn miniature dog to protect.

There is a sudden sharp bark. A...well, really big, deep bark. A Dumpster-side bonging bark. It is followed by a snarl Grizelle the white tiger would not disown.

The guy falls over backwards. The snarls emanating from the region of his throat intensify as he tries to gargle out words like "No. Get away, you damn brute!" I watch four big gray paws with big gray claws straddling his fallen lumpy form.

The man twists onto his stomach to run-crawl away, pursued by giant paws.

Behind me, Arthur is producing cute, little snarls that escalate louder the farther the fleeing guard is away.

I wait, then watch the big dog's return as he sniffs and circles along the dirty ground to the closed metal door. There he paws it, snorts, and gives a canine whine that would raise the hairs on the back of your neck even if you were a Rhodesian Ridgeback. Or King Kong.

I snake out a forelimb, holding Arthur back with the other. The Big Bad Wolf impersonator is following my scent in this area perfectly. I nudge Arthur and hiss in his limp ear.

"This big boy is not going anywhere. He is on my track. You are his kind. Get out there and introduce yourself."

"N-n-no."

"Come on. You are Arthur, King of the Britons—"

"I do not even know who or where the Britons are. My Mamatina did not tell me."

"Your Mamatina and my Mamatina and that guy's Mamatina are not here, but we three are. It is time to Manchester up or whatever breed you are and assert your noble name and title. Get out there and ask him to account for himself. You are too small to eat for a monster like him to bother with, too easy for your little bones to get caught in those big fangs."

"*Oooh,* bones, fangs. I am not even allowed to watch cable TV. Only reruns of *Mr. Roger's Neighborhood.*"

"You are in Mr. Ogre's Neighborhood now."

I grab Arthur by the scruff and sling him out onto the gasoline-slick pavement. Oh my, that will really do in his most recent groomer-administered bath and manicure.

Okay, this may be rather pusillanimous of me, but I am caught between two extremes of a breed not mine.

My under-Dumpster narrow perspective is like looking out the viewing-slit on a Panzer tank. Panzer. Sounds big and feline panther-like, does it not? I watch four huge paws stop, scrape around, and reach one huge limb out to Arthur, whose tippy-toes shivering in their knit slippers sound like a flamenco dancer who's wearing footlets instead of nail head-bottomed pumps. Why not? He has a lot of Chihuahua in Little Him.

"Your scent here is new," the Big Dog tells him.

"Yes, Sir. I have just escaped from bondage inside. I have never trod this ground until now."

The Big Dog lowers his big nose to the battered asphalt and concrete. "True, pipsqueak. I seek She Who Came Before."

Arthur speaks up in a sudden flow of high, squeaky voice. "I would not know about that, Sir, but the-big-black-alley-cat-under-the-ugly-metal-box was here before me. He would know more than me, even though I am Arthur, King of the Britons."

The Dog raises his huge, fanged head. I am mesmerized to see his eyes are not canine-brown, but a Karma-like pale blue color. Almost human.

He and his darn nose are pointing at right where I am hunkered down. He starts pacing toward my Dumpster, one strong leg crossing over the other like a catwalk model.

"*Fee Fi Foe Fum*, I smell the blood of a cat the size of Thumbelina's thumb."

I, ah, do not quaver. One of those paws will only reach three inches under my shelter and I have four shivs to make it pay for the intrusion.

"Where is My Girl?" the dog demands. "She has been here. With you."

He is way more coherent than your average Rottweiler, say. I pride myself on speaking in many tongues with various species of so-called Dumb Beast, as erroneously slandered by humans. I have never encountered a member of any species so close to human conversation.

I produce a big Cheshire cat grin. "Your girl. *Heh-heh.* I have heard of a boy and his dog but—"

"Silence, cat," he growls, going down on his forelegs, which are intruding several huge sharp nails into my safe space. "Where is My Girl? You were here with My Girl, and disappeared inside."

"Well, yes. Can we talk? Without claws. Your Girl is safe, and I led her to safety inside, but she must miss you mightily."

"I had rogue canines and machines to take down, and so lost track of her."

"She is alive and well, inside here as you sense and see, and will soon be taken to a safe place near here." I get an idea.

"I am a private investigator, Sir Dog." I do not have to tell him his "Girl", obviously Miss Lilah Lane, is going to the Crystal Phoenix. "I can track her progress and report to you at a place where we can meet later."

"Here," he says. He sniffs the air. "Not. Others arrive. *I* will find *you*."

I search my memory desperately for some common meeting place.

"I have your scent," I am told. "We have never met before, but from now on I can find you anywhere." His glowing blue eyes and wet black snout loom even closer toward my face. "Anywhere. Any time."

Well, is that a convenience, or a threat?

No matter. The big canine lug has dashed off.

As I stretch to extract myself from the tight space into the open, Arthur stutter-steps over and leans against my shoulder. "Woe is me. What will become of me, Sir Midnight?"

Sigh. I thought I was preserving evidence, but where can I stow King Arthur for safe-keeping? Who would believe his name even? Much less respect his runty size? And the knit booties?

A desperate idea occurs. Midnight Louie will have to act as a diplomat and a godfather at the same time to pull off this scheme, but it is the only way.

"Put your trotting booties in gear, King Arthur, we are going on a knightly quest."

21
"Jane Eyrie?"

Alone at last.

What am I, chopped liver? Irma kvetched.

"Or what is Achilles, for that matter? Don't lecture me. I've... *we*'ve crash-landed on Cream of Wheat," I told her, throwing myself back down on the cushy bedspread, right atop its central gold-and-silver lamé image of a phoenix rising.

Careful with those battered boots!

"Not touching a filthy sole to a stitch on this five-star bedding." I sat up, feet firmly on the carpet, and pulled the three rattling shopping bags over to shake out my new duds from the hotel gift shop. Glitzy tourist stuff, but outrageous glitter was how to be overlooked in Vegas. Achilles danced around my feet as I leaned over to tug off my black motorcycle boots. I glanced up to make sure the fancy door hardware was set to "lock", then began dropping off my clothes as I lurched toward the bathroom and the promised Jacuzzi spa.

Promise fulfilled. Achilles bounced up two carpeted steps to a filling sunken tub. He sniffed the array of bath bubbles, powders and soaps and lotions arranged in fancy bottles along the wide white marble rim, sneezing a time or two.

"When I'm soft-scrubbed back to normal," I told him, "you're going to be down to your digger-dog toes and up to your topknot in cleansing bubbles, baby boy!"

His expressive ears lifted and then drooped. I wrapped my bare arms around his surprisingly sturdy body. "So good to have you… back, buddy. From where? How? You're a Wichita native. You've never even met Quicksilver."

Achilles just gave me a happy doggy grin with tongue hanging like a limp pink zipper pull out the side of his formidable fangs.

Now for some long overdue Me time.

Me too, Irma chortled.

So I gave my bruised and scraped body a slow lowering into the hot water, relishing even the first allover stinging sensations on my abrasions, and then a wave of melting relaxation as I bonelessly slid into the water and put on the jets, puttin' on the Ritz.

Hot water drops rained on Achilles. He shook his floor-length coat, more gray than white, and retreated to the marble floor.

I sighed as I stared through the bathroom's open double doors at the giant black screen of the hotel room window that framed arching comets and pinwheels of galaxies forming a new zodiac, just for me. The Las Vegas hotel rooms real "night-lights."

Then the nightstand phone in the other room rang.

Nuts.

Had to be a wrong number. Nobody knew I was here.

Except the hotel owners, the TV interview show hosts, the police detectives and lieutenant, the Six Deadly Sins and Snow, and probably every dang one of the ten Fontana brothers by now.

Grabbing one from a thick pile of aqua-colored bath towels, I exited the Jacuzzi with the prissy-footed care of a cat on a two-inch wide windowsill, and wrapped my torso with the bath sheet.

This could have been an episode of *I Love Lucy*. (I watched a lot of retro TV in the group homes.) So picture this: I stubbed my toe on the desk chair's merry-go-round of radiating steel legs and hopped on one bare foot, dripping, while almost knocking the phone off the desk.

"Yes?"

"Max Kinsella. I'm suggesting a pow-wow since you're one of two mysterious ladies starring in Spellbinder's show tonight, and the other one is uncommunicative."

"Max Kin—? Oh, the other magician."

"You do know how to mangle the male ego, Miss Lane. I know Lieutenant Molina. It's far better to satisfy her thirst for information before she has to go searching and bringing little nooks and crannies of your life and background you never dreamed of into the light of day."

"'Pow-wow.' You want to meet me for a talk?"

"Precisely."

I checked my new Crystal Phoenix shop watch. "Downstairs in fifteen minutes."

"Too public for talking. Your room will do when you've dressed."

I glanced at the shopping bags on the bed. At least I *could* get dressed now...wait!

"How do you know I'm *not* dressed?" I squinted at the window. A hunk of lit-up Las Vegas was blotted out by solid black.

"Oh my God. Are you Spider-Man?"

"I prefer 'cat burglar.'"

"I prefer *you* out of my line of sight. If you *can* get into my room, I'll be in the bath area getting dressed, and I warn you, I am armed with a Tibetan staple gun, so don't try anything funny."

"Some new martial arts gizmo?"

"The product of ancient Shaolin warrior monks. They could defy gravity and hover, you know. Did not need to use stagecraft trickery to window-peep."

I grabbed my bags and whisked back through the double doors to the bathroom and locked them.

Thank goodness I'd bought new underwear. A woman always felt more formidable wearing underwear.

I was sure Matt and Temple would vouch for the guy, but I'd sensed tension between him and the lieutenant, so I wasn't buying him having any business at all in talking to me.

I'm a fast dresser and lightweight jeggings make sense in Vegas. I'd found some Cuban-heeled red booties at the attached shopping mall and a huge tote bag to match.

Achilles lived up to his name by immediately nosing my leather ankle boots.

"Poor boy." I surveyed Achilles' still disheveled coat as I donned a black Tee and my new black-satin baseball jacket with *Lost Vegas Hellionaire* in rhinestones on the back.

"You can't escape the doggie beauty parlor appointment tomorrow. Now, come on out and show this Max guy who's alpha dog in this suite."

I threw the bathroom double doors open as Achilles and I made our debut for a first Las Vegas formal appearance.

Max, who'd easily cracked a narrow side-vent window of the huge main window, was a symphony of subtlety in various textures of black, and raised an arm to his eyes to ward off bling when I turned to flash my rhinestones. "In Vegas, obvious is the best disguise. You have good instincts, Miss Lane."

"Thank you."

"About that."

"About thanking you? I do have *some* manners."

He pulled a length of buckled black webbing and leather from his linen sport coat inside pocket and threw it on the bed, dead-on the bejeweled eye of the crystal phoenix.

"About this and what's in it, Miss *Lane*."

Caught, Irma wailed in a whisper.

I picked up my upscale, downsized fanny pack and belt, but he wasn't done lecturing me.

Meanwhile, I found and successfully turned on my cell phone. Apparently my device was not lost in space or time.

Max was still dissing my belongings.

"The buckle is a toy, the license ID is wildly not kosher for L.V., and the name is six twists of the dial warped off. I'd have expected better from a smooth operator like you."

"Sarcasm won't help me now."

"No, but I can. You'll find a past-muster ID for Lilah Lane inside your skinny Minnie Mouse fanny pack. "

I sure didn't want his hands on my fanny pack. "Magic or elves, I hope?"

"Better. I know people who know people. "

Achilles had been tilting his head back and forth during this exchange and now decided his move. He leaped onto the foot of the bedspread, planted his fluffy, wet, muddy feet and loosed a series of seriously throaty growls at our visitor.

"Achilles has a good question. Why would you help us?"

He nodded at the dog. "When housekeeping gets an eyeful of that bedspread you'll need an advocate."

"Oh, Achilles! *Down!* Maybe I can wash the spread in the Jacuzzi."

Max laughed. "Van and Nicky don't bite. Dog paws on the bedspread is a none-issue compared to an utterly phony ID."

"It isn't phony. That's, ah, that's my sister's stuff. I musta grabbed the wrong cards. I needed to get out of Wichita fast."

"This 'Delilah Street' is your sister?" he studied the license under the desk lamp. "Different hair-do, but face is pretty close, so why is your surname different?"

"Step-sisters. What's wrong with the driver's license? She's had it for years."

He shook his head this time. Apparently I was getting more and more hopeless. "Obviously, again. It doesn't have the Homeland Security omni-chip that gives you a pass for all purposes. Isn't she going to get in trouble without it?"

I sighed. "Not as much as I am with it, I guess. I haven't heard of this new omni-chip, but so what? They won't need a driver's license to convict me of murder."

"Which leads me back to my dinner invitation."

"And me back to my wondering why. What's in it for me besides what's on the menu?"

"We have so much in common. You're a stranger who strangely appeared on a magic show stage with a murdered woman lying not thirty feet from you. I spotted the murdered woman lying not thirty feet from you while concealed up high backstage, so we're both logical suspects. You hit your head, you say, and are confused on specifics. I hit my head and broke my legs and went on the run in Europe before I returned, so I'm a reliable usual suspect. Someone needs to find out about the no longer living Celeste Novak. You, or perhaps your convenient step-sister, were a TV reporter, you claim, which is next door to being an investigative pro."

"So it's the head cases putting their heads together. Okay, but I'm taking Achilles. I can use my useless fanny pack belt for a lead."

"That's right, you lost him once today."

Not quite right. Quicksilver was still among the missing and Achilles hadn't been among the living until the Fontana boys "found" and "returned" him. The Quick and the Dead, that was my mini-dog pack now.

One reason I wanted out from the hotel was the hope that Quicksilver was missing me as much as I was missing him and he'd have a better chance to find my scent on the streets.

"Is there a diner that accepts dogs?" I asked.

"I know just the place. Has a dog in residence. And sometimes even a cat."

"Cool." I tossed the contents of the fanny pack on the bedspread and picked up a silver bullet.

Kinsella's expressive eyebrows did their power lift.

"Lipstick." I waved my tube. "Creative packaging these dangerous days." I shook out my slightly damp mane of hair. "Gotta do something so I don't look like I just escaped from Alcatraz with water wings. Or a coal mine chain gang. And I should get some antibiotic cream for facial scrapes in the hotel gift shop."

I stuffed the driver's license, lipstick case and my hotel room card into a jacket pocket.

"Looks like you're used to life on the run."

Not worth answering. I fastened the fanny pack around like a harness, then called Achilles to heel. He did it perfectly, like he'd never been gone. Dead and gone. I swallowed the lump in my throat. If any enemy ankles or heels lurked in biting range, he would do his protection thing and be a happy dog.

"Well, aren't you the perfect Las Vegas couple out on the town," Van Von Rhine declared when we encountered her in the lobby. "I was just going up to see if everything was satisfactory in your room, Lilah."

Both Achilles' ears and my expression drooped a little. Bad dog. Bad girl. "Achilles got a bit exuberant on the bedspread before I could rinse him off from the accident site grime."

"Not to worry. That's why we have a huge hotel laundry. I'll take care of it right now."

She trotted away on hotel business, a coolly efficient ice-blonde with a warm heart.

I noticed the subtlest frown flicker over my escort's features. Maybe he hadn't wanted Van Von Rhine to see me leave with him. I'd sensed awkwardness between him and not only the homicide lieutenant, but the Temple-Matt couple. Like most performers, he had a strong personality and couldn't always subdue it.

Never mind. I could handle it. Right now, I needed a guide to who I was and where I was, which states seem to have collided like Dolly with the Inferno Hotel window-wall, and shattered.

22
Hot Dog in Sin City

So where do you hide a leaf? In a forest.

That is a question in a famous mystery story.

Where do you stash a maybe-murder victim's purse pooch?

I would say at the high-end purse shop at the Bellagio, but that is too obvious.

Somewhere truly safe and unexpected. Somewhere where someone can keep an eye on nine pounds of faux Chihuahua-Husky.

Now that King Arthur sniffs the night air of the Hellfire back area, he shivers.

"It is not cold in Vegas," I tell him.

"But I do not have the slippers-matching sweater my Mamatina bought for me. You were in such a hurry we…, uh you left it behind, Sir Midnight."

Now that he mentions it, he is part something called "Mexican Hairless" and I realize the little dude's coat is pretty skimpy. *Drat!*

"We are going someplace warmer. Mush. You won't feel cold when you get your feet in gear."

"I do not like this place. It is stinky and my knit slippers are getting greasy."

"That is why we are leaving it."

"For where?"

Where to be or not to be. That is the question. Where can I drop off a hot dog? Somebody will no doubt miss this over-priced pipsqueak.

"I bet your Mamatina paid a pretty penny for you at some fancy kennel before you were even born."

"Oh, no. My Mamatina picked me personally. Just me from all the others. And I picked her. I am not only a king, I am special. I am a 'rescue'."

"Oh. Well, congratulations. I am going to 'rescue' you again, but first we will get somewhere safe where I can…" Grill you like a swordfish steak, comes to mind, but I forbear to say it aloud.

Where do you hide a nine-pound black dog? I suddenly know the answer, as in "Mama Knows Best".

"Okay, King Arthur. We are travelling 'tail, hop, skip, and jump'. You know what that means?

"Noo…"

"We *tail* a vehicle, *hop* on, *skip* out later and *jump* off. Got it?"

"What is a 'vehicle'?"

"Uh, car. You know 'ride in car', I bet."

Now he is shivering with excitement. "Why did you not say so? We are Outside to go Ride in Car." His scant little tail pounds the back alley asphalt. "Have fun."

"Yeah. Remember. I say 'Hop'?"

"I hop." That sounds like a chain restaurant, but what the Hellfire.

"I say 'Skip'."

"I get ready to…"

"Jump off to the street."

That is how we become hobos riding not the rails, but the delivery van routes. With online ordering, the transportation system throngs with UPS-style vans and trucks doing promised-time deliveries all over the country. Driver-side doors are always open and they are watching traffic, not very short hitchhikers.

Critters with a low-profile and black like us can Hop, Skip and Jump free feet-sparing transportation if you know where you are going, and I do. At least King Arthur is light on his tootsie slippers and we leave the Strip and its bright lights behind.

We are soon in the Circle Ritz neighborhood and within hoofing distance. But I am not heading there. Instead, I guide my charge to the nearby police substation.

He begins to pant and trot faster.

"Whoa, slow down," I order. My breed is unexcitable and does not pant except in extreme heat.

"Treat, treat," his squeaky voice chatters. We're coming up to a parking lot with fast-food wrappers near the building's back door. The odor is beguiling.

"Slow down, Your Majesty," I urge.

But those slippered feet were made for the hyperactive fox trot and he runs his runty little body right into the middle of where I had him headed.

You would never hear such hissing unless it was a snarl of snakes jumping away from a broken steam pipe. The security light casts the shadows of dozens of undulating eels on the back wall. Medusa herself, the serpent-tressed Gorgon monster of myth who could freeze any critter to look her in the face into stone, could be casting her long paralyzing shadow here.

This is when my Royal Pain takes it into his big-eared head to plant his footlets and let loose an aria of ear-piercing canine indignation and challenge that would wake The City That Never Sleeps.

I manage to clap my mitts over his snout. *"Shhhh!* This is where we are hiding out. You do not want to irk the police officers inside this station. They will keep any dangers away."

"S-s-snakes," he sputters through my tender pads. "I hate snakes."

"Those are not snakes."

By now someone inside the police substation has turned on a spotlight. I sweep Arthur away with me into the shadows near the fence shrubbery. A tall silhouette in the doorway looks around, shrugs, and shuts the door, muttering, "Cats."

That is so unfair! The yapping culprit was a dog. Apparently I am agreed with, because a low vibration begins all around us. The sound is so deep and threatening that Arthur, King of the Britons, cowers against my side.

Arthur starts toward it to make another noisy, overambitious challenge even as the shadows develop eyes by the dozen, iridescent red and green irises decorating the dark.

"Is this creature a friend of yours?" a raspy voice demands from the shadows.

I get him in a headlock that will muzzle him and say, "No, Ma. He is a Chihuahua mix, a refugee from south of the border seeking asylum."

23
Déjà Vu

"I can't complain," I told Max after we left Van in our wake. "Everybody's been so helpful and so darn nice. And now you're taking me to dinner. Why?"

"Perhaps because I'm not sure who you are, and because *you* are not quite sure of who you are, which is a dangerous state. I know. I've been there. Head injury in my case. Head knock and some deft prevarication in yours, I think."

"And we're both suspects for the death of Celeste Novak."

"I'm Molina's favorite go-to suspect, but not seriously in this case."

What he said so lightly covered a lot of time, peril and angst, I guessed.

Back story, back story. The past is prologue, Shakespeare said, and here I was landing dead center in several people's pasts, all unknown, especially the dead woman's, and including parts of my own.

I returned to what I knew.

"Van von Rhine is a doll. If I were her, she'd be bristling with tough questions for me," I commented to Max as we walked away, me bristling with questions for him.

"That's what I'm here for," Max said, with enough of an Irish twinkle that I could take him seriously, or not. Kind of freaky. We shared the same Black Irish coloring: black hair, blue eyes, but no freckles. In heeled boots I was a five-ten or so to his six-three or four.

I peeled off from his escort to buy necessities still locked in the trunk of my spirited-away Caddy and stuffed them in the big jacket pockets, smiling as I thought of the both suave and kiddishly enthusiastic Fontana clan. I could see why all-business Van Von Rhine had married the kid brother of the lot. Whatever, I knew Dolly was in indulgent hands and now—however, whyever, forever, I hope—Achilles and his joyous terrier bounce clung to my side again.

"Must be annoying," Max said as we waited for the parking valet to retrieve his car, "to replace every detail of your everyday life."

"I'm just relieved to know you *drove* here. After that twelfth-story window appearance, I thought you might have flown."

"It's you who has the Superman girlfriend name."

I groaned. "Everybody always does a riff on that." Well, he was the second, after myself.

"Or a stripper name. That an option?"

"Dream on, and guard your ankles." Achilles snapped his jaws with a short, rough bark.

Max sighed. "Look. You need a job. You need a place to stay. Can't you just phone home?"

"Can you?"

"No. My place was burned down."

"*Was* burned down. Didn't do it all by itself?"

"You *are* a quick pick up on nuances, even with a dented head. Yes. '*Was* burned down.' Yes. It was a legacy Vegas house, once owned by Orson Welles."

"What! Someone burned it down on purpose? That's…that's a crime against the culture. I'm so sorry, Max."

"I'm doing fine. I own a former nightclub building. It's dark now, but it's all one big playhouse for me, so I camp out there."

"I'm still shocked to hear about the Welles house being destroyed. I'm a huge fan of vintage films."

His pleased smile allowed me to glimpse the professional magician's usually buried teenage glee in surprising an audience. "Then we're going to just the right place tonight."

Magicians always strive to make you curious, too.

I hate to say it, but with Max and Achilles alongside me, I felt as dashing and tart as Myrna Loy playing Nora Charles. Look her up. She was something.

Max continued to surprise me, though I'd never admit it to him.

His car was an old-fashioned black sedan, a Maxima, of course, both bold and discreet. Instead of driving it to someplace blindingly be-lit and ballyhooed (Like Bally's) on the Strip, we prowled the quiet, dark streets of a neighborhood village of sorts. I absently fingered the charms on my silver bracelet as I peered out at The Magic Mushroom Muffin restaurant, a lit store with customers still browsing called the Thrill 'n' Quill Bookstore, with—I leaned nose-close to the deeply tinted passenger window to be sure—a striped brown tabby cat sitting like a prominently placed literary novel in the central window. Its amber eyes blinked as we passed. Or winked. A warning signal, perhaps?

We were approaching a swirl of hot-pink and turquoise-blue neon that called my name. *Café Noir & Déjà Vu Bar.*

"We're dining French?" I asked.

"It's a café and bar, yes. And so much more."

Achilles, who'd curled up on my new red boot toes in the dark passenger well, looked up, his white locks quivering with excitement. He'd been inactive for a long time in that vase. The car swung around the café's side to park.

I was stepping out as soon as it stopped, untangling Achilles' makeshift leash and my feet, and then meeting up with Max at the car's rear. I open my own doors. And shut them too.

He gestured me around the corner.

The café's black-light exterior lamps, used in the clubs to make mostly naked strippers' skin look electric blue-white, made Achilles' swaying floor-length white coat luminous.

Cocktails a hot-pink neon moon boasted. I felt at home already.

Speaking of "already", a cursive line of neon spelled out *Café Noir and Déjà Vu Bar*, complete with the French accent marks.

"*Déjà Vu*," I read aloud with a corny French accent. "That means 'already seen' in French, but I've never known about this place."

Max's sweeping arm gesture matched his words. "This is an up-and-coming new venue in a just-off-Strip neighborhood. The round marble-faced building we drove past houses the Fifties-built Circle Ritz apartments and condominiums. I lived there once, but Temple and Matt do now, in combined upper and lower units. The landlady is a hoot, and owns these buildings. Not likely there's room in that inn at the CR for you, I'm afraid. Let's discuss this sitting down."

The front door with its glass inset was wide enough for me and Achilles to enter side by side. The twenty-something male waiter comprehended some signal from Max behind me and led us to a table for four on the sidelines. Normalcy was feeling nice again.

Whoa! A curly-coated black-and-white dog, off-leash, came bouncing over to our table, and feet, barking.

Achilles tap-danced again on his hairy paws until his nails scraped wooden floor and he *arf*ed back, tilting his head. Then commenced black noses sniffing in concert and dogs turning end to nose and more dwelling on scents.

"Achilles!" I ordered, tightening the makeshift lead.

A willowy woman with short, fluffy hair and a long, floaty skirt came rushing over. "Asta! *No!* I'm so sorry," she told me. "He escaped his lead and darted in from the back. Asta! Be good. Good dog." She clipped a lead to his collar. "Someone will take your cocktail order in two shakes of a wire-haired fox terrier's tail."

She and the curly-coated dog swept to the rear area. She alone emerged a moment later to tend to other tables.

Achilles whimpered and curled around my boots.

I sat stunned too. Dog and woman had been black and white and gray all over. I was used to CinSims, of course, but when had the Inferno Hotel and Casino lost the lease on the Nick and Nora Charles "family", including dog, of CinSims to this tiny off-Strip venue? Was Snow losing his mind? Or was I? I had shamed Snow into reuniting the entire "set" from two different hotels a few months ago, after I solved a virtual murder at the Inferno, and *now* he'd given up leasing rights entirely?

I turned to Max Kinsella, tranquilly seated and reviewing the menu. "Since when have the famous Las Vegas CinSims been moved around willy nilly? Nick and Nora deserve a really massive Strip audience."

Max looked puzzled. "I beg your pardon? CinSims?"

"Cinema Simulacrums."

"Nobody uses that antique term anymore. They're just called celebrity impersonators."

"Even the dog?"

"Especially the dog," Nora said, back again and a bit breathless. "Asta thinks he's the star. *Your* dog is stealing his limelight. My husband will soon take your cocktail orders. *If* he's not gotten too cozy with a bottle of Boodles, his next favorite sleeping partner to me." She smiled impishly. "I'm so happy, darling girl, to overhear that you believe our little act merits star position on the Strip. From your lips to Hector Nightwine's ears."

I turned to Max after she had swooped away again. (Asta. Still a silly name for a dog.) "Are my eyes crossed?"

"And charming baby blues they'd be if they did."

"Can the flattery. What is this place?" I'd not forget that "Nora" had mentioned my so-far elusive landlord, Hector Nightwine. Nor that Max hadn't blinked either of *his* baby blues at the name or remark.

Max was shrugging now. "The latest in Las Vegas entertainment. A harking back to the classic films of yesteryear. Your dog seems to be getting into the spirit of things."

"If I had wanted to be 'getting into spirits', I would have gone to a medium. Or a bar."

"Well, this is a medium-level bar. And, your order taker awaits."

I looked up at a black tie-attired middle-aged gentleman with an anemic mustache (not Tom Selleck, for sure) swaying discreetly over our table with pad and pen—yes an actual ink pen, in hand.

"So good to see you, Nick Charles!" I greeted him, meaning every syllable.

"And I you as well my dear, darling…"

"Lilah!" I got that in fast before he called me Delilah. "Lilah Lane."

"Yes. Er, yes, Lilah. Dee-lightful Lilah. Delilah…"

He was understandably confused.

"Lilah Lane, Nick. *You* remember."

"Frankly, my dear, I don't."

"I'll have an Albino Vampire."

"Very good, Miss Dee-lightful…Lilah? And the gentleman?"

Max was laughing into his hand, knowing what ID I had carried. "He's doing a great job of pretending he knows you, but the drink? An Albino Vampire?" He leaned even closer to whisper, "Did you have our dee-lightful Christophe in mind when you ordered? The man would be livid. But then, he already is."

"The Albino Vampire is a cocktail of my invention, yes."

"You sling booze too?"

"I'm an amateur mixologist."

Nick Charles always came to the rescue of a lady. "I'll have you know, sir, Miss …dee-lightful, ah…Lane."

I nodded encouragingly.

"Miss…Lane. Is a queen of the modern cocktail. I highly recommend her concoctions."

Max laughed again. "Sounds bewitching. I'll have an Albino Vampire too."

Nick bowed and retreated.

"May I ask what I'm having?" Max leaned in to whisper.

"The recipe is secret."

"Maybe bartending would be a job for you. Except you'd be working when we creatures of the night—"

"Like magicians—?" I raised my eyebrows and crossed my legs.

"—would be working too."

"I could concoct a cocktail in your honor, I suppose. Just to annoy Christophe, since you seem to be rivals."

"Yes?"

"The Maxi-Magnum. *Hmm.* Tall, dark and charming. Black Russian ingredients are out. Maybe a Tom Selleck Magnum."

"Too much for me."

Two Champagne flutes filled with a creamy-white concoction were lofted to the table in front of them by a young waiter who looked suspiciously like Mickey Rooney.

Max was leery.

I liked inspiring that look on him.

"So," he said. "What's the bloody red blob at the bottom, and do I need a straw for this vanilla malted milk?" Max asked.

"The blood-red Albino Vampire bottom is a shot of Chambord raspberry liqueur," I explained. "And I hadn't thought of using a straw to imbibe every last bit, but that might work very well." I stood. "I'll get a couple straws from the bar."

I dashed away before he could react. I needed more from the bar than straws.

The chrome-and-red-leather swivel barstools were all taken, but I squeezed in next to Nick Charles, who was directing his conversation with all comers by using his full martini glass as a conductor's baton. And nearly, but never, spilling a drop.

"Of course," he said, "we were not willing to drive all the way from Los Angeles to Las Vegas in our heyday," he pointed out. "Eventually Mrs. Charles realized the desert oasis clubs here were in need of her glamour and my cultured conversation. So the whole family packed up and arrived and was in immediate demand."

I looked past the busy bartender, a lively brunette, to gaze deeply *into* the mirror backing the shelves of liquor bottles. Hedy LaMarr stared back at me while other familiar CinSims milled in the even dimmer background behind her.

Nick turned to me. "What brings you to Vegas, Miss, uh, Delilah?"

"It's 'Lilah' here," I whispered.

He nodded with the solemnity lent by plenty of gin. "Oh, yes, I see. I too find a pseudonym useful on occasion. Although my detecting days are over. My wife has declared me retired."

"What a pity. I'm in a bit of an awkward place regarding a dead body—"

"Was the corpse in an awkward position or yourself?"

"Both. I fear I'm a police suspect and must solve the case myself to stay out of the slammer."

"That *is* a dilemma. Been there myself." He waved toward the mirror. "Mrs. Charles, your commiseration is required."

That brought Nora from behind the bar and sweeping over to us. "Dearest girl, I was afraid we wouldn't see you again after that brouhaha at the Inferno. Thanks so much for persuading Christophe to buy our leases from the 'Thin Man' series so we could share the same venue again."

"It was outrageous to separate you three, and blackmail on my part to get you all together again, actually."

"What an enterprising female," Nick said with an amiable sway of both smile and posture. "Reminds me of Nora after I first introduced her to the gentle art of applying pressure. She got several fur coats out of me for it."

Nora faux-slapped his shoulder with her tiny silver mesh Whiting & Davis evening bag. "That was long ago. Wearing fur is dead now."

I blinked at her airy logic as she turned to me again. "Speaking of fur, is that adorable little white dog Asta is trying to mount yours?"

I turned, aghast. Achilles was showing his teeth at the famous canine film star and gargling warming growls in his throat. Asta suddenly whined and ran off.

"Oh, dear," Nora murmured. "A slight confusion of gender. And," she asked, "the lovely lonely man sitting at the table staring into space is yours also?"

I regarded Max, who was studying the clientele.

"An acquaintance only. You remind me, Nora, that I need to compose a signature cocktail for an Irishman named Max. Call it, 'Maximum Impact', perhaps?"

"If that's how you feel about him," Nora said.

"Nora should have an idea about Maximum Impact." Nick leaned lovingly and sloshingly toward her piquant profile. "She has some Irish in her. I used to call her 'Silky Sullivan.'"

"After a racehorse in your day?" I envisioned Nora as a svelte, spirited champion thoroughbred.

Nick shook his head. "Not at the track, though I often am to be found there. Silky Sullivan is a boxer, not the canine kind. A boxer, wasn't he, heart of my heart? Possessed of a punch that would make a strong man swoon like a day-old lily and go six feet under."

Nora remained loftily serene. "Your memories of the sporting life will not help our girl here create a new cocktail."

Their banter had already inspired me. "I can call the drink a 'Maximum Punch'. Now to start with some innocent Bailey's Irish cream."

I called the bartender over.

"*Si, si,*" said Carmen Miranda, the slinky nineteen-forties Latin singer-dancer with a bare midriff and high headdress of fruits and flowers. "Come behind the bar with me and we will shake up the place." She jumped up to sit on the bar.

I jumped up to join her, then spun around and, presto, another jump and I was behind the bar.

"We'll make a 'Fruit Cocktail' together," I said.

By now, Carmen's exotic looks, metal and porcelain jewelry, stunning even in black-and-white, and shoulder-shaking, hip-slinging moves provided a rhythmic clicking background to my impromptu feat of mixology.

I asked her for a tall glass, Bourbon, the V-8 juice, a lemon half, horseradish, hot *and* Worcestershire sauce, and shakers of Parmesan cheese and chili powder, plus a tall footed glass.

"*Ay, caramba,*" she groaned, "you are cooking up quite a hot mess for that man named Max."

Fulfilling that list kept Carmen Miranda's hip and shoulder ruffles shaking, but she whipped all the ingredients into a line before me. I rimmed the empty glass with the lemon and twisted it through the Parmesan and chili powder pile. Presto! The shaken ice and ingredients became a rich, full-bodied crimson drink in a chili and cheese-rimmed glass. *Ay, caramba!*

I thought Max Kinsella, my co-murder suspect, deserved his own hot, blood-red sweet spot.

Finally, I brought the drink to our table held in both hands, to applause from the diners around us.

He rose like the big little gentleman he was, like a Fontana brother. And Achilles jumped up on my leg while Asta sniffed my boot soles.

"Your Albino Vampire is getting warm," Kinsella warned me.

"Your Maximum Punch is getting cooler. What can we eat here?"

"The celebrity film stars and the cocktails are the major attraction. Déjà Vu serves pricey bar appetizers, but they'll hold you over until morning. Meanwhile…" He lifted his new signature drink for a toast, "Here's to our both being as innocent as holy water when it comes to the death of the Green Fairy."

I surveyed the menu. "You've seen how flat my wallet is."

"You'll just have to rely on the kindness of strangers then."

"Blanche Dubois' line from Tennessee Williams' classic play *Streetcar Named Desire*. Vivian Leigh in the movie. I don't like to rely on anyone."

"I rely on you landing on your feet. Consider me a future employer."

The prices didn't have the cents listed or those tacky dollar signs fast food places threw around like dice. Irma provided commentary.

Fava Bean prosciutto bread, mint 15
Too Hannibal Lector for my taste.

Blue Crab garlic cream, jalapeno, tomato compote 15
Delish!

Misticanza heirloom radishes, goat cheese vinaigrette 18
Not consuming vegetables with a better heritage than me.

Marinated Beets pistachio, grapefruit, crema 19
Marinating beets sounds like vegetable abuse.

Octopus alla Piastra romesco verde, pistachio, orange 22
I hate grabby food.

Steak Tartara Piemontese wagyu beef, hazelnuts, black truffle 24
Not eating steak rare enough to bite me back.

I ordered the moody crab and hot like Carmen Miranda tomato jalapeño, the cheapest choice.

Max ordered the savage steak and funereal truffle, the most expensive.

He paid, but I kept track.

24
Ritzy Rooming House

I was relieved to leave the bar, walking beyond the talk and laughter into this quiet, charming off-Strip assembly of quirky shops and restaurants. Max seemed to crave strolling for a change.

"So what's with all these people in black and white and gray clothes and makeup?" I wondered aloud.

Nobody called them CinSims, but they had an eerie parallel to the fangirl and fanboy Cinema Symbiants who haunted the Inferno Bar and other venues that featured celebrity CinSims. Admirers of the genuine CinSims (a contradiction in terms, I know) would dress up and don ghostly makeup to match the film images of the actors.

Max explained. "Vegas has lasted so long because entertainment celebrities were the big draw since Frank Sinatra and the Rat Pack and Shirley MacLaine and Sammy Davis, Jr. Nowadays, with jets, it's so close to Hollywood. Clubs started using Technicolor holograms in their decor a few years ago. There'd always been a market for celebrity impersonators and recently they perform as the vintage stars in their black-and-white personas. These 'Nick and Nora' franchise actors are well paid and it's a fun gig because they're always improvising. It's almost a magic act."

"Like the all-white 'plaster statue' figures in the Venetian hotel public spaces, who move so slowly that tourists try to catch them doing it."

"Larger than life illusions."

I nodded. Of course, I couldn't tell him that in *my* Las Vegas, the CinSims were real cinema images blended onto reanimated zombie "canvases".

"Don't look so glum," he said. "You're about to meet my former landlady and now entrepreneur, Electra Lark. She owns all the land around here. I phoned her and she can put you up for a few days while you recover and look for a job. Van would hire you in a minute."

"For what position? I don't want charity."

"If I were proposing charity, I'd hire you myself as an assistant. Don't worry. I'm not concocting a new act at the moment."

"What does an idle magician do?"

"This and that."

A neon flash from the Déjà Vu sign behind us skimmed a small patch of black ahead. Achilles strained forward on his leash.

"That darn cat," I said. "If I hadn't followed him, I wouldn't be a suspect in a murder case."

"And you wouldn't have had a place tonight."

"We should being getting back to the Phoenix, instead of ambling around here."

He stopped at the landscaped entry to the big, round white building. "No need. This is where you'll be home after tonight, I hope."

"It doesn't look like a homeless shelter," I said. Not even the black cat had accompanied us here.

"Look," Max said. "Electra's in the lobby awaiting us."

I was successfully diverted from the Mystifying Max's current job opportunities by an ample peacock-blue-and-tiger-lily-orange-printed muumuu wearing a seventyish woman whose white curly hair sported swaths of temporary matching colors.

The energizing Technicolor shock, as in *The Wizard of Oz*, woke me up from the fifty shades of gray crowd I'd been associating with at Déjà Vu. I waltzed through the open glass door Max held open.

"Welcome, Lilah," the woman said so warmly I expected a paper lei to appear and float down over my head. So Max had phoned ahead.

"Such a pretty, old-fashioned name for a pretty, new-fashioned woman."

Not Max's description, I assumed.

"Oh. My goodness! Does your dog have eyes under that fountain of white hair? It could do with a colored swath of purple temporary dye like Princess Puffy-powder Persian on You-tube."

Achilles stopped his animated greeting dance in front of Electra and growled.

"Oh." She stepped back.

"He's telling you he's a *boy*," I said. "No purple swaths. No furbelows for him beyond a tidy black-tie topknot holder like the Asian martial artists wear on their man-buns. Achilles is a Lhasa Apso, a Tibetan 'warrior' breed that guarded the ancient Dalai Lamas. And so he will guard you."

"Achilles was also a strong man of myth," Electra agreed. "My Birman cat, Karma, would love to meet him! She's psychic, I swear. Her breed protected the Buddhist monks below Nepal and Tibet and are known as the Sacred Cat of Burma for that position. Karma is reclusive, sadly, but she may warm up to a fellow phenomenon, even if he is canine."

I decided not to mention Achilles' ankle-nipping tendencies since he was disarmed now, sensing no danger to me.

"All of Achilles' topknot ties and my worldly goods are in the trunk of my car," I said, "which is in for rest and rehabilitation from Gangsters and the Fontana brothers," I said. "I charged some clothes and necessities at the Crystal Phoenix gift shop, but I can't pay for a room until I find a job."

"Then you'll just have to accept one on the house. I may have just the room for you." She turned to Max in his recent role of silent backup for me. "And you, Max Kinsella, you may not live here anymore, but you need to come up and see me sometime," she said, parodying Mae West's famous sexy invitation to Cary Grant in *She Done Him Wrong*.

This Vegas was as classic film crazy as mine. That gave me hope the confusing bits I remembered that seemed slightly "off" here would merge with my memories, two translucent images finally sliding into focus over each other. That feat might take awhile, I realized.

"Are you motorcycle friendly?" Max asked me.

Before I could answer, Electra clapped her hands. "Great idea. She can ride the Vampire while waiting for the car to be ready."

"The vampire!" Was I wrong? Did these people accept a world of werewolf biker gangs and vampires?

"It's an English motorcycle." Max had turned to me. "Rare vintage, a Hesketh Vampire. Screams when the speed ramps up. Otherwise a motorcycle is a bike is a ride."

"She can use my 'Speed Queen' helmet," Electra said.

"I have to get some new leathers," I objected.

"Matt and Temple live here," Max said. "Temple can show you every retro clothing store in town tomorrow. So, Electra, Miss Lilah Lane is good for the night?"

"That would be something you would know better than I."

I hoped a serious blush didn't show on my naturally graveyard-marble pale face. This portly older lady had the sassy Mae West repartee down pat, but it was still hard to picture her on a motorcycle.

Electra leaned close to me and whispered, "'Speed Queen' was a brand of famous clothes washing machines in the middle of the last century. Which, alas, I'm old enough to remember. Anyway, you must be beat." Electra's hand on my shoulder nudged me toward the fancy elevator door in this tiny lobby area.

"Maybe I can do something for you with the fourth floor, longer term, meanwhile you can use my guest room."

"I was supposed to sleep at the Crystal Phoenix tonight. I need to thank Van Von Rhine for instant shelter. And all the new toiletries and stuff I bought in the hotel shop are there."

"I have a closet full of muumuu nighties for you, dear. And I'll have a Fontana brother explain to Van and fetch your gear from the Phoenix room by morning." She pulled a cell phone from a floral-print jungle of hidden muumuu pocket.

"Isn't it awfully late to disturb the Fonanta brothers?"

"Oh, my dear, a woman is never too late or too old to call on the Fontana brothers. It's one of life in Las Vegas's little bonuses."

Maybe, I thought, that's why I cringe at the idea of greeting a Fontana brother in an Electra Lark muumuu first thing in the morning.

"And at least you have your little dog with you."

Achilles, at my heels as, had hopped onto the elevator, which was now burping to a stop and opening its gilded doors.

"I do wonder," Electra said, "how Karma will deal with a dog."

"Karma's been pretty good to us so far today…and night."

Electra smiled at my referring to Karma in the sense of being Fate, and I felt instantly welcomed here too.

The place clearly dated back to the nineteen fifties and would have fascinated me normally, but I was as beat and beat up as she said.

"About the dog—" I began.

"He'll be fine. You'll see in daylight that grass surrounds the building's front and side yards and you can pick up after him then. The rear has the pool and parking lot."

A pool too. Wow.

I heard a muffled slam of a car door behind me as Max left. Everybody was finding me and passing me on. I knew my orphaned past made me oversensitive to abandonment, even if it was *me* doing the abandoning. How was I going to sleep tonight knowing Quicksilver was out there somewhere under the natural and unnatural skies we both thought we knew and I was finding awfully alien?

Electra, it seemed, would leave me no time to brood.

"Now this little old elevator may be small, like your dog, but it has done its duty for decades. I didn't want to tell Max I'm a bit tight on rooms. When he used to live here—"

"I know Max used to live here, but why do you keep his motorcycle on site?"

"I like to take a little spin now and then, just like the Speed Queen washer."

"Why did Max move out?"

"He didn't tell me at the time, or his roommate, which was worse. You know magicians. Always need to have something you don't know up his or her sleeve. Anyway, I've lost a unit now that

Matt and Temple have married and combined their separate units into a two-story. It *is* gorgeous though!"

"Who was Max's roommate?"

"Oh, Lilah. I don't know if I should reveal that. I don't want to look like a nosy landlady."

I suspected she was as nosy or more so as anyone. "I understand. I was just wondering, Max is so attractive. It's hard to imagine him single and alone by the phone…"

"Poor boy. You're right. He *has* been left out." She eyed me from my brush-starved tousled raven hair to my Cuban-heeled red booties. I bet she fancied herself a matchmaker, too.

"*Hmm.* I suppose you have a 'need to know', so you don't make a blunder now that you've met the Crystal Phoenix and Circle Ritz gangs. Temple was Max's, um, roommate, along with Midnight Louie, of course. And then he was just gone and I thought he was never coming back."

"Midnight Louie?"

"Not Louie, *Max!* Louie would never leave. He is our guardian, mascot, pest. But Max did leave abruptly, and then Matt moved into the unit above Temple."

And then…Max had left behind an unintended vacancy of the heart as well as the home, sweet home.

I *thought* there'd been some hidden past connections among my new friends. I felt like someone playing 3-D chess from *Star Trek* in the dark. Great. I'd dropped in on the aftermath of an unintended ménage a trois. Not including the cat.

Apparently my time here in Vegas Nouveau was going to be very French.

25
The Three Muzzleteers

There is nothing like overhearing your nearest and dearest describing you to a new acquaintance as a pest. Resident *"pest"!* Miss Electra Lark must have been taking courtesy lessons from Christophe, who could use a tongue-lashing or two, preferably from his personal Big Cat.

Of course, I cannot take public umbrage and give away my superior intelligence, so I lurk discreetly as I follow Miss Lilah Lane's safe arrival at her new possible digs. I was dismayed earlier to hear Mr. Max Kinsella proposing she become an easy rider around Vegas until her large and ridiculously commodious car is restored.

Motorcycles are noisy, unstable machines, with little space for stowaways except a cramped saddlebag or two.

Obviously, I am not fond of the cramped quarters, the competition with noisy motors when striving to eavesdrop, and the flat-out risk factor of a fatal fall.

It is possible that I must let Miss Lilah off her leash for a while. I hate to miss any racy conversation, not to mention clues, but a motorcycle is built for two, maximum, and I no longer can take riding saddlebag unless it is an emergency.

However, I *can* stay safe at home and learn much. I must ask Karma what she knows of this hitherto never mentioned "fourth floor".

Meanwhile, Miss Electra is telling Miss Lilah she can "bunk" in her guest bedroom on the penthouse level for the night.

What? That penthouse is the sole and single and singular domain of the High Priestess of Hoity Toity, the Psychic Princess of Prognostication, the luckily one and only Karma, Sacred Cat of Burma.

Even My Miss Temple has only once been invited into Miss Electra's living quarters.

(I, of course, had trespassed once or twice, unbeknownst to our esteemed landlady, just on principle.)

Now a *dog* is getting the red carpet shoo-in treatment? I am not going to miss out on this event. However, the little tousle-pot clings to Miss Lilah's heels like a lamprey eel with lockjaw.

Before I know it, the elevator lofts up and stops. Miss Lilah and Mr. Achilles are through the penthouse door right behind Miss Electra. I am left kissing my own reflection in the black semi-gloss painted door.

Not allowed. I race for the back stairs and gallop down three floors to floor two. Despite the remodeling, Miss Temple and my former place is the only unit where my frequent attempts have made the front door Louie-accommodating. I know just where and how high to lunge to spring the lock mechanism. Presto. Inside. Only now I have to clamber up the new spiral staircase, spring open the French doors to the balcony, hurl myself onto the thick, knobby palm tree trunk in the dark of night, scale it like a firefighter, leap off onto the penthouse balcony and...

...and collapse against the French doors, which give way to reveal the noxious sight of Karma and Achilles sitting side by side. If you like cream in your coffee, this bland duo of white and buff fur is tailor-made for your nightmare mornings-after.

"Lou-ie," Karma chides. "You could have broken your neck."

"Well, I did not. Why are you sharing shoulder-space with a dog?"

"Those old species biases are so passé, Louie. Besides, Achilles' and my ancestors have protecting Buddhist monks in common, although only his have guarded a Dalai Lama in Tibet."

I could swear she had said "tidbit". "Is that a new brand of chow?" I ask.

"Strange you should evoke another Asian breed of dog," Karma mused. (Karma is the type to "muse" ceaselessly.)

"How?"

"Well, the Chow Chow, of course."

"Of course I know chow," I mutter into my whiskers. Dog chow. Oh, pardon *moi*. Whiskers technically are "vibrissae". I see Karma is trying to impress the new mutt.

She deigns to enlighten me further.

"Achilles and I, both descendants of warrior breeds, have been channeling our most ancient forebears."

"What fun. If I am going to channel anything, it will be the black leopard in the show half a mile up the Strip. Why was everybody out to kill monks in the olden days anyway? They were not very sociable, did not have a huge group of BFFs to promo them, or sit on easily reachable treasure to snatch, as far as I hear tell."

"That is the *telling* phrase, Louie. As far as you can speculate." She puts her rear in gear to come and whisper in my ear.

"I must ask you to shed your insensitive self. We stand—"

"You stand. I sit."

"And a good thing. You sit in the presence of one recently raised from the dead."

I realize Karma is serious. I look at Achilles. He is basically a bed-flopper. One long hair part of feet-obscuring white locks up the back, a forehead fountain of forelock, black button eyes and nose peering through the hairy curtain. I admit I can see him taken for dead and stuffed and left in a broom closet for a decade or two.

I also realize that in some weird way he reminds me of Mr. Snow Christophe, My Miss Lilah's apparent enemy. Oh, my. Did I just give Miss Lilah My Miss Temple's pet form of address?

Back to business. "What is this fourth floor I am hearing about for the first time?" I ask Karma. "I have never known anybody to mention it."

Her blue eyes grow alarmed. Then she rubs against me in her soft fluffy coat so powerfully I am almost knocked off my feet. She is not a bad-looking dame, but too flakey on the top floor for my taste. Her move on me puts Achilles out of earshot, but Lhasa Apso (what a giggle-worthy name!) ears are long and dangling and hairy, so he is not likely to overhear us anyway.

"Do *not* go on the fourth floor, Louie," she hisses a trifle hysterically. "It has an ugly aura. Miss Electra only uses it for storage, and you know how much money she is losing on an entire floor of residences."

"How long has it been unused and forbidden?"

"Forever."

"You claim knowledge that goes back that far?"

"Well, since the building was constructed." She has wrapped one supple paw around my shoulder and now her claws dig into my muscular neck. "I have already told you a Wolf Moon is full. You have met a dog who one night ago was a pile of ashes in a jar. I myself number lives in the three figures. How many lives do you think a low-brow alley cat like yourself has, Louie? You are the walking symbol of the eerie holiday, Halloween, and often hated and hunted for your coat color. Can you afford to continue to scoff at the supernatural?"

I am momentarily speechless.

Out from the mountains, a lonesome single wolf wail sounds.

That breaks Karma's spell.

Calling Central Casting. No one is going to spook me with some sound effects and a purported formerly deceased purse pooch. I have a more important dog on my mind. Little King Arthur, who has, though he knows it not, lost a significant other in the real world of non-refundable mortality.

Karma seems to read my mind. "Do not toy with the time of the Wolf Moon, Louie."

I listen to the next distant howl. "I have one word for you. Coyotes."

Such a perfect put-down and return to reality.

Such a shame Miss Lilah Lane chooses that moment to come through the open French double doors to find our little triumvirate.

"What's this? A critter convention?" She pushes through us to the balcony edge.

This is the fifth floor penthouse, toots, it is dangerously high, I want to tell her.

She jerks back, as if she heard me, but her sole focus remains on the dark beyond the illuminated Strip.

The howl comes again. On cue, I think.

"Quicksilver," she whispers to the desert wind.

Okay. I am unnerved. If this fluff-puff Achilles can come back from the dead, like he and Karma claim, what do you suppose a dog with a wolfish howl like that can do if he gets a new ticket punched on the immortality express?

26
Maximum Punch

Max settled into his new futon for the night while visions of Albino Vampires and Brunette Bombers danced in his head.

Sleeping at the apex of the glass-covered pyramid once known as the Neon Nightmare dance club made him feel like Tarzan tucked away in a high-tech jungle aerie, without Jane or Cheetah. Or Lilah and Louie? *Cut it out, Kinsella.*

A swing on a handy bungee cord would have him on the first floor, with a choice of sleek, dark restrooms, an echoing stainless steel dream chef's kitchen, an awesome wine cellar, and one finely stocked and glamorous bar set like a shining temple of mirror and diamond crystals and blue sapphires and precious topaz tawny liquors.

The enormous smoked glass mirror reflected a mute 3-D interior of black on black and sometimes the face he glimpsed in that mirror wouldn't be him. Sometimes, out of the corner of his eye, it would be Gandolph. Or Kathleen. Or her lost daughter he'd found. Or, when he was hungry in more ways than one, Revienne.

His moody memories ultimately made him laugh. *Rather large and grand for a bachelor pad, Kinsella.* Sometimes he awoke looking for and missing the house and furnishings burned in Kathleen O'Connor's last destructive act. Nothing remained of his mentor but a laptop. Max had defied falling smoldering embers and weakened timbers to reclaim it. It held the last thoughts and maybe wishes of Garry Randolph, the mentor behind Max's magician's mask, and a father figure lost to the guns of a sectarian fight he'd never had any part in, and whose physical memory had been further demolished in a vicious arson attack.

And among the ashes were Max's own magical appliances, paper flowers, trick boxes and assorted artifacts of his stage career. Also that extravagant, exotic Asian mother-of-pearl-inlaid opium bed, more like a latticed throne room, oft-times scene of sleep, sex, and dreams.

No, the sleek, hard dimension of this building without a name was a better shell for a man with no direction home, or rather too many homes in his history, and nothing new on the domestic horizon. The Abyss. The Nightshade.

Lilah Lane's mind had a delicious dark streak that ranged from commercial to too bloody personal.

Max rolled over on his monkish sleeping roll and knew one nightmare was done at last. Kitty the Cutter had come to a closure with her brutal past and no longer needed to take it out on the Las Vegas innocents she'd harried so hard.

Max sighed. Yet… Vegas life would be duller without her death threats looming. Had he come to that?

Bette Midler bawling out "I'm the Boogie Woogie Bugle Boy of Company B" awoke him. It was a more optimistic ringtone selection than "Taps".

Max clawed the covers for his phone and input the code fast. No daylight slipped into the building. The phone claimed the time was 8:30 a.m.

"Sleep well, prime suspect?" a woman's contralto drawl asked.

"*You've* probably not yet been to bed," he groaned.

"I'm not that dedicated. This case is a puzzler. Especially puzzling is your sudden new acquaintance in town and on the crime site."

"You mean Temple and Matt's, Van von Rhine and Nicky Fontana's sudden new acquaintance."

"*They* didn't take her to dinner at a bar."

"Had me followed, eh?"

"And to bed—"

"Now, wait a minute, Lieutenant…"

"…to bed at Electra's place, all above-board and boring. You disappoint me, Kinsella."

"Better you than her."

"Ah. Not disinterested, I see."

"What do you want?"

"Just you to do more of the same old black magic you do so well. Continue to represent the legendary hospitality of Las Vegas."

"Pump her and report to you. You have no old unsolved murders to hold over my head anymore."

"Except this new one."

"Pish posh."

"You apparently have nothing better to do…no more rumors of a new show in the works."

"You forget. I'm homeless."

That stopped her cold.

Max shouldn't have lapsed into neediness, but a black curtain descended when he was reminded of his double loss. The Northern Ireland death of his mentor and the real house owner, Garry Randolph, in a hail of bullets meant for Max.

And now the house was here no longer, as well, burnt down to its blackened bones.

How much did Molina know about that international stuff? About Max's entanglement with various versions of the IRA since he'd been an American teenager abroad for the summer? She had FBI and other federal law enforcement contacts. Probably knew more about why the IRA had a price on his head since he was old enough to drink Guinness. More than he thought. But not enough.

"Kathleen O'Connor. If that woman ever comes near Las Vegas again," Molina vowed as if she read his mind. She spoke with casual coldness, "I'll get her for a slew of charges, including arson and stalking, but I figure you've taken care of her in your own sly and secret ways."

"Something like that." Max smiled. He hadn't hurt Kathleen the way she tried to destroy others. He'd simply diverted her nuclear-level nastiness to an equally nasty object. Islamic terrorists. Kitty was something of a feminist, though she didn't know it.

And she had diverted him to another secret cause. Born to an unwed mother who had been betrayed into a short life of forced humiliation and death, she'd been kept as a child for a corrupt priest's pleasure. One fact about Kitty's brutal past had seared his soul. She had been forcibly taken from her mother not as an infant, but as a mother-bonded toddler, the better to exploit her.

During the time Kitty had been stalking him and making Vegas nervous, Molina had come to use him as more than a "confidential informant", but an investigator. Maybe it had something to do with her being a single mother, and a Tiger Mom, at that, but she had a bad habit of relying on an "outside 'inside' guy".

It seemed the position was up for grabs. His cover was blown on the international scene, and that life was insecure and "no fun fast" without Garry, who was his mentor in magic as well as secret agent gigs. He might as well accommodate the local law.

Max sensed a touch of Kitty's orphaned iron edge in Delilah... Lilah. Self-sufficient to a fault. Skeptical. Femme Feral. Not the softer side of Sears. Likely not a cold-blooded murderer, but she might become a loaded gun. His loaded gun. Time to take her out for a trial run.

But, first, he needed to learn more from Molina than she could learn from him.

27
Magic Mushroom

Someone was ringing my doorbell. My door*bell!* Well, Electra's doorbell. Imagine. A real cello-mellow gong-style interior doorbell. The Circle Ritz had doorbells, like on a vintage radio show. Wonderful.

It was 8:00 a.m.—early, but Fontana brother service was 24/7 with a large designer tote bag awaiting me outside Electra's apartment door. I was already out of my florescent muumuu and dressed in my blue-denim jeggings and a blowsy white tunic shirt. I slipped on soft-soled black flats, and Achilles' brisk nails clattered over the parquet wood floor after me to the door.

I opened it to Temple Barr, her curly red hair accessorized by a pale yellow pants suit. Matt Devine's calm blond presence behind her said loud and clear that he had her back.

I could see why. Temple was smart, fresh, and insightful. And fearless. A guy could feel obliged to protect her charming yet somehow savvy innocence. No group homes in *her* history.

"Good morning, Lilah," she said. "I see Electra found you a bunk bed." Temple peered into the darkness behind me, frankly curious. "Funny. Electra is really shy about having people in her penthouse, and I just realized I've never met a tenant who lived on the fourth floor before. Maybe there are family skeletons."

"That floor's not quite up to code or something. Could just be the air conditioning. Nothing worrisome, Electra said. For now, I'm here, and I'm so grateful you brought me to the Crystal Phoenix and Max introduced me to the Circle Ritz."

"You're welcome." Matt smiled mysteriously. "And now we're here to take you somewhere else for breakfast. The Magic Mushroom."

"Is that out of *The Hobbit*, or from a San Francisco 'Summer of Love' LSD usage manual?"

"Quick and witty," Temple said, looking back and up at her spouse. "A program possibility?"

"Give me a minute to do something interview-worthy," I protested. "I'm a long way from being settled into this community."

"A five-day-a-week TV show burns up potential guest possibilities fast," Matt explained. "We're walking 'guest' scouts."

"We'll be considering Achilles for a spot any day now," Temple added. "He's such a cutie. I imagine he'd have a great story to tell if he could talk."

I could only agree with a nod and a smile. Coming back from the dead, and especially from your own ashes, would be quite a dog's tale.

Temple glanced down at my feet. "Fun shoes. You don't need height, like I do. Stop teetering on that door sill and push your toes out one by one. Don't be shy. I'm not."

"Uh. I don't know about leaving Achilles alone in a strange (if only they knew how strange) place."

"Electra makes sure her tenants are pet-friendly. Of course, the area has always been Midnight Louie-friendly."

"My wallet is still lost. I'll owe money wherever I go for a while."

"Then don't owe it. You're on our show tab, under 'research.'"

"Me? Research?"

Temple took my arm.

Achilles growled softly.

Something dark emerged from behind Temple's black patent leather high heels…a black cat face.

"Oh." Temple kept looking down. "Do they need separating?"

"Heel, Achilles," I ordered, hoping a new authority in my tone would make him obey and he'd walk in step with me. I took two steps. He sat instead. It was a start. I said. "Sit. Good Boy." Next time.

The cat leaned its muzzle forward and sniffed Achilles's nose, as if he had a bouquet, like wine. Louie lifted his upper lip and long white whiskers.

Achilles circled around and did a play bow to the black cat, forelegs on the ground.

Apparently obeisance was the proper response. Midnight Louie lifted his head, turned and went on his way.

"At least they didn't shred the welcome mat," Temple said.

"I have a welcome mat? I do!"

That's one thing the Enchanted Cottage went without.

I must start thinking of Now, not the ever-so-recent Then. We all went down on the richly paneled and brass-appointed toy elevator.

"Small spaces," Temple noted, "are always classy, and the most lavishly decorated."

"Rather like you," Matt told Temple. They smiled at each other like newlyweds.

I wanted to pinch myself. Was I now in Munchkin Land or what? This was all backwards. The harrowing chase, the claustrophobic underground escape. Now the tidy and welcoming village.

Achilles brought me back to earth in one doggy dash. A shake of a rear leg and a fruitful stream against the trunk of a palm tree.

A stroll took us to a whimsical storefront with mushrooms painted on the glass like side curtains and round tables for four with old-fashioned twisted metal chairs.

I was suddenly ravenous. A narrow menu mocked the usual categories: appetizers, main dishes, desserts, beverages. You checked the boxes like on a hotel in-room menu and fresh-faced college kids served.

Achilles had found a picket-fence-enclosed supernaturally green (for Vegas) patch of sward adjoining the patio and occupied himself sniffing for all preceding clients.

"The muffins are shaped like giant mushrooms," Matt warned me. "One is a meal."

I ordered a Pocketful of Rye muffin with dark chocolate and walnuts and a ginger and almond latte from a list of various exotic coffees.

"What occasion are we celebrating?" I asked.

Came a silence. "There's some disturbing news," Temple answered. "In other words, it's a case of no news."

I looked at Matt for clarification.

"We'd been planning to have Celeste Novak on our talk show about her Green Fairy gig, along with Christophe, of course, and the more than striking Gwen, who transforms into the white tiger."

Where the Hellfire had Grizelle been? She was the absent person, not this mythical Gwen.

I pictured the list of characters. The Green Fairy, the White Tiger with emerald eyes, and the White Magician. Spellbinding indeed on TV.

"The thing is," Temple said, leaning confidentially closer, "Celeste's performance and bio entry was strangely sketchy."

"And Christophe's?"

"He'd been performing in Europe, Australia, and South America. This is his Vegas debut. Years ago, Siegfried and Roy also made their names in Europe. They and their white lions and tigers are in retirement now, after Roy was dragged offstage and paralyzed by a tiger years ago. They insist it was a freak accident."

"So they defended the tiger?" I asked. A key question, because they'd been going long and strong in the Vegas I knew, where Snow was a rock star, not a prestidigitator.

Matt nodded over a mouthful of muffin. The spreading tops were as large as a saucer.

"How is Celeste's background vague?" I asked Temple.

"I was a reporter before I switched sides, so to speak, to PR, public relations, where spin is king. So I could understand a performer exaggerating her credits. That's called puffery, but her background was a terse summary, like it'd been written by an accountant. You know how it is, when you're a reporter and you can't find much information that should be there, you…take the muffin by the puffed-up top and dig until you get a satisfactory answer."

I laughed at the idea of doing breakfast battle with these humungous muffins. "So what was missing about Celeste?"

"She was purportedly living in Iowa, where there are plenty of Novaks, but only one Celestine in her age group. No Celeste."

"Change of name for performing purposes," I said promptly, getting ultra-nervous, given that I was sporting two names myself at the moment. *Why* had I told those fibs? I didn't expect to run into a horde of people who knew each other, intent on being Good Samaritans when I just wanted to go off by myself and find Quicksilver, no questions asked.

"You were a reporter, Lilah," Temple said. "You know how we never let go of a mystery or an anomaly until we know what's behind the whole story."

"Yeah. Stubborn little diggers, like Achilles here."

Speaking of which, he was out of sight behind the oleander bushes, which could be poisonous, so I got up to bring him tableside again. "Stay," I said, and he did.

I resumed the issue of who the dead Green Fairy had been. "Celeste must have had some newspaper performance notices if she was good enough to do a *Cirque du Soleil* show."

"No, her résumé indicated she was in the uncredited 'company' or understudy roles. Besides, the onstage audition is ninety percent of the hiring process when it comes to high-wire performances."

"She could do the high-wire acts, though?"

"More like a change-of-form act," Matt said. "We were given fresh tape of the show, since the Green Fairy sequence had been recently added, and the bit was amazing. We can copy it for your DVD player."

"My what?"

"Oh, that's right, Matt. She's not set up house here yet." Temple turned to me. "Were all your worldly goods in your car?"

"It's old Detroit. The trunk alone has the capacity to tote the corpses of six mob hits, easy."

Matt laughed. "Or six Fontana brothers. Those old fifties car trunks were the size of a hot tub for eight nowadays."

"I've gotta see this fabled vehicle," Temple said, grinning at Matt. "Maybe I should get something more substantial than my Miata. I'll check with the Fontana boys on how the tune-up is coming along, and tell them Lilah is camping at the Circle Ritz. With Achilles?"

"Electra has fallen in love with him. Thinks he's a watchdog born."

I sighed briskly. *Please*, get the spotlight off me and mine until we know what's what. I returned to the murder at hand.

"So Celeste, poor girl, was getting a huge career boost from playing this Green Fairy. I passed a place along the Strip with a Green Fairy neon sign, but it was called Absinthe."

"Vegas is ever-changing," Matt said.

"That's the truest thing in Vegas." Temple shook her curls. "I came here just a year before Matt did," she said, "the iconic hotel-casinos all had foot-pounding, huge, impressive driveways to the main buildings, Caesars, Bally's, the MGM-Grand have been crowding their frontage space with tent shows. Mini-shows, cabarets really, evoking the prime nineteenth century Parisian cafés. Absinthe and its vivid green color was a favored liqueur of the soon-to-be world-famous artists. The wormwood in the drink recipe gave them delusions. Liquid forerunner of much more potent modern LSD. All really deliciously decadent."

"Beyond merely decadent." Matt shook his altar-boy golden head. "The process of drinking Absinthe became an almost religious ritual, and like all rituals, required certain 'sacred' objects. You could say the Green Fairy was their high priestess, an immaterial one, but implanted strongly in their addicted minds."

"*Ooh.*" I shivered in the bright fresh morning sunlight. "Sounds spooky."

"Here." Temple thrust her cell phone face toward me. "I've got the recorded version of the illusion. The stage is black except for a huge vertical green glass candle in a ten-foot-tall glass canister with a flame burning on top. As the candle wax melts and drips down the sides the contents change into green smoke."

The tiny image kept me rapt. A miniature Christophe kept stalking around the cylinder, swirling and snapping his black-velvet-lined cloak with its inner universe of alien constellations.

I watched the small living image, fixated as eerie music played.

Then, I saw the change. "It's like the canister is filled with water, green swirling water…with a green, swirling, long-haired mermaid spinning inside. Holy cow. You'd almost think she was naked."

"This *is* Vegas, Lilah." Temple was watching me fondly, almost like a mom would, I thought, had I ever had one. Like Max Kinsella, a PR person relished surprising people with wonder. No surprise they'd been a couple once. I had to wonder what broke them up.

"Keep watching," Matt advised, smiling. "It's a really subtle strip act."

The swirling substance was thinning. I watched the mermaid melting into sinuous wisps of smoke and diaphanous silk, undulating upward to vanish into the dark above the "human candle" and then high above the stage.

While we'd been watching the woman vanish, the giant absinthe-green candle had solidified again, a woman's form clearly outlined and struggling to escape, to breathe air. A hand and arm broke through, bare and struggling. The audience gasped. I did too, despite myself.

One more circuit of the white-cloaked figure and another hand clawed to break free. So Houdini had writhed in old films while executing a finely plotted yet agonizing escapist trick.

The imprisoned woman was faceless, and expended so much energy with her hidden limbs flailing, we were now wishing for a moth to break through its chrysalis to take wing.

The magician halted to make a mighty sweep of his cloak directly in front of the waxen prison. A burst of flame exploded from the open top, followed by a woman draped in gossamer wafting up into the flies.

The cylinder interior, its interior smothered with rotating green smoke and shadows, cleared to reveal the Green Fairy painted onto the ornate label of giant an Art Nouveau vintage absinthe bottle, while glittering green "moths" fluttering and floating down made the cylinders into an hourglass.

As the audience sighed at the stunning tableau, the Green Fairy became 3-D again. Draped in semi-concealing sheer chiffon, she again ascended out of sight, sprinkling green "fairy dust" over everything. Between that moment and me entering the tunnels to ultimately glimpse and not recognize her supine body lying ahead of me in the secret passage, Celeste Novak had met death.

But not on Temple's cell phone screen. There, the absinthe cylinder spun down and out of sight.

"You know what strikes me?" I said.

They waited with bated breath and muffins upraised.

"You never really see the Green Fairy's face. There's always some veiling. Swirling water or smoke covering her features."

"Makes the mythic figure more mysterious," Matt said.

"What do the in-house posters show?" I wondered.

Temple put out a palm. "Let me see that phone. I'll check the montage before the show footage, starting with the huge Strip neon sign, then moving through all the posters inside the casino to the Looking Glass Theater entrance with its ten-foot-high posters."

Luckily, I'd entered the theater from below, never having to confront a ten-foot high poster of Christophe, almost large enough to emulate his ego.

Temple eagerly tapped through the sequence. "You're so right, Lilah. While the Green Fairy's body is artfully revealed, her face is even more artfully concealed."

Matt leaned away from the miniature image.

"You're suggesting the Green Fairy's identity might have been switched, Lilah?" he asked.

"I'm thinking identity is the common conundrum we're facing in this crime."

Including mine.

28
Achilles Heel

It *is* high time for me and the new temporary (I truly trust) dog-in-residence to have a heart-to-heart. If I am not careful, I will lose my primo position as iconic house mascot as well as house detective.

I have found it something of a burden all these years to have a resident feline seeress prophesying from the fifth-floor penthouse like some Drag Queen Dalai Lama. At least Karma keeps herself and her "Sacred Cat of Burma"-ness and all things weird and woo-woo to her top-story queendom.

Now, having a canine Karma surrogate bouncing around unfettered in the house and on the grounds is as bad as having Magnum P.I. doing ditto to the bloodthirsty resident Doberman Pinschers on Robin Masters Hawaii estate on TV.

This Achilles individual has been flashing his snooty Asian pedigree upstairs, downstairs and in my lady's chamber without answering to a higher power long enough.

Luckily, this Flopsy, Mopsy and Cottontail dog with white floor-length hair and bowties in its top-knot more resembles a long-haired show rabbit. Not much of a candidate for the protect and serve crowd.

Achilles may have been a famous warrior in ancient days, but he had a weak heel and probably toes. My toes and their retractable shivs make me a cousin of superhero Wolverine in comic books.

Anyway, it is too much that Achilles, the mere dog, has hogged breakfast duty and tidbits at the Magic Mushroom with my live-in roomies, now Mr. and Mrs. And the new girl, who has a puzzling weakness herself. For dogs!

We have done the dog-cat do-si-do around the place, encouraging murmurs of "How cute they are together!" from without-a-clue human associates.

I accost him privately out by the pool. If we tangle and fall in, his long hair will weigh him down while I will be as sleek and agile as an otter. The able operative always weighs the odds for any eventuality.

Achilles is reclining under the shade of a spreading elephant ears and canna lily plants. Even in the shade he is panting, displaying the large pink tongue dogs so often do. We cats are content with keeping our tongues to ourselves.

"What is up, Achilles? Hot enough for you?" I remark as I flop down on the green grass plot that is so complementary to my vivid eye color. I can barely see the dog's brown ones through the thick hair, a benefit of this breed, in my opinion.

"*Garrrgh*," he says in lieu of a shrug. "Assuming a calm, meditative position and mindset overcomes overheating."

Already with the annoying New Age allusions! "Snag any tasty muffin crumbs at your breakfast?"

"It was a business breakfast, so I did not get the usual attention. However, some bacon bits and Vienna sausage made the trip to my vicinity."

Vienna sausage! I love Vienna sausage and seldom get it. I stretch my neck out to inhale the aroma from my companion's white mustache and beard. The fellow reminds me of the White Wizard Gandalf on cable TV in *The Lord of the Rings*. He shakes his abundant facial hair and several crumbs fall out.

It is all I can do to resist snagging some. I do not do dog leavings.

"So," Achilles says, "your girl is not into Vienna sausage. A pity."

"My Little Doll, Miss Temple, is not much into cooking. She is good at presentation. What about your, uh, Big Doll?"

"She orders out a lot. However, during our earlier association in Wichita, I was able to sample the exotic taste of vampire blood."

"You bit a vampire instead of it biting you! Not that I believe in vampires, but that would be quite a feat."

"It was a feat, all right. My mistress was not fond of vampires even though they were *the* rock-star date in her crowd. So she tried a night out with Undead Ted, the news anchor at the TV station where she worked. If she had been inter-species mind-speech-enabled then, I could have told her he was a narcissistic nothing, but she kind of suspected that.

"He could not even wait to spend money on a dinner out, but tried to get her in the blood-donating mood by bringing her flowers with X-acto knife blades taped to the stems."

"The cad!"

"Once her fingertip was pierced like Sleeping Beauty's and bled, he went all supernatural leech on her. The guy had fangs like an East African gaboon pit viper, long, curved hollow tiger claws crossed with drinking straws. He would have drained her in six heartbeats.

"While she was fighting him off, I did a snapping turtle chaw on his heel. He kicked me off and fled, but no one knew I would get blood poisoning from vampire blood and shortly die at the vet's."

We were both silent. This was serious talk.

"About that," I finally said. "What was it like to be a vase pooch?"

"Boring beyond belief. Luckily, my brilliant girl found a black porcelain funeral vase engraved with the most powerful Dragon image, five-toed like a person. When she was driving any distance, she kept the vase in her glove compartment. She knew I loved to "ride in car". I believe when her car hit the ground hard coming here, the vase stopper jiggled loose and some of my ashes escaped, animating the power of the Dragon and reconstituting me."

"I get it. Like powdered soup flavoring. Everything, er, operative?"

"I was fixed, Louie. Do not frown. A celibate life allows me to concentrate my *chi* and enhance my spiritual and psychic energy."

"Yeah, right. Well, if you are a model of woo-woo mysticism, I am a model of hard science innovation. It is a long story, chronicled in my *Flamingo Fedora* casebook. I am unable to sire offspring, but I am still four-on-the-floor and fully equipped from the factory, like the old car ad said, if you know what I mean."

Achilles' black button nose sniffs at my declaration. "The life of the mind and spirit is superior to mere material pleasures."

"Not in my book! You did suck those Vienna sausage bits right down, did you not? But congratulations on getting a second run."

Achilles lay his face on his paws and looked wistful. "I am uncertain, though, of how much use I can be to she whom you call 'my Big Doll'. I am not sure what a 'doll' is."

"Listen. You are man's best friend, and your girl's too. I am sure you will rise to the occasion, maybe not literally, when your protection is needed. Now, bowtie and ears up. Do not be glum! I can always use an inside source when I am pursuing a case.

"For some reason, your Miss Delilah-Lilah has brought a smattering of your world's extra-sensory perception with her, and she and I are more than somewhat on the same woo-woo wave length. Do not tell Karma. She will know soon enough.

"I am the one with nine lives here, and do not forget it, Achilles. Even though Karma boasts of one hundred and ninety-nine lives, I am the one living on the mortality line out here in real life."

"Do you know which one of your lives you are on, Louie?"

"Ah, not exactly, probably for the best. Okay, Achilles, you're a stand-up dude. Stand up and we will shake on it." He did. We did.

I still think teaching dogs to "shake" paws is lame. A cat would never stand for it… but it is better than sealing a doggie deal with a kiss. *Argh.* Dog slobber.

29
Speed Queen

"**What kind of** Muumuu Queen keeps a vintage motorcycle in her yard shed?" I asked at ten that morning. The glaring Vegas sun in the Circle Ritz's parking lot highlighted Max's black hair in rusty red, like it did mine, probably.

He'd turned up, fully black-leather clad from boots to gloves, announcing it was time to see if the Hesketh Vampire motorcycle was the ride for me until I got my car back.

"Why would Electra want a motorcycle?" I persisted.

"Electra is a game old girl. Age does not wither...et cetera. I was short of condo cash when Temple and I got to the Circle Ritz. I gave her the Vampire as collateral."

"Game is right. She even lent me her leather jacket."

"No wonder you're swimming in it."

"Any port in a storm." I pushed up the leather sleeves past my charm bracelet and ended my morning-sun-awakened vampire squint by donning black sunglasses. "I feel so Christophe world-view all of a sudden."

"You'll be wearing a motorcycle helmet soon enough and can ditch the shades. How are you familiar with a high-end Vegas act like his?"

"*Please.* The word 'familiar' in any respect related to Christophe gives me the Halloween shudders."

Max laughed.

"Wichita has the massive Emerald City Hotel-Casino. He did a gig there. You know, the whole Elvis thing of throwing scarves into the mosh-pit fan babes. Only Snow used the scarves to draw them close for a smooch. 'The Brimstone Kiss' the swooning fangirls called it. The newspapers named him 'Cocaine for the Promise Ring set'. That's how the whole 'Snow' nickname came about. Disgusting! Like old-time rock star fans throwing underwear and room keys to the stage. Or vice versa."

"Something of a Puritan, are you?"

"What's the use of yearning after some phony personality on a stage? The roadies will only let a few knockouts through to the star's room, and all those other girls are left feeling second best."

"Better he seduce them all, then," Max said, amused by my feminist indignation.

"Maybe. If he got tired enough, he might come up with something better to do than rake in cash and kisses." I looked at Max as I accepted Electra's "Speed Queen" helmet to don. "You do any of that obvious crowd sucking up in your act?"

"Alas, no. I didn't even have a shapely assistant. I worked with doves."

"Another docile creature, like the famous rabbit. White, but no tiger."

"Which may be why I don't have a new act in the works. It's hard to find something different yet excellent."

"This motorcycle does the job for me now," I said. "And then some. Gorgeous fairing," I noted as I walked around the front. "What's with the scowling chicken decal? Not very big, bad vampire."

"That's the Brit sense of humor. They underplay everything. An English lord developed the machine, but the Vampire model was only manufactured for one year, nineteen eighty-three. It's heavy and high-riding, but you have the height to manage it. I'll take you for a short spin to get the feel of the Hesketh, and then you can solo."

By then I'd straddled the machine and had my legs braced. "Why'd you invest in it?"

"Rare things appreciate. Besides, it's called a 'vampire' for the horror-movie scream the engine makes at higher speed. Even better than a police siren."

"This I gotta hear."

"I put 'M' as in motorcycle approved on your new phony driver's license, but you don't want to get caught. So let out your primal scream someplace discreet, please. I'd be legally liable for scaring the horses."

Being a passenger on a motorcycle was not only ceding control to the guy or gal up front, it was getting really up close and personal. Kinda like a zombie jamboree, only back to belly and belly to back. Sorta a zombie jamboree, as the song went. After I donned my black leather workout gloves, I mounted and placed my boot soles on the back pegs. I debated what to do with my hands.

Awkward. I have to place at least one hand on Max's side, and the choice is up to me, all options a form of intimacy I in no way wanted with this guy. How not to give him a free thrill and still keep balanced if he's taking a curve deep?

"Remember," he said. "The engine will shriek at a certain speed. Do *not* let go."

Of what? I balled up my fists, thrust them into his jacket pockets and curled my fingers tight around the interior leather of the lining.

Arms around the waist? Not until the third date.

Whoo! Irma whooped. *We're off. Better hang on like a girlfriend.*

No thanks, girlfriend.

Once we were out of the lot we moved into street swoop and sway and soon were roaring up onto I-15 northeast toward the Valley of Fire. Electra's helmet muffled the wind and traffic noise. I began to relish looking around without having to watch the traffic.

In daylight, the landmark Vegas hotel behemoths looked naked, their colors flat without the zap of spotlights and neon. The traffic flow was thick with cabs and Lyft and Uber vehicles as the Vampire danced like a dragonfly over lily pads among them.

I could feel the heavy hair on my neck lifting and flying along too. The vibration of motor, well, more fun than a spa jet.

"Look right," Max shouted back to me.

I looked at the row of Strip landmarks flying by, then at the onramp we were racing to the next big intersection. Other motorcycles in a pack.

"Your gang?" he shouted. "Lobo jacket insignia."

No... *You and Dolly lost those damn Lunatics,* Irma reminded me.

"Look at that police dog!" Max exclaimed, swooping us into the right lane even though it would soon merge with the motorcycle pack.

Yup, there was a lone motorcycle cop on the gang's tail, but his dog was racing and gaining on the pack as they neared the intersection, leaping and pulling the mid-pack riders down by their jackets so their rides spun out sideways and took out the following bikes in one huge spinning mass. The motorcycle cop must have called for assistance. Cop cars wailed from behind to stop and take fallen riders into custody. At the front of the pack, the K-9 dog was snarling and worrying the fallen bikers' upper arms until a cop could come to roll them facedown and cuff them.

Max had taken an exit. So we were stopped on the bridge over the action. I looked down. That was no German Shepherd or Belgian Malinois K-9 dog. It had the Siberian Husky's blue eyes and a wolfish genome, its silver-gray coat. His head lifted toward me to sniff the air. I would recognize that head tilt, ear cock, muzzle anywhere.

Quicksilver!

And here my face was an enigma behind smoked glass and my scent a combo of new clothes and tall, dark stranger.

"I've got to get down there!" I shouted into the wind.

But the light had changed, the traffic flow had surged forward, and my words lofted into the wind behind me. My view of the scene below was blocked.

We crossed the second light when it turned green and growled into a Whataburger parking lot on the corner.

Max doffed his helmet. "What were you yelling about back there? The cops grabbed that gang for speeding, or maybe dealing speed. It's all over down there."

I could no longer see Quicksilver. Cops rolled the bikes to the entry ramp side for towing. Hand-cuffed bikers, the ordinary tattooed and truculent human kind, were crammed into the back of squad cars. Maybe the dog was no longer visible because he was leaving in one particular cop car. Or maybe he was far back, retracing the path of his pursuit, sniffing the dangerous edge of the traffic lanes for a mirage. Me.

I walked to the edge of the lot. Stood there and mentally called his name. Seeing just traffic in its eternal flow and slow motion. Just me already not quite the same, looking for my lost dog.

And him really not the same at all.

"Remind you of the gang chasing your car?" Max had come up behind me, helmet in hand.

I had started at his comment, and shook off my fixation on Quicksilver.

"A session with the wind and road-feel sometimes vibrates some ideas in my brain into going supernova."

"And—?"

"Let's get Vlad the Impaler on wheels back to the Circle Ritz, and I'll tell you."

"I can't wait." Max saw me into position on the bike. He swung on in front of me and grabbed his helmet, looking back to say a last word before we revved out of there.

"We're going to fly like a bat out of hell, so you better hang on with both arms."

"So Dracula appropriate," I commented as I took up my helmet. "This is only the second date, so you're escalating my rules on the touchy-feely timetable."

"Then let's skip to three and get that over with."

"Okay. You don't look like the ticklish type."

So I wrapped my arms around him and we took off into the instant wind and whine.

By the time we rolled back into the Circle Ritz lot, my body had adapted to the entire vibe, the balance, the rock and roll and soul.

When the Vampire stopped, I got off. Max balanced the bike on its kick-stand, but I kept my Speed Queen helmet on.

"I'm ready for my solo now, Mr. Kinsella."

He removed his helmet and laughed at the classic movie line I paraphrased. "There's even a Sunset Road, if not a Sunset Boulevard, in Vegas. Have at it."

I hated to start and take over a guy's "baby" in front of him, but riding a motorcycle was like a motorless bike when a kid. The brain remembers. Max was right about the weight. I felt like a motorcycle cop on a Harley hog as I rolled out of the parking lot. Only one place to go. Into the mountains. I soon spun up the ramp to Highway I-95 and waltzed in and out of traffic until I found a paved sub highway likely to end at an abandoned gravel pit. Or a dumped dead body, if you had my imagination.

I patted the pack behind me, relieved to feel the shape of a water jug. Shouldn't have ventured so far without checking.

The overhead sun beat down on the heavy metal, on my borrowed leather jacket, the helmet. I let the engine out and it started to roar and gain speed and throb, and then its shrill full-throated scream seemed to be chasing me down the road faster and faster almost overtaking me—Holy Hesketh—until the road led up a low hill and I pulled back on the reins. "Whoa."

I'd stopped at the top of a ridge, one of the desert's furrowed forehead wrinkles repeated to an infinity of sand below me. The mountains were at my back, the sand's oceanic ripples tapering off before me, the scent of sagebrush and gasoline in my nostrils. The Las Vegas Strip was a scatter of cardboard images baking like gingerbread castles in a small clump below, flashing a bright gleam here and there.

I took off the helmet and balanced it on my hip.

Then I bellowed into the faded, dry distance, "Quicksilver! Quick! Quicksilver," in all directions. Several times, until I was hoarse.

For a moment the Hollywood-set profile of Vegas shimmered like a mirage, and I saw not the Mirage Hotel's golden glass triple towers, but the dancing fire spires of the Inferno Hotel.

Yet the desert remained still and silent, a mantle of heat, except for the scuttles of crawling, creeping things along its dried-out seabed. Lake Mead beyond the city was a small teardrop of blue set in the white-washed thick rim of salt on a Margarita. The water ended at the bright white wall of Hoover dam, an engineering marvel of its time with almost nothing to hold back now.

I felt as empty as the landscape without Quicksilver. And Ric. And the sweet and scary home Las Vegas I had known. Achilles had found me. I would find them both. I turned the Vampire around to get it back to its owner.

30
Sorcerer's Apprentice

"Oops. We've got a discontented chaperone," I said when the Vampire throttled down to a stop in the parking lot near the shed.

I nodded at the black cat crouched atop a black Buick Enclave for camouflage.

"Maybe he's delivering a message," Max said as I dismounted.

Standing again on unmoving ground had me a trifle disoriented and saddle-sore, like getting off a horse, even though the height was much less.

Max rolled the beast into the shed and I followed to hang up Electra's jacket and helmet. He stashed his outer gear there too.

"For next time," he told me. The silky designer tee he wore under the jacket reminded me of the Six Deadly Sins' body-hugging yet disguising body stockings. This tee did nothing to disguise Kinsella's elegant long muscles, the steel-string strength of a guitar string.

"Am I hooking you back on motorcycles?" I wondered.

"You're hooking me back on thinking like a criminal, which is how we get ourselves untangled from the suspect list. We need a longer list."

Midnight Louie had finished a detailed sniffing of the bike, our boots, which we couldn't change until later, and the shed.

We'd glimpsed the deserted and tranquil Circle Ritz pool area, so nodded to it simultaneously. The cat tagged after us, but we'd barely sat on a pair of sun-warmed lounge chairs when a white, long-haired bowling ball came barreling toward me. Achilles joyously lunged at my ankles, I bent and pushed him back, then it was lunge and push back, again and again, him growling in mock-aggression.

"He's a determined sort," Max said. "I can see he'd make a good watchdog."

"Electra thinks so too. She adores him, and vice versa. He lived with me before in one apartment, but now he's got a whole building to call home. He's a special dog, full of life and energy." I put my sunglasses on. Quick, before I teared up, thinking of my wonder dogs, one lost, one found. "The pool's really glaring in the sun."

Max ignored my cover-up. "You know, Delilah-Lilah, if you want to overcome being a suspect, you could clear up the discrepancy in your dogs, as well as your name."

A chill crept up the back of my head. You don't say anything to threaten my dogs.

"That Rin Tin Tin reincarnation that was attacking the biker gang, that's the one who attacked the bikers when they chased your car into the back of the Hellfire Hotel. He's your 'lost' dog. Not the one the Fontana brothers found by your stalled car, which is this one here."

He nodded at Achilles, who was going nose to nose with Midnight Louie, wonder of wonders.

Imagination, do your duty, Irma ordered. "People were offering me a hotel room for the night. I couldn't foist two dogs on them."

"*Hmm,*" Max Kinsella was unconvinced, and I wasn't going to try to sell him on canine reincarnation.

Achilles, tongue hanging out and panting from play, leaned against my leg while I ran my fingers through his long, silky ear hair.

"Guess every woman likes to be mysterious," Max said, "you more than most. What you want the most often comes to you when least expected." He smiled to himself. "That happened to me once in Ireland. It can happen to you here."

I'd glimpsed that shadow in his eyes again. It faded like a passing cloud, which had just cooled and subtly darkened the pool area. But his smile remained sunny.

"This conversation has gone to the dogs, and cat." He nodded at Louie, who seemed to be listening to us most attentively, as Achilles did.

"We need to know more about Celeste," he said, "and who better to learn from than her coworkers? Every stage show is a family enterprise, with members drawn willy-nilly from the talent pool."

I nodded. "So. Are you or am I going to get the audition list for the Green Fairy role out of our unfriendly neighborhood magician?" I asked.

"An audition list." Max nodded, pleased. "Checking out Celeste Novak's defeated rivals for the Green Fairy job. Aren't you the clever one?"

"Won't the police detectives have gotten that?"

"Probably, but they won't share and they won't be able to interview the suspects with their guards down, as candidates for a replacement job."

I caught my breath before it drifted out over the pool. "Oh, that's right. You're a supposed magician too. You need staff."

Max laughed, immune to my jibe.

"That settles it, Lilah. Neither of us have the stomach to humbly seek aid and information from the spellbinding Christophe, drat his tricky charismatic soul."

I didn't comment that suspected vampires don't have souls.

Max grinned. "This other course has the advantage of ensuring you're gainfully employed, which will prevent Molina from labeling you a rootless person of interest in a murder."

"Employed? By you? How?"

"I'll announce I'm casting aerial assistants for my new show. They'll come in droves, many who auditioned for—and failed to get—the plum Green Fairy gig with Christophe."

"What a huge task. You could get dozens of applicants. You couldn't keep track of so many, even if Jill the Ripper showed up."

"Keeping track will be your job."

I made no encouraging murmurs.

"You'd be my personal assistant."

"No." I folded my arms.

He frowned.

"Show manager," I said. "What good is a recommendation for a flunky job?"

"You're aware the title doesn't matter? They're both mythical jobs, like my vaunted magic show."

"You'll still have to write me a reference."

"You trust me to do right by you?"

"You I trust if I keep my eyes open. So far. Snow not."

"Why the instant dislike?"

"He reminds me of someone I used to know."

Max shrugged. "Anyway, I own a huge empty performance venue, perfect for holding auditions."

"How will you get the word out you're hiring?"

"Simple. I don't want to compromise Temple and Matt's classy TV show with a phony audition call, so I'll go to the sleazier side of Vegas media. A guy called Crawford Buchanan. Writes for the *Las Vegas Scoop*."

"So we'd really be auditioning all the women who show up for the Likely Suspect role. I love it. We need to get more on Celeste's professional as well as her personal background. If she had experience in a *Cirque du Soleil* show, she must be in a performer's union. We could check that out with a computer search."

"You sound like you've done investigative work before. I confess I've as often been the subject of an investigation as an investigator."

"I did notice that hard-boiled homicide Jane, as in 'Dick and…' has it in for you."

He bowed his head modestly. "The formidable Lieutenant C. R. Molina. I had the misfortune to find myself on a murder scene just before I needed to skip town. I was cleared eventually, but a cop never gets over having wasted time pursuing the wrong man."

"That holds true for the average woman."

"The voice of experience?"

"I don't pursue men unless they've done something monstrous." I had been thinking of a particular werewolf mobster. Kinsella looked so startled by my intensity, I qualified my statement. "That's the reward of being a TV reporter, I can expose crooked moguls and penny-ante cheaters both. Crusading reporters never run out of stories."

"Just so you don't turn your crusading eye on me."

I shrugged. "You know what? I could get a lot closer and a lot more out of the rival performers if I was one of them. Could I fake having aerial chops?"

"Let's find out," he said. "Tonight. At my place."

Hmm, Irma purrs wickedly.

"Can't miss it," he said. "I'll text you the address. Wear flat shoes if you have any. Eight o'clock?"

"Great. Sounds intriguing."

But first I had another assignation. One that would shock his sockless shoes off.

31
By Heart in the Dark

"I hear your car has inspired 'engine envy' in the Fontana brothers," Homicide Lieutenant C. R. Molina said, leaning back in her desk chair.

I hadn't told Max Kinsella Molina had scheduled me for a witness interview. She'd been on his mind and I wanted to form my own impression of her.

And now I had wheels. The police department building was obviously new. Its flashy glass façade suited Las Vegas. Inside, it was the TV-series almost-newsroom look: acres of desk cubicles and a few perimeter offices.

I did a rapid cop-style assessment after following C. R. Molina into a cubby-hole office. Five-eleven and wearing loafers. Probably so she didn't intimidate the men too much.

That almost black, blunt-cut, jaw-brushing hair-do. Message: "I care about my job, not my hair".

A hint of south-of-the-border cinnamon tinged her complexion, but something wildly "else" had produced that paper-cut sharp jawline and blazing blue eyes, Bottom line: a navy pantsuit blazer that said: "I'm armed, are you?"

Well, ma'am, only with my mind and mindfulness at the moment.

"Engine Envy," I repeated. "I guess you could say that's men for you. I collect—rescue—vintage clothing and other articles. I found my 'enviable' Caddy buried by hay bales in a Kansas barn."

"And now it's basking in automobile La-La Land with the Gangsters crew. How'd you get here without it?"

"Motorcycle."

"Aren't you transportation talented! A Hesketh Vampire is your steed of the day, I assume. My, my, Miss Lane, as a damsel in distress you're inspiring some notorious personalities in this town to play Galahad to the rescue. Not to mention the women flying to your side. Temple Barr, PR whiz. Electra Lark, grandmother entrepreneur. So you're rooming at the Circle Ritz?"

"How did you know?"

"Max Kinsella stables his precious Vampire motorcycle there. He *loaned* it to you? Must be smitten. Or bewitched."

I ignored the jabs, pushing for a full bio. "I'm staying at the Circle Ritz just until I can get myself and my stuff together. The space envelope there is tight. Unless I bed down in the shed with the bike."

"Somehow a very disturbing image, and too darn hot. Don't move without telling me."

"That's the usual 'don't leave town' message?"

"You *are* a person of interest in a suspicious death. Brand-new in town. Breaking into the underbelly of a major hotel-casino and ending up thirty feet from a possible murder victim. Your fingerprint tracks will confirm your story. Or not."

"It's verifiable that a motorcycle gang was after me. The apparently famous Fontana brothers can confirm that. They found oil slicks and tire tracks."

"Hooray for them. More to the point, Miss Lane, my accident analyst officer not only found those traces at the car site, but she tracked the pursuit back to the Strip. A lone woman at the wheel of an open convertible was sweet meat to the Lobos gang, but your vintagemobile was powerful enough to outrun them."

"Lobos. That means 'wolves' in Spanish."

Molina consulted her paper forms. "You thought their T-shirts read 'L-something', so you told my detective. Not exactly the right name, but the very right game. Bad mojo biker gang. Lobos. You were lucky to come out of that encounter with just that forehead owie and a few bruises. Have you been checked for concussion? I recommend it."

"There's been no time…"

"Make it. I don't want my prime and only suspect at this point kicking off."

"Well, thanks. Why suspect me?"

"Because there were only two ways of getting at the deceased once she was established in her backstage position. The Kinsella method, from above in the flies, and *my* favored option, from the performance tunnels below."

"Some iffy premeditated murder," I said. "Max Kinsella's presence was an afterthought to the TV hosts' visit, and I wouldn't have been there at all if I hadn't discovered an escape route from the back alley. The biker gang ensures that I entered the premises with no forethought."

"Via the hotel H-vac system. Tried by myriad cheaters, liars, and thieves before. Only *they* were breaking *out* with their stolen goods."

"I'd have never noticed the metal door if that cat hadn't been pawing and sniffing it."

"Cat? A white dog was reported at the scene, but not a cat."

"I was in the hotel's back alley. Hence, it was a big black alley cat. I've since met him in imposing fursome, and heard he's a known moocher along all the Strip hotels. Lots of high-end food must go out in those Dumpsters."

"Midnight Louie." Molina's expression was deadpan to the point of evoking a stone statue lining the Caesars' driveway. Only these statues were dead-white marble and mostly naked.

"And this guide-cat led you through air-conditioning vents and the magic complex of under-stage passages. Must have been a tight fit all the way."

"It was a big cat."

Lieutenant Molina leaned back in her desk chair until it squeaked for mercy. "And you're a big girl," she said.

"So are you," I answered.

"Not built for squirming through mechanical conduits, though I know an ex-magician with that modus operandi. How do you know Christophe, our new 'Spellbinder' on the Strip?"

"Not 'know', 'know of'. He performed at the Emerald City Hotel-Casino in my hometown, Wichita."

She nodded. "We did find a record of that."

I was so shocked I bit my lip, which was still sore, to avoid making a spontaneous sound. *Oops.* For the first time, a memory of my past had been verified in this topsy-turvy Vegas I was struggling to figure out. And it verified the most lavish and outlandish Strip performer since Liberace…Christophe. Verified by the most hard-nosed female cop I'd ever met. (Not that I had made a habit of meeting hard-nosed cops of any gender.)

"No record of you, however," Molina pointed out.

My heart hiccupped. The Mystifying Max's phony driver's license was all right for superficial ID, but I had nothing solid documenting my current *nom de guerre*. He might be able to cook up something more if he felt charitable, or, more likely, if he thought I could help him out in some way.

But I was on my own here, a condition I was used to, and…I'd noticed a framed snapshot on the table behind the getting-impatient lieutenant. Sturdy pewter framed her standing with a teenage girl almost as tall, both in dressy clothes for some event.

"Not having a 'record' used to be a good thing," I said with a rueful laugh. "I don't even have a proper birth certificate. I was found abandoned as an infant on Lilac Lane. 'Baby Lane,' they called me at the hospital. That's where they got my first and last name."

"They?"

I shrugged. "I have flashes of milling around on the floor with lots of little kids, pulling on impossible-to-don boots. Kansas winters are heavy on cold and snow. And naptime, when the steel railings on the bed slammed up and down, and dinner, with some nameless witch telling me if I didn't eat my vegetables, I wouldn't get dessert. I didn't get dessert."

Molina was looking appalled. I was pretty appalled myself because that was my life, only I ended up being named for Delilah Street, which didn't exist in Wichita. Yeah, crazy. Yet I grew up there.

A mystery from the git-go. I felt a tad bad about playing the mama lieutenant. I'd made up "Lilac Lane" on the spot, but I needed time to figure what-why-when-where-who I really was.

"You know the routine," I said. "Alternating institutions and foster homes, and toward the end "foster" brothers and fathers with 'inappropriate' ideas."

"What do you mean, 'toward the end'?"

"I ran away. Nobody much noticed. Call it 'opting out'. The system burns out social workers, so they constantly change. And records had gone from paper to digital, with some information lost beyond finding." I smiled. "My record specifically. I had a social security number for a passkey. No more group 'homes' for me. The only thing that kept me sane there was watching old black-and-white movies all night in the TV room with a long diamond-dust nail file in my hand. Could go straight for the eyes."

So there I went and "committed" truth. Spoke truth to power.

We are fried, Irma wailed. *This is one tough mama.*

That was what I was counting on. Her recognizing another one.

"School?" Molina asked.

"By the time I left, I could ace the GED." I smiled at these memories. "I found an elderly pawn shop widow who employed me if I got my GED, no questions asked. That's where I got my eye for vintage, that and the old movies I'd kill to see in the foster homes."

Not for her or the record to know: All that was when I was "Delilah Street" and I was building a new life here in Vegas and I'm only staying in this weird do-over until I can get back to my old one, particularly to find *mi amor,* Ricardo Montoya. If Snow was here, Ric had to be too. Didn't he?

"Ultimately I worked myself through college in communications and got a TV reporting job," I finished up for her.

"You make it sound easy." Her chair squeaked again.

"It was necessary."

She abruptly changed topics to rattle me. "Was your dog all right?"

I nodded. "Looked like he'd been doing the tango with a grease monkey. Just needed a bath. Achilles is a long-haired Lhasa Apso. White."

"Lassa, er, Alpo?"

"Apso. Short legs, long hair. Short jaw, strong fangs. I call him the Tibetan staple gun. Lhasa is the capital of Tibet. His ancestors were bred to protect the ancient Dalai Lamas. Would-be assassins would be nipped in the ankles until they fell. Being downed by four of five Lhasa Apsos as they set to work would have you wishing for the release of piranhas."

She actually laughed. "'Achilles heel' was the Greek mythical hero's one weak spot. I get it. You *did* get yourself through college."

"Seriously. If you arrest any Lobos soon, check for ankle wounds."

"You have led an adventuresome life, Miss Lane, but I don't take formal statements. My detectives do."

She stood, which cued the door behind me to open and I walked out to meet the detective pair. I saw Detective Alch's thick salt-and-pepper hair and mustache. He was just parting from a coworker, a nondescript middle-aged man who had been…frankly staring at me before his head quickly turned away. I wasn't that much of a babe.

"This way, Miss Lane."

Drat! Detective Bellamy was directing me in the opposite direction as Alch headed toward us. I wrenched my head over my shoulder and caught a last glimpse of the other man. Not familiar with the military-short haircut at the nape of his neck…

Going, going, gone.

My next gig was the typical interrogation room, as bare and transitory as expected. Cigarette burns pocked the laminated tabletop. A waft of cleaning fluid invaded my nostrils and set up camp with an undercurrent of what I imagined to be sweat, blood and tears.

No tabletop handcuffs or ankle locks, though. The blank, black observation window nowadays reminded me more of a huge HD TV screen than an oil-slick-black giant peephole.

I asked the first question. "May I sit?

And off we went, into All About Lilah.

I didn't worry about the peek-a-boo window on my world at the moment. I doubted Lieutenant C. R. Molina needed or cared to see or hear any more of me.

Alch hit the Record button. "Detectives Morris Alch and Phyllis Bellamy with witness Lilah Lane." He gave the time and date, then he turned to me. "We'd like your account of the biker gang attack behind the Hellfire hotel."

"It started on the Strip. I heard the bikers before I saw them since I was driving a convertible. They swooped out of nowhere like a bunch of giant black wasps. Maybe twelve on Harleys. They were howling and hooting and edging up on the driver's side but my car has three hundred and twenty-five horses and we could outrun them. That meant breaking the speed limit, so I turned off to lose them in the tangles of access routes behind the hotels."

"Really?" Detective Bellamy was openly skeptical. "Some rough bikers surround your vehicle and you're worrying about breaking the speed limit?"

"I was brought up in the Midwest. We're rules followers. Besides, my dog had gotten excited and I didn't want him jumping out on the Strip in that traffic mess."

Alch leaned forward. "This was the 'little white dog' found on scene after you'd escaped the bikers by entering the hotel's ventilation system hatch?"

No way could I mention my formerly dead dog must have magically escaped the bubble-packed funerary urn in Dolly's roomy glove compartment.

I just nodded, and lied repeatedly between nuggets of truth. "My dog, Achilles, is super smart and can bite like a buzz saw. When I'd tumbled out of my car to the alley and that cat accidentally showed me an escape route, he wouldn't come when called. I had to push on alone. Not that I wasn't worried about him."

"So you didn't specifically exit into the Hellfire Hotel from the Strip?"

"No."

"Didn't you spot the twenty-foot-high marquee for the *Spellbinder* show?" Bellamy asked.

"No, everything became a blur when I realized I was a target. Any port in a tsunami."

"Why did you describe the Lobos name on the bikers T-shirts and jackets as 'Lunatics'?"

"I just saw the capital '*L*'. They sure rode like lunatics. Even in the Midwest, we know what biker gangs are, and also know that iconic actor Marlon Brando shooting a movie is no longer among them."

"*The Wild One*," Alch chortled into his mustache. "Famous biker gang movie before you were born," he told Bellamy, then turned to me again. "Right?" I nodded. He couldn't know I'd seen every old black-and-white film in creation during those unsettled nights in the group home.

Bellamy looked confused by the film talk. Alch smiled at her and said, "When my regular partner, Detective Su, gets off special assignment she'll fill you in on the Noir film mania gripping Las Vegas venues now."

"Wasn't happening at my department in Reno," Bellamy said, sounding relieved. "When did you realize you were being herded into a dead-end alley?" she asked me.

"When I had to brake fast and got tossed out. I came to a few seconds later with cat whiskers tickling my cheeks and the gang guys making growling circles like ground-bound vultures. My dog wasn't in sight and I didn't want them messing with him, so I followed the resident alley cat into his favorite escape hatch."

"They didn't follow you?" Bellamy asked.

"Most bikers carry too much suet to be comfy in cars, so…on their hands and knees into mechanical tunnels just to further hassle a poor lone woman, no."

"And," Alch asked, "you went all the way through the tunnels and by luck came straight to that trapdoor and up and out onstage? You didn't spot anyone else moving down there, show crew or the person lying in a muddle of green veils and sequins and such farther along the route?"

"No. I only saw a faint glimmer from distant work lights. The tunnels were meant for repair people wearing headlamps and performers who knew the tunnels and trapdoors by heart in the dark. The trapdoor to the stage set was marked by a thin sliver of light. I made for it and heard Christophe booming something like 'and here—' so I took that as a cue to exit that claustrophobe's nightmare."

"What about the cat?"

"The area was black and so was he. I don't know where he was by then. Not making fresh with his whiskers on my face, for sure. I figured someone was expected onstage and I would have to do in a pinch."

I suddenly imagined what I'd said being replayed on a tape-recorder.

"'In a pinch', I just said. I guess I have been. Pinched, that is, but I'm not pleading guilty of anything."

Bellamy and Alch exchanged glances, but didn't laugh.

32
Neon Notions

"**What an awesome** place."

I stood on the black glass floor, a reflected shadow in midnight leather shoes and jeggings. I turned around, looking up into the vanishing peak. Horizontal bars of neon marked the "stories" that surrounded the pyramid's interior.

"It was part disco nightclub and aerial magic show. A huge neon Pegasus horse figure flew over the apex of the pyramid roof."

"That's why it was called the Neon Night*mare*. What are you going to call it now?"

"I don't know. Suicide Watch. It almost killed me."

"How?"

"I used to 'cliff-dive' from the peak on a bungee cord."

"Ten stories maybe?"

"You've seen that heights don't bother me. Do they bother you?"

"I don't know. I'm sure you're determined to find out."

Meanwhile I found myself drawn to the bar. Or, rather, the mirror behind it, which had a darker tint.

"Finding something fascinating?"

"Besides rows of ridiculously expensive hard liquor? Is there a mirror tint? My eyes look almost green."

"An illusion," he said. "There are a lot of green glass liquor bottles standing against the mirror."

I was startled. I'd seen a lurid unfamiliar image of myself in the green room serving tray, and the facial blood had distracted me then.

Maybe, Irma said, *more than we know has changed in transit.*

"How about calling the building or the bar In Transit?" I suggested.

"Not bad."

Max had bent to pair his face with mine in the reflection, his laughing Irish eyes next to mine. Blue eyes like mine.

"My eyes used to be green," he said. Nostalgia warmed his voice. "Early in my career. Before personal issues took me into the deep end of love and war. I'd used vivid green contact lenses. Hokey, but maybe I was subconsciously capitalizing on the Midnight Louie 'look' without even knowing he would come into my life."

"Midnight Louie…? Oh, my guide cat. Say, 'Subconscious' is another good club name."

His "love and war" phrase had intrigued me. I'd sensed a shade of black, some dark, long, deep, wide nagging wound, beneath Max Kinsella's perpetually cool and controlled façade. Temple Barr had the unflagging compassion and spirit a man like him would need. Her loss might still sting.

"I've got the perfect name this time," I told him. "Nightshade."

"Isn't that usually preceded by the word 'Deadly'?"

"If it's a plant. You can keep the 'night' in the name yet still have a new concept that's whatever you want it to be."

Max walked around the bar to pour two fingers of Scotch into crystal lowball glasses and slid one in front of me. I loved being the sole customer in this huge, empty bar.

"Nightshade. That's genius." His long, agile fingers pantomimed his words. "Serpentine vines and unfolding, floating, flying flower petals. I envision illusions twisted within layers of deceptive shapes and motions and allusions."

I was doing a bit of envisioning myself. "The house Nightshade cocktail would be served in a fabulous custom blown glass sort of… chalice. And a great snarled crown of tangled neon thorns would circle the exterior top of the pyramid, making the word Nightshade as iconic as any Strip hotel name, as bold as the HOLLYWOOD sign in L.A."

"By Jove, I think you've got something. Maybe I *should* make you manager."

I'd never seen him so animated.

He clapped a hand to my shoulder. "Forget worrying about what the eyes in the mirror tell you. They so often lie. We've got a mountain to climb. Come on."

He led me by the arm to the black glass sidewall. An unseen black staircase showed glinting silver, lit riser edges diminishing into the upper level.

Lucky I'd changed into ridged, rubber-soled flats that laced up my ankles and legs. They became my mountaineering ballet flats as I started to scale a dark fairytale's glass mountain with Max Kinsella's hand lifting mine and me higher and higher.

I pulled myself and him to a stop.

"There's a hallway off to the right. Is this building modeled on the Egyptian pyramids with their secret byways and rooms?"

"Merely office areas. This *used* to be a hot magic show-nightclub business when I ran it. A cabal of unemployed magicians took over the building after my 'accident' when I was AWOL on other matters and had no one in town to handle it, but it was always mine and they scattered on my return."

"You could employ them again and get some free time."

"For what or from what?"

By then we'd reached the building's interior apex, to stand on a large platform. Below us, swords of opposing LED lights intersected like flaming red, blue and green arrows.

"Cool," I said, to prove I wasn't intimidated. I was. "Why were you gone?"

"Because someone clever interfered with my nightly bungee jump apparatus. I always checked the cord at the top, but I was distracted and it broke at the midway point. I crashed into the wall of the main floor, between the doors and the bar."

"How'd you do?"

"I used my legs to rappel off the oncoming wall. That did 'break' my fall...and both legs. And a lot of glass. My head hit where the glass had already fallen off, much bad luck for the plastic surgeons' bank accounts."

"So you were…are a daredevil magician."

"Circus Circus Hotel-Casino's shtick had been aerial acts above the gaming tables for decades, but it was considered a kiddie-friendly venue, so nothing that exciting. Then *Cirque de Soleil* overwhelmed Las Vegas with far more sophisticated aerial acts, even an x-rated one. Imagine, an entertainment company from good neighbor Canada created the most successful brand in the world. Other shows had to 'up their games', quite literally, from the stage into the air. Not a problem for me."

"And you're still not afraid of heights after that Lucifer-level fall?" I looked down.

Irma must have joined me. *Ooh, girlfriend, very far and very dark and very hard. Let's not let go.*

"With all this black mirror, it would be like falling into your own image," I imagined.

"The ultimate in ego, maybe, like Lucifer. I suffered some head issues with the impact. Mostly memory loss or memory stuttering, I call it. Good memories can remain foggy and distant forever. Bad ones don't let go so easily."

I was having a bad memory flashback right now, about some nasty hotel-casino owner knocking me out and suspending me over a stage in a sexy routine because I was…I was the image of an anonymous, but hot naked corpse on an episode of *CSI V: Las Vegas* TV franchise. Memory or dream?

Nightmare.

I didn't know my fists were closing and opening until the magician put a bungee cord into their grip.

"You can't let a bad landing unnerve you. You can't let a rattled brain deter you. Most of all, you can't let what someone else has done hurt you enough to evolve into a fear."

"Is that why we're up here? Playing games with fear?"

"If you let it win, you're lost. Now. I'm going to repeat my show-closing bungee dive for the first time since the attempt on my life. If I survive…"

I was edging back against the wall so I wouldn't be peering over the edge anymore. Death was nothing to trifle with.

"In that case," he went on, "if I survive, I'll climb back up to the maiden in the tower and swing you down with me. Nothing for you to do but hold on. And hope. And I'll make you my manager."

"Assuming I want to be. I think you'd be hell on wheels to manage."

"My sentiments exactly. Don't creep back against the wall. If I die, I want a witness."

"Great. Terrific. So thoughtful of my finer feelings."

Without another word or look, he swung out over the abyss.

That was the name for his new act. Abyss.

I leaned as far forward as I dared. It wasn't a straight shot down. No. He was catching the bungee cord up and looping and twirling, then plunging and then stopping upright in air, plunging again.

And landing like a ballerina on point, in super slow motion, on the black mirrored floor.

He looked up and bowed mockingly. "It's much more impressive with strobe lights," he called to me. "But I'd need a light board operator. You'll have to use your imagination."

My imagination was in overdrive. And the dominant thought was how easy it would have been for Mr. Max Kinsella to use his Spider-Man aerial tricks to kill the Green Fairy and pretend to find her body.

33
Trust Issues

Heights were not an issue with me, but independence was.

I didn't wait for Max Kinsella to climb up to the girl in the tower to swing her to freedom on a braid of her supernaturally long hair. I could never grow mine past my shoulder blades anyway. So much for Princessdom.

So I donned the flat leather workout gloves from the flat pack on my rear, wrapped my hands around the anchored bungee cord, and swung out into the laser lights, sweet bells of freedom chiming.

Once free falling, I discovered I could shift my weight into the path of a particular streaking color and waft more slowly or faster. Green was a leaf, swirling rather than plunging. Red was a brake, allowing me to hang in what felt like thick gelatin stasis. Blue was my deep breathing rhythm holding me still on a frigid azure horizon.

I twisted and turned, then looked straight down into myself as I headed for my own image.

Hmm, no brakes on this artificial umbilical cord. I tried adjusting my weight or spinning, but not quickly enough.

Max came plunging down after me, below me, grabbing the cord just below my feet and twining around and around so I suddenly slowed and hung on as I twisted tight, and then twisted undone, and finally stopped cold, as he had.

The floor was an ankle-breaking fourteen inches below my virtually barefoot and vulnerable feet.

He held onto my waist as my stiff-clenched fingers uncurled and fanned back from the cord, which rebounded up like a whip past my face.

My ballet flats were now the toe shoes coming gently to earth, thanks to Max easing me down and landing beside me.

"Impulsive," he said.

"Not usually."

"You have an idea what Celeste Novak did, saw, how she felt?"

"And I also have an idea of how a second aerialist could interrupt, disrupt, confuse, corrupt her act and take control and kill her."

I looked pointedly at Max.

A cell phone rang. It was Bette Midler with "Boogie Woogie Bugle Boy of Company B".

He bolted for the bar where his cell phone lay, maybe to avoid a comment.

"Yes? You're kidding. Yes, I'm listening. That was just a phrase to give me time to think. That should draw a crowd of possible suspects. Thanks, Temple. Christophe won't be crazy about your covering the hiring process. I know you will. 'Bye."

I'd come to the bar to eavesdrop better. "What's up, besides us?"

"That was Temple."

"You think?"

"The Hellfire is holding open auditions for Celeste's replacement. Temple wants to 'cover' the process."

"That'd be a lot simpler than faking new show auditions here."

He shrugged. "That lets me off the hook of pretending to create a show I'm not ready to work on.

"I'd have less control over your situation and welfare at the Hellfire," Max said as he looked up to the building's apex, the top of his own personal mountain.

Don't be shy, Irma prodded me. *If Caesar Cicero tried to hijack you for a stage act, you must have some show biz chops.*

"Can you really teach me enough rope tricks this fast?" I asked him.

His gaze came abruptly down to earth.

"Seriously? After that crack about a second aerialist being a prime suspect?"

"I bet everybody involved in that stage show has some gymnastic moves, even Christophe."

"Yeah, but the Green Fairy routine is more about steamy titillation than acrobatics. I'd worry more about you being convincing in that part—"

"Thanks!"

"They cast on the girl's looks. Sorry, that's show biz."

He stepped back and looked me over from head to toe and back again. I had kicked the ankles out from under jerks for that. And then Achilles had bitten them on the way out.

The speculation in his narrowed eyes was intense. "Tall enough, but too heavy, no way ethereal," he murmured. "Leather workout gloves…way too suggestive of a gym rat. *Aha!* Black satin opera-length gloves with leather palms and fingers. Instant signature look. I know where to get them. *Hmm.* Leggings and tunics… Russian peasant with overtones of Goth Girl. And too much hair. Maybe go for statuesque."

By then I had crossed my arms and my foot was tapping, although that would have more effective had I been wearing boots.

He stopped musing and laughed at me. "I said steamy, not steamed." Back to musing mood. "The girl's got the nerve, can she broadcast the verve?"

"You've got the nerve! 'Too much this and too much that.' If you don't stop talking trash about me *to* me, you'll need your casts and crutches again."

"Spunky too."

"You bet your smug mug, Mr. Grant."

He laughed again. "I can picture you as a punk Mary Richards via Mary Tyler Moore. Better yet, if you work at it, I think you can pass as an aspiring aerialist."

He looked down. "The ballerina flats with textured leather soles will work, as they did here. Implies dance training. Acceptable, but not too much of a statement."

He looked up. "Front hair braided into a coronet and the back twisted into one of those tight, snobby fashion-model buns on the nape of your neck."

"You must be a control freak to date."

"I'm not dating, I'm giving you a designer undercover makeover. Get a tape of the *So You Think You Can Dance* tryouts. Get a midriff-baring top and full-coverage but flirty bottom, not too ballet or jazz, more Broadway, in blue-green."

"Any more orders?"

"Yes. I'm calling Temple back right now. She'll take you to the right resale shops and even spring for lunch at the Crystal Phoenix. Vegas is packed with second-hand fripperies, and she'll get what I mean and you need. Meanwhile, I'll start showing you the ropes now. I'll even give you moves to use if another aerialist tries to sabotage you."

I nodded, my stomach fluttering. Was I really going all out for this? I thought of troubled Celeste behind the grace and glamour of a "muse" that brought men despair and death. Trying to float like a butterfly might sting me like a bee if I made a beginner's misstep.

"I won't let you fall," Max said with absolute certainty, guessing my second thoughts. "But you do realize if you're successfully cast as the Green Fairy and snooping around, someone could try to kill you too."

If I didn't kill *myself* trying to play Tinkerbell first.

34
Kit for Tat

How *is* a dude supposed to set priorities when his business and social obligations are being shaken, not gently stirred, like a James Bond martini?

The advent of Miss Lilah Lane (or Miss Delilah Street in pseudonymous clothing) has me twirling like a puppet on string, trying to keep up with her various to's and fro's.

She is rapidly making a circuit of not only my nearest and dearest and their doings, but of some of the most unsavory individuals in town.

I cannot begrudge Mr. Max Kinsella taking up (literally) new interests, since the many stresses and losses in his recent life and times, the direst being the withdrawal of his past love, my Miss Temple, into matrimony with another.

Believe me, I feel for him in the circumstance of our joint bereavement.

That zebra-print coverlet at the Circle Ritz holds forever fond memories for us both. I particularly remember a green silk chiffon dress thrown casually across it, left for me to *del-i-cate-ly* rearrange with my shivs into a soft pile on which I could impress all my twenty-some pounds for a nice long luxurious nap.

So thoughtful of Miss Temple, although she must have apparently had a bad day when she returned and hurled several harsh words at me in her distress at the rough ways of the world. "Pristine vintage from the fifties" and "Bad, Bad Boy" were particularly hurtful, but I hold no grudges.

I am, in fact, much intrigued by Miss Lilah Lane. Miss Temple is stalwart and smart, but Miss Lilah seems to share some of the agility and grace native to my breed, which Mr. Max is now discovering.

One who has recently lost a beloved mentor could do worse than to have a new pupil to train. You see I have this human psychology down pat, as in the "pat" of little cat feet.

Also, although it has taxed my patience mightily, I have also been cultivating new acquaintances, as it seems the new Swiffer mop may be a permanent Circle Ritz accessory. To hear him and Karma go on about past life matters is truly mind-numbing.

Meanwhile, I have learned now that I will have to "do time" exclusively at the Hellfire, where both Miss Lilah and Mr. Max will be probing the death of Miss Celeste Novak full-time.

I also learned that my two large and little dolls in detecting are going to link up tomorrow.

At least this case has taken me here. I love visiting again what Miss Lilah Lane has declared to be the 'Abyss'. It is dark inside and out, and my natural camouflage environment for eavesdropping and crime-solving.

Abysssss. So feline, so serpentine. No room for clunky canines here.

That is Miss Lilah's only drawback. It will not take long for me to ankle over and cozy up, so that she learns to appreciate the subtle, silent, slinky cat as the superior partner in crime-solving. Especially when I nail the murderer.

35
Vintage Trek

The Looking Glass Theater and the Spellbinder show was beginning to wear on her, so Temple was delighted to spend quality time with Louie's new find, the mysterious young woman with the huge old car. Temple liked vintage, but that didn't extend to cars: too expensive and too impractical, although Gangsters was a whiz at stretching them into chic and shiny custom limos.

A red Miata convertible was a perfect fit for five-foot-zero Temple Barr.

She paused at the front of the massive, and deserted, Neon Nightmare building. She loved the black glass pyramid surrounded by a sunbaked empty parking lot. She couldn't help worrying how Max was doing now that his old family secrets and misunderstandings had come into the open, resulting in glorious reunion and resolution during the after-party of her wedding to Matt. Max had followed a heroic path, but heroism requires sacrifices. His relationship with her had been one of them.

Matt being Matt, he was as happy as she that their wedding was a stage for Max being born again into whatever professional and personal path he wanted, or wanted enough to fight for.

Now, Max was apparently taking this scruffy stranger under his wing. She could be a killer, and looked far too healthy to be the homeless, carless, dogless waif she claimed to be. Was Max finally seriously contemplating resuming his magician career? Did this woman have something to do with that? Was he breaking precedence and considering her as an assistant? "The Mystifying Max" had always lived up to that performance name onstage and off.

The woman in question exited the building alone, squinting her eyes against the sun while she donned polarized mirror sunglasses. Mid-twenties maybe. A bit young for Max, Temple sniffed, now that she herself was thirty. He must be…Lord, how could she have forgotten after them not celebrating a couple years of birthdays together? Thirty-four, was it?

Did it matter? Temple admonished herself. No longer her business. At least this girl was a far cry from the subtle and polished French woman who'd fled with Max through Western Europe. Revienne. Possible spy and maybe lover on that long, long trek.

Beautiful name and another lofty female. Well, Max was six-four. This one seemed quite tall to Temple, although not intimidatingly towering like Lieutenant C. R. Molina. Temple eyed Lilah's outfit, wondering what her style was. Temple would never wear that funky black satin baseball jacket sporting a tourist phrase, "Lost Vegas Hellionaire". The jeggings were serviceable denim-look and her footwear—a critical area to Temple in sizing up other women—she had worn red Cuban-heeled ankle boots Temple could endorse and maybe even covet. But today it was lace-up ballet flats, and Temple could tell Lilah wore at least a size eight or even nine, not five like herself! No way they could ever bond enough to exchange clothes anyway. Lilah. Old-fashioned name but new-fashioned attitude.

"This sports car might be a bit cramped for you," Temple called in greeting.

"Ragtop. Red. I dig it. It reminds me of my red-leather-upholstered Caddy convertible, only this is dollhouse size. Don't worry. I bend, not break."

"I bought it when I was still single."

"And you're recently not single, I hear." Lilah casually jackknifed her long legs into the passenger seat while Temple concentrated on not being envious.

Lilah smiled. "I hate to say 'Congratulations' like you finally 'caught' one, but your hubby is super nice."

"Thanks. You're not married, I guess."

"One significant other. MIA. Before that, it was me and my dog."

Lilah had stared straight into the windshield when she mentioned her significant other and dog. Temple caught a fleeting expression of grief or worry crinkling the corners of her eyes.

She guided the car away from the curb. "Max was not specific or expansive, as usual, but he wants me to go shopping with you to find some used *gym* clothes?"

Lilah's laugh rang up and down almost a full octave. "I understand you're queen of the vintage shops. I got into that for a while, but Wichita isn't loaded with designer finds. Mr. Kinsella had in mind some chorus girl leotards and tights."

"Leotards and tights…? *Wait!* Is he using you to get inside the Spellbinder show? You're not a magician. Or a seasoned performer. It could be dangerous if you try to perform."

Lilah shrugged. "He and I are both suspects, me especially. Might as well as get inside the operation to defend ourselves."

"Oh, Max is such a fraud! *You*'re the one who's really on shaky ground. Or *under*ground in your case."

"That homicide lieutenant seems as ready to growl and bite at him as that huge white tiger."

"Molina does that. It's some eternal game of cat and mouse they've got going." Temple didn't want to betray Max's counterterrorism agent history. "He was 'accidentally' near another murder victim at a Vegas hotel awhile back and became a handy 'usual suspect' for Molina. I think she knows better, but they sharpen their games on each other."

"Magicians like to pretend they know more, and do more, than they do," Lilah said. "It's all showmanship."

"So you distrust magicians in general, Lilah? I noticed some sizzling antipathy between you and Christophe. Speaking of bite-ready people, you notice that Christophe's super-secretary and his Big Cat are both called Grizelle? Makes me I wonder who is named after whom."

Lilah quirked me a smile as quick as a wink. "You're pretty observant yourself, Temple. Like in the 'Woman or the Tiger' illusion I accidentally crashed, I think the human Grizelle came first with Snow, and then he acquired her namesake Big Cat."

"'Snow'. Short for 'Cocaine'. Not a role model. The show film emphasizes his addicted groupies writhing in the mosh pit. Really over the top for a magic act. You'd think he was a rock star."

"So does he," Lilah answered with a wicked grin.

She turned in her seat to peep at Temple close-up in turn. "What about that Little Cat That Could leading me into this mess. He seems to be yours?"

"Oh, Midnight Louie is nobody's and everybody's in this town. He managed to crash a huge publishing convention at the Convention Center. Twenty thousand people and two company mascot cats, Baker and Taylor, kidnapped. I was handling local public relations, so it was up to me to get the uniquely eared Scottish Fold cats back and catch and kick out His Royal Hindness."

Lilah glanced to my high heel on the gas pedal. "And you chasing him down while wearing"—she peered into the shadowed car floor—"something rare and French. Charles Jordan four-inch heels from nineteen-seventy."

"Say, you *do* know your eras. This will be girly fun."

"For you, Temple. Most vintage shoes and clothes come in small-to-tiny sizes. Not applicable to me."

"It figures that size zero-to-six women would be clothes horses and save their expensive items."

Lilah shook her thick dark hair. "Size zero. I can't comprehend that. Maybe my thigh can."

"Never mind. You're going to be in vintage real-women size heaven. I'm taking you someplace that's not for me, but tailor-made for you. Reprise. Showgirl clothes and accessories. Everything Tall and Towering, Blingy and Blinding. I felt three years old and like I was invading my mother's closet when I peeked in once and saw Onstage Oz, all Technicolor and sparkly."

There it was, dead-ahead, down the block from their car, the name Reprise outlined in round yellow theatrical lights.

"This does look fun!" Lilah craned her neck to eye the place's front façade in the aging strip shopping center line-up.

Temple loved the shop's name. Reprise meant a recurrence, a renewal, a repeat performance, so right for showgirl costume retreads.

She whisked the Miata up a short gravel drive to park along the building's side, turned to exit the car, then paused.

"Say, Max isn't having you audition for the dead woman's part?"

"That's info not shared. But he'd warned me it could be dangerous."

"*Hmm.* Well, I am not going to let my indignation at his careless love of daring and danger ruin a satisfying make-over expedition for you.

"Once we do this," she told Lilah, "we'll fulfill Max's prescription for the hair next at the Crystal Phoenix salon. And then we'll have a late lunch and disassemble Mr. Mystifying Max from head to foot, brain cell to bunion."

"Bunions. Really?"

"Wouldn't know now. Just sounded good. PR woman hyperbole." Temple turned off the motor and pushed down on her high heels to get out of the low car. With Lilah still sitting she was taller for once.

"My Aunt Kit treated me to a hunt for the perfect wedding gown, and I am passing on the favor to you. Not a wedding gown, the experience," she added hastily.

Lilah shed the car like a snail its shell as she stood. "Well, I just hope this getup we're looking for won't be a matter of until death do us part for me."

36
Lou's on First

Since I also feel obligated to check on the little doll...*oops*, my error.

Miss Lilah Lane is not petite like my Miss Temple and I suspect her dollish quotient nears the level as that of my esteemed mama, Ma Barker, who runs the Las Vegas Cat Pack with a steel claw and sharpened fang.

I will have to find an appropriate "pet" name for her. I know! My Great Big Beautiful Doll. Who needs to rely on a Big Handsome Fellow for backup. I am sure Miss Midnight Louise would take offence at my old-fashioned gallantry, but what she does not hear or know is okay by me. Maybe I will shorten that to my GBBD.

Anyway, since I led Miss Lilah Lane into the Hellfire's noxious underbelly, where she encountered discomfort and embarrassing disclosure, I want to make sure my minions at the Phoenix are properly caring for another not-so-big stranger.

So I ankle out to the pool area at the back of the hotel and take a sentimental stroll to my old office in the canna lilies surrounding the koi pool. I moisten a toe in the shaded and murky water, hoping to catch glimpse of gilt and silver fins doing the hula through the water lilies.

The scene is so idyllic I could puke from feeling good will for all my fellow creatures, even prey, when I am bowled over almost into the arms of a trident-wielding pond statue of Neptune, god of the sea.

"Cut that out!" I do a one-eighty on my shivs and confront a bright bouncing ball of fuzzy and fiery orange, like a wayward tennis ball hurled at sixty miles per hour. I discover it is only one ultra-orange-striped kitten.

"Mr. Midnight, Mr. Midnight, you came *back* for me," is his shrill greeting. "You disappeared after your exhausting climb of Mount Mirage to hurl the Ring of Bondage around your neck into its fiery maw, and then the volcano exploded and swallowed your white bowtie collar, or maybe it was black, hard to see against all those flames, and you brought me here and I thought I'd never see you again."

"Well, Never is Now and you did, kid." I reject a "here's looking at you" addition as clichéd.

"The name is Punky. You did not forget? You gave it to me. You said it was more macho than Pumpkin." He rests his chin on my shoulder and gazes up at me like an enamored puppy. This must stop.

I shake off my ruffled top coat and brush away any stray orange hairs that make me look like a Halloween knick-knack in waiting.

"So are you here on a case?" Punky is now running around the koi pound, dipping in a rash paw and leaping back, sprinkling water on me.

"I did not come here to get a birdbath and I was already blessed by a priest at a ceremony for domestic companions," I state, removing myself from the pond vicinity. "Besides, those upper-class fish are biting."

"Why did you drop by, drop-off daddy?" comes a new voice on the scene.

I freeze at those arch and chastising tones. My maybe (okay, finally acknowledged) offspring, Miss Midnight Louise, is certainly here now, and on *my* case.

She looks me up and down with her usual hauteur. Hauteur means she has a big head and a nose in the air. She has not inherited my cool muscular buzz-cut black coat and dandy white whiskers. She has a little long-hair from her mother, cathouse house cat, black Satin, and black silky whiskers, but her temperament when it comes to me is one-hundred-percent scouring pad.

"Speaking of Punky," she says, "I see you are associating with a human of the punk rock school."

"I know nothing of Miss Lilah Lane's education, but she is from out of town and needs some hip feline guidance to Sin City."

"She needs more than a little. Miss Lt. C. R. Molina sent two detectives sniffing around the Phoenix to follow up on your rescue's well-being and her actions on the one night she was booked in here before Mr. Max Kinsella wafted her away. I overheard the Phoenix folks attributing the police visit to a murder not thirty feet away from Miss Lilah Lane when she crashed the Hellfire Hotel Looking Glass Theater magic show, following your dubious lead. Do I hope in vain that you are not involved in murder most magical?"

That gets my back up. I arch like a Halloween cat and inadvertently scare off Punky. He retreats under the pierced plastic lounge chairs circling the pool, amusing himself by patting the sweat drops from sunscreen-basted people browning into the color of sizzled bacon.

Unfortunately, without the orphan kit within hearing distance, Miss Midnight Louise is free to give me a large corrosive piece of her mind. She leans forward to breathe fiercely into my whiskers.

"You had some nerve dumping that bundle of unflagging energy on me. He is as orange as He Who Shall Not Be Named and having him for a second tail is hampering my undercover operations as Crystal Phoenix unofficial house detective, a position *you* created."

Miss Midnight Louise was never one to hiss and run. As she takes a deep breath to heap another monologue of grief on my head, an unwelcome interruption occurs. Punky on springs.

"Mr. Midnight, Mr. Midnight! Are you on another dark and daring quest, like throwing something else into the Mount Mirage volcano? Are you, are you? Can I come too?"

Miss Midnight Louise jumps on this opening. "Of course, my darling itty-bitty Punky-wunky."

Louise's baby kit talk leaves much sincerity to be desired, since she has embraced the procedure that makes motherhood impossible.

"Mr. Midnight would adore having you accompany him."

I give a mighty sigh.

I have but one option for safely storing a stray kit. Ma's cat pack. Maybe I can sell Punky as a guard for Arthur during his protected witness program. Maybe Ma will not clip me across the chops for using her operation as a safe house.

Maybe.

I sigh as I contemplate another tedious trek to Ma's clowder.

"Okay, Punky," I say. "We are travelling tail, hop, skip, and jump. You know what that means?"

He shakes his fluffy kitten head and widens his big eyes that may be green or yellow.

"We *tail* a vehicle, *hop* on, *skip* out later and *jump* off. Got it?"

"It is a game, Mr. Midnight! Will there be exciting fire and thunder at the end of it?"

"Probably so, Punky. Probably so."

Ma Barker is her own special breed of volcano.

37
Lilah in La-La Land

"**Reprise.**" Not a repeat performance for me, and I hope not requiring resurrection, like the clothes inside this shabby-funk shop next to a taxidermist's workshop.

What kind of an off-Strip world had I gotten myself, and "my little dog too", into?

I was glad I'd left Achilles at "home" with Electra at the Circle Ritz, because he'd be storming these floor-length gowns and trailing trains for ankles to ID and supervise.

Temple had led me around front as proudly as someone escorting a seeker to a fabled hidden kingdom, like Shangri-La or La-La Land East. Lilah Land. Had a ring to it.

Decommissioned department store mannequins from decades past starred in the showroom windows, bracketing the large glass door announcing "Reprise" written diagonally in large glitter-laden looping letters.

The other next-door shop was a fifties movie theater turned into what might be an R-rated peep show. I didn't stare long enough to be certain.

As I walked in behind Temple, her high-heeled clicks announced our arrival to all the frozen-in-time ladies, but I noticed no sign of human habitation.

The floor was wooden, but old and scuffed. A similar condition retail case with glass top and sides held a well-used computerized cash register.

Meanwhile we could explore a maze of the eerie vintage mannequins, all six feet tall with shoulders linebacker-wide, propped at various angles on metal rods impaled in glass bases. Calling Vlad in aisle three.

They wore a chorus line of sequins and feathers, but then you noticed many long fingers were broken off. A casserole dish on the display case held a serial killer's assortment of painted, truncated knuckles and fingernails.

Despite air-conditioning, a miasma of dust and stale cigarette smoke hung invisibly over every inch. I wanted to sneeze just looking at the crowded landscape.

"Looks unpromising here," Temple said in low tones I had to stoop to hear. "The stuff on the racks farther in is what we're going for."

I nodded, thankful I didn't need to concern myself with a bikini bottom trailing a peacock tail's worth of dust-choked ostrich feathers dyed turquoise and yellow and red, nor the matching towering headdresses.

We wended our way back into the maze, around circular hanging blouse and skirt and pants racks and taller long dress racks. Amongst them we spotted, but did not attract the mutual attention of, a sad beagle-faced man reading a thick, yellowed paperback book.

"Can you say creepy?" I whispered to Temple.

"That's why I brought you for protection. I've wanted to explore this place for years."

She darted off to page through the racks, returning with an armful of short items that looked like kiddie clothes.

"Um, we are looking for something for me to *wear*."

"Workout and dance wear is mostly two-piece nowadays. Come on, I'll find a dressing room."

I would never have found one because of mistaking it for a clothesline, like they still had in Kansas. Two sheets on a rope bridged a concrete block corner. Beyond it, was an old wooden chair and an unframed long mirror leaned against the wall.

A hand with long red fingernails shot through the slit in the sheets. "Try these. If you want an opinion, I'll hop inside when you're dressed." Temple's oddly disembodied hand pinched the sheet gap closed.

"I see why it takes two to manage a private try-on," I said.

"I concentrated on smoky silver-gray with a hint of green for the colors, so you can *imply* the Green Fairy without going overboard. You'll be a blank slate for the costumers and choreographers to work their magic on."

"Good idea, I'm sure," I grumbled. "Why does this top have eight crisscrossing straps, like a bra for an octopus? You could strangle yourself getting it on. Oh. *Oops.* Maybe she did."

"It's the style, besides the name of the magician is Spell*binder*. There's a lot of bondage and captivity in most magic acts."

"Can I say 'creepy' again?"

"Max never did that." Temple thrust in an arm for collecting my rejects. Great to have a girl guard at a split-sheet dressing room curtain. I'd never had a gal pal, except Irma.

Back to Max. Where we both kept going. Old Blue Eyes without perfect pitch.

"Good for Max," I said, "but he's not the magician I'm trying to work for."

"No? You're working for him already."

"Not being paid. I work for satisfaction. I want to find out who killed Celeste and how and why. It's so sad she had no family or friends."

Temple's soft laugh stirred the flimsy sheet. "And just how is she that different from you?"

We're stronger, Irma said.

Lame, though, to have an invisible friend at my age.

Hey, I do a lot. Take the twisty, strappy top. And the skirt bottom with the cascading ruffle. It'll cover your butt and that's what you want when you're going aerial and undercover.

I thrust the clothes through to Temple this time.

"Okay. Not bad. Let's move on."

I stood by while Temple did her thing at the cash register. She shifted the slinky garments through her hands like she was evaluating cleaning rags. She pouted in indecision. She looked into her tiny rainbow-striped coin purse, flashing a wad of one-dollar bills.

By then Paperback Snoozing Man was droopy lidded.

She asked for the "best price," sighed, and said, "Oh, all right."

We stood outside in the sunlight, holding recycled chain-store plastic bags, inhaling the just-ironed fresh and starchy desert air deep into our lungs.

"Twelve bucks," I said. "You're quite an operator."

She handed me the bag containing my audition costume. It wasn't heavy. "Let's hope you're 'quite an operator' too."

38
Wash, Dry, and Repeat

Our last stop was the hair salon.

I relayed Max's hairdo description to the fashionably coifed stylist and was smoothly moved from station to station and process to process. This new show pony emerged with mane washed, dried and braided, and hooves polished.

All the while, my mind was on the audition and my undercover role. I'd investigated people and situations for Perry Mason, after all, and partnered with ex-FBI agent Ricardo Montoya taking down demon drug lords trafficking in zombies. If I found this Vegas weirdly off-kilter and possibly kinder and gentler than my usual hunting grounds, plenty of crime and punishment still abounded here. Clearing myself and nabbing a killer would be an excellent start to becoming a "normal" rather than paranormal investigator, if anything in any version of Las Vegas had ever been normal.

Still, imagine me, Lilah Lane, aka Delilah Street, un-adopted orphan and Las Vegas paranormal detective, sitting with Temple Barr under the elaborate skylights of the Crystal Phoenix Hotel's Crystal Court restaurant, everything light and bright and clean and sparkling. And perfectly normal through and through.

Except for having murder and Max on our minds.

"How did you and Matt meet?" I asked as we continued to talk while holding unread menus.

"He moved into the Circle Ritz, into the apartment just above me, as a matter of fact."

"That was after Max Kinsella moved out."

"Skedaddled, is the word," Temple said sharply. "We should figure what to order."

"Good idea." I looked down at fancy cursive lettering that was hard to decipher. "There's more to that 'skedaddling', I take it."

Temple sighed. "I guess I'll order the same old favorite."

"Are we talking Max or menu?"

"Look. He left so abruptly to protect me. And it turned out some thugs were on his trail. And Molina was after them both."

She looked up from the menu to me, and blinked. "Say, that new hairdo gives you such an elegant, regal look."

I patted the crown of braids. "Queen La-de-da Lilah, that's me. All the better to win a chance at replacing a murder victim."

"You don't seem scared."

"I dumped 'scared' before I hit puberty and had real reason to be."

"You have to admit Max knows his theatrical effects."

"He assured me the Absinthe act was all special effects. That the Green Fairy mostly spun on a rope and was pulled up and down. No death-defying stunts. More like a mobile chorus girl. I can't believe he himself took that huge dive into the Abyss twice nightly. Guess he paid for it."

"How much else did he tell you?" Temple sounded miffed. I'd forgotten Max had been…what? Her first great, if not first, love.

"Did he take you from the apex down with him on a bungee dive?" she asked.

I nodded, reluctantly.

She winked at me. "Quite a rush, isn't it?"

"Ladies?" a youthful male waiter had appeared at our table. "Something to drink before ordering?"

We eyed each other, rueful.

"Could you give us another minute?" Temple shrugged. "We've been talking too much."

He nodded and waltzed away as silently as he'd arrived.

"The service here is really discreet," I said.

"You want a cocktail? Something light and girly? In honor of our successful shopping expedition."

"Girly is a first for me."

"Drinking girly or shopping with a girlfriend?"

"Both."

"That's it! Cosmopolitans all 'round, my friend."

"You're amazing," I found myself saying. "I don't know why you and Max didn't work out."

Whoops, Irma said. *We don't do 'girl talk'.*

She was right. What was coming over me? Was I channeling lonely, disconnected Celeste?

Luckily, the waiter returned swiftly, we ordered—Temple's "same old" was a Cobb salad, and I went for chicken Caesar, which sounded like a cowardly Roman emperor, come to think of it—and then we talked business. Men.

"First, no way can I fool Snow at the audition that I'm not me," I said, "no matter how redone I look. I'm counting on him taking perverse enjoyment in employing the person who inadvertently 'pranked' his show."

"And this, ah, dissonance between you isn't personal?"

"As far as I can remember, which is not reliable, no. I hope I can sleep on these braids, because the audition is tomorrow."

"Let's toast then," Temple said with raised cocktail glass, "to your success and being *careful.* The murderer is likely connected to the show."

As we clicked wide glass rims, I spied something suspicious in the beds of lavish greenery woven through the luncheon tables.

"This is a strong drink," I said after the first swallow.

"Shouldn't be," Temple said.

"Well, looking over your shoulder, I'm seeing double."

She turned, looked left and right, and up to the spectacular ceiling.

"Down," I said.

She looked to the ground level and a profusion of elephant ears plants.

"You're not seeing double, Lilah. It's Midnight Louie and his, uh, associate. Louie sort of owned the Crystal Phoenix and grounds until this longer-haired black female stray showed up, and stayed, also fed by the hotel's star Asian chef. Louie took umbrage and visits only occasionally, so we…Nicky and Van and the boys named the new mascot Midnight Louise. We almost never see them together now."

"Really? That Mr. Midnight showed me the way out of a tight corner. Here's a toast to Midnight Louie and his kitty clone. Too funny. A cat snit over hotel residency. And they're so cute together."

Glasses clinked and lunch began, but the cats had vanished by the next time I looked for them.

After I finished a delicious Caesar salad, which name now had a darker connotation for me, Temple snatched a black charge folder from the advancing waiter.

"Temple, I, um, will pay you back for the clothes and lunch and pay for the shiny nude color tights you copped, er, borrowed from the Four Queens dressing room when I get a job."

"When you get the Green Fairy job," Temple said with a smile. "Don't worry! The Four Queens have dozens of extra chorus-girl pantyhose at all times."

"And here I'd sworn not to wear pantyhose ever again when I came to Vegas."

Temple giggled. "You're breaking that rule big time! Forget money. The Phoenix was my biggest public relations client before Matt and I got the TV show gig, and I can comp anything here for life."

"Comp?"

"All charges are on the house. Complementary."

"You could do some heavy gambling with that."

"I don't believe in luck, so I don't gamble."

"What about gambling on me?"

"Lilah, you are so darn…interesting I consider you a tutor. You know, when I first met Max, I secretly envisioned myself in bustier, heels and fishnet stockings as his assistant. He explained to me petite assistants make the tricks look more suspicious than with bigger women squeezing into small spaces. Also, he didn't use visible assistants in his act."

I nodded. "He had Men in Black behind the scenes like the Six Deadly Sins."

"So did Houdini. And Max used no animals but doves."

"Gosh, Max is a pacifist compared to Christophe and his man-eating tiger."

"Not exactly." Temple signed the bill and stopped the conversation on that ambiguous answer.

I couldn't help feeling I'd been taken to lunch by Mother, not that I'd ever had one. Temple had been so gracious and fun, part of her job, I suppose.

"By the way," Temple said, as we left the restaurant behind, "we'll be picking up a freshly groomed Achilles when we leave."

I stopped cold. "No! How?"

"A Fontana brother collected him from Electra and he's been getting a beauty treatment at our dog salon at the rear of the hotel while we've been girly at the front."

"I'm amazed." I felt near tears, which was a place I fight not to be.

She took my arm. "You should be amazed. It's a surprise."

By now Temple and I had walked the relatively short distance to the main entrance and stood under the hotel's dazzling canopy of light and refraction.

Two parking valets were panting to drive our presumed cars around from the garage, but Temple fended them off with the news we were awaiting a ride.

We were distracted by honking and jerky maneuvering among the cued-up cabs. These days, cabs weren't the long-used blue or yellow low sedans, but tall, hulking SUVs you couldn't see over or past, and so high that kids and seniors could barely crawl into them.

A pair of polished chrome bumper bullets slowly hove into view like the prow on a majestic ship of the line, drawing wolf whistles from valets, bellboys herding luggage carts and male passengers ignoring wives and girlfriends.

Dolly glided into sight, low and long and black, and as sleek as my newly named Abyss's exterior sheathing, top down and the seats occupied by four, no *five* Fontana brothers, two in front—one to drive and one to ride shotgun holding a dazzlingly white and fluffy Achilles—and three shoulder to discreetly padded shoulder in the back.

That was when the wives and girlfriends started wolf whistling. Last came an Albino Vampire-colored stretch limo with *Rides to die for by Gangsters* emblazoned in black on one side door.

I couldn't help giggling. I just couldn't stop it. This was a pop-up parade with my glamorous vintage used car the lead float. I was giddy with laughter that was three parts surprise, relief and hysteria. I was reminded of the slowly descending hot air balloon in *The Wizard of Oz* film drawing the crowd's awed attention.

The wizard—driver—put Dolly in Park and came around to present me with the keys on a sparkly chain.

"Better than new, Miss Lane. Special alarm. A gnat couldn't land on it without triggering World War Three."

It started pouring Fontana brothers as the clan opened doors and surrounded Temple and me like a pastel Ermenegildo Zegna picket fence. Offered arms wafted me around to the driver's seat, which I found had been left in my ideal position. Surely some lush, corny music was playing somewhere like those angel-on-earth fantasy Forties movies that still merited annual reruns as Christmas classics.

Achilles was almost escaping Fontana arms to slather my face with happy dog kisses, as Aldo, or maybe Ernesto, gently but firmly contained him.

"We'll follow you home," Armando said, shutting the heavy wide door on me and loading my shopping bags into the back seat.

"Home." To the Circle Ritz. Home. I almost choked up like Dorothy. After all, we were both misplaced Kansas girls.

Armando nodded to the hotel doors and the cheering crowd.

Julio (I think) was shutting the driver's door of Temple's Miata. She waved from her much lower position and pulled out in front of Dolly.

I put my arms out to embrace and claim Dolly's giant pizza-sized steering wheel. No puny wheel-cover-sized steering wheel would move a 1957 Cadillac Eldorado Biarritz. It took muscle to maneuver all that massive metal.

How good it felt easing the foot pedal into that familiar slow, steady acceleration. So our makeshift automotive show headed down the long driveway to the Strip. All I was missing was Quicksilver riding shotgun. And Ric waiting for me at the Enchanted Cottage behind Hector Nightwine's mansion.

39
Dishing Lilah Lane

Miss Midnight Louise and I grab a quick under-the-table consultation near our two lunching ladies.

"Did you hear that?" I ask my long-lost daughter, Miss Midnight Louise, as we watch. "New tenants at the Circle Ritz. A girl and her car."

Actually, Louise was never lost, but I did not recognize her, at least as my daughter, until she had proved herself as my assistant. So even before the Me, Too age, I had to found Midnight Investigations, Inc. and make her a full partner.

You will kindly observe that my business name specifies no gender or species or marital status, although I confess I cannot change my old-fashioned manners, taught to me with nail and claw by my own clowder boss and mama, Ma Barker, of using honorifics in address.

"So," I ask Miss Midnight Louise, "what do you think of the new dame in town, whom I rescued from the Lobos biker gang?"

"She is strapping enough to rescue herself, I think. Even your precious Miss Temple has Big Cat grit, despite her dainty size."

"I could say the same for you, Louise."

"Hmm, you must want something." Yet she preens, shaking out her heart-shaped luxurious black ruff and running her nails through it before continuing. "From what you have told me of your latest case, which you stumbled over in the company of Miss Lilah Lane, she is returning to the scene of the crime to gather evidence. She would be better off maintaining her role of suspect and avoiding exposure both professional and personal."

I swallow a sigh. "I will have to shadow and herd her, as usual. She is truly a Babe in Toyland. And she has an unfortunate liking for the canine kind."

"They are often silly and dependent, but sometimes useful," she agrees. "So, you need the Circle Ritz covered while you hound the footsteps of our large-footed lady."

Miss Midnight Louise raises a petite paw and smoothes it with her tongue, then runs it over her eyebrow hairs. She is a trifle vain.

I, being just a plain American domestic shorthair, come with a neat, plush all-over buzz cut. I do not have ruffs, but some discernable ridges, like the snack chips called Ruffles. If anyone is inclined to call me "Ruffles" because of that, he or she will find Free-to-Be-Feline kibble clogging the kitchen sink. My Miss Temple has drunk the Kefir and is on a health kick that makes it not safe for me to eat and drink the dedicated offerings in her and Mr. Matt's snazzy new two-story condo at the Circle Ritz.

Midnight Louise is still mulling doing solo duty at the Circle Ritz while I investigate at the Hellfire. "Speaking of canines, what will I find in residence?"

"You may recall Scotch and Soda from our most recent case here at the Crystal Phoenix. Bluff, hearty active boys who were a tad resistant to direction—"

"Stubborn as a sore toe," she interjects morosely.

"This is a different breed, discovered in the Asian mountains in the nineteenth century, cousin to a Tibetan terrier—"

"Terriers are terrors, harriers, digger dogs. I well remember that Scottie and Westie combo." Her ruff shudders to the feathered black tips. "I should get hazardous duty pay for herding one. What are the particulars?"

"Name of Achilles."

"Like the human heel?"

"I prefer to think of the ancient Greek hero."

"Who thinks of ancient Greek heroes these debased days? So. Same size and weight as the Scottish twain?" she asks.

"Yes, but…"

"'Yes, but' are the two most wishy-washy words of tongue and pen."

"…but more elevated, spiritual."

"Oh, slap a rabies shot on me now! You mean like Karma, the so-called Sacred Cat of Burma—more like the scared Cat of Burma—reincarnated as a New Age dog?"

"The times require us to be more broad-minded, Louise. Achilles is a Lhasa Apso, a refugee from ancient Tibet, which has been ravaged by outlanders. Plus, he is a darn good little ankle chewer."

"Oh, very well. I will babysit this martial arts, mystical Kung Fu type while you maintain your guide duty with his companion. I doubt you will inspire her to a more favorable view of *our* mystical breed."

"You might be surprised, Louise."

"That is an even more foreboding statement," Miss Midnight Louise grumbles as she grooms her toe hairs before we head back to the Phoenix entryway, where she will have to find public transportation to the Circle Ritz.

I'm shocked to find the ladies who lunch have passed on second Cosmopolitans and are no longer at the restaurant table. *Holy Hot Elvis!* We must catch up to find where they go.

We slither and slink though potted plants and dark-colored pants to arrive at the main entrance to find a buzzing crowd blocking our way.

Enduring murmurs of "Oh, look, how cute, kitty cats looking for a ride", we work our way to the front row. A huge black car surrounded by Fontana brothers is pausing in the driveway, purring throatily, like a femme fatale in a noir film.

How I love Miss Lilah's ride! It is the biggest car I have ever seen outside of a stretch limo, and the black convertible top is down to showcase the most indecent, succulent swath of channel-sewn crimson leather to honor a mid-century modern car showroom.

Oh, my throbbing nose, my itching dew claws and shivs!

There, in the passenger seat, sits a creature wearing a long platinum silver wig from its perky topknot to its painted toe nails. Achilles has gone boy toy.

Armando Fontana is stepping up to Miss Lilah Lane with a keychain while his brothers cluster around like a wall of *Vanity Fair* models.

"Your ride, Miss Lane," Armando says as she steps forward to take the keys. "All botoxed and buffed and in A-one condition"—

only *I* have ankle-rubbed close enough to hear the last part—"and you appear to have had an enticing remodel yourself."

He must be referring to her oddly knotted and twisted head hair.

"Thank you…Armando, is it?"

"At your service."

"I hope Achilles wasn't too much trouble."

"Not a bit. We dropped him off at the Phoenix groomers and he is now bathed and trimmed and accompanied by a shopping bag of treats and toys, including four highly consumable high-heeled leather shoes donated by the Phoenix's Four Queens chorus girl act. If you should prefer to wear them, you may add them to your wardrobe instead of Achilles' menu."

"But that would make me almost six feet tall."

"Yes," said Armando, bowing and inclining his head to Miss Lilah Lane's.

"I can see your point," she answers, pretty in pink cheeks as she turns quickly to her reclaimed car and dog.

"Thank you all so much," she said, opening her arms to the entire crowd, which now includes Nicky and Van. "From Dolly and me and Achilles."

It is a moment touching enough to put a lump in a giraffe's throat, but something butts my shoulder.

"Outa the way, Pops. My ride to my Circle Ritz assignment is here and I gotta make like a rug on the floor of that classic car and get to work. *Ciao*."

That is the last I see of her in this mob.

That girl does have primo sleuthing potential. Both of them.

40
Three Women in a Bar

How amazing to return to the Hellfire Hotel the next day—after exotic Retro Ragland and then the Crystal Phoenix elegance yesterday—and see the Wicked Wormwood Bar had customers in Bermuda shorts and designer tennis shoes seated at the vintage café tables, bare knees knocking the undersides of oaken tabletops.

"Isn't this amazing?" I asked Temple, who was escorting my made-over self to the theater area where I'd be trying out shortly for the Green Fairy role.

I remembered the attraction was scheduled for a soft opening, not ballyhooed, but serving anyone who bellied up to the Belle Epoque bar.

The fully populated Cinsim cast of characters took my breath away. Figures in black-and-white and the ever-popular gray skin tones sat at the tables, staring into absinthe glasses holding the signature liquor in living poison-green color.

The celebrity impersonators wore clothing from the 1890s, most obvious with the women as usual. I identified Edgar Degas, Vincent van Gogh, Oscar Wilde, and a snowy-haired Mark Twain even, in his signature white suit. Also an Englishman slouching down at a corner table, wearing checkered caped greatcoat, and a slouch hat. The women, corseted and stately, remained standing, skirts sweeping the wooden floor, elaborate bustles draped at their rears like waddling goose derrieres, bonnets tilted coquettishly down over their eyes.

One caught *my* eye. Her lavishly curled and coifed hairdo was of the period, yet she was wearing a white 1970s pants suit with a lacey ascot cascading from the neck and dainty white lace-up Cuban heels, and smoking a petite brown cigar. Plus, she was beyond gorgeous and had attracted a circle of the guys in Bermuda shorts.

I had to go up and even the odds.

"Your ensemble is gorgeous, but rather out of period, isn't it?"

"Au contraire, my dear. My great friend, Sarah Bernhardt, wears such 'walking out' men's clothing when she sculpts her large art pieces, for much more freedom of movement than corsets and heavy skirts layers provide. And we two walk the streets of Paris in them, for a lark. Please do not call us 'streetwalkers', though."

"I didn't know the great actress sculpted."

"Like many creative women, Sarah is talented in more than one art form."

"And you're not drinking absinthe," I commented.

"So last century, don't you think?"

Her fluttering eyelashes mocked my observations.

"Actually, the last *two* centuries," I said. "This is the 21st century. Frankly, I'm waiting for Flash Gordon to check in any second."

"Who's the guy in the corner with the pipe and the top hat?" Temple, who had followed me, wondered. "He looks familiar."

"A private consulting detective. Do you need one?" the woman asked. "Irene Adler, songbird and diva detective," she announced in a clipped Bette Davis way. "Here in Paris by way of London and New York. I may suit better."

I waved a spider web of smoke away. "Actually I *am* an investigator of sorts myself, and I've had my fill of other people's mysteries. I have enough of my own."

"Me too," Irene said and winked.

My movie-mania head was swimming. Irene Adler was an American opera singer and actually *"The* Woman" to Sherlock Holmes, the only woman to outwit the legendary detective. In the 1880s!

"What film did you star in?" I asked, knowing of none.

She laid her smoke down in a bar ashtray announcing Hellfire Hotel around the ceramic edge. "A good question. I'm really just hired help, but my true self starred in a famous, fabulous 'lost' film of the cinema world."

"*Metropolis*?" Temple asked behind me. I knew the 1927 Art Deco silent film masterpiece had been salvaged and now basked in the limelight it deserved.

"Star? Oh, my dear, no," Irene said. "I was an underpaid and underappreciated second banana to some overrated Brit actor playing Sherlock Holmes."

"There have been several such film roles since," I said. "And distinguished American actors playing Sherlock Holmes as well."

"But not distinguished actresses playing me?"

I thought of Morgan Fairchild's abominable caricature of Irene in some TV movie and remained silent. Gayle Hunnicutt was my favorite.

Irene Adler went on. "I, like Sarah, appeared on film. The silent film of *Good Night, Mr. Holmes* is still lost to early cinema history, but, fortunately, acting wasn't my main art form, and that early experiment didn't dash my operatic career. Divas of my time would perform with brooches and bracelets and rows of precious diamonds and pearls affixed to their costumes to boast of the wealth of their lovers. I prefer to be mistress of no one but myself. I still debuted at La Scala in the title role of *Cinderella*, wearing a magnificent diamond necklace *loaned* to me by the American jeweler, Mr. Tiffany. He and I relished the publicity and he was thankful for my finding some 'lost' historical gems he hired me to locate. It was an alliance of business man and business woman, nothing more. And most successful for us both."

I noticed Temple nodding at me as she eyed my glamorous new acquaintance. "I couldn't help overhearing about the Tiffany necklace incident, Miss Adler. It reminds me of the greatest publicity 'hound' of your century, P. T. Barnum. Publicity is my game too."

I agreed. "Free advertisement for Tiffany and publicity for you, and everyone involved upright and ethical. No Me Too moments."

Irene Adler looked confused but smiled at our praise. "Self-enterprise does have its drawbacks. The other women in the cast put ground glass in my dressing room rouge pot. However, I didn't need or use that artifice and left the engagement with my complexion uncompromised and my name and reputation on the rise, all without ever having to go *tediously* horizontal."

"And then?"

"Then 'The Man' got all the film roles and recognition, ad infinitum."

She took a delicate drag on her cigar and blew smoke down the line of gloomy noted and notorious gentlemen at the bar huddled over their absinthe glasses.

Temple sent a dainty hand clap after Irene Adler as The Woman moved back deeper into the bar to nod at the man in the top hat.

"I love these celebrity impersonators," Temple told me as we walked toward the outer tables. "The actors really study their periods and subjects. Irene Adler was indeed the only woman to outwit Sherlock Holmes, and she's given me a really good clue for *our* situation.

"What if the Green Fairy murder motive was out-and-out professional jealousy, nothing personally motivated?"

"Interesting angle," I agreed.

We sat at a table for eight for those who wanted to watch the absinthe bar like a living drama. A Vegas soap opera, so to speak.

"We hopeful Green Fairy auditioners are not supposed to linger near the bar," I told Temple. "Weird because my face would never show in that Green Fairy stunt, thank goodness, even if I got it. But the place is already thronging with women candidates, and they tell me some were in the first auditions with Celeste."

"How soon is the audition? I see you're wearing some of our shopping booty and your hair remains perfect.."

"Thanks. I didn't sleep much. In an hour."

"Speaking of ground glass in the facial cosmetics, what's the jealousy quotient among the women who are auditioning for the second time?"

"Celeste was certainly a fish out of water, and the general feelings that she got the part ranged from resentment to shrugs."

"Suppose this is a case of 'The Ground Glass in the Rouge Pot'? Another performer sabotaging Celeste. How could it be done?"

"With absinthe so present, poison, I suppose. Yet the liquor is safe now. Possibly any date rape drug?"

"Too effective too fast. With 7:00 and 10:00 p.m. shows, it'd be difficult to control. Pros don't drink before shows."

"Celeste was not a pro."

"One thing, those anonymous 'Sixes' are like those Spy vs. Spy black crow cartoons. Anybody could be inside those burglar body stockings and I try not to ever forget that."

"Good." Temple leaned near and put a hand over mine. Her earnest gaze drilled into mine. "Remember, those body stockings cut both ways. You are among friends, whether you know it or not."

"That's what Celeste thought. Apparently erroneously."

She didn't have an answer.

41
Trying, Very Trying

Another word for "Audition" is "Try-out". Emphasis on the word "Try".

So here I was, heading into the Hellfire's bright, crowded, noisy heart, darting in and out past gamblers who preferred to sit at slot machines or stand at more expensive table games when I was going to have to fly shortly.

Chorus girls' dressing rooms always look like Henry the Eighth is alive and well and still collecting wives and heads. That's because a long shelf runs under the high ceiling with featureless female heads holding the elaborate headdresses that give Las Vegas showgirls shoulders and necks of steel.

We wannabes came trooping in, jeans- and jeggings-dressed women in loose tops, huge tote bags slung over our shoulders like Santa's toy sack. Light street makeup-made faces an almost blank slate, so we looked more like a militia on the move. I'd seen "off-duty" showgirls before, hair in messy knots and ponytails, faces shiny from makeup remover, hurrying to all-night grocery stores to get home to husbands and kids. So I knew how to blend in with this group.

The occasional exception—a woman wearing bright eyeliner and shadow and heavy lipstick to the audition—would be frowned upon as a vulgar, attention-seeking "amateur". Me being new to the "profession" and unknown was bad enough.

We coagulated clot-like in the long hall of dressing rooms.

"Ladies," an unseen male voice resonated from the dressing room receivers, "welcome back. Most of you know the drill. You've been given a card on which to write your name, age, specialty, agent and contact information. Take a number from the large plastic container and leave your information sheet with the gentleman sitting at the table. File into the dressing rooms to change into your rehearsal clothes. You'll be called to audition in groups of three by the chit numbers."

A booming gold rush of athletic women to the big jar with numbers quickly reversed course in the scramble to grab places in the long line of dressing rooms. What a relief. My number was 14, so I'd be in the fifth group.

Gym Class Confidential, Irma trilled like an old movie "Coming Attraction" announcement. *Thirty flirting, fighting, feisty babes, all after fame and fortune and the dangerous dudes who may be gentleman friends…or fiends."*

I attached myself to a knot of twenty-somethings coming unraveled as they sped back and forth. Celeste had been twenty-eight and might have done the same thing when she auditioned.

In the first dressing room I could enter that wasn't full, I grabbed an empty wooden chair, cozied up to the mirror lit by a frame of small bright bulbs and slammed my tote bag to the tabletop to claim the spot.

A huge aluminum bucket of energy drinks on ice was soon emptied. I snagged a can but figured my beginner's nerves were all the "pseudo-speed" I could handle.

"What a mob," I remarked to a woman next to me.

"You should have seen the first audition call," she answered, flashing a lightning glance at all the heads and legs around the room. "Mostly runners-up here. The ones who almost made it. They think."

"You?" I asked.

"Yeah." Her fingers spread out an array of combs, brushes and makeup. "Raven," she identified herself with a nod, probably citing a nickname. Her sculptured dark bob was blacker than mine and accented with feathered purple-pink highlights.

"Lilah." I spilled out the meager contents of my cosmetic bag to establish sisterhood. "Kind of queasy, though, the thought of replacing a dead girl. Isn't anyone here worried that might become a habit?"

"Listen, a second chance in Vegas is rare. And a gig as Green Fairy Girl in a major show like Spellbinder is even rarer." She stood and hoisted a stocking-clad leg and strappy high-heeled sandal on the chair seat. Her long fingernails teased the shiny showgirl panty hose tauter up her seemingly endless legs. "You get a little star with your name on it on the posters and in the show program."

Raven grabbed the pantyhose waist. A little jump pulled them even tauter. She glanced at my legs.

"Those sheer smoke-patterned leggings are cool."

"Or varicose veins," I joked. "I took a vow never to wear pantyhose again when I hit Vegas and its desert heat. Do I need spike heels to compete?" I eyed my Max-approved laced-up ballet slipper flats.

"You could be more competitive taller, but who knows? Something as simple as an eye or nail color could make the difference, and you'll never know it."

"What made Celeste the winner last time?" I idly rolled the different tubes in front of me. My Black Irish coloring gave me eyebrows and eyelashes that didn't need emphasis from a mascara wand. I had a reason to be suspicious of mirrors. Delilah Me used to see an unexpected twin sister, Lilith, in mirrors.

And with my pale skin, even soft shades of lipstick seemed pasted on. During my cosmetic self-evaluation, I was startled to realize that had I been born Latina, my coloring mimicked that of homicide cop Carmen Molina.

Raven studied my face. "For instance, your using green contact lenses would be a plus for casting directors thinking 'Green Fairy' and 'absinthe,'" she said.

"But my eye color wouldn't show in the illusion all the way up on stage."

"Still, they'd help your name and image stick in casting directors' minds."

"Little details like that get performers roles?" I shook my head. "What was Celeste's coloring?"

"Brown and brown," Raven shrugged. "So blah. So Midwest. Some directors like a bland canvas. There are always no-prescription color contact lenses."

"Did Celeste ever really fit in here?"

Raven straddled her chair to take weight off her feet. "Now that you mention it. No. Like you don't really fit in. This is your first tryout, isn't it?"

"Yeah. My car crashed getting into town. Everything I own was in it. People I hardly know have been helping me out."

"Funny. With Celeste, it was the same thing. Unlike you, she also had this sad, little girl lost vibe, I guess. When she…died, I thought it was an awful shame. I sensed she didn't have her life together, through no fault of her own."

"So she wasn't a pro. And she wasn't a naïve hopeful?"

"Oh, she was Naïve with a capital *N*. And timid. Really didn't have the *See Me!* attitude for this work. They even made an exemption for her, so she could have a purse pooch in the dressing room. Someone said it was an emotional service animal."

"What kind of dog?"

"A little black yappy Chihuahua-mix thing. We had a betting pool going on what other breeds could be in there. Pomeranian, some said. One of the Six thought Schipperke, a Belgian breed. Celeste didn't care. She called it Arthur. *King* Arthur and dressed it in purple plush socks. Even had a little crown for it, and a 'King' in rhinestones name tag along with its rabies and other collar tags."

"That dog would be hard to miss."

Raven rolled her eyes. "So over the top. But maybe, poor girl, it was all she had. Never talked about a boyfriend. Never talked about much."

"Was she hard up for money?"

"Probably. All we gypsy dancers are, but sometimes the pay is sweet. And it's better than stripping. Not as profitable, but better for peace of mind and body. Celeste hit the jackpot when she won the tryout. Everybody was jealous when she got the job. She was only okay. I didn't think she was the best, but she'd definitely had a gymnast past. Gymnasts do one here-I-am moment at the end of their routines. Stage performers are 'on' like a neon light all the time."

"That's not needed inside that swirling smoky gas concoction that fills the Absinthe tube."

"A knockout figure is, and she sure had that in spades. Gymnast lean is for the birds in that routine. I have a theory." Raven leaned toward the mirror. Her lashes needed mascara and she caked it on. "Every girl is born with either a great face *or* a great body. In my case, great legs."

Raven leaned back in her fragile wooden chair and kicked her right leg almost straight up onto the table.

"Amen to that."

"The 'men' is the important syllable." Raven arched her foot in its stiletto-heeled black patent shoe, shiny like her nude-color tights, shiny like lip gloss and shiny like plastic.

"From what you said earlier, did Celeste have some secret Sugar Daddy looking out for her?"

"She came and went to and from the theater real fast. Didn't stick around to gossip, for sure. Every night a Six would escort her out to get a ride home."

Raven lowered what some circles would call a "gam", and pursed her lips. "I don't know. She sure got all the 'exceptions', all the breaks here, except the dying part. I don't know if someone was looking after her, or just plain *after* her."

"Not Christophe?"

When she stopped hooting with laughter, Raven frowned. "No. Odd guy; sexy as hell, but all business around the girl assistants." Raven paused, then said, "You know what bothers me about Celeste's death?"

"What?"

Is this it, girlfriend? The killer clue?

Hush, hush, Irma, so I can hear it.

"That little dog went missing after her death. Everybody forgot about it. Not Martie. She's a dog person and just doted on Arthur. *She* thought to check when things calmed down with the police arriving and all, but the carrier was empty and his leash was chewed up and left behind."

"It escaped?"

"Hard to imagine that shy little dog gnawing through a leash. Nobody heard or saw it, and it could whine up a storm when Celeste was out of her dressing room."

"Did anybody else look into finding the dog?"

"In this huge hotel, with all the secret entrances and exits from the stage and understage area to where the dressing rooms are? It would be like trying to find a mouse in Disneyland. Maybe she'd left it at home that night."

"Maybe. That's even worse! Did someone check where she lived?"

"That's the police's job. We didn't know."

"But a dog that human dependent would be lost without his companion."

"Gollee, have you got a thing for dogs like Celeste and Martie, or what?"

Or what.

Raven stopped patting on powder to keep the sweat down. "Maybe the S&M Supermodel personal assistant, Grizelle, got him."

"Does she hate dogs?"

"I don't know, but I'm sure her better half, the tiger, would have snapped King Arthur up like last night's steak if it had a chance."

"Surely the tiger's fed enough to quell its carnivore nature."

"Sweetie, carnivore natures never die."

I shivered, dramatically. I had ridden that tiger. By happenstance. And had this been the Inferno Hotel and Snow was a rock star rather than a rock-star magician, I'd have known (along with some other tipsters along the Strip) that gorgeous black Supermodel type, Grizelle, was a shapeshifter with a secret tiger in her tank.

"The Lady or the Tiger illusion is almost as great as the Green Fairy gavotte," I mentioned. "Do you ever see human Grizelle cozying up to tiger Grizelle?"

"Never. Christophe interacts most with the tiger. He has that Big Cat trained to an amazing degree. She's just a huge striped pussycat around him. I wouldn't worry if you got the job. Snow's always onstage with the Big Cat when it's on and the Green Fairy illusion is a center solo act."

"What I gotta worry about is getting the job." I held up my number. "Since you tried out, would mind telling me what to expect? I don't count on winning, but I'd still like to try my best."

"Sure, kid. There's no sense in backstage jealousy. I've auditioned a zillion times, and it's usually some fluke that puts one girl ahead of another. So no point in being a dog in the manger."

She eyed my few cosmetic bag items. "You should slather on more of the green eyeshadow. Green sells in this show. Think Grizelle tiger-green eyes."

"Thanks." I picked up my new eyeshadow, found at a small Strip shop called Chez Shezmu, and brought up the intensity. *Hmm,* lipstick. I know the range to wear with blue eyes, from Lt. Molina's Barely There Natural Maroon lip gloss to showgirl hot pink and fuchsia. But red with green unfailingly says Christmas. Not the desired effect.

I eyed the clear top of one of Raven's bandolier's worth of makeup tubes. "That lipstick black?"

She nods. "Close. Deep purple black."

And who had recently called me "Goth Girl"?

So over, that look…but… I traced a careful outline and filled it in.

"Say, kiddo, that does have a certain *pow*. That's attitude."

"Thirteen, fourteen, fifteen," the invisible announcer called.

I stood. Time to go and show off my *pow* and my ominous lips. *Wow,* Irma agreed, *ready when you are.*

42
Going Through the Motions

I linked up in the hall with a curly blonde pixie-type on spike heels and a woman with long red hair on spike heels. Talk about feeling flat-footed going to an audition.

"Hi, I'm Casey", said the blonde. "Lilah," I added. "Martie." She tossed her red hair like a horse's tail switching away flies and said, "Introductions are useless. I'll be competing after you two will be gone."

Casey and I exchanged looks. *If I can sabotage that witch, I will,* Irma vowed.

A gnawing sensation in my stomach told me Martie was probably right. At least I'd get myself into Celeste's former private dressing room later. A rack of sheet-covered costumes outside one dressing room door stood on a swath of fallen green glitter, sequins and metallic ribbon, below it, enough for me to spot small animal footprints in it. I'd be back as soon as I could to inspect *that* dressing room.

One of the Six Deadly Sins waited for us to mount ye old circular metal mesh staircase to the stage level. Guess who scampers up with the speed of a gazelle escaping Grizelle? Guess who keeps catching high heels on the pierced treads? That Max was spot-on when it came to flat-soled footwear.

Gluttony, I saw as I leaned around the Sin to view his, or her, mortal sin name on his back. Another mute, faceless Six awaited in the stage-right wing.

Behind him, the Green Fairy illusion components on the empty stage looked more mad scientist than enchanting magical moment.

Black-painted platforms and risers held a giant test tube of glass or Plexiglas about ten feet tall surrounded by an elaborate Art Nouveau web of thin gilt metal leaves and flowers. I'd seen some small exquisite private European elevator cars like that in the old silent movies I ODed on during my foster home youth.

A lone man paced the area. Terribly tall, and thin, and old, yet wearing leotard and tights that revealed ropy muscles and steel posture. An ancient ballet and aerial master, I supposed. One judge. One judge to rule them all. He held a clipboard and his bony face seemed to be pinned to his shaved skull by one arched eyebrow.

Gluttony addressed us. "I assume all you candidates have seen this illusion in person or at least on film. I hope you all have availed yourself of the dressing room water. Performers must be hydrated. Also, you must stretch at least fifteen minutes before the routine begins. Not necessary today. The audition is a simple up and down one on aerial silk, composed of minimal stretch for safety. Posture is paramount. Consider yourself as the strong, straight root of a beautiful unfolding lily on a puppeteer's string. The effects will flower and flow around you. You must maintain elegant posture throughout, whether the root spins or lowers and raises. You must keep your toes pointed at all times."

Was Gluttony a glutton for punishment?

Foot cramps, here we come, Irma whispered.

Frankly, it sounded like a life-size Barbie doll would serve as well as any one of us.

"We are not requiring you to do more than vertical moves now. You are merely to show us the simplest moves, a foot twist and a knee-lock in actual performance. When you are finally lowered to touch down on the inside of the absinthe column, you'll be ready to elevate your arms gracefully and disappear in a whirlwind of fog. That will not happen today. Only the new Green Fairy will learn that performance protocol. So today you will walk onto the stage to perform certain moves, and be asked into the offstage green room for the final selection. Or not. If not chosen, please return down to the dressing rooms and collect your belongings. Thank you for your participation."

I looked at the setup and my blood ran, raced, pulsed like ice water through my veins.

Three empty, hanging cables resembled a gallows high over the stage. Three cables dangling in a row maybe ten feet apart with a scaffold behind them. Each a different type. Each capable of swinging into the others. We'd have to mount a long set of metal ladder-like stairs against the stage wall to select our favored cable and jump off.

And that would be a race.

We three started toward the stairs, eyeing the dangling performance cables.

"Oh," Gluttony added. "Ladies wearing spike heels will kindly leave them off before they mount the stairs to the platform."

I walked right up to the stairs on my ballet flats, no longer feeling like the shrimp of the chorus line. Meanwhile, my rivals were hopping on one leg and scraping their heels together to pull their shoes off, their skimpy skirted derrières in the air. That judge didn't look derrière susceptible.

The others were racing up the stairs to push me aside. There definitely was a "first to fall off" aspect to this audition. My rivals looked like they'd had gymnastic and maybe even high wire training.

On the other hand, they hadn't gone hand-to-hand with demon drug lords along the Mexican border. I mean, of course, *demonic* drug lords, as they all were, even in this kinder, gentler Las Vegas I'd driven me and mine into.

And I suppose I could count in-tandem Abyss-diving with Max Kinsella an advantage too. Plus, I hadn't showed up to an athletic tryout in ankle-and-arch-buster silly shoes. From the film on Temple's cell phone, the Green Fairy's modus operandi of movement would be reminiscent of belly dancing. Not on my résumé but probably every girl had mocked those iconic moves from preschool to college dorm rooms. No stunning skills required here.

Still, I couldn't underestimate the others' desperate will to win.

"Grab on and climb, ladies," our watching ringmaster urged, "Pick your poison."

I had jumped several steps up the ladder first and, once on the horizontal scaffolding, rushed to embrace my bungee cord on the far end. Casey and Martie jousted each other on the stairs, with Martie grabbing the purple aerial silk in the middle and already doing flashy twists in the air that destabilized the less elastic aerial silk left for Casey on the end.

The middle silk was best for flashy, free-flying acts, Max had said, doing the splits on them fifty feet up. For going up and down with turns and frills on the way that fit the restricted space of the Absinthe tube, the lowly bungee cord, originally designed to attach tanks and Jeeps to parachutes for airdrops from military cargo planes should be able to handle Little Me.

I hoped. I was relying on a year's worth of rubber strands, 365, masquerading as an ordinary climbing rope.

Martie , next to me, gave me a wicked glance, then twisted her purple silk so her airborne splits, legs splayed like wings, swung into my and Casey's cords, forcing us to swing off-center.

I wrapped an ankle around my bungee cord and spun fast and hard, then unspun like an ice skater, straight under myself, twirling into a blur and my head sure knew it. I had once determined to learn how to "spot" like a ballerina, snapping my head out of a spin at the last possible nano-second, and that was second nature now.

While Casey and Martie tangled each other's cords, my superior height and body-weight—go, girls of stature!—kept me the still, solid center of the trio.

All three of us slowed, stopping dead center on our cords, just as the verdict was rendered.

I couldn't help glancing at Martie, with a warning. Her gaze was fixed on the judge.

We all blinked to watch Snow walk out of the wings and take the clipboard from him.

"Ladies," he said, with nods at all three.

"Casey, you are young and fairy-light, but it takes strength and experience to appear so. You are dismissed to try again another day.

"The good news, Martie, is you again produced a creative, dazzling array of amazing elasticity in your upside down splits, twirls, poses. You owned your space, and beyond.

"The good news for you, Miss Lane, is you demonstrated stability and endurance. You did what was asked. You kept your toes pointed and your head on straight. You made your marks and boundaries. You will be the new Green Fairy."

"Her?" Martie practically spat out her indignation. "You choose the dull, uninspired, untested new nobody on the scene. Again! It makes no sense. It's rigged."

"Every illusion is 'rigged', Martie. Runner-up is a good position. We're resuming The Lady or the Tiger illusion shortly, and could use you as the Lady now that Gwen is out of the picture."

I watched Martie's eyes flash on the word "use".

She pouted, then made it "pouted prettily", lifted her head imperially, shot me a venomous glance and stalked out off the stage.

Snow didn't notice. He headed to the double doors of his office, the silent judge gesturing me to follow.

I felt like the new Miss America as I strode through those doors.

Snow ignored me. He was busy sliding a pile of legal papers across the frosted glass surface of his immense free-form steel desk.

"Sit down. Sign here," he instructed without looking up as someone closed the doors behind me.

"Martie is right about me, you know," I said.

"Modesty becomes you, Miss Lane, although your magnificent new Green Fairy costume will not be."

"I'm not afraid of the Big Bad Wolf."

"That's why you won."

I set about reading the long contract, in triplicate before me.

"You can just sign. I won't change an iota of it. You don't have to read every comma and asterisk."

I gave him—his blamed noncommittal black sunglasses—my levelest glance. "I do. That's why *I* won."

43
Dotted Lines

I squinted at the even fine print paragraphs after the inserted asterisks.

The contract was about forty printed paragraphs on legal-length paper that folded three times.

Snow's super-white shiny French manicured fingernails tapped the desktop, all dead tip and no quick. "The position is for a performer, not a reader. Forty other women are swooning for this job."

"It's this nondisclosure clause. Where I swear to keep quiet about the mechanics of your 'professionally produced illusions'. I can sign on to that.

"But…'in all media invented or not yet invented and everywhere in the world and the universe for all time'. Isn't that a bit broad?"

Snow's fingernails stopped tapping. "Forty women. Sign or leave."

"Um, as you know, I'm new in town, and my car was chased by a motorcycle gang and my dog leaped out of the car to challenge them and got lost for a while, so he has separation anxiety issues, not to mention the trauma of us both fleeing fifteen Harley motorcycles. Any chance I could keep Achilles in the dressing room area? He's only twenty pounds or so."

"Grizelle does not like dogs."

"The woman or the tiger?" I smiled coyly.

"Both."

"The previous Green Fairy had purse pooch privileges."

He was silent for a moment while I reran Clint Eastwood's "Do you feel lucky?" speech from *Dirty Harry* while he was aiming a really big gun, bigger than Molina's Glock, at the downed perp's face, through the Moviola in my head.

Do you? Irma asked. *Feel lucky?*

Film directors used to scan production reels through Moviola machines in the very old days. Sometimes I thought I was a walking Moviola.

Snow was smiling. "You remind me of someone I once knew who insisted I reunite the Nick and Nora Charles 'family' of celebrity impersonators with their movie dog. Asta. Silly name."

"Did you do it?"

"Yes, and a chore it was to find the identical breed in a trained dog. Then I let another venue buy it for a five-year contract, at three times what I'd paid for the package previously."

"Guess you owe that person—*Us*, Irma shouted—thanks."

"Perhaps."

My hand still hovered over the signing line. "Why did you choose me for this job?"

"Miss Lane." He shook his head and his shimmery long white hair, probably because rolling his eyes behind those movie-star sunglasses would be counterproductive. "Being around you is like being in a Superman movie."

"You could call me Lilah."

"*Miss Lane*, dozens of women in high heels have lined up in the hot sun, standing for hours to apply for this job, this featured role, and you blow in here on your size nine flats with your dated Greek goddess hair-do and get what they all want."

"I'm always suspicious of what everybody wants."

"Then you want something else. You are nosy and annoying and you don't like me, nor do you respect what I do. Why would you apply?"

"Maybe I thought you might grow on me?"

He leaned forward to challenge me with his bug-eyed sunglasses. "But not at this close a range." I said. "Why would you hire *me*?"

"One reason?" He leaned across the desk so my reflection enlarged in the black convex lenses of those darn, affected glasses. "I thought you best evoked Celeste's slow, sinewy dance moves, like absinthe in motion, a Delilah tempting a Samson before cutting off his hair and eradicating his strength."

Delilah. I cleared my throat and my voice, and tried not to look at his long, flowing white locks.

"Like Delilah," I repeated.

"That's what I wanted." He still was in my face like a hooded cobra. His voice went low and very precise. "A woman like that Biblical temptress and man-trap, Delilah, and here you are, Lilah, in the flesh, right in front of me signing a lucrative contract with a name that's half of hers. Delilah."

Could *he* rub it in!

Nobody can say we don't shimmy, shimmy like our sister Kate in the old song now, Irma breathed.

"I take that as a good omen," I said demurely.

The comparison had finally flopped. I was pretty sure Samson wasn't a guy who'd go in for French manicures.

Snow sat back abruptly. "And because I don't want another Green Fairy dying in the show. Hiring you has a double benefit."

My turn to nod. "Either I'm nosy enough to find out the Who and the Why of the Green Fairy death…or, I might perish next. A win-win for you, clearly. I'd appreciate your delaying any formal announcement of my achievement so I can chat up folks in and around the show for a while longer without any hullabaloo. I can discreetly learn the job when the theater goes dark during the daytime. Danny Dove told me he will help. And I'll need copies of the exceedingly illegal and personally invasive forms *I* filled out for every other contender, from Celeste's group and now my own."

"The police have all that."

"I have the ears and lips of the contenders. And, believe me, you learn a lot more from a bunch of women in a dressing room than in the U.N."

I leaned forward to pick up the long black ballpoint pen with "Spellbinder" written on it in rainbow glitter. I sighed, but kept "Tacky" to myself. I didn't know whether I'd been hired or endangered, but Temple had been right to sense dissonance between the rock-star magician and me. He'd known Delilah me as an investigator in our mutually turned somewhat inside-out pasts.

As I signed, he said, "Given the risks, you can keep the damn dog, but just in the dressing room."

Yes! I'd lost Quicksilver. Achilles wasn't going to leave my side if I could help it. And not in this snake pit.

As I pushed the pen and signed contract over the desk toward him, my silver charm bracelet tinkled on the glass desktop. Not like a dog, like metal.

"Interesting charm bracelet," he commented. He leaned over to inspect it, his long wavy, white hair brushing my wrist.

A visceral shiver thrummed through me. I suddenly knew I'd gotten it in a scary, unnatural way. Unwanted, like a virus. And unreturnable. That was why there was no clasp to open and shut, and it was too tight to pull off over my knuckles.

"You gave it to me," I said before I could stop myself.

He said nothing.

I examined the charms again. Yup, the new fluffy dog face was still there along with Quick's formidable wolfish profile, and now… either a silver Tinkerbell or…the Green Fairy.

"It looks like you believe in fairies, Miss Lane," Snow said. "I hope they believe in you."

44
Stranger Danger

There was something about the words "I got a new job" that is beyond satisfying. Especially as a stranger in a strange world who could now pay the rent. Find and store food. Eat out and pay the bill. Hunker down at night alone in a safe cave.

Something so primal.

So what if I'd probably face the torture chamber from an Edgar Allan Poe nightmare at my orientation session tomorrow. What could happen to me zipping in and out of an enclosed giant glass test tube in clothing emulating nudity while suspended on Spandex bands with weird-colored gases of unknown composition flowing around me? Where another woman had died doing that trick? Forewarned is forearmed, right?

That all faded to black. Nothing, for an ex-TV reporter, compared to the mantra, "I've got a job".

Two, actually. Though Max Kinsella hadn't offered a salary yet. *Aha.* Now I had more Green Fairy auditioners' info and suspicions, and even a salary for him to match. And not peanuts either.

I took the escalator up to the Hellfire's third floor and the bridge to the attached parking ramp. All of Vegas that was not hotel-casino and pool or the occasional golf course was parking ramp or lot now. And, though less glamorous, parking made plenty of moolah too.

There was a bar (of course) before the exit to highly stacked cars, gasoline fumes, and hot, arid summer air. The Not-Hot Spot bar had cushy chairs and big round cocktail tables that could always accommodate a few more conventioneers or post-wedding parties, and all the usual suspects had plunked down in all the chairs.

I owed myself a celebratory though solitary drink, I decided. I dragged one heavy unoccupied chair to the one small round table left vacant. Getting a waitress when they were all toting trays for nine around would take time. So I took in the population and mused on why guys still wore dark business suits that screamed "over-heated" in Las Vegas. Must be hotel execs or corporate types who could never shed their power suits.

Now, look at the Fontana brothers. They had managed to have their cake and eat it too, in every color and flavor. Their pale, pastel, designer Italian suits were miracles of lightweight wool and yet showed off the guys' eternal "cool".

Thinking of them had me craving a banana daiquiri or something else summery and frothy. Then I realized a waitress was approaching my tiny table, courtesy of a dark-suited man seated at the adjacent bar boardroom contingent.

I nodded graciously at the guy and put my mind on Frothy again. "Are you familiar," I asked the thirty-something ash-blonde, "with the Fontana brothers?"

"Don't I wish."

"Well, I want something pretty but muscular, that tastes as good as their suits look."

"Huh." Her weary hazel eyes sparkled. "There *should* be a drink like that, shouldn't there? Give me a couple minutes while I clear the monster table."

"Sure." I put my cross-body flat purse on the table.

Mr. Navy Suit caught my eye again, so I nodded and mouthed my thanks.

He hefted his full wineglass with a questioning look. The table was now empty and he wanted to join me. I'd been sitting alone here for a while.

Flash evaluation. Close shave didn't banish a dark beard shadow. That sounded dangerous, but his white shirt and navy suit was as neat as a Mormon's. Probably mid-fifties, in good shape, but way too old for my style. Married with kids. Not about to be a nuisance. Safe to chat up.

He easily pushed the massive chair over and put down his wineglass. "My group folded and left just before my wine order came. At these prices…"

"I hear you."

He smiled ruefully, "I heard you mention the Fontana Brothers. They are quite a local phenomenon, aren't they?"

"I guess they're a Vegas institution. They're so gallant. Helped me out with some car trouble on the Strip."

"You a tourist?"

"Not anymore. Do you work here too?"

"No, I'm based out of town. Come here on business every so often. Not into gambling or other nonsense."

"You are a rare man."

He had confirmed my impression that he was a rules follower, not wild card. I was about to ask him what field he worked in when Hazel Eyes reappeared, bearing one drink on her plain brown bar tray that had other tables a-buzz.

The stemmed margarita glass had a glittering rock-crystal sugar rim and held brandy-rum-color booze bedazzled by a foaming white top layer. So appropriate to my new job and work environs.

"*Ooh la la.* Just what the therapist ordered. What's it called?"

"The Fontana Flip." She winked.

"What's in it?"

"Our bar guy whipped this up when he heard the name Fontana pronounced. I'm told it's a smoky, almost burnt flavor rum, 100-proof bourbon, lime juice, rum liqueur, pimento, rum syrup, some bitters and six drops of absinthe for bite. The foam on top is egg white. The egg in the mix is 'flip' part."

"*Hmm* sounds both manly and sophisticated, something a girl could sip on while dreaming of unforgettable hot- and cold-running nights of yore in Rio. I'll pay now."

I got out the cash and an almost matching tip. It doesn't hurt to have pals at the workplace.

"You must be celebrating something," wine-sipping man said.

"My new job." *Two jobs*, Irma corrected. *One above board, and how; one under the table. Just like Vegas.*

"A toast then." He raised his wineglass. I lifted my showgirl of a cocktail.

I was glad he wasn't asking about what my job was, keeping it impersonal. Nice guy. Here's to the kindness of strangers.

He chuckled as I pushed the mint garnish aside and swallowed a mouthful of potent nirvana through the straw. I knew hearing "rum" three times was a warning. My shoulders suddenly relaxed. I'd been more keyed up about this assignment than I'd let myself know.

"You've got a new career just in drinking that cocktail," he said. "Enjoy. Take it slow and sober and keep safe. Don't drive too soon."

I was amazed. I saw his wine was still almost untouched and now had a tip beside it.

"It was nice chatting with you," he said.

"Yeah. What line are you in?" Maybe he was a minister.

He paused for a second as he pushed back the chair. "Accountant. I'm an accountant." He smiled, apologetic. "Pretty dull work."

"Now that I've got a job I might need one. What's your name?"

"Bucek," he said. "Frank Bucek."

Before I could ask for a card he was swept away by a noisy group crowding into the bar and grabbing his empty chair.

I took his advice and held my own solo ground, slowly sipping my way into my mellow version of Margaritaville. Ric was there, and Quicksilver.

I had a feeling this would be my last beach party moment for a long while.

45
Molina, Molina, a Bird That Sings

Max was sitting alone at his own bar at three in the afternoon, drinking sparkling water from Baccarat crystal, and examining his black elephant building, The Abyss, according to Delilah-Lilah.

The juxtaposition of the names always amused him. One was for a seductress, one for a great-aunt, and she was neither. Must make her a bit bipolar.

Max decided he'd had enough of abysses. Abyssi?

"Nightshade" was more promising. It had the decadent touch of Absinthe without the gloomy olden-day baggage. Nightshade could be sleek, modern, whatever he wanted it to be. Better trademark the name.

Maybe he *should* hire Lilah as a manager. Then she wouldn't be risking herself in undercover work, and for what? To allay suspicion of herself. He slammed the glass down.

Now was when he really was needed in the Hellfire flies.

He started to rise, but "Boogie Woogie Bugle Boy" was being hailed.

He recognized the caller and swiped the cell phone.

"Lieutenant Molina, what can I do for you?"

"Leave town?"

"You've got that turned around, haven't you? The police usually—"

"I'm not 'the police usually'. We need a meet. You prefer Sunrise Park or Sunset Park?"

"Vegas always covers its bases, even in the matter of park locations. Sunrise. The usual picnic table?"

"Twenty minutes."

"Ah…"

"You are dressed and up doing things? Or did I interrupt your beauty sleep?"

"No. I'm just surprised. I thought those dear dead days of crisis and collusion between us were over."

She sighed. "Apparently not. Tell me your sudden new protégé is *not* hanging out at the Hellfire's Green Fairy auditions, hoping to break her head again. And tell me you don't know about it, and then we're done."

"Fifteen minutes now. I'm on my way."

With the zillion bustling attractions along the Boulevard known as "The Strip", the city's desert parks were quiet, calm and mostly hosted family groups of residents.

Max took the black Maxima from the three vehicles parked against Neon Nightmare's back service area. He smiled to recall he now had a drink named Maximum Punch named after him.

He wondered if Molina would ever be so honored.

She was waiting for him, her personal Prius parked in the small empty lot and herself a sandy-tan figure sitting on a picnic table, her loafers on the attached bench. One hand held a big Styrofoam coffee cup.

He walked up, but she was already questioning him from afar.

"How the heck did you get hooked into Miss Lilah Lane's predicament?"

"I was scouting the show for Temple and Matt and spotted the Green Fairy's body, for which I was rewarded with instant police suspicion."

"Yes, yes. But you could have let Miss Lane walk off into the, er, the Sunset…Park." Her long arm of the law made a sweeping gesture westward, where that opposite park from Sunrise lay.

He jumped up on the picnic table to sit on her non-gesturing, coffee cup side. "Something's made you grumpy today, and you're taking it out on me. Do you have a small new assignment for slightly unofficial info?"

"'Grumpy!' You don't know me well enough to diagnose my mood. How much do you know about this woman?"

He caught himself before he said, "Delilah?" He shrugged. "Lilah Lane is new to Las Vegas. Young women like her throng to town looking for something, mostly work along the glamorous Strip. You know how most of them end up. Busted and broken-hearted."

"Not this one. No. She's actually auditioning for a dead woman's role, probably tutored and egged on by you. There is so much going on here that Mr. Mystifying Max Kinsella doesn't have a clue on."

"You still have people watching the Spellbinder stage show? What about finding this missing Gwen woman? You can't deny you considered Lilah a suspect."

"Considered. Past tense. That was before I had a chat with her and my people interviewed her as a witness."

"She has a sketchy background," Max admitted, "but she also has a lot of grit."

"And wouldn't you, if you were abandoned as an infant and named for the place you were found, schooled in group homes and ran away from would-be abusers to get a job and a GED and work your way through college?"

"Dammit." Max let his shoulders slump in shock. "You *are* an ace interrogator." After a pause, he murmured, "I should have brought coffee."

"Here. You can have mine. It's cold." So was her tone.

He sipped it anyway, thinking. Molina's daughter must be graduating from high school herself in a couple years. Molina had been a single mother in a macho world for a long time. He was facing Mama Bear. Clever of Lilah to have come clean on her iffy background in a way to sway Molina. He set the cup down to prepare for verbal battle.

"So," Molina said. "Is your interest romantic?"

"In Lilah? Lord, no. We're co-members of the Cracked Head Society and she has some survival instincts, and she also was under suspicion…"

"So Kinsella and the Kid are going to smoke out a killer. New stage act, playing nightly. Only someone has already ended up dead. You need to get her out of there."

"I can't tell her what to do. She's not a quitter."

"Then I'll arrest her."

"You can't."

"Try me."

"She's already signed a contract with Christophe. She just texted me."

"Screw Christophe."

He killed a comeback to that, although the thought was mind-blowing. "Lilah's an inside woman now. She says the creepy Deadly Six Sin characters are ideally placed to have messed with Celeste's equipment, or to semi-strangle her, or drop her twenty feet, or…"

Molina's fist hit the wooden tabletop between them. The lightweight cup toppled, spreading cold, wet coffee on his thigh.

He jumped back to avoid more.

Molina was fully steamed at him, He could drown in coffee and she wouldn't throw him a donut.

"You two have forced me to tell *you* need-to-know information."

"That bad?"

"I don't know what agency you served with or what oath you took during your counter-terrorism days in Europe, but whatever that was you have to swear, to me, that you will never divulge to anyone what I'm about to tell you."

"Come on, the local fuzz aren't that uptight."

"It isn't the Metro Police. It's the FBI. It's the U.S. Marshal's office. It's military intelligence."

Max could feel his blood draining out in the still cool morning air. He got it.

"God help us," he said sincerely. "Celeste Novak, or whatever her name really is, was in the witness protection program."

"And not protected in my town, on my watch."

"Why put her in a stage show?"

"Hiding in plain sight, besides, that's what she could do. Almost Olympic-level gymnast in high school. And I don't know, but I think somebody else under witness protection or involved in the same case bolted or was kidnapped, just before things heated up around Novak and she was brought here."

Molina was vibrating with frustration. "And you and your Circle Ritz pals have been practically living at the Looking Glass Theater among a nest of assassins and secret agents from the very time of Celeste's murder on."

Max pulled out his cell phone. "We have to fix it. Lilah's got the Green Fairy gig. She just texted me on the way over. She's rehearsing and could go live on short notice."

46
Bring in the Clones

"There's no going back," Max said. "I don't care about those other agencies, like you have to. Believe me, I've been an unwanted and undetected extra on intelligence operations many times. You now have Lilah on the ground, and me underground or overhead."

"Those underground passages benefitted the murderer?"

"Maybe. Think about the Six Deadly Sins. That's how magicians cast their hidden helpers, like clones. All limber men and women about five-nine, Lilah's height."

"Not romantically interested in her, eh? I suppose you have her shoe size too."

"Temple would know. They had a recent retail-bonding expedition to get Lilah audition clothes."

Molina rolled her eyes. "What happens right under my nose. I will never understand how a clothes-spending spree cements female friendship."

"That's because you wear a uniform by day, but by night, don't kid me, you like wearing those slinky, velvet, thirties gowns when you sing the blues at the Blue Dahlia."

"That's still a secret and the same oath you swore earlier is still in force."

"So you've got a *secret,* secret pair of agents. My first role is to protect Lilah. If I…we happen on a killer, so much the better," Max said.

"The protected witness is dead. Why would the second Green Fairy be under threat?"

"I agree that's not likely. But maybe it wasn't Celeste Novak who was killed, but *whoever* played the Green Fairy."

"Oh, now you're getting too counter-espionage-y for a simple homicide cop."

He laughed. "There's nothing simple about you, to have gotten to your rank starting in the days when minorities and women were pushed to the bottom rather than the top." Max shook his head. "I could never make it in such an inflexible system."

"That's not bad. There's always some value in having a rogue element to disrupt procedure that's gone asleep at the wheel or off the rails. Not the case here. We have more cops of various stripes than robbers. I'm afraid we're going to fall all over everybody's size nine or twelve, or *five* feet."

She eyed him hard.

He gave her the answer she wanted. "I'll see nothing happens to Temple either. She's on the fringe now, thank God."

Molina sighed. "Why is it when you call or I meet with you, I always sigh?"

"You're sweet on me?" Max said with Tom Selleck waggling eyebrows. "No kidding, Lilah's a mixologist and she *almos*t named a drink for me after Tom Selleck's *Magnum* character."

"Too much information. Don't see the resemblance. Seriously, I have to spill one last forbidden fact. Again, your gonads are on the line. The coroner found ethylene glycol in Celeste Novak's body."

"Ethylene glycol. Sweet-tasting, odorless and *not* colorless unless…"

"It's found in vehicle anti-freeze. It's bright green to warn humans, but domestic pets can lap it up under the family car with irreversible fatal consequences."

"The perfect absinthe substitute," Max marveled. "I wonder. That last ingredient in Lilah's Maximum Punch cocktail was several drops of absinthe. Do you suppose she's seriously hostile to me?"

"Devoutly to be wished," Molina said. "Everybody nowadays knows the notorious historical effects of drinking absinthe are debunked. Any wormwood issue is gone. The drink is legal and safe."

"Unless it's *not* absinthe."

"Why was Celeste so overprotected in this show and on this set? From Lilah's description, she was shy, almost timid, except on the aerial cables, and needed an emotional support dog to function. She didn't seem the rogue spy type," Max said.

"Not *her*. The husband is an Army intelligence officer who had gone AWOL. Still missing, despite a multi-service task force hunting him. He had a very high security clearance involving Russians. Need I say more?"

"Suspected traitor or victim?"

"Motive not clear."

"So they embedded his wife, Celeste, in the chaos of a magic show, where everything is designed to make you realize you can't believe what you see?"

"The thought was the elaborate setup would make it easier to monitor the situation. They've had people watching her all along."

"Watching Lilah now?"

Molina nodded.

"Not fond of their track record, Carmen." He'd never used her first name before.

She recognized an emergency need to hook-up when she heard one. "Work your unofficial miracles, Mr. Magic Man. I'm still on the homicide case. I'll have detectives outside the stage area. You realize the good guys as well as the bad may get trigger-happy now that everything has gone sideways."

Max smiled and shook his head. "That's what I said to Lilah when she decided to go inside to clear herself. Maybe she can do even more."

"No way I'm approving putting a civilian in more danger, even if the spooks did it."

"I'm with you. The murder is key. How about a friendly neighborhood demo of method and opportunity? My place. Showtime at eight p.m. Might be enlightening."

"Max Kinsella. Born to bemuse." Molina shook her head. "Neon Nightmare. So well named. I'll be there. Should I dress to arrest?"

"You're always arresting, Lieutenant. Handcuffs optional."

"Fifty Shades of Blarney."

She jumped down from her picnic table throne, annoyed that he'd talked her into a vague assignation. Someday *she'd* surprise *him*.

47
Overkill

Lilah Lane, wearing a silky black turtleneck top and a white felt fedora with a black feather band, stood behind the long, sleek, black glass bar inside the Art Deco black pyramid that belonged to Max Kinsella.

Behind her on a glass shelf sat an absinthe bottle in a 3-D green skeleton face bottle. Four "customers" lined up in front of her. Matt Devine and Temple Barr, Max Kinsella and Lt. Carmen Regina Molina.

A fifth sat on the bar to her left, twitching his tail with impatience, but all else remaining as still as an Egyptian mummy cat while subtle breaths of air-conditioning tickled Lilah's black feathers into a Samba motion.

"Welcome to Nightshade," Lilah said in a sepulchral tone.

"Nightshade," Temple murmured, "I like it. *Mucho* marketable."

"And appropriate," Max added with a twist of lime in his voice, "since we're watching a poisoning in progress." His cell phone was positioned to film this.

Lilah smiled at them both. "How good that our friendly, deserted neighborhood bar will keep our experiment from the prying eyes of the public at Hellfire's absinthe bar."

Lilah gestured to the two identical glasses in front of her.

"Item: two Absinthe glasses with the one-ounce absinthe bowl on the bottom and the flaring ordinary cocktail glass upper portion.

"Here is a skull-shaped green glass bottle of Absinthe."

"I love that design," Temple said. "So spooky. The skull's reflection in the black mirror bar top is even more sinister."

"And here," Lilah tilted the bottle and poured green fluid into an empty shot glass. Then she reached under the bar top to bring up another shot glass from the well, "is one ounce of green anti-freeze fluid."

"The two shot glasses are remarkably identical and relentlessly bright green in color," Molina said.

"So." Lilah's wrist flicked that hat farther back as her silver charm bracelet chimed against a glass. She was settling into her Cabaret Host role. "I pour an ounce of each liquid into each empty absinthe glass. Then I balance the slotted absinthe spoons on each glass rim. Put a sugar lump on top. We'll skip setting the sugar lump afire, but that could be done, perhaps to distract."

She drew two small pitchers filled with a clear liquid out from under the bar top.

"As my audience focuses hard, hard enough to squint and discern the sleight of hand, I pour the frigid ice water over the sugar lump and it trickles down through both pierced spoons.

"And, presto! The 'louch' effect occurs in both glasses as the green 'absinthe' in the bottom turns milky. I could add a few more drops of green absinthe to each drink for a final kick, but that's perhaps...overkill.

"*Voila!*" Her hands haloed the two glasses, twins in every respect.

"No sleight of hand, just sleight of mind and chemistry at work."

"Miss Lane, that is amazing." Molina folded her hands on the bar, and then leaned in and down to balance her chin on them and squint at the glasses. "How on earth did you get the anti-freeze to 'louch' like the absinthe?"

Lilah did a little song and dance behind the bar. "I like-a-*louch* and you like-a-*louch* and we both like-a-*louch* the same..." She put a little shoulder shimmy into it like Carmen Miranda.

Molina seemed mesmerized for a moment, then she said, "No songs from the *Meet Me in St. Louis* movie, however adorable you were in the Tiny Tot Orphan dance recital."

Lilah chuckled and pulled up from the well a quart bottle with the word *OUZO* in script on the label.

"Ouzo, of course!" Max still looked a bit dazed from the Lane-Molina exchange. "It's a Greek liquor. Like absinthe, it contains anise, a licorice flavoring. And it goes from clear to milky in the presence of ice or cold water. So *no one* would suspect from the taste this glass didn't contain absinthe. And Absinthe newbies would be even more naïve. This killing was demonically clever."

"I imagine," Matt said, "seasoned absinthe drinkers might notice a difference, but, in my observations at the Hellfire bar, drinkers are so enchanted by the transformation ritual they concentrate on the look of it, not the taste. That reminds me of the Transubstantiation during every mass, as the host and wine are turned into the body and blood of Christ. People become absorbed in their belief system symbolized by the process."

"The same for magic acts," Max said. "It's always about transformation, from captive to free usually. Here now, gone the next millisecond."

"Like life and death," Matt agreed.

"And we're talking outright murderous trickery, in this instance." Molina eyed the faux absinthe glass, and sighed as she calculated the deadly time table. "Celeste must have taken the drink before the first show. The effects would manifest in about six hours, during the late show, starting with dizziness and progressing to delusion. It wouldn't kill her outright, but caused her fall and the fatal head blow."

She stood. "Pour both contents into the sink." She put her hand out and Max put the cell phone—hers—into her palm.

"You may have to show your act to a jury someday, Miss Lane. Most ingenious of you, and the killer. Congratulations for your solution, excuse the pun, to the ethylene glycol issue. First-class work. I'll share this with the coroner, who will do further tests and may have more comments."

Molina smiled. "And now I'm going home to savor a nice, factory-capped Dos Equis beer. Color me amber." She actually clapped Max on the shoulder goodbye. "*Adios.*"

She nodded around and her flat shoes echoed on the nightclub floor like one person clapping, very slowly and deliberately.

Lilah sighed. "What she didn't say…who, where and when."

Temple looked up from checking her cell phone.

"I confess. I don't have a clue. Pour us something safe and amber-colored too, Lilah. I'm at the end of my investigative leash, ready to kiss my PR smarts goodbye."

Matt put his arm around her. "My money's on you, Temple. You never let a phony, or a liar, or an outright killer escape your tracking-down skills. I would not want to be someone who'd done someone else wrong in your neighborhood."

"It's called being an investigative reporter," Temple said. "I follow my heart and sense of justice. And you're right. No one can slide away sideways and shut me up."

48
Werewolf Moon Rising

I must be psychic despite myself.

There I am, having modestly installed myself at the Neon Nightmare—excuse me, Nightshade Bar—as a witness to Miss Lilah Lane's socko performance at the Wicked Stepmother Gourmet Cocktail Poisoning School of No Return, when I get paged by the Empress of the Empyrean.

Ever since Miss Lilah Lane turned up in my social circle I am intercepting unwanted mental static on my keen but distant psychic circuits.

Now Karma seems to have me on instant redial.

So now I am to be hauled away from my seasoned detective peers, like Miss Temple Barr and Miss Lt. C. R. Molina, to the Circle Ritz for some crazy astrological mumbo-jumbo involving a Circle of Three calling upon the Werewolf Moon to save all our hides.

First. There are no werewolves except on late-night cable TV channels.

Second, I would not be so rash as to deny the existence of the Moon, but it is just a dead rock that had enough pedal to the metal to latch onto our unenterprising little planet and hitch a ride to obliteration in the sun some zillion years from now. (I am not a climate change denier. My personal climate gets whipped around daily by forces of nature like Ma Barker or purported immortal shamans from Shangri-La-La Land.)

In the face of that, my nine lives pale.

And I am not risking a single one on a dubious venture drawing on what Karma assures me are "savants of several species worldwide".

Bunk.

Then she tells me Punky will act as an "acolyte".

What? Contributing to the delinquency of a minor? I cannot believe Ma Barker would approve such a travesty.

I sigh, leap off the mirrored black bar as silently as a wraith and race to the parking lot to await hitching a ride to the Circle Ritz. Mr. Matt Devine's silver Jaguar seems a fitting possibility.

I am one with the black asphalt under the silver Jag, communing with the scent of forbidden virgin interior leather awaiting my imminent arrival, when I hear Miss Temple Barr's muted high-heeled approach and Mr. Matt's subtle footstep shuffle. (Everyone knows Cat Heaven is next door to Leather Limbo, where fields of owners' former footwear are there assembled for Olympian wrestling, gnawing, slashing and piercing exercise.)

I slip into the back via Mr. Matt's driver's side, not a sign of favoritism, but a bow to the fact that long pants keep my lush furred sides from betraying my presence.

Unfortunately, I am forced to eavesdrop on what I have termed "married couple event summation".

"Lilah Lane is a bit of a showman," Miss Temple comments.

"A fox with moxie."

"Matt, that's a rather slick summary, coming from you."

"I'm picking up some of your PR speak. She certainly shares Max's dramatic streak."

"Don't think he has not noticed. And for a mysterious stranger without any discernable background credentials, she seems to have won over Lieutenant Molina."

"Not a mystery. Lilah arrived in town homeless and alone, and preyed upon. Molina may be a tough cop, but she's also a Mama Bear. How is Mariah doing, by the way?"

"Molina Jr. is doing great. Hitting the touchy transition to high school like a precocious hurricane, from what little impression I get. It is hard being a cop's kid."

"Hard being a single mother," Mr. Matt said. "I had one."

Huh! Try being Ma Barker, I think. I had not considered her that way, but she is a single mother to an entire clan. Thankfully so, because she has taken in my off-species refugee and hyperactive kit.

We are soon at the Circle Ritz parking lot where I ooze out the door behind Mr. Matt and split to the lot's far side.

It amazes me that my favored humans are so oblivious to Ma Barker having cleverly set up her clowder right on top of the police substation just an oleander bush divider away from the Circle Ritz parking lot.

It is an ideal situation: secure, teeming with fast-food tidbits, and near my drop-off donation site for excess Free-to-Be-Feline kitty health kibble to counter the unhealthful burger bits.

Arriving there now in the dark of night is not an ideal situation because the security lights make me an easy target. I am greeted by an orange fireball, screeching, "Mr. Midnight, Mr. Midnight." Right on Punky's tail (still kitten-short and pointy) comes a second squealer, "Sir Midnight, Sir Midnight!"

At nine pounds and ninety-five percent black, Arthur, King of the Britons, looks right at home milling around with the rest of the clowder, but he has lost his slippers.

Ma has shown up to give me a welcoming punch on the shoulder. She is still her rangy, scruffy black self, yellow eyes gleaming and ragged ear cocked.

"We have a new Wise One among us, Grasshopper."

I cringe at my baby kit nickname, but look over her shoulder to see a huge black longhair reclining in the classic "meatloaf" position on a discarded red velvet sofa pillow, front limbs tucked under like a Chinese sage and only a faint glitter showing between its slitted eyes. I cannot tell if it is male or female or fixed or not. Its vibe is entirely neutral.

"Spooner," Ma informs me in a gravely whisper to my whiskers, "gathers all evil influences surrounding the clowder and projects them into a landfill in Death Valley."

Nice work if you can get it. I spot chicken McNuggets artistically spaced around the pillow. Ma is getting up in years and I fear she is prey to scammers.

I am just adjusting to the new weirdo in the cat pack when the dust mop with shark teeth bounds over from the Circle Ritz grounds.

I am speedily being outnumbered.

I nervously eye the Circle Ritz façade and spy Karma's pale form on the penthouse balcony. Apparently she can participate in place. Also yammer long distance.

"You, Midnight Louie," I hear her voice crooning, "will join minds with the ancient shamans to summon the power of the Werewolf Moon to protect us and ours during this perilous astrological period."

I look up to make sure there is a moon in the sky, as I do not want to waste whatever pitiably small mystical power I have. Yup. Round and full and the usual mottled so people can make up what they see on its surface. The green cheese notion is long dead, a good thing because cheese that is green is spoiled rotten.

I check in with Achilles, who is "smiling" amiably with an ungoverned tongue the canine breeds are prone. He seems about as impressed as if his person had told him he was having Alpo for dinner.

"So," I say to him. "I have heard you bit a vampire in defense of Miss Lilah Lane. I do not believe there are such creatures, but if there are, you were very brave to think you could do that."

"Thanks. They were common in our neighborhood. I died of blood poisoning."

"The vampire blood is poisonous, like anti-freeze fluid?"

"Maybe just to dogs. Not to worry, I am on my second life now. And since I have found another Asian savant in Karma, I am not susceptible any longer. But we need three to invoke the Werewolf moon and that is why you are here."

"The Tibetan and Burmese Twain cannot accomplish this mumbo-jumbo by themselves?"

"We need a less sensitive third entity to stabilize the psychic bolts. The triangle is the strongest form."

"That sounds more than somewhat condescending, but if this will let me get on about my business of protecting my people, do your extra-sensory thing."

There is a sudden mental silence.

Karma breaks it. "You should know, Louie, participating will cost you one life."

"My being this third leg and making the whole deal go will cost me a life? I should get extra."

"Using power always has a price."

"Uh, do we have any statistics on that life part? Like, say, one out of one hundred?"

"The usual nine is the only number known since the Egyptians and may be just human whimsy."

"I have little faith in human whimsy. Is there not some sort of bookkeeper in the universe who knows how many intact lives a guy has? Like an insurance company?"

"Louie, Louie, Louie. No one knows. Not even I."

Well, what I do not know cannot hurt me, right?

I gaze around to see Ma sitting like the number one pin in a bowling alley at the front of her entire gathered Cat Pack—the Havana Brown ninjas, The Tabby-striped Stealth unit, the undercover Black Tide, the White Ghost warriors, the Parti-color ground troops.

I stand in front of her, and Achilles has placed himself between me and Karma, looking up to her balcony where her eyes shine a sinister red.

"So," I ask, "is there some sort of ceremonial dance or howl—?"

A wind without sound hits me in the kisser, freezing my tongue in my mouth. Hope Achilles gets a dose of this. Behind me I sense a strange vibration rising like a tide.

The bee hive-like buzz at my rear gets louder, but I am trapped in place and cannot turn to look. And then I realize it is not insects but the combined purr power of Ma's clowder.

I sense it as a wall behind me and brace my feet just in time to see an aurora of absinthe green and magenta lightning travel from Karma's glowing red eyes, flashing over Achilles' white coat from head to tail and filling my field of vision with blinding light that almost knocks me over until I sense the sea of solid furry bodies and soaring purrs holding me up on a psychic wave.

A wolf howl rises in the night.

Everything around me softens, the light, the purrs, the massed cats. Achilles is shaking out his glamour tresses. Beside me, Arthur is licking his slipperless forefoot. Karma is stretching on her balcony and disappearing indoors.

Much ado about nothing, I think.

Then I see a lean wolfish shape prowling the edges of the property like a cold gray bolt of lightning. Maybe Miss Lilah's impressive dog Quicksilver is fully present on the scene and ready to rock 'n' roll.

49
Freaked and Fled

Truth to tell, Matt thought she was a champion amateur detective, but Temple Barr was not happy with herself about her role lately. She had been present at a death almost literally taking place underneath her feet, and had not a clue.

Not one clue, and here she was co-host and chief researcher for *Las Vegas Last Night.* She was supposed to know this town from top to bottom.

The fire and fury over the Green Fairy death, as horrible as it was, had overshadowed an unfollowed thread: the simultaneous disappearance of a reliable performer named "Gwen".

A TV-show co-host had a certain caché, recognizability—aw, heck, power—in an entertainment town like Vegas. So Temple cozied up to—who was she kidding—Christophe's head lady, the snooty supermodel, Grizelle.

Temple had long been aware her short stature encouraged insensitive people to underestimate her. She had long used it. Call it the pseudo-Ditsy factor.

First, she would tackle Christophe, then Grizelle, who was far more intimidating.

Christophe leaned an elbow on his desk, then his face on his hand. Both were unnervingly snow-white and death-pale. She gave herself a lecture on how being born albino was a disadvantage and such people were sadly discriminated against. "Bleeding heart liberal" was not a dirty phrase in her book. It was a synonym for "How'd you feel if it had happened to you?"

So she pitched Christophe straight out. And he listened.

"How can I help you 'pull together this fabulous TV segment'— sounds rather wormlike—on my magic show?"

Temple snuggled confidently into the huge leather chair facing his desk. Her feet didn't touch the floor despite three-inch heels. "I have a radical idea. Me and my cell phone, at large, with a cinema *verité* edge."

"A cinema *verité* edge?"

"I can't promise, but it *could* be submitted as a short film to the, well, Oscars. Or lesser film competitions. I *can* promise it won't have been done before."

"So your cell-phone interviews will give your viewers a spontaneous insight into the workings of a major Vegas show?"

"I couldn't have put it better myself."

"While you snoop around and interrogate my cast to find clues to the Green Fairy death. I agree that that is most unheard of and audacious."

The constant sunglasses made Christophe devilishly hard to read.

"You're right. It's risky and the police wouldn't like it at all."

There was a long pause.

"I suggest you start with Miss Lane."

Now was not the time to stutter out her surprise at his agreement. "She does seem to have an intriguing backstory."

"Intriguing *lack* of backstory."

"You could look at it like that. I'll get started. Background is my bag."

Temple escaped and made her way down to the dressing rooms, where she quickly discovered the missing Gwen's surname was Owens. If that wasn't a stage name.

She asked the way to the Green Fairy dressing room, deserted at this daylight hour. Once there, Temple sank onto a lumpy Goodwill velvet sofa opposite the long makeup table shelf and the mirrors.

She spent a few moments mourning the former resident. Everyone fought and survived and sometimes lost. The place had an odor of cosmetics, dust and dog, testified to by a sadly collapsed and empty canvas carrier in one corner and a white pad diaper pile in the opposite corner.

She filmed the empty sadness of the room, which would soon be Lilah Lane's.

Green glitter and sequins littered the floor and tabletop. A fluffy, white-feathered-rimmed velvet powder puff, was embroidered with the poignant saying "There's No Place Like Home".

Poignant because uprooted Celeste, fleeing death, as Max had told her, had found a home among the tawdry glamour of a Vegas show. That hopeful frippery hung from a wall nail and trembled in the draft from the air conditioning vent above the stage sound speaker. That reminded Temple that every dressing room was linked to the stage sound system. For cues. And possibly could have been bugged. What a palace of paranoia the Spellbinder show had become!

Temple heard a bump against the dressing room door and jumped along with a tiny leap of her heart. A curly blond head peered around the door edge.

"Danny Dove!" Seeing him lifted her sinking spirits.

"What are you doing here?" they each said simultaneously.

He answered solo first. "I'm consulting on choreography for the acts. The cast changes require fine-tuning."

"I'm looking for information," Temple said.

"Clues, you mean." Danny gave a sage head nod. "Ask me. Showgirls confide in their choreographers even more than in their hairdressers. My dear, the intimate secrets I hear."

"You're always so confide-able in," Temple said with a hug. "Who's playing 'The Lady' in that exchange with the Tiger bit now?"

"Martie. She was runner-up for Green Fairy, but now this dark horse, Lilah Lane, has that locked in. Luckily, Lilah's a quick study and, frankly, a big improvement over the film I've seen of the original."

"Heard anything about this 'Gwen' who went rogue and whose whereabouts nobody seems to care about after the Green Fairy death?"

"Gwen Keljic," Danny said promptly.

Temple's jaw dropped. "How'd you dig up a real live messy surname?"

Danny explained. "Lilah Lane somehow coaxed the autobio sheets for the women who auditioned from Mr. Big, and she consulted me. Our pooled info and rumors gave us a better picture.

"Gwen was from Flagstaff originally. Danced chorus in Reno for a while. Strong résumé. Playing the Lady in 'The Lady or the Tiger' act was a plum role—she would have been very excited. Zero reason to bail, my petite shamus, but…anybody could do the bit, as you saw with Miss Lane. You're right. Gwen's the forgotten woman. Hadn't been here long, was just beginning to make friends."

"You got all that info already?"

"I may work with the chorus girls, but I treat 'em all like solo stars. Trade secret."

"*You're* not working backstage now?" Temple asked.

"Not much, but I can hang around and try to get more of a lead for you on the Missing-in-Action Gwen."

"That's right. It's worrisome Gwen's still MIA and continues to be AWOL. The way Celeste was."

"Gwen should have been in place under the trapdoor when Lilah and Midnight Louie got there," Danny said.

"Maybe Gwen spotted Celeste's huddled body on the floor farther on. She could have freaked and fled."

"So could have Celeste at something else. Maybe an out-of-place Six, say," Danny said. "Only she was too late to escape what Gwen feared."

Danny clasped Temple's wrist and leaned close. "Two featured performers, both women, one dead and one missing. Stay away from backstage and the circuitous under-stage tunnels, dear heart. I would *miss* you."

"I'm not involved in the show, or in competition for any roles. I'm just a visiting TV host who could pluck one of them out of obscurity for a guest spot. Why would anyone want to hurt me?"

"Yes, you've got a legitimate reason to hang around." Danny frowned. "So many people float around this production maze down here. The Sixes come and go like malignant reverse-image ghosts. We already know this. Someone, or even two, with really bad intentions could find cover in this crowd."

50
Done and Gone

Danny's warning only made Temple fret more.

The name "Gwen" struck Temple—with her modern non-girly, non-gender name—as so old-fashioned, like "Lilah", as a matter of fact. Her performance name, though, Gwen Owens, had some assonance, as the poets put it, at least.

Had fiery film dancer Gwen Verdon inspired Gwen Owens's first name and then career? Did her parents name her Gwendolyn? Were they youthful English Lit graduates, enamored of Oscar Wilde's *Importance of Being Earnest* pun-titled play featuring an imperious Lady Gwendolyn. Or was the name influenced by Guinevere, fatal queen of the Arthurian cycle of tales?

Thinking of which, where was Celeste's beloved dog, Arthur? That name pinged a Monty Python Brit comedy series memory in Temple's brain.

Argh! Names. Who would name a baby girl Gwen? Maybe the baby girl herself, later in life?

Temple considered the Celtic origins of the name 'Gwen' and started searching the Internet for Gwen Owens. Had that ring to it. Would be remembered. Looked well in type. A dream of a name. And it was on the IMDb. The International Movie data base. A bit part in a 2011 B movie, but….

She found an Owens on the first Hellfire audition list. And Gwen Owens on the Green Fairy runner-up cast list!

This woman had gotten the call, came in to audition, been runner-up for the Green Fairy part, and won another role, the "Lady" part of Gwendolyn, and then that one fatal night she got into costume and just…vanished.

All big entertainment cities have small off-map motels with cheap rent-by-the-week rooms for performers down on their luck. Being 'down on their luck' means being performers in a hurdy-gurdy, somewhat shifty, thrift-shop world.

These places reminded Temple of Las Vegas's shabby-chic resale shops behind dusty glass windows and doors, those expanding endlessly *Twilight Zone* dystopias occupied by pre-robotic clothing store mannequins. Talk about "boulevards of broken dreams".

Finding the maiden name Keljic was a huge break. Performance names were often bland by design and Gwen had used one to perform. But Keljic was ethnic and easier to trace.

Temple only had to try four places before finding the Blue Mermaid Motel near Downtown had a resident named Keljik.

The time was right. Temple had always found 11:00 a.m. great for catching people in. She had the Miata parked in front of room 42, second level, in minutes.

Gwen Keljik answered Temple's knock, clearly expecting housekeeping. Her face was slightly swollen and sleep creased. She was a dye-dark brunette in her hard forties.

"Hi. I'm Temple Barr and I'm helping Danny Dove with his projects at the Hellfire Hotel and—"

"Danny." Gwen's face looked instantly troubled. "He must be so disappointed in me."

"Not disappointed, worried."

"Who did you say you were?"

"My name is Temple—"

"Oh, I've seen you on TV with the cute guy."

"That's my husband, Matt Devine. Great name, no?"

Now that the family/public connection had been made, Gwen almost seemed eager for company.

She opened the door fully. "It's a mess in here." She gestured to a chair and sat on the foot of the unmade bed. Paper remnants of fast food orders littered the bedspread and newspapers covered the table and chairs.

"If you've seen our TV show," Temple said, "you know Matt and I cover entertainment, but also personal and social issues."

"Yeah. Is this a survey or something?"

"No." Temple glanced to a strewn newspaper. It was the issue reporting Celeste's death. "You've read about what happened to Celeste?"

"Yeah. So what."

"People were concerned when you left the show so suddenly."

"That's nice. I just didn't feel well enough to go on." Gwen picked up the bedspread edge and wrapped her arms around it.

The slow, monotone tempo of her responses screamed "depression".

Temple leaned forward in her chair. "Did you know that Celeste's dog, Arthur, disappeared the day she died?"

"Arthur? Arthur's dead too?" She veered from zero to sixty into panic. Gwen sat up and started thrashing the news sheets around. "It wasn't in the paper."

"No, no. Arthur's just AWOL. Missing. Maybe another performer took him after Celeste died. Martie or, or—"

"Tina. She was Martie, but sometimes went by Tina."

"You don't know your sister performers' surnames?"

"Oh, I guess not. We move around so much. We had a 'Martha' on the craft services crew, so Martina, she went by her nickname, "Tina". Celeste really responded to the name 'Tina' for some reason, and she was pretty down to begin with, so Martie played up her nickname "Tina" around Celeste. Poor Celeste was a basket case, really. So nervous. Not getting that easy camaraderie with the cast and crew. Just jumpy. She kind of buried herself in the Green Fairy act. I couldn't perform in that freaking glass test tube, but it somehow gave her peace. And that sweet little dog calmed her down, and Tina, I mean Martie, lavished treats and petting on 'Arthur, King of the Britons', she called him.

"Between the dog and Tina and me, Celeste was just starting to get at ease with herself and us and the show, and then..."

"She died."

Gwen shut her eyes in silent acceptance.

"Listen. When you were getting into place for your entrance as 'The Lady' you saw Celeste fall, didn't you?"

Sometimes an interviewer had to hit hard.

"No! Yes! I didn't want to. The lights were dim, but the costume sparkled. We're all about sparkle, aren't we?"

Temple kept on topic. "Once Celeste hit the ground, the risers to the various stage boxes would hide her presence. Why didn't you sound the alarm?"

"It was the middle of the show. We're saturated with a 'show must go on' mentality."

"And the show would stop in a few minutes anyway? When you ran off and failed to make your entrance?"

Gwen remained silent.

"You were gone long enough before Lilah found her way to the trapdoor that she bungled getting through in time for your missed cue."

"Lilah? I don't know her. I just wanted to get away."

"Do you have any idea who might have taken Arthur?"

"Arthur? No. I was too panicked to think of him, but pets aren't allowed here, anyway. I just turned around and got myself out of the understage area and out through the housekeeping area, to a quick side exit from the hotel."

"So you didn't see or hear any motorcycle gang outside the back of the hotel?"

"Motorcycle gang? I heard some clanging and maybe engines, but my car was parked right near that side entrance, so I just left."

"In costume and all?"

"Uh, yeah."

"Your street clothes and purse or wallet with your ID and your driver's license remained in the dressing rooms area?"

"Well, yeah." Gwen sighed.

"Be glad I'm not the police. How'd you get them later?"

"Martie met me, and handed them over. I knew I couldn't go back after dropping the ball. I don't know how you got my address."

"Once I knew your real last name, I checked with Grizelle. She gave it to me from your employment sheet. She was happy I could save her a trip. You should be too."

Temple reached into her large hot-pink tote bag and pulled out a plum.

"I have your letter of termination and last full check. Grizelle has highlighted all the contracted conditions of employment with the show your going AWOL violated." I handed her the fat manila envelope. "She gave me a message. No recommendation."

Gwen shuddered for effect. "I'm not sorry. That Spellbinder show is a very weird setup."

Temple leaned inward. "But you are *very, very* sorry for something else, aren't you?"

"What? No! You're crazy."

"At least I'm not the police. Talk to me or talk to them."

"Why should I? Who the hell are you?"

"Someone with a built-in lie detector who's very committed to solving how Celeste died."

Gwen drew her knees up on the bed and huddled her arms around them.

"Look," Temple said. "This is show biz. There's no time to waste. Everyone's forgotten about you and moved on. You've been replaced by the next girl in the audition hierarchy. If I were you, I'd cool it and try to get work in Reno under another name."

"I can't cool it!" Gwen put her face on her knees and started sobbing.

Temple whipped the facial tissue packet from her tote bag like a seasoned psychotherapist. PR people acted in that capacity sometimes.

Gwen was—once more with feeling—over-sharing. "When I saw Celeste dropping, just dropping during her act, totally out of control, all I could think was that I might be next. I didn't want to be seen watching, so I spun around and vanished down the tunnels."

"Who would see you down there?"

"Those creepy black Sixes are always slinking around. Sure, they're backup and string pullers for the acts, but they hover like these sinister spy-spiders. And all us girls are changing costumes on the way to the stage. Spiders looking, looking, looking all the time. We're used to it. We don't think about it. But maybe we should."

Gwen pulled a gob of tissues out of the packet and buried her face in them.

After a minute, she looked up with painfully red eyes. "I'm not, like, the most popular girl. But Celeste, Celeste was really not fitting in. And Martie, she adored Celeste's little dog and would feed it treats, so she was always around between shows or acts. And that was good for Celeste. She had the chops to do the Green Fairy gig, but was nervous. It was kind of, what would you call it? Weird that they chose her.

"Anyway, I was passing Celeste's private dressing room with her "emotional support" dog in there. Like any of us other girls would get an emotional support lizard even, and Martie was in there cheering Celeste up and they were laughing, so I went in."

"That's performing," Temple said, "hurry up and then wait around a century."

"You got it." Gwen paused for a deep sigh. "There was Ms. Martini…sometimes Martie called herself Ms. Martini because she liked to invent cocktails and because of her nickname, Tina." Gwen hiccoughed as her inflamed eyes focused on the past. "She was turning around in the middle of the dressing room feeding that little dog treats and he circled too as she was saying 'Auntie Tina, Tina, Tina has a treat for tiny Weena, Weena, Weena', and Celeste was laughing like there was no tomorrow, which there sure isn't now."

Gwen's clutched fingers had started wringing. Temple took Gwen's wrists firmly in her hands. "Girls just having some hard-earned fun. What are *you* so guilty about?"

"We teased her. We teased Celeste. Because she was so straight-laced. Martie, Tina, had found out she'd never drunk absinthe and I hadn't either, so she said we'd have an Absinthe Christening Party, and brought out some glasses and funny spoons—don't they use spoons for hard drugs—?"

Temple waggled her head skeptically. "Sometimes, but the absinthe spoon is just a fancy cooking sieve."

"That why they call it 'cooking' drugs sometimes?"

Gwen had been as naïve as Celeste, Temple saw. If anybody had anything to answer for that it would be "Auntie Tina, Tina, Tina".

Gwen licked her dry lips. "So Ms. Martini…for some reason we found that nickname a gas, we were all giggling, produced, like, this big blown-rose-shaped perfume bottle filled to the neck with green liquid and the cutest little silver bottle of ice water," she said.

"And she pulled out—her backstage bag was almost as big as your tote bag—one, two, three, I swear she had more in there, of those bubble-bottomed bar glasses. She said she'd 'borrowed' them from Gaston at the absinthe bar setup.

"We performers were forbidden to show up in the absinthe bar, in costume or out, to keep our 'mystique' with the patrons. So this was our secret little girly dressing room work-around.

"She put out these three glasses, like the shell game with three cups and one pea under them that's always not showing up where you think it is. Or showing up where you think it is not.

"Tina poured the green stuff into the bottom of the three glasses, set up on the makeup table, and did the…what was it, the cat ran away with the spoon? But it was more like the dog in our case. And three spoons to run away with.

"Then she spun the wide thick silver bracelet off her wrist and it's a liquor flask with a screw cap on the top. So clever and fun!

"Martie balanced a spoon on the first glass rim, put a sugar lump on it and then on our two glasses as well. She poured some clear liquid from the flask into it. Presto! The green absinthe turned the color of skim milk and looked so innocent. She did the same with glasses two and three and handed them to us. We clicked rims and drank it. It tasted like licorice 'swizzle stick' candy!

"And we just laughed, us all, and after twenty minutes went our separate ways, leaving Arthur leaping up on Martie's…Ms. Martini's lower leg, poor thing, hoping for more treats, but they were all gone, I guess."

Gwen heaved another giant sigh. "Don't you see? I helped *kill* Celeste, because we weren't used to that kind of alcohol. I egged her on. I know I felt a little buzz afterward. And Celeste went on for her act and fell and died and I had to get away from there before I did the same thing too."

Gwen frowned. "I felt more normal once I was out of there, but I didn't deserve to. I was just lucky and Celeste wasn't."

Temple remained perfectly still, thinking furiously, holding Gwen's hands and gazing into her tear-smeared face.

Gwen needed to be in a protected witness program, but even that hadn't saved the last woman.

So much for taking pride in tracking down people, Temple scolded herself. Somebody else might be just as good at that, or had followed her and now was a threat. She had to get Gwen someone to watch over her.

The options were not pretty.

Temple dug her cell phone from her tote bag and called Max. Then (gulp) Molina.

Now she only had to sit tight and imagine in what order they would react and what recriminations would flow from them both when they next saw her.

She was babysitting a witness to at least manslaughter and Lilah Lane was soon to become the new Green Fairy and target for a possibly psychopathic murderer.

51
Six Wrong Turns

Tonight I would hear "Lilah Lane" announced from the Looking Glass Theater stage.

I can't help thinking of Celeste for my first onstage performance as the Green Fairy. I wish her spirit peace as I wait to "appear" onstage. I've beaten back anxiety and claustrophobia with Danny Dove's tutelage. Like the Force, he's promised to be with me. And somehow Celeste is too, because I've cared about what happened to her.

Celeste and I can breathe deep, float, waft, become a muse, a magical creature lighter than smoke, each in our own way.

I've designed my own "act" to a degree. I decided for the lights to come up with my arms crossed on my chest Egyptian mummy style, then sliding unbound down my side. All magic is escape, someone told me. I smile. Escape from binding, the binding of others and the binding we do unto ourselves sometimes.

I am the Green Fairy. I am a metaphor. For imagination, for creation, for destruction, for the search for beauty and freedom, for the search for each of us by Death.

The haze, the layers of smoke and mirrors, the veils of my costume unfold and waft weightlessly. To everything there is a season. With full stage lights and effects, I can sense the audience in the dark, like the curl of a gigantic cat with black fur dreaming around me, wondering at the illusion as I raise my arms and my filmy wings, moth like, and my body elevates through the clear tube, past the lavish gilt and silver filigree enfolding it, into the dark, workaday reality of the stage.

Steady, steady, turn, turn, turn. Irma and I have made this into a meditative state, the steady pull of my invisible harness and the visible green velvet rope lifting me out of sight, pointed toes and all. All the while turn, turn, turning for the absinthe season, the sweet delusion, the wispy, fragile illusion. I lift my head back to see my assistant Six awaiting on a black scaffold to safely transfer me there while my image seems to fragment to the audience below and dissolve into a dream and assume the position of the Green Fairy depicted on the Art Nouveau label of a giant absinthe bottle.

Then they'll clap and whistle wildly and I will be up, up, up and awaaay. Me becoming my own beautiful balloon.

I am past sight of the audience and am feeling the triumph of a performer Raven was talking about. I have finished. I played my role. I am walking on air, I am mighty—"the mighty Delilah" Shezmu, the Egyptian god of slaughter as well as wine, perfume, and exotic oils, called me in another Las Vegas after I rescued him from the Afterworld. Mighty Shezmu, are you also the god of absinthe?

My chest harness lifts up from a mighty yank and something, someone grabs me by it and starts to turn the velvet rope, now slack enough, around my neck.

Turn, turn, turn. The blood is pounding in my chest and my throat, which was shamelessly swelling with pride, bites back at my own cardinal sin, Pride.

I pull both legs up, kick out hard like the swimmer in space I seem to be. That reverses the turn, turn, turn tightening, but my vision is turning dark. I see black upon black, Six and Six and Six and one Six too, too tall.

He grabs my hand and I slowly slip from his grip, not onto the safety scaffold no longer safe, but down to the backstage area below. My feet hit hard, despite bent knees.

"Run," Max gasps. "All the way out. Run, Delilah, Run!"

Delilah. Am I Delilah? Or Lilah?

I run, not surprised to find Achilles growling at my heels. He always comes to my defense, alive or dead.

So here I am again, on the run with my little dog too. Achilles at my heels is doing his Dalai Lama darnedest to nip me into faster speed and drill my eardrums with a lapdog-shrill siren while I try to grasp who I'm eluding. A witchy tiger-woman, a straw man, a hidden wizard, and/or Six kinds of spies and assassins with fifty-three ways to help me kiss my life goodbye.

And maybe some good guys or gals in the gang.

Oh, and I'm again following the bobbing tail of a Black Cat guide into Wonderland-cum-Westworld.

I have nothing for weapons but my wits, and little for clothing but a Victoria's Secret body stocking, which thankfully is slippery enough in these big metal air ducts to let me eel on through.

My nose tells me I'm racing into Rankland near the tiger's cage. Gnawed bone, tissue and blood to my left, some sort of roar to my right.

My cover, if I was ever naïve enough to think I had one, has been what they call "blown".

So when I realize I have taken a wrong turn and am following the tiger entrance to the enclosed outdoor bell jar marketed as the "Tiger Retreat and Tropical Garden", I realize I'll be facing down Grizelle in her Big Cat persona.

Actually, this makes me more confident. Just as I'd had a Flashback Moment about my charm bracelet's past as a Silver Familiar courtesy of Snow, I feel in my bones that at least I'd faced off the white tiger before. But then did I have Quicksilver with me to distract the Big Cat?

Whatever. I'll just have to do it solo.

So I run, barefoot…until I emerge from the tunnel, almost standing up, and face a huge and temporarily blinding bubble of hyper-lit tableau, daylight under glass at 11:00 p.m., bordered at the enclosed steel foundation with rows of rapt tourist faces looking in.

I gasp for air, which is warm, moist and tropical. It makes me want to lie down, panting, beside the spotlit free-form pool and meandering stream edged with elephant ear plants and other oversized greenery and nap before the attendant arrives for my hot stone massage.

The blazing white poured concrete towering walls surround me like an idyllic Greek island, overrun with beautiful feral cats, and on one elevated lounge area an unmoving huge elegant white tiger is staring right at me. Green-eyed, but with majesty, not Envy. I feel Achilles' little body trembling alongside my calf from exertion and tension.

He is *not* going to be tiger meat and have to come back from an urn ever again.

I turn to retreat, but black, sinuous figures slither amid the lurid blooms and huge, shadowing plants.

As for the white tiger, it deigns to stand. Anyone who has ever been *this close* to such a magnificent creature, the beauty of the markings, the emerald eyes the size of saucers, the powerful shoulder bones moving in balletic harmony, the soft pillowing seduction of those immense pink-padded paws…

All of its moves are unconscious, motivated only by a need to know its environment, its survival needs, its safety. Yet a ballerina could study for years to master the poetry of this Big Cat putting one paw forward.

Okay. Enough shock and awe. I knew this was really Snow's shape-shifting security chief and she had never liked me, maybe because I never much kowtowed to rules.

Right now, I would take Achilles in my arms, bow backwards and tiptoe out the entrance from which I had come.

But a glance backwards shows someone has shut the cast-iron grille between here and there.

I look forward for an exit into the watching audience, who, aghast, are skimming nervous hands over the glass and metal to find some sort of egress point for me.

This is a seamless bubble, folks, for your own protection. Thanks, but keep yourselves safe.

The tiger continues its leisurely, elegant catwalk toward me and Achilles.

I'm about to take a long-needed breath. Then I glance at the audience.

Grizelle on her slashing high heels looms a head above the onlookers, trying to calm them down.

I look at the tiger.

I look back at the woman. She smiles and waves. *Expletives deleted,* Irma crows.

Not everything in my Vegas Now jibes with the Vegas I drove and was driven-out of.

Oh.

Avoid small, quick movements. Cats are genetically programmed to chase and, um, quiet prey.

Irma has apparently done a Google search for me on Big Cat behavior.

I crush Achilles against my chest, realizing my ribs and shoulders are aching from the attack onstage.

I look back to the exit and spy at least two stalking Sixes. Why are they after *me*?

An impact on the plastic bubble surface above us lands with a thump.

I'm looking up at four spread hairy legs with splayed claws scratching tracks into the curved plastic surface.

The dome vibrates with a muffled howl.

The Big Cat flattens its curved ears and looks up, annoyed.

Quicksilver. His claws are tap-dancing on the curved clear globe surface, seeking traction, trying to distract the Big Cat from me.

I cry, "Kitty, Kitty, Kitty, Nice Kitty."

Not going to work. We'll wear ourselves out and tiger Grizelle will blunder into satisfying her curiosity about intruders into her realm with death by unintended mauling.

Behind me the screech of a metal hinge either scorches my nerves or raises my hopes.

I look. Snow has stepped through, the man in white.

"Sixes," he ordered, "out, before I throw you into the tiger pool."

They backed away, foiling me as I try to read the names on their backs.

"You," the eternal sunglasses face me. "Quiet and still for once."

It wasn't "Run, Delilah, run!" but I listened.

He turned to the tiger, which had so stealthily come so much closer to me and Achilles I could see its pale eyelashes.

I couldn't have moved if I had wanted to.

Snow stepped between us and the tiger. I saw him reach up to push the sunglasses up on his head.

The huge tiger's head tilted like a kitten's.

Snow gestured it closer.

It came. Its forelegs rose a bit.

I held my breath.

Its lifted forelegs lay on Snow's shoulders.

He staggered, and held, and gritted evenly between his teeth. "Delilah, back away through the tunnels."

Above us, Quicksilver whimpered softly and lay down on the now scratched-to-heck dome.

I bet I owed Christophe a small fortune in damages.

By then I was in the open archway where a pair of hands pulled me father into the now friendly dark.

"Steady, steady," said Danny Dove. "Great performance, in both arenas."

It was hard to watch Quick disappear from view, but I hung onto Achilles and we all, whoever was down here, walked silent and shaken toward the glow of a gaping open stage trapdoor and whatever light was to be found in the Looking Glass Theater.

52
Paw de Deux

Crowds of excited, departing people chattering like chimpanzees confined to quarters with a glut of gossiping parrots have me pushing forward against the flow, whiskers flattened back.

I cling to the exit walls from the Tropical Tiger Retreat and Garden attraction, dodging smelly flip-flops and sweat-soaked tennis shoes.

My usual agility, aided by my prickly four-on-the-floor, produce a little walking space for me. I can slow the people down to make room when they pause to remove that troublesome burr in their anklets (me!) that suddenly pricked them.

I must be sure tell Achilles that I am no slouch at heel nipping too.

"What an amazing act!" I hear from above my head. "I did not expect the magician to be a tiger-tamer too."

"It is all a con. The tiger was never going to get the girl. Sure was big, though."

"Those creepy Men in Black must have been animal trainers."

"I do not think they should have allowed the trained dog to taunt the poor caged tiger."

"The whole thing was fake. A phony chase scene to liven up the exhibition."

Or deaden it, I think.

Right now I am in search of the "trained dog" before he can run wild again. I need to play matchmaker pronto. I am not looking for the first exit from the hall designed to funnel people back to the Strip. I have more elevated aspirations.

When they go low, I go higher.

I hear the muffled buzz of human voices and dash cross-traffic toward it, leaving tripping feet and whining children in my wake. I arrive at an unmarked door closing just slowly enough for me to execute emergency tail-tuck and roll through it.

The door closes on nothing essential of me but a few wafting black hairs.

I am at the bottom of some service stairs. Excellent. I leap up a few, then the door below opens admitting people sounds and a flashlight beam.

"Hey, you, alley cat! Get outta here."

For once I am happy to obey. I bound up the plain concrete steps like a Slinky on Speed in reverse. My momentum sends me barreling through a swinging door at the top of the stairs. A tumbleweed roll has me landing on my feet.

There I am. In broad daylight with the clear blue sky above and the lush green Tropical Tiger Retreat and Garden under glass below me.

Something big brushes past me to leap against the door to the roof area.

I hear the lock engage and the foiled security men pounding the metal.

I turned to find myself face-to-knee with a much bigger four-on-the-floor.

"Mr. Quicksilver, I presume. We have met before."

The dog's long, professionally fanged snout pushes close enough that his big black wet nose almost smothers my face.

"You," he snarls after a deep sniff, "were the sniveling feline under the Dumpster where My Girl went to ground."

"I was the fast-acting feline that guided her *under*ground to safety while you rounded up and dumped those bully boy bikers. Nice work. The Lobos are a bad lot."

He snorts.

I wipe off my face with a front mitt and without comment. I am not a fan of dog slobber.

Quicksilver seems to know that, and grins.

Oh, what a big mouth you have, I think. *And teeth.*

"Lobos are easy prey. Nothing compared to the Lunatics from north of Las Vegas."

He lies down on his stomach, forelegs stretched out, to face me more directly.

Okay. I concede that if we were in an animal act his jaws are big enough to take my whole head into his mouth. Need I mention that I am not intimidated?

He tilts that huge head, curious. "The Lunatics vanished."

"The Lunatics are real wolf-men. They are banned here. This other hairy human gang is in charge here."

"Sub-standard in any world! And what do *you* do here?"

"I am Midnight Louie. *Sir* Midnight to some, including you."

"Sir Louie could sound like something tasty to eat."

"You are thinking of sirloin. Get this. I am no one's food source. I am a facilitator and private investigator."

"*I* should investigate *you*. I told you when we met I could find you anywhere, and it appears you have the same facility."

"Well, somewhat," I say modestly. "You can scent your Girl on me. I have a personal Girl too. I know how it is."

"She rescued me from imprisonment and certain death."

"How annoying it is when we are going about minding our own business on the street and they seize us and put us in a crate for sale or slaughter."

"I get you, bub, I was up for adoption when My Girl sprung me. As I have come to understand over time and via overhearing, she herself was shuffled from shelter to shelter in her youth."

"Awful, I say, what they will do to their own species too. I have gone back inside undercover at times, once to rescue two of my breed."

"You do not look like an action film hero."

"I am paying it forward after My Girl rescued me from a short life on the Mean Streets without the condo comforts I have become used to."

Quicksilver shakes his head. "I do not seek comfort. I am a defender, a warrior."

"Me too. Only I require certain creature comforts I am sure you have experienced, if you would admit it."

"The Enchanted Cottage does have brownies tending the fire on chill desert nights."

I nod, stupefied. A fireplace would be nice at the Circle Ritz. Where is this automated up-to-date "smart" cottage? This I gotta see.

"Anyway, Quick, my boy…"

"I am not your boy."

"My fine fellow. I think there is one thing you would want to do beyond all others and, if my ears do not deceive me—and they are as sharp as yours if my nose is not—that is on the way."

He stands, ears pricked, no longer distracted by me now that what I had expected has transpired.

"You cannot go in," a man beyond the closed door bellows. "We have orders to contain that dangerous animal."

Sounds of a spirited discussion ensue.

Another bellow. "It could be a mad dog. Foaming at the mouth."

Comes a raised familiar voice: "You will see a whole different flavor of 'mad' if you do not open that door and let me through."

"Lady, you are not allowed."

Something hits the metal door and bounces a bit. I wince.

The door swings open to reveal two security guards in brown uniforms looking dazed and holding onto bits of gauzy green silk wings while a tall man in black holds them each in collared custody with one hand.

I would not differ with Mr. Max Kinsella if I were them.

In storms the angriest Green Fairy I have ever seen. She is wearing black leggings and boots that show signs of hasty donning, and long shimmering green sleeves and scarves. Her eyes are hooded in green glitter. Her lips are purple-black and her hair is a frazzled hive of black hair and green rhinestone spiderwebs.

She hurls herself onto her knees before me. I *am* Sir Midnight by decree of King Arthur.

Wait.

She has not even noticed me. It is actually the dog she hugs like she is never going to let go. "Quicksilver."

He sits there looking majestic, pleased, and a bit embarrassed. He is not a tongue-bath dog like Achilles. He is more of a majestic tail-wagger. And though I do not claim extensive study of Dog, as I do Human, he is one ecstatic canine. His tail slowly wafts its hairy tip back and force across my face. I sneeze.

Then Miss Lilah Lane looks over Quicksilver's luxuriously furred silver-gray shoulder and notices me. He might not be so bad to curl up next to before a fire. For her, that is.

Anyway, she gives me this Look, and winks.

Like Quicksilver, I am not displeased, but I do not wag anything. That would be a rude gesture.

53
Six Deadly Sins in
Search of a Solution

It was déjà vu all over again.

I'd again been rescued from an attack on the fringes of the Hellfire Hotel and had to answer for myself, whatever name I used.

Except now, as I looked around the green room area crowded with sitting and standing people, like a celebrity criminal courtroom, I knew most of these faces and loved a few, mostly furry; liked others; and, as for the others, meh.

Were this a play, I would say we had a mixed "house", or a confusion of who were actors and audience. Except one of the "actors" could be a murderer.

I was back sitting in my defensive couch corner, Achilles at my feet again. There's a "love".

This time Quicksilver was sitting by my side, overwhelming the upholstery.

I'd ordered him off the furniture when he'd jumped up, but Snow had told him, "Stay."

Quick had hesitated, sniffed in Snow's direction and wrinkled his snout, then jumped up and lay down. He'd placed his graceful forelegs across my thighs as a shield, and kept a surgically sharp stare on Grizelle, the woman, standing behind Snow. *Good dog!*

Dog disdain did not ruffle my contracted boss, Christophe, sprawling in his former place down the sofa. Matt Devine and Temple Barr sat opposite him, as before.

The Six Deadly Sins massed at the far fringe of the room, more in a lineup rather than a group, fidgeting like nervous children.

Then there were those new few good men, vigilant, hard-eyed, pacing slightly like Grizelle, watching the scene as keenly as Quicksilver. Some, although in street clothes, had a military bearing. I wanted to say "at ease", but I knew no one would be until this was over.

Lieutenant Molina had pulled a dining chair away from the food and drink table, and maneuvered it around next to my sofa end. I wasn't sure whether to feel protected or hemmed in.

And Max Kinsella? Always the impish bad boy, perched on the sofa table behind the empty sofa opposite us all (for a quick getaway?), his feet on the furniture cushions, like Quicksilver.

Midnight Louie had elected to sit by Max's feet on the sofa cushion.

At either corner of Max's long empty sofa sat a woman. Martina Antonovna on his left, Gwen Owens, cuddling Arthur, on his right. The little dog waded over the cushions to confer nose-to-nose with Louie, then jumped down to the floor and trotted speedily back to jump up to his soft spot on the couch with Gwen. His four feet sported fresh knitted absinthe-green slippers. He seemed to arrange his spindly legs to best to show them off. Almost everybody smiled. Not Martina.

The ghost of Celeste hovered over us all.

An abstracted man in a dark suit bustled through the double doors. "Sorry, paperwork."

"Mr. Bucek!" I said, surprised.

"Frank," said Molina and Matt in tandem, also surprised.

"Sir," said one of the buff men in cargo pants and T-shirt and muscles. He did not sound surprised.

Frank nodded to acknowledge us all. "This operation is over. Citizens here need to know what they cannot discuss about the onstage death of Celeste Novak and its details. Lieutenant Molina, I remand Miss Martina Antonovna to your custody for whatever charges your jurisdiction deems proper. You may have to fight our foreign security branches.

"The Marshal Service does not deem that Miss Gwen Owens needs witness protection, and I don't believe she should face any charges, so you may depose her and grant such protection services you think necessary as we sort things out."

Gwen's voice throbbed as she clutched Arthur and asked. "Can I keep the dog?"

Bucek smiled. "I think the SPCA need not be brought in to consult about that.

"Now, all you civilians need know is that this death had a national security element. In fact, several law enforcement arms have an interest in the dramatic death of the Green Fairy.

"I believe a vague reference to drugs might satisfy the news outlets."

"But Celeste didn't do drugs, ever!" Gwen argued. "You're dirtying the reputation of a dead woman, a victim, to keep things quiet."

Bucek regarded her with compassion. "I'm not through." He strolled around the far edge of the room like a lawyer showboating. "We can't forget. This is a magic show environment. There's always been a teasing now-you-see-it, now-you-don't procedure about everything that has happened on this stage."

"Thank you," Snow said.

"Don't take a bow. That made things tough for law enforcement."

Grizelle stepped forward, almost forgetting herself and growling, I was sure. After all, she was security head.

"And that further betrayed victims," Bucek said. He strolled to the gathered Six Deadly Sins, literally backed against the wall, and restive. He looked them over. "Like Roger Mayfield, Major Roger Mayfield." He shook his head. "For the same reason it was not so clever to hide Celeste Mayfield, under a maiden name, Novak, and behind a disguised person in a magic show, it provided a disastrous hunting ground for her stalkers."

"There are seven," a childish voice said, as if announcing the emperor had no clothes. This one had too many, I realized.

Gwen was still sheltering Arthur between her side and the couch. "When I found Arthur gone after Celeste fell, I knew somebody else wrong was here."

"Somebody other than Miss Antonovna, who resorted to poisoned absinthe to handicap her performing rival."

One of the apparently now seven black figures—who's counting with a flock like them, and someone had counted on that all along—burst from the group to jump a sofa and pounce on Martina in her corner.

"It's Envy," I cried. "Stop him."

I needn't have worried. The plainclothes guys were on him and Quick obeyed me so fast he was at the guy's throat.

"Miss Lane. Resist calling on your dog, or you will have to leave." Bucek stepped toward me.

"I didn't mean for Quicksilver to…"

Achilles lunged for Bucek's ankles.

"Or the other one. Dogs, plural. Contain them, or I will have them contained."

Both dogs desisted, growling low at the threat in Bucek's voice and posture.

Somebody smirked. I think it was Snow.

The unmasking drama at the couch was too vivid to interrupt. The hooded man's arms were pulled back for cuffs and one rough pull pushed up his features as the hood was stripped away.

Bucek checked the sin name on the black body stocking back.

"Envy. Hole in one, Ms. Lane."

"He'd been defensive of Celeste early on," I said. "If he's her husband on the run, why risk coming here?"

"To protect her," the man said. The *black* man, one not automatically assumed to be the husband of a white woman. Had racial stereotypes" confused the motives and issues? Ethnic ones sure had.

"Too late," Celeste's AWOL officer husband said bitterly. "That Russian bloodhound had already planned her death, created a clever poison, as their agents so often do."

"Dirty laundry, Major. Not in public," Bucek warned.

"Danny Dove was onto it early," I said, smiling toward the Six still against the wall. One of them pulled back a hood to showcase a Brillo pad of blond curls and stepped away, hands spread in surrender.

"The dance guy engaged the killer at the top of the illusion stage works?" a deep voice muttered.

I didn't give Max some credit for that, and he didn't take it. Danny had been there first and always.

"I told you I had your back," Danny told me with a warm smile. He looked around, concentrating on the muscle boys. "Put some steel in your steps, fellows. Try dancing."

Temple got up to hug Danny and pull him down to sit next to her and Matt. I gave him a quick salute.

As for Roger, no longer AWOL, he sat cuffed between two of the muscle boys. His story, and I bet it was TV movie quality, would be given in private, maybe under oath.

Bucek stood before Snow and shook his head. "And you, Mr. Christophe. It may be good business for a magician, but you created the perfect cover for spies and killers, and paid them well to boot."

Someone snickered. I think it was Max.

Bucek continued laying out his case. "The Six Deadly Sins were all the same general size. Their work was strenuous and their elasticized body-stocking costumes tenuous. Body-*stalking* costumes, really. Backup costumes were readily available if a Six got a run in his or her costume. Anyone roughly the right size and physical condition could be inside that getup. Could observe and learn the moves for certain acts, could melt away. We know two trespassers who co-opted the Sixs' built-in anonymity. Danny Dove, who wanted to protect Miss Lane. Roger Mayfield, who came to protect, and then hope to avenge his wife's death.

"With these two unmasked, we believe we have the current five Six corralled here. Step forward and remove your hoods, please. Let's be methodical and go from left to right."

The first stripped off the hood. Strawberry blonde. Next, red-haired guy. Then, Latina woman. Two left of the five. Number four hesitated, then complied. Detective Bell, still successfully undercover. Bucek nodded approvingly.

And last, a smart step forward, a brisk unveiling of brown hair…

"Celeste!" Several people shouted in surprise.

"She's alive." Roger's voice shook with joy.

Celeste turned to him, her expression dissolving into love and tears streaming from her brown eyes. Brown and brown. I noted idly the name on the back of her costume was Wrath.

Roger turned to Bucek. "Now you have your data secure. She's hidden it all along. She's clever at that. This proves I was protecting it. Celeste, baby, how'd you fool them all? Even me? I believed you were dead."

"Roger's innocent," she told Bucek and the room. "You can see and hear he went AWOL to draw the enemy agents away from his wife."

"Yes, this is over," Bucek said. "Mrs. Mayfield, I apologize for your trauma. We'll collect the data and take you and your husband out of the eye of the hurricane and into protective custody."

Shaking her tear-slick face, she wiped it with the back of her hand. "Like your protective custody worked. You don't understand. You've got it all wrong, so sadly, sadly wrong. I don't know where your precious damn data is!"

That silenced everyone.

"Celeste?" Roger asked. "What's wrong, baby? We're all right now."

"No!" Her voice throbbed with pain and frustration. "I'm *not* Celeste."

Sheer confusion resulted in astounded silence. Was this domestic drama without end, or high stakes espionage?

"Novak," Temple said into the silence. Musing aloud. "Celeste said she'd been born in Iowa. I checked. There was a *Celestine* Novak on my Internet search. But no Celeste Novak. You're Celest*ine*. You're a second Tina."

Two plainclothes guys took her arms and gently seated her in an upholstered chair, partly custody, partly compassion.

"Celeste had dusted her ballet slippers free of Iowa by then," the unveiled Celestine said. "Yes, twins. Yes, an enforced childhood dancing and gymnastic act. 'Celeste and Celestina: Terrific Tiny Tots'. Same costumes, same steps, Same seedy travelling circus circuit. That's mostly gone now, and so, I guess are we. Yes, us both sick of it, and each other by our teens. Separate ways. We scrubbed our Wikipedia page. I worked as 'Tina'. We always secretly followed where the other was, but kept the gate up."

Her eyes reddened again as she looked at all of us, including me and Snow and Bucek and Roger Mayfield. "It had been hell for Celeste to take up performing again. She'd always been the introvert, me the extrovert. Her only slip was starring in high school gymnastics, a solo art. Shy, yet she still craved attention and that 'achievement' on her record got her put back into performing when her life was in danger! She did it to take the heat off you, Roger, to save your career and reputation. That anxiety, and then the jealousy and pressure from the auditions was too much. She called me after many years to help her cope. Too late."

No one spoke. Law enforcement people had to be questioning the depth of their research and the depth of the sisters' sacrifice and despair. We amateurs at solving other people's mysteries had to wonder how we'd feel if our own pasts and identities had been stripped so bare.

Roger's troubled face said it all. Being pressured to betray his country and thinking his disappearance would solve everything… ultimately he both saved his wife from foreign attack and yet lost her utterly to a petty rivalry. That was the case, *if* Martina wasn't a Russian agent, but only the living embodiment of a bitter rival to the bitter end.

The one certainty? The secret data Celeste had put her whole heart and soul into saving could be lost and in danger of circulating forever.

I had to intervene. "I need to take Arthur for a few minutes."

Everybody blinked at my seeming non sequitur.

"Celeste's beloved emotional support dog would know what is what."

They looked at the little dog yawning and licking his socks.

They looked at me. I was getting used to everybody looking at me as if I were crazy.

Especially Quicksilver and Achilles.

"Walkies, Arthur? Outside? Good boy!"

I picked him up as he ran to me and we left the green room together.

54
Last Act

My Miss Temple has performed flawlessly in the green room at deciphering the clue of the Celestial twins, but I know now I can also trust My GBBD to give me my cue at the exactly right moment.

I am waiting beyond the doors as she comes out with Arthur in her arms.

I am very thankful Miss Lilah is not usually the "picking up" type my breed must tolerate on very infrequent occasion, but I respect the need for speed now.

I trot ahead as we cross the stage that has been the scene of magical illusion and all too material motivations as Envy, Wrath, Pride, Greed and also scheming, spying, and slaying and other unofficial Seven Deadly sins.

The theater seats are empty and half-lit, the stage is still.

One single hanging bulb is lit in the stage's left wing. The "Ghost Light", a bare bulb left on every night in theaters over the world so no one can stumble on the empty stage in the dark. Also lit to commemorate what ghosts may linger after the show is over. Tonight it still beams for Miss Celeste, who had so recently and momentarily been taken for rising from the dead.

I get a shiver up my spine. Normally, I pooh-pooh superstition but am a bit shaken now, thanks to Karma acquiring some partners in woo-woo in Miss Lilah's canine retinue. I will concede that we "dumb" beasts have instincts that sometimes verge on the mystic.

Enough of all that. We are on a firmly corporeal quest now.

The backstage spiral staircase to the dressing room reminds me of the mini-version at the Circle Ritz.

Arthur wiggles to be put down as we near our goal and Miss Lilah complies.

Together we three push through the ajar dressing room occupied by the Green Fairy and her successor. I should say successors, because I am sure Miss Lilah Lane has no desire to see her name in lights or don tights again to seemingly evaporate and reappear twice a night.

"Is this it?" Arthur asks me. "Is this the end of my quest, Sir Midnight?"

I check to ensure that the thoughts conveyed while we are innocently touching whiskers or rubbing jaws or even faking a spat, are not communicable to humans. Miss Lilah has proved to be a little too sensitive to secret languages once or twice.

"Yes," I tell Arthur.

I watch Miss Lilah pause to look pensive and gaze at the common dressing room clutter, all sparkling with absinthe-green fairy dust. She has lost all thought of us as she shifts through the costume rack, fingers the veils, moons over Miss Celeste's makeup trays.

"Listen, Arthur. To remain King of the Britons you must take this token of favor back to the green room and present it to the, uh, new chancellor."

"What is a chancellor?"

"Like a, a dog show judge. And you must bring it to the judge personally. You are the token bearer."

"That sounds very important."

"It is, and here is your token, not much of a heavy burden."

I glance at another glittery shiny object, low-hanging useless glitz on the wall.

"Oh, Sir Midnight, it is my Mamatina's Mussentouch." Arthur's tiny snout turns away, brown eyes averted so I see the whites of his eyes. Most disconcerting. My breed has developed a third eyelid to avoid showing a glimpse of eye-white, but we are generally more genteel than dogs.

"You *must* touch it. You must carry it in your teeth, deliver it personally."

"*You* do it. Then Mamatina can be mad at you."

"This is for your own good. Your own credit. Mamatina will be very proud of you."

"Would I see Mamatina again? Really? You said I would not."

I am beginning to understand Miss Midnight Louise's impatience with Punky.

"Look. You can bring it right to Mamatina, see. She will love that. I guarantee it."

Gee whiz, I am sounding like I sell used cars and suits.

"There it is!" Miss Lilah exclaims and snatches for the prize.

There is not a morsel I set my mind on that escapes my capture. I seize it right out of Miss Lilah's fingers and run.

"Louie," she cries. "Louie, drop that now!" she orders.

Arthur adds his confused yips to the noise.

I am out of the dressing room, down the hall and up the spiral stairs, hearing pounding feet and tiny claws scrabbling behind me. She is gaining on me. I had not calculated that Miss Lilah Lane's stride is much longer than My Miss Temple's, especially with her wearing flat shoes. The nerve to take athletic advantage when I am used to the handicap of high heels should I ever find it necessary to elude Miss Temple! Miss Lilah is quite the savage competitor.

I perhaps have slipped a bit in my lung capacity, not to mention some three-course Dumpster dives lately. I thunder across the stage and wings and arrive at the green room doors, panting.

By then Miss Lilah, panting herself, has gotten the idea.

I push my nose against Arthur's. (Forecast: wet, cold and drizzly. *Ugh*.)

She kneels to Arthur, King of the Britons, and keeps the prize up to his sniffer.

"Arthur, do you 'fetch'?"

His ears perk. He gazes at me. *Outside, ride, fetch?* The sacred trinity of doghood.

I nod.

He seizes the featherweight burden bravely and boldly in his tiny teeth, a bit of marabou fringe under his nostrils looking like snowy mustache, and trots straight through the double doors.

Oh, it was hard, so hard to let that tempting cat-tease turn into a soon-to-be soggy doggy toy. But this is for Miss Celeste and Arthur. Sometimes it is more rewarding to step back from center stage and watch another take a bow.

Even if it is a dog.

55
Arthur Takes His Throne

Maybe fleeting stardom as the Green Fairy is spoiling me.

Imagine, expecting that returning to the green room would get all eyes on me, Lilah Lane.

Achilles and Quicksilver deserted furniture to flank me quietly and in doggone good order.

Before that miracle had been noted, and Arthur came high-stepping through the double doors, no one even noticed Midnight Louie had returned.

Toy in mouth, Arthur surveyed the crowd, then ran to Martina hand-cuffed in her corner.

There was no more Mamatina, but there was a Tina.

He stood on his hind legs and turned.

Tina, Tina, Tina. Weena, Weena, Weena.

And he dropped the "There's No Place Like Home" powder puff from Celeste's dressing room at Martina's feet.

I caught my breath, and then the G-men pounced.

Arthur pranced and turned, so proud. Martie, Martina. Tina, Tina, Tina.

What she gave her soul to possess, she could have had at the call of a dog whistle.

I looked back to the double doors.

Midnight Louie sat there, grooming his green-powdered muzzle with his front-shived paws, looking like the cat that ate the bird that sang. Corinna, Corinna. Martina, Martina. Martina was a false friend to man, woman, and dog.

Had serious matters like top secret data and death in the wings and onstage not been the recent obsessions, it would have been amusing to watch grown men bear a dressing room frippery turned dog and cat toy away for examination, x-ray and/or experimental surgery, whatever spy guys do. I am no Jane Bond.

I *am* happy when I see Celestina sit next to a still-dazed Gwen. Arthur, befuddled to lose his prize, had followed her over. Celestina lifted her arm holding her fingers shut on an imaginary treat and circled her wrist, saying softly "Tina, Tina, Tina" and "Weena, Weena, Weena."

Arthur yipped for joy and went up on his hind toes to spin.

Apparently Celestina had befriended Arthur in the dressing room and played his special game as well as Martina had. I wondered. Maybe Celestina in her Six guise as a fellow performer had secretly revealed herself to her sister. They'd kept their kinship hidden for decades. Maybe Celeste had known her sister was *there* among the Six to watch her, even take over the Green Fairy role on occasion.

I looked at Snow, who was leaving without a word to me. Ingrate! His sunglasses were fixed on the two women and dog on the sofa. *Hmm.* Was Arthur going to have joint custody? Would he remain a dressing room dog with *two* loving companions?

Was Christophe capable of sentiment?

I saw Bucek was chatting with, actually chatting with—not warning or instructing—Temple and Matt.

I had to say goodbye to my anonymous drinking buddy, so I walked up to him when the group broke up.

"Frank Bucek, drinking partner and 'accountant'. You warned me. That must have been against the rules. You warned me I was in danger. Everybody official seems to know who you are. Am I to be so honored?"

"FBI. That's the business of making people 'account' for their crimes. Whether you needed my advice or not…"

"Oh, I figured staying sober and driving carefully after drinking a Fontana Flip was very good advice to someone in the risky business of being the Green Fairy."

"Will whatever Celestina may be guilty of, including nothing, impede her in getting custody of Arthur?"

"Why? Do you want him?"

"I want to be sure he has a good home."

"Celestina is probably guilty of thinking about killing *you* for possibly killing her sister to get her job. Now that Martina has been outed as the killer, she should be satisfied. I don't know if that kind of wrath is prosecutable. If you help her get Arthur, you might sleep better."

"About Martina Antonovna. Is she a spy and zealous killer, or just a jealous, killer competitor?"

"Maybe a bit of both. Who knows? We will. Soon."

"Give my best to Scully and Mulder. Could the producers have come up with scruffier names? I think this Vegas area is fertile ground for some new X-File cases. When you're back in town, let me buy you a Fontana Flip sometime."

"I understand you're quite a mixologist yourself."

"You've seen the recording?"

"It's making the rounds of law enforcement types on their off hours. You're getting quite a fan base, Miss Lane."

He left. Now what did he mean by that?

Someone chuckled beside me. I turned and had to look up. Still wearing my running flats.

No one was around us. Max always managed that.

"Thanks for the onstage 'lift,'" I told him. "It took a lot of upper body strength to support my weight and duel a Six trying to throttle me. Who was it?"

"Martina. Olympic gymnast. The thighs on that woman. Could crush a Mini-Cooper."

"Please. Too much information. She's off to no-man or woman's land, isn't she?"

He nodded and looked down. Quick's head was leaning against my hip and Achilles was the usual foot-warmer.

"Glad you got your partners back."

"I always have my partner's back."

"Me too. Another movement entirely. Let's do it again sometime."

"Dinner or…"

"Dinner's a good start. Or breakfast."

It's a good thing that dogs don't blush.

Me too.

Tailpiece: Midnight Louie Goes to the Dogs

I am now the poster boy for "being careful what you wish for".

I have finished an epic run as a primo feline P.I. on the cozy-noir side of the Mean Streets in the mystery book game, with 28 Alphabet-titled books published over a quarter of a century of changes in the national fabric. This feat makes clear that my detection smarts and deep understanding of the sometimes deficient human hearts and minds, i.e., of murderers or murdered, satisfied readers and demanded a new series of my detective cases.

I dared to be a bit flattered.

Never presume.

I came back all right, but my collaborator had a shocking new situation in mind for me.

I do not object to meeting a new Great Big Beautiful Doll human to protect and follow, while still having My Miss Temple on the crime-solving scene.

What else could a polyamorous guy want?" (You will have to look up that big word in the dictionary yourself. I hardly know what it means except that I am a born babe magnet and have more great dames around now than usual.)

My new debut (that may be a redundant phrase, but I am an action kind of guy, not a word wimp) was exciting with cover portrait contribution by artist Cindy Grundsten of Sweden and my Miss Carole adding her, ahem, original touches.

But Miss Delilah Street not only had an identity crisis being dragged back into my more normal Vegas of the 21st century, she has an unfortunate weakness for Close Encounters of the Canine Kind.

Need I say more?

I must confess My Miss Carole has strayed before, as far back as 1992 when she gave a Samoyed dog (big, all white, admittedly gorgeous) Rambeau, a sidekick role to her world-walking heroine, Alison Carver in the *Taliswoman* fantasy trilogy, which turned out to be only two books through no fault of our own. Our bow to our many readers awaiting a third adventure. We are still regrouping after all that angst.

And in this adventure, the participation of rescue dog, Arthur, King of the Britons, by way of Monty Python is the result of his mistress winning him a role at a charity auction for literacy at Malice Domestic annual mystery convention in Bethesda, Maryland. Below are photos of Arthur relaxing at home and of how he pictures himself when battle-ready.

Appearance and photos of Arthur courtesy of Joni Langevoort

Despite my literary rivalry with dogs, in no way do I discriminate between species. I know I should be grateful that I am still wanted in these sadly stressed times. But if you could find it in your hearts to adopt black felines, as I was, you will be assisting a superstitiously avoided and, dare I say, underestimated furperson of the feline population.

And I must alert you. Anything a dog does in these previous pages, or any others written by Miss Carole Nelson Douglas, I can do better if I put my mind and sharply shived mitts to it.

Very Best Fishes,

Midnight Louie, Esq.

Want Midnight Louie's print or e-scribe
Scratching Post-Intelligencer newsletter?
Contact Louie and Carole at PO BOX 33155
Fort Worth TX 76163-1555
Or sign up at www.carolenelsondouglas.com.
E-mail: cdouglas@catwriter.com

Tailpiece: Carole Sums up a Lifetime with Louie

It's only natural that I would create noir fantasy investigator Delilah Street and her more fantastic version of Midnight Louie's Las Vegas. Few know that in the early eighties I wrote high fantasy novels that were "surprise" bestsellers of hundreds of thousands of copies. (They'll be reissued after Midnight Louie's first Quartet of books is republished in the next two years.)

With my inborn love of animals I was fearless about adding the whimsy of fantasy to any genre, even one as realistic and "logical" as mystery, so it's no wonder a stray black cat from the Classified Ads turned out to be my writing career's lucky charm.

Midnight Louie is based on a real-life homeless cat with an uncanny gift for landing on his feet. We only "met" once decades ago for an interview, but my "allowing" Louie to have his own voice on the newspaper page in 1973 has driven my fiction writing career through forty years of exciting twists and turns.

1972: St. Paul newspaper reporter is assigned to interview touring Golden Age Hollywood and Broadway director, novelist, playwright, and actress Ruth Gordon's Fifties feminist husband, Garson Kanin. He sends an effusive Thank You note. "My friend Phil Silvers says he has never won an interview yet, but he never had the luck of you."

1973: "The real and original" Midnight Louie is flown almost 2,000 miles from an upscale Palo Alto motel to St. Paul, Minnesota.

He is a solid-black stray cat named by the motel residents. His skill at surviving by eating the costly koi fish on the grounds had him marked for the pound, from which a mature black cat would not emerge alive. But sharing an apartment in St. Paul with his rescuer, her lawyer husband, and two fixed female cats was not the life for any of them.

1973: St. Paul daily newspaper reporter and cat-lover spots a three-inch long, costly classified ad offering said "Midnight Louey" to a good home for one dollar. Curious, the reporter meets the cat, writes a feature article, and—in one crucial moment, fingers suspended over the typewriter keys—lets the cat tell the story in his own voice. He finds a home in the country, free to roam.

1974-76: The reporter, feeling cramped by the glass ceiling, pulls out the first three chapters of a historical Gothic mystery started in college and finishes it.

1977, spring: The reporter is again assigned to interview Garson Kanin. He is still effusive about her writing. She dares to mention her novel, hoping for a New York agent's name. (She soon finds one on her own but...think of it: Garson Kanin takes the novel, unread, to his New York publisher).

1977, fall: Reporter sells *One Faithful Harp* (now publisher-renamed *Amberleigh)* and a second historical novel, to a major NY publishing house...which swallows up another house and it's...

1980-81: the two books *finally* come out.

1985-90: Now launched, the ex-reporter needs more book sales. She dreams up an innovative four-book romance-with-mystery mini-series framed by Louie's inimitable voice. Never been done in the short romance field and, with other book sales to publishers, solves the money problem.

1990: Author sees a lack in the mystery field and becomes the first woman to create a Sherlock Holmes spin-off series, and the first author to make a woman from the original Holmes stories, American opera singer Irene Alder, the only woman to outwit Holmes, the protagonist of her own mystery series. The first of eight series books, *Good Night, Mr. Holmes,* becomes a *New York Times* Notable Book of the Year and wins mystery and romance awards.

But Louie is not satisfied to be left on the shelf, so to speak.

1992: the first Midnight Louie mystery comes out, *Catnap* (retitled *Cat in an Alphabet Soup* in e-book).

1992-2016: 28 books of the Midnight Louie alphabetically titled mysteries finish a long storyline of Louie's four human associates with *Cat in an Alphabet Endgame*.

2017-present: As Sir Arthur Conan Doyle couldn't shed writing Sherlock Holmes, Midnight Louie's clamoring fans want more. So does Carole. She imports the female protagonist from her paranormal version of Louie's Las Vegas as a new character in the continuing series.

2018: *Absinthe Without Leave*, the first book in a new Midnight Louie Café Noir series debuts.

Forty-five years in the life of a writer with Midnight Louie.
Thanks to you, and you, and you, our always loyal readers.
Did she and Midnight Louie live happily ever after? So far, yes.

ABOUT THE AUTHOR

www.carolenelsondouglas.com
www.wishlistpublishing.com

CAROLE NELSON DOUGLAS is the award-winning, bestselling author of sixty-four novels in the mystery/thriller, women's fiction, and science fiction/fantasy genres.

She is noted for the long-running Midnight Louie, feline PI, cozy-noir mystery series (*Cat in an Alphabet Soup, Cat in an Aqua Storm, Cat on a Blue Monday,* etc.) and the Delilah Street, Paranormal Investigator, noir urban fantasy series (*Dancing with Werewolves*, etc.). Midnight Louie prowls the "slightly surreal" Vegas of today, narrating interlarded chapters in his alley-cat noir voice. Delilah walks the mean streets of a paranormally post-apocalyptic Sin City, fighting supernatural mobsters with Louie's wile, wit and grit.

Douglas was the first author to make a Sherlockian female character, Irene Adler, a series protagonist, with the *New York Times* Notable Book of the Year, *Good Night, Mr. Holmes*, and the first woman to write a Holmes spin-off series. Her award nominations run from the Agatha (mystery) to the Nebula (science fiction), including Lifetime Achievement Awards from *RT Book Reviews* for Mystery, Suspense, Versatility, and as a Pioneer of Publishing for her groundbreaking multi-genre work. She has won a clowder of Catwriters' Association first place Muse awards, and is a four-time finalist for the Romance Writers of America's Rita® award in four different categories.

Her short fiction has appeared in many anthologies and several Years' Best Mystery collections.

An award-winning daily newspaper reporter and editor in Minnesota, she moved to the sunbelt to write fiction full-time and has been inducted into the Texas Literary Hall of Fame. She does a mean Marilyn Monroe impersonation, collects vintage clothing and homeless cats, and enjoys Zumba, but has never danced with werewolves. (That she knows of.)

Visit Carole at https://www.facebook.com/CaroleNelsonDouglas
Twitter @CNDouglasWriter
And write her at cdouglas@catwriter.com

Made in United States
Orlando, FL
23 February 2022

15088208R00186